The Naked Book Club

Jennifer Aline

A MERLIN HEIGHTS BOOK

Dedication

To my family, friends, and the "Writer Mamas"
who've been there every step of the way.

To the therapists who helped me through my
darkest days.

To the dance instructors who taught me to
freely express myself.

And to my brother, Matthew. I will forever
dedicate every book I write to you. Thank you
for always pushing me to create, imagine, and
write from the heart.

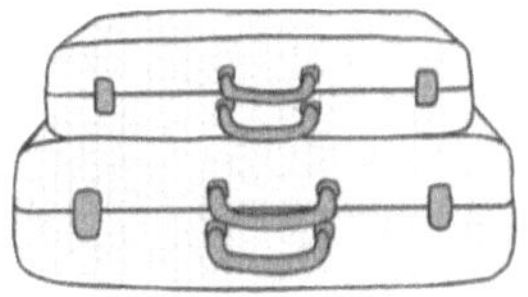

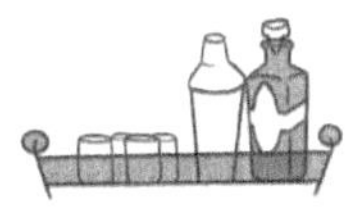

Author's Note

Dear Reader,

THE NAKED BOOK CLUB is a fun, steamy story about self-empowerment, sex positivity, and the power of friendship. However, this story also tackles some darker topics, such as postpartum depression, anxiety, codependency, and verbal and emotional abuse.

Before you dive into Nel and Rosie's story, remember that everyone reacts to trauma in their own way and heals at their own speed. While some may easily walk away from a traumatic situation, others may need years to get themselves to a healthier, happier place. It's okay to feel stuck, or frustrated, or unsure on your healing journey—that's part of being human. No one situation is the same as the next, and it's important to recognize that.

I hope you read THE NAKED BOOK CLUB with an open mind and an understanding heart with the barriers Nel and Rosie face. I also hope you giggle, relate to, and swoon over some characters and situations you run into within these pages!

Thank you,

Jennifer Aline

Content Warnings

- Alcohol use and discussions involving drugs

- Curse words

- Discussions surrounding verbal and emotional abuse

- Tears. Lots and lots of tears

- Toxic codependent relationships

- A lot of messy buns

- Prenatal/Postpartum depression, anxiety, and mental health struggles

- Damage to the heels of stilettos (I mean...this can be traumatic...)

- Mentions of BDSM and on page use of sex toys

- INTENSE SIPPING...like, a lot. You've been warned.

Chapter 1

Nel

She couldn't stop crying.

Well, *we* couldn't stop crying.

After readjusting Mae over my shoulder, I placed the binky back between her pink, pouting lips for what felt like the third time in fifteen minutes. When it seemed safe to sit down on the couch—an act I knew the repercussions of—I hunched in front of the laptop like the exhausted gargoyle I was.

I'd spent the first half of my therapy session hauling both my laptop and Mae around the apartment, hoping to find somewhere to continue the appointment. I'd placed her in her floral boppy just to hear her screams grow fiercer. I tried the overly priced swing my older sister bought her, but she was not having it. As I hurried us back to the original spot on the couch, I eyed one of her thousand rubber binkies sitting pristinely on the kitchen counter.

I stopped in my tracks and squinted at it. It looked like it was laughing at me.

The second it hit her lips, the cries softened.

Why was it that once *her* tears began to slow, *mine* sped up?

"I'm *so* sorry this happens every time we do a remote session. I'll see if one of my sisters can watch Mae next time. Or maybe my mom, but probably—"

"Never apologize. This all comes with the territory," Dr. Delilah said calmly. "Why don't you take a sip of water, Nel. Then we can get back to where we were."

As always, I did what she said. The liquid was a relief to my throat—a throat rubbed raw from nights of holding in sobs as Mae screamed into my shoulder.

"I don't even remember what we were talking about," I admitted.

Damn you, Mom Brain.

Delilah laced her fingers together. "You were talking about the letter your Theía Elena sent you."

No wonder Mae decided to throw a tantrum when this topic started.

I wanted to throw a tantrum as well.

I mean, I guess I kind of had.

"Oh. Yeah. That." Looking down at my daughter's face, I watched her eyelids twitch shut, dark eyelashes painting her sienna cheeks. I set her against a carefully constructed pile of pillows, making sure the binky was secure between her lips. "So, the letter said she's moving back to Greece in six months and is selling the house."

"The house your apartment is in, correct?" Delilah asked.

I nodded. "Yup. *This* house. I have to move in six months, and I cannot afford anything that's halfway livable or has at least two bedrooms. I was lucky she offered up this place for me last year. She even cut the rent in half. I just don't know where I'm going to go or what I'm going to do once I'm out of here."

The thought of moving out and paying full, legitimate rent made me want to vomit.

"Six months may not seem like a lot of time, but you *do* have time. Think about your life over these last six months. It probably moved both quickly and slowly since having Mae. You have that amount of time now to plan and prepare," Delilah explained.

She wasn't wrong.

Since welcoming Mae into the world six months ago, life seemed to move in both slow motion and at warped speed simultaneously. If I'd learned anything since becoming a mom, it was that the world was a distorted version of the one we'd grown up learning about, the one we grew up expecting.

"I've looked at some apartments, and I can't even afford a down payment," I said softly. "The freelance work coming in is so inconsistent. It barely pays the rent *here*."

"You have freelance work coming in though. That's great!" Delilah adjusted the red curls falling in front of her eyes. "Have you thought about any other job opportunities you may find interesting?"

I'd thought about jobs and finances more than the average adult should—even though I still didn't feel like the average adult. Yes, I was thirty years old with a baby and a place to call my own—well, sort of—but I still felt like the college student attached to her roommate's hip. I still felt like the twenty-something grabbing brunch with co-workers or my younger sister. I even still felt like the cool, collected English tutor clad in cropped sweaters and Converse sneakers working odd hours at Merlin Community College.

Cool and collected had turned into a puddle of uncertainty in the blink of an eye.

It took too long to get to the point of cool and collected for it to fall apart.

"Yeah, I'll start looking a little bit," I muttered. "Maybe I'll take on a few virtual tutoring clients if Hallie or Nora could watch Mae. I'll...I'll reach out."

"Those are great options, Nel." Delilah leaned back in her chair, her bright-pink lips twisting. "I do think that is time for today. I'm glad you have some ideas brewing. Slow and steady. It will happen."

I hoped she was right.

She had to be.

Bam, bam, bam!

The moment I clicked off the video chat, my apartment door vibrated with consistent, solid knocks. My heart danced, and Mae wriggled against the pillows, the binky falling from her lips.

I would not let that stupid binky win.

Placing it back into her mouth and cuddling her to my chest, I walked down the few steps leading to the entrance. Peeking out through the thin window framing the door, all I saw was the shadow of someone carrying a large bag—or maybe a pile of blankets—and rain pouring down behind them. As the shadow knocked again, they kept readjusting whatever they were carrying, low grumbles whispering toward the door.

This was it.

This was why I listened to all those terrifying crime podcasts and read all the dark romances.

They'd trained me for *this* moment.

If only I'd placed that baseball bat by the door like I'd meant to months ago.

Instead, there was a folded stroller in the corner.

"No one is home!" I shouted before realizing what the fuck I'd done. As the shadowed face turned toward the window, I shifted so we were hidden directly behind the door.

"Nel. It's Jude," a low, familiar voice said. "And Rosie."

If there was air still in my lungs, it disappeared when I heard those names. My feet were frozen to the floor, and my heart was back in palpitation mode.

Shock and surprise and confusion consumed me. I hadn't seen my college roommate since she left Merlin Heights to travel with

The Bare Assentials around three years ago. She hadn't returned for any visits and was silent on all social platforms since leaving.

Well, that wasn't totally true. Her burlesque profile was still active and growing by the day—or at least it was the last time I looked at it. There was always a new picture marketing her next gig or a video highlighting some of her spiciest moments during a show. But her personal accounts had all gone dark—along with our friendship.

Once she'd gone from Rosie the Roommate to Zesty Zi of The Bare Assentials, I was nothing to her.

Or at least it seemed that way.

As for her brother, I hadn't talked to him since he left Merlin Community College to hostel hop across the country. Last I knew, Jude set up camp out west with a couple friends around Birch Bay. Or maybe it was Eastsound? It was somewhere near Seattle, and since I had zero geographical knowledge, my brain just assumed I'd never see him again.

Why the fuck were they at my door?

And how the hell had they found my apartment?

"Nel? I know you're standing right there." Jude's voice sounded through the solid wood of the door—his gruff tone soft at the edges. "It's me. Can you let us in?"

It was him. It was absolutely his voice. But why wasn't it Rosie's voice? She would have been the first one to speak up and storm straight through the front door without knocking. She would have probably charged my fridge, grabbing a beer and a cheese stick before even giving me one of her obnoxious bear hugs.

Yet, her softer-spoken twin was the one doing all the violent knocking.

"What name did you call me in college?"

There was a beat of silence before this "So-Called Jude" shuffled closer to the door. "I called you Penny after you told me your full name was Penelope. You kicked me in the shin, and I never called you that again."

You're only worth a penny.

The sentence still stung my ears. It had been years since Grant—the high school boyfriend I'd do anything to forget—said that to me, but it felt like seconds since his words originally left their mark.

The wound still felt so fresh.

I slowly twisted the handle. Standing in the doorway was Jude, his long, dark hair and denim jacket soaked from the rain. His kind, brown eyes stared through me, bringing every college memory we had together to the forefront of my exhausted mind. In his arms was a very damp and—from the looks of it—very drunk Rosie. She was wearing nothing but flat, combat-style black boots reaching up to her knees and a long-sleeved, sequined dress barely covering her pale thighs.

"What the actual fuck?" I whispered, my eyes hopping from Rosie's drunk ass to Jude's tired gaze. I watched his dark eyes flicker to the sleeping infant in my arms, and his eyebrows lifted before returning to mine.

"Can we come in?"

Chapter 2

Rosie

The smell of charred grilled cheese surrounded me.

A cool washcloth, smelling of lavender and something else, dampened my forehead.

I was wearing an oversized sweatshirt and gym shorts that *definitely* were not mine.

Was that red pepper hummus and pita bread I smelled?

Talk about sensory overload.

"Nel?" My voice sounded foreign. The second I whispered out the word, a high-pitched squeal echoed against the inside of my skull. My eyes started throbbing, and my brain began vibrating more than my damn Magic Wand did...and that thing could *vibrate*.

If this was hell, at least it had hummus.

And apparently, screaming demons.

"You're alive," Jude said, his voice somehow making its way through my hands as they mimicked earmuffs. My eyelids twitched open, and for the quickest millisecond, bright light flooded my gaze. A blurry version of Jude's stupid, scruffy face came into view before everything went dark again.

I flopped my hand in his direction, pushing his own away from my face. "Don't touch me."

Then, the asshole did it again.

The rough skin of his thumb and forefinger lifted both of my eyelids open, and I shot up, elbowing him away. "What the fuck, Jude?"

He reached for a glass of water with a thin, content smile before jutting it toward my face. "Drink this. Now."

Then the sound started up again. The squeal was deafening. It took every muscle not to drop the glass of water onto the floor and curl into the fetal position against the pile of carefully placed pillows to my right.

The pillows were actually some of the softest I'd ever felt.

I wanted to dive into them and hide from this sound forever.

"What the fuck is that?" I said, scanning the room with squinted eyes. This was *not* Jude's place. This wasn't even a place Viv would be found staying the night at. Small, plastic toys covered the floor, and beside the television sat a pink-and-gray swing with yellow stars dangling above it, rotating in a circle to some kind of hushed, instrumental music.

This was *not* the kind of swing I'd find at Viv's.

The scent of burnt cheddar pierced my senses again. "It smells like Merlin Community College," I whispered. "It smells like—"

"Oh my gosh, you're okay." Nel's voice silenced the wails coming from the hallway, and my eyes connected with her light, blood-shot ones. She skittered toward the stove and poked a pan with a spatula. Grabbing a plate from the drying rack, she placed the sandwich onto it before walking in my direction. "I thought maybe the post-bar meal we used to devour at three in the morning may still do the trick. I know it's only eight o'clock at night, but it's worth a try."

I stared down at the sandwich, the edges crisped to perfection with the most beautiful splotches of black strewn across thin, artisan bread. "This is probably the most divine thing I've ever seen."

"There she is," Nel laughed, setting the plate on the coffee table before shuffling back toward the kitchen counter where she scooped up a bag of chips and a small tray. "I thought this may bring you back to life."

Red pepper hummus and overly seasoned pita chips.

This was fucking heaven.

Once I felt the hot, melted cheese slide down my throat, practically giving me the best orgasm of my life, I finally took in my surroundings. With each bite of sandwich and each crunch of pita, I realized I was sitting in a small apartment that, to my knowledge, was Nel's. It was pouring outside, the rain attempting to break through the thin walls of the house—a Cape Cod-style home she seemed to live on the first floor of. Once Jude saw color return to my face, he plunged his body into a recliner beside the little pink-and-gray swing, the stars still spinning.

I lifted my hand and pointed at the swing, my mouth filled with crispy cheddar. "What's that?"

Nel followed my finger, and her neck muscles tensed as she faced me. "That's Mae's swing."

"Who?" My voice was muffled. I was definitely chewing with my mouth open.

"Mae," Nel said, her voice hesitant. "She's six months old."

I blinked, my eyelashes sticking together from the lingering mascara. "Huh?"

"Mae is my daughter."

I wasn't sure why this brought back the spiraling headache I'd felt minutes earlier. The squeals, the screaming, the nonstop sound. It made sense the noises weren't the demonic wails of devils pulling me down to Hangover Hell—they were the demonic wails of a child.

Nel's child.

She had always been very open about wanting children someday. It was just hard to believe that someday was, apparently, now. And she was, what, thirty years old? Her having a baby shouldn't have shaken me harder than the orgasmic smell of grilled cheese had.

But it did.

"You...have a kid? Why didn't you tell me, Nel?"

Nel shrugged, sliding down onto the floor and crossing her legs beneath her, leaning back against the couch. "I texted and called you when I found out I was pregnant. You must have gotten a new number or were just too busy on tour. I didn't want to stalk The Bare Assentials on social media just to let you know. So, I stayed quiet."

"You *should* have stalked me! I *love* being stalked!" I shouted, my voice shifting back into one I was familiar with.

I thought back to the last few years, digging into my memory to find any recollection of a call or text or message from Nel mentioning she was pregnant. I'm sure I would have noticed a message like that, and if I had, I would have driven back to Merlin in a heartbeat.

But as I watched her remove her glasses, drying them on the corner of her shirt before placing them back onto the bridge of her nose, my stomach sank, knowing I hadn't been there for her.

I mean, I hadn't been there for her much at all during our twenties either.

Had I *really* just, I don't know, disappeared?

Shaking my head, I tried not to let my emotions control me. They never had before, and hell if they started taking the reins now.

"Nel, who's...who's the dad?" I asked.

"Come on, Rowe. You can't just ask that," Jude said, adjusting himself so he was at the edge of the recliner, his arms over his knees. He still hadn't taken off the denim jacket he was wearing, and the hood of the navy-blue sweatshirt he wore beneath it popped out awkwardly at the collar. His dark hair was pulled into a knot at the top of his head, and the clean-shaven face I'd last seen him with had transformed into a face clad with a short, scruffy beard.

Jude looked like a classy homeless man—if that was even a thing.

Not that I had anything against the homeless.

I just wasn't used to this wilder, more disheveled version of my twin.

Nel faced Jude, shaking her head. "No, no. She's fine. I mean, if this were the other way around, I'd want to know who the father was."

"Well, you can only get pregnant when a penis is involved," I said with a snort. "And I haven't been near one of those since high school."

"Touche," Nel said with a nod. "Are you and Viv still…a thing?"

I cleared my throat and reached for a pita chip, scooping up way too much hummus with it. "The dad. Who is he?"

Nel pulled her knees into her chest, her chest lifting and falling slowly. "His name is Landon. You wouldn't know him. He lives in Greyport."

Jude shifted in the recliner again, fiddling with his hands in his lap.

I could tell Nel was trying desperately to move on from this discussion—Jude too. I also knew she was not good at keeping things balled up inside, and I sensed this was one of those things. "Okay. Is he your boyfriend? *Was* he your boyfriend? Or were you engag—"

"He was a one-night stand." Her words came out fast and heavy, as if it was the first time they'd ever been spoken aloud.

"And I know what you're going to say, Rowe. I know, I *never* have one-night stands...and you're right. But I had one."

Jude cleared his throat, shifting in his seat again. This time, I eyed him warily.

"Nel. You *really* think that's what I would say?" I asked.

"It's *exactly* what you'd say," she said, her face drained of emotion.

"I guess you're right. Yeah." I took the final bite of grilled cheese, chewing it for much longer than necessary to relish that crunchy, cheddar perfection. "Okay, so you're doing one-night stands now. That's great! You're putting yourself out there!"

"Watch yourself, Rowe," Jude hummed from the recliner.

"It was my first one-night stand since...like...college." Nel's voice was hushed, her legs still tight against her body. "I'd forgotten to refill my birth control that week, and when I went to Thirsty Theodore's with some co-workers, they saw him looking at me. He was cute, I guess. Since he was just visiting his cousin for the week, it would be a one-and-done kind of thing. Something I could get out of my system and move on from."

She shut her eyes tight and took a deep breath. Looking down at her from my spot on the couch, she seemed so fragile as she set her chin on top of her knees. She'd always been the introvert to my extrovert, the collected to my chaotic. But from here, she looked small—*too* small.

This was a shell of the roommate I'd once had.

"Huh. Okay," I said, wiping my hands on my sweatpants—or, *her* sweatpants—before my ass hit the floor, and I snuggled up next to her. "I'm guessing he's not in the picture?"

She shook her head. "I never even got his number. He left the next morning to head back to Greyport, and that was it."

"Wow. You had a *real* one-night stand, Nel." I could sense Jude's stare burning a hole through the side of my face. I ignored the heat and maintained my focus.

Nel turned toward me, her thin, dry lips lifting slightly to pinch her cheeks. "I was embracing my inner Rosie and stepping outside of my comfort zone. Honestly, it felt good walking over to him and flirting. I felt—I don't know—empowered."

"*You* walked over to *him?* I'm so proud!" I was honestly shocked. Though she'd once been the queen of bar top body shots and a professional at sneaking alcohol into the campus suites, she'd always been hesitant initiating any kind of activity or discussion with future partners. The fact that she'd walked right up to this guy and started talking to him blew my mind.

"Yeah, well, it happened. He's gone, and Mae's here." She snagged a pita chip, dipping the tip of the cracker into the hummus. "Don't get me wrong, I love my daughter. You know more than anyone I've always wanted a family. It's just...I don't know. It's just been harder than expected."

"The timing," I said, my voice quiet. "The timing of it all. It wasn't what you expected, right?"

She looked up, and her mouth fell the slightest bit ajar. Her indigo, familiar eyes. Her soft yet significant voice. Her energy injected me with a comfort I didn't know I was in withdrawal from until now. Just being back in her presence helped me let go, breathe, and bend at the seams.

Seams that were starting to tear.

"Yeah." Nel nodded and let her knees fall to the floor, stretching her long legs out in front of her and wiggling her socked toes in front of the recliner Jude sat in. "The timing definitely wasn't ideal. A lot of things lately have been working off their own time-frame...not mine."

"I get it," I whispered, taking a handful of crackers and dipping them all into the hummus at once so I wouldn't have to look as serious as I was starting to feel.

Because I did get it.

I really, *really* did.

Chapter 3

NEL

Jude stepped into the unforgiving rainstorm, and I cupped his elbow to slow his steps. His eyes hit mine, and my heart jolted in a way I hadn't felt in...well, years.

"Jude." I took a step back, my hand falling from his elbow. "Rosie and I are going to Spellbound Beans in the morning. You know...like we all used to do."

"Oh, I remember," he said as he ran a hand over his beard. He'd had such a baby face at MCC, clad in button-downs and skinny blue jeans with some band from the early 2000s peeking out from beneath the collar. His voice was still soft but with a little more grit at the edges than I was used to. "Do you know where The Vintage Press is?"

"That's the comic book and gaming store right off Main Street, right? Isn't it across from Wine Thyme, or a few doors down from it, or something?"

Jude nodded, sweeping the thick hood of his sweatshirt over his head. "I've got a project going on next door to The Vintage Press. Stop by around ten."

A project?

How long had Jude been back in Merlin for if he was working on a *project*?

"Will there be coffee, though?" I asked, raising my eyebrows with a jut of my hip. "After the night we've had, caffeine is imper-ative."

"There will *definitely* be coffee," he said with a grin. *That* was the smile I remembered. The one that took up a little too much space on his face, causing skin to crease at the edges of his eyes. "Goodnight, Nel. Thanks for not leaving me in the rain all night." The earthy night air hugged his frame as he disappeared from my life yet again.

However, this time, he wasn't gone for good.

Rosie and I needed to talk about whatever the fuck happened last night over some monstrously caffeinated coffee. Being the coffee snobs we were, visiting Spellbound Beans seemed like the natural next step in our mind-boggling reunion. But after Jude's mysterious mention of his *project*—a project with coffee at hand—we'd make a quick stop there before getting caffeinated for the day.

Turning onto Main Street, huddled up in our heaviest coats, with Mae hugging my chest in her carrier, it was still a bit surreal that Rosie was here.

Not that I was at all upset about seeing her.

I was just...I don't know, surprised.

She was the first person I called once I realized that staring at the four positive pregnancy tests for an hour wasn't going to change a damn thing. Though our friendship started dwindling a year or two after graduation—around when she tried supporting her mom a little more—Rosie still naturally felt like the first person to talk to.

Maybe it was because she'd been the person I called to save me from a horrendous date if I needed to "help a friend with her car" or "drive my friend to the hospital because she was in labor"—an excuse she'd used way too many times. Whenever I finished the same romance novel she'd been reading, I called her to gush about how incredibly hot the sex scene in the car or office or childhood bedroom had been.

She always finished books before I did and hated waiting.

I loved watching her squirm as I took my time, absorbing every word on every page and rereading the previous chapter just to get back into the character mindset.

Yes, I was happy to see her. But her visit was a shock to the system after a few years without my best friend.

Well...more like my entire twenties without one.

If she'd ghosted me once, couldn't she ghost me again?

Why wasn't I focusing on *that* instead of the stir of excitement I felt just seeing her back by my side?

"Did he say what he was doing down here?" I asked Rosie as we hesitantly trudged onto Willow Drive and away from Main Street. It was busy for the morning after a freak rainstorm drenched the village streets, forcing snow mounds to become ponds at every corner. In a town famous for wicked winters lasting through springtime, a jarring rainstorm in mid-February was just another unexpected plot twist to add to my growing list of them.

It was just like Rosie to bring a little chaos the second she touched back down at her home base.

"He didn't say a thing," Rosie said, wrapping her scarf higher over her lips. "If this project is any farther down this way, we're going to end up near those sketchy lofts...holy shit! We're almost to where Isaac lived! *You* know this area, Nel!"

I sure did know this area.

How did you forget yet another shitty boyfriend?

Rosie lifted her chin in the direction we were walking, elbowing me gently. "It was right up there, wasn't it? The night you guys broke up, we had to sneak out because the cops were called. Wasn't Isaac's brother getting a bit too mouthy with his girlfriend in the bathroom or something?"

I had been the more sober one between the two of us during our college escapades, but I remembered the night Rosie was talking about as clear as all those double lines on the pregnancy tests. We'd taken off the peep-toe pumps we'd forced our feet into and raced down the metal stairs out onto the cobblestone street—*this* cobblestone street and the only original one Merlin Heights still had. I'd never run so fast, my heart pulsing like hummingbird wings.

"Yeah, his brother was being an asshole. Isaac too." After that night, I ignored Isaac's constant texts until he finally gave up on me. "I remember."

Her laugh faltered, and she straightened her arm in front of us, as if protecting a child in the front seat of a car. "What the fuck are they doing?"

Instead of putting together a makeshift tent on some sequestered beach or stopping by the nearest hostel to take a shower, we found Jude standing on a ladder outside a storefront. He held a drill in one hand and some kind of laser measure in the other as he threw a prideful smile our way. Inside one of the windows was a shorter, stockier man with dark skin and coveralls, spraying down the glass. He seemed to be nodding to the beat of an upbeat folk tune playing from a speaker somewhere inside.

No, it wasn't coming from a speaker.

Someone was *actually* playing music.

On...a mandolin?

What the hell was happening?

"Uh...Jude?" Rosie shouted, throwing her hands in the air.

The music grew louder as a blond musician strode out the front doors. His smug smile oozed confidence. He looked like he'd walked straight out of some cliché surf movie, but with unkempt, dirty-blond hair falling just above the shoulders of his sweatshirt instead of salty, golden locks flowing in the wind.

If this were a movie, he would be walking in slow motion while strumming his mandolin.

From the look on his face, he probably thought that was what he was doing instead of walking through the entrance of…well, I wasn't quite sure yet what this was.

Jude made his way down the ladder and tossed tools into a bin by the front door. His beige sweatshirt looked like it was used as a practice paint palette, his black jeans dusted with hues of grays and greens and blues. "Nice to see you're alive, Rosie." Jude wiped gloved hands over his chest before rising up onto his toes in hopes of seeing Mae. "Is there a human in there?"

Mae's cheeks smushed together against the blankets hugging her, a knit hat covering her dark hair. "She's in there. She's nocturnal, so right now is prime sleep time. I've given up trying to change her schedule since she started cutting teeth."

"Gross." Rosie winced. "The phrase *cutting teeth* sounds like a scene from a horror movie."

I shrugged, rocking side to side as she wiggled against my chest. "I mean, you're not totally wrong." I met Jude's gaze, the man with the mandolin behind him switching to a song with a slower, bluegrass-inspired rhythm. Honestly, I didn't hate this vibe. "You said there was coffee. I need some."

"With Baileys in it," Rosie added. "You got Baileys, right?"

"Rosie, it's ten o'clock in the morning," I said, my head falling forward in shock. "How can you even think about alcohol right now without dry heaving?"

Shrugging, Rosie took Jude's silence as a no. "Coffee. Where is it? I skipped Spellbound for *this*."

"Well, you're standing in front of Spellbound's newest competition," Jude said, crossing his arms and turning toward the storefront.

"There's no competition," the man in coveralls shouted from the window as he waved a rag in the air. "Everyone will forget about Spellbound and their asshole manager once they visit Java Jude's."

Facing Rosie, I watched her eyebrows practically hit the knit hat covering her pin-straight hair. "*What*...did that guy just say?"

I pointed to the first three letters Jude had finished mounting to the storefront minutes before we'd arrived: JAV. "We heard correctly."

"You're opening up...a coffee shop?" Rosie asked, her hoarse voice dripping in shock. "Since when did you become a bigger coffee snob than the two of us?"

"Since we met Marty and Dale in Seattle and were introduced to the best damn coffee farm on the planet," an abrupt voice said from the doorway. The musician began in our direction, the mandolin swung over his back and his hand outstretched in Rosie's direction. "Sebastian Cohen. You must be Rosie. I do see similarities between you two now that you're here in the flesh."

"Twins freak me out," shouted Coverall Guy, dropping the rag into a bucket. His eyes darted from Jude to Rosie behind his tortoise-shell glasses. "But I see it too."

Rosie ignored the comments. "And now you're some hipster barista? What the hell happened to you out West?"

I wasn't sure exactly why Rosie was angry.

I mean...we had VIP access to coffee now.

I didn't see what the problem was.

Jude's shoulders slumped, and he rolled his eyes, scooping up the tools he'd thrown into the bin minutes earlier as he started back up the ladder. "Oh, come on, Rowe."

"Obviously, *something* happened," I added, Mae's eyes flickering open from within her blanketed cocoon. I pointed from Jude's boots up to his face and then back down again before circling his body in the air with my index finger. "Hipster or not, this whole transformation is kind of intriguing. I want to know how this all happened, but bring us to the coffee, Jude."

He nodded toward the door propped open with a paint can and led us to a concrete countertop lining the left side of the space. I ran my hand over the soft, cool material as I took in the massive espresso machine humming behind the counter, industrial bulbs dangling from the planked ceiling above, and the built-in bookshelf near one of the windows where piles of comic books sat waiting to be organized. While I typically leaned toward a more vintage, passé aesthetic—or "grandma vibes" as Rosie liked to call it—the dark, smooth concrete counter did something for me.

"What's with all the gray?" Rosie asked, tossing her hat onto the closest table. "I don't hate it, but it's just very...gray. Oh, *that's* what we need, Nel." A drip coffee pot sat beside the espresso monstrosity, and Rosie flew behind the counter, snagging one of the many ceramic mugs off a floating shelf above it. Mae stirred and when I looked down into her cocoon, her pupils were wide and darting from lightbulb to lightbulb overhead.

I reached into my coat pocket where I stashed a tiny octopus-shaped rattle, a pocket-sized plush octopus, and three extra binkies in case the one in her mouth disappeared—as they typically did.

I had an unhealthy obsession with Atlantic pygmy octopi.

Octopuses.

Octopodes.

There were too many plural versions to keep track of.

Rosie poured me a hot cup, and after arguing with Sebastian about the difference in taste between oat milk and almond milk, Sebastian finally pointed out the tiny fridge under the counter where milk cartons, creamers, and flavors lived. We wandered toward the window on the other side of the door where she collapsed into a leather wingback, and Mae and I stretched out on an orange floral sofa—one plucked straight out of the 70s.

"So, are you back for good?" I hesitantly asked Rosie, taking a sip.

Rosie squinted out the large window overlooking the cobblestone street. "I don't want to be, but I think I am."

"Why'd you come back?" I hated prying, but there was no way around the question game we both were about to play.

It had been almost three years since the two of us sat down, chugged coffee, and talked about...well, anything and everything. Even before that, our early twenties revolved around occasional video chats, memes, and a sprinkling of text messages here and there. But it was about three years ago, after a handful of vague texts—mentioning The Bare Assentials and the name *Viv*—when our communication dialed back. I hadn't questioned it, really—mostly because I was so wrapped up in the tutoring program I'd started at. I was building new friendships and expected she'd do the same.

But I also expected she'd still be just a text or call away when I needed her.

And she hadn't been.

"I was kicked out of The Bare Assentials on Wednesday." Rosie's voice was gravel scraping stone. She wasn't one to show emotion. I often cried enough for the both of us, but I could tell saying this aloud was a major punch to the gut. "They had to cut the troupe in half because of budget issues, I guess. And after the *heel incident,* I just wasn't going to make the cut."

I scooted closer to the table, my brow furrowed. "What *heel incident?*"

A heavy sigh fell from Rosie's lips. "In December, I started feeling pain in the arches of my feet. In January, my physical therapist said I have plantar fasciitis and should avoid high heels...which is hilarious, *right?* I mean...what burlesque dancer *avoids* high heels?"

Rosie's arms flew up in the air, forcing out a painful laugh. My eyes opened wider as a memory sparked, and I said, "You weren't wearing heeled boots last night."

Lifting her foot above the table—practically into a standing split—she wiggled a combat boot in my direction. This one wasn't up to her knees like the night before. It went to a little above her an-kle and looked pretty worn. "I, now, am one with the combat-boot life."

"Shouldn't you be wearing, like, special sneakers?"

"Hell no. I've already said goodbye to heels, and I will *not* give in to the God of Granny Sneakers." Rosie released her ankle, and the boot slammed onto the ground, enunciating her point. "I also wear inserts with everything…so that helps. A little."

"Rosie, I'm so sorry," I said, knowing an apology did nothing to change that we were sitting in the same jobless boat together.

It also wouldn't change her *very* aggressive opinion when it came to footwear.

"Maybe my brother will hire me as a barista!" she shouted, looking over my shoulder toward the counter behind us where Jude now stood. "I can striptease on that big cement block back there and bring in the big bucks for you guys. I'll dance barefoot too. Feet bring in lots of money these days."

Jude shook his head before removing his knit hat—one almost identical to his sister's—and tossing it onto a metal stool. "The three of us got this covered…and we can't afford to hire anyone right now anyway."

"Did someone say *striptease*?" Sebastian sang, strolling back into the coffee shop while strumming a lazy tune on his mandolin. "I support this. Bring on the skin."

"And *this* is why I'm not a penis person," Rosie said with a dramatic eyeroll, finally taking a sip of her coffee. "What do *you* do for this place, Samson? Are you just the roaming coffee shop bard or what?"

"It's Sebastian, dumbass!" Jude shouted from across the room.

Sebastian let out a chesty laugh before tapping his foot against the cement floor. "I'm the guy making magic happen behind the scenes. I just finished the website, contacted three of Merlin's major news channels, and got us an ad campaign on the My Cup o' Joe dating app." He slowed his strum and raised an eyebrow at Rosie, throwing a cocky smile her way. "I'm now on bard duties for the rest of the day, m'lady."

Jude chuckled at Rosie's silence from behind the counter where he was now stacking more mugs on the shelves. As if right on cue, Mae's squeal cracked that silence, and I rushed my knuckle between her lips, eyeing the pacifier on the floor by Rosie's boot.

"Dammit," I mumbled, rocking Mae back and forth as Rosie handed over the pacifier. After scanning the walls around us and failing to find a clock, I grabbed a plastic bottle with a baggy of dry formula inside from my diaper bag. It looked like I was sneaking drugs into the shop using my daughter's bottle. "Jude, can I fill this back there quick?"

He nodded toward the sink, and I scooted behind the counter where we stood hip-to-hip as I filled up Mae's bottle with luke-warm water, shaking it until the formula turned into something edible. My back found the brick wall behind me, letting my tense muscles loosen as I pressed the rubber nipple between Mae's lips.

Everyone around me seemed to hold their breath until the moment Mae's cries fell quiet. I could almost feel a simultaneous exhale the second she began drinking.

Jude watched the scene unfold from beside me as I peered at him over my glasses that now sat on the very tip of my nose. Throwing my head back—barely avoiding the wall behind me—I attempted to slide my glasses back to their usual spot.

I failed.

Miserably.

I attempted again, and when I brought my face forward, the glasses fell off my nose onto the hard floor. Jude snagged them, setting them back on my face and slipping them to where I'd failed getting them to seconds before.

My heart raced to a beat I was oddly familiar with.

It had been ten years since that beat played.

"Thanks," I said, cheeks heating. "Multitasking is both easier and harder now."

"You could have just asked me to fix your glasses, you know." Jude's thin smile peeked out from beneath the dark mustache meshing into that impressive beard of his.

"I know you, Jude." I couldn't help but mirror his grin. "You would have taken my glasses hostage for fun."

"That was *one* time." Jude smirked before setting the final mug onto the floating shelf. "I learned my lesson when you flipped your entire suite upside down looking for them...for three hours."

"And they ended up being under your damn pillow the whole time!" Rosie shouted, swinging herself onto a stool in front of me. "Okay, it's your turn to play this little game, Nel. I assume you're not working right now...or am I wrong."

"You're not wrong," I said, rocking side to side with Mae content in my arms. "I'm hoping more freelance work comes in soon from the college or maybe I can start virtually working with some students I tutored before I had Mae. Responses from the college have been slow, and I *need* to get my finances to a place where I can move into another apartment in six months. My Theía owns the house I'm in now, and it's going up for sale in September."

"Fuck family. In the end, all they do is break your heart and break your bank," Rosie grunted, eyeing the fridge where we'd grabbed creamer from twenty minutes before. "There really isn't any Baileys in there? We could use some."

Jude looked over his shoulder through unfazed eyes. He stood at the far side of the counter where he now held a hammer, preparing to install supports for the giant painting leaning against the wall.

He turned back to face the wall without a response.

"Do you have a place to stay, Rosie?" I asked, placing the bottle on the counter and scooting Mae up against my shoulder. The question rolled off my tongue before I could swallow it down.

Did I want to live under the same roof as Rosie again?

Would things be the same, or—worse—would they be *so* different now that years had passed?

But when my eyes locked with Rosie's in front of me, a slideshow of memories flipped through my vision. All I saw were moments spent laughing at SultReads book club and nights when we walked back to our suite with the sunrise, barefoot with heels in hand. I was surprisingly clinging to the good of our past rather than the bad, and that was positivity I had to run with.

Because I knew how quickly that mindset could fall.

"If you need somewhere to crash...you can stay with us," I continued. "I know kids aren't really your thing, but if we split the rent, it will save us both a ton while we look for work."

"Do it!" Jude shouted, two nails jutting out from between his lips. "I don't want her ass staying on our couch, Nel."

"Yeah...the couch is kind of my bed anyway," the man wearing coveralls stated, appearing at the counter.

Had he been there the whole time?

I expected Rosie to ponder this idea for a few heavy minutes. Instead, the look on her face mimicked one of a child promised candy before dinner.

Not just candy—cake. With rainbow sprinkles.

And so much whipped cream.

"I'm in. Take me. I'm yours." Rosie reached forward, placing a hand on each of my shoulders as a toothy grin filled her face. "Viv is still touring or else I'd just stay in some hotel with her. She doesn't really have a home base either right now. That lucky bitch wasn't cut from the troupe. I guess The Bare Assentials need someone with *perfectly* healthy arches like hers to bring in the big bucks."

Viv.

My shoulders slumped a little at the sound of her name. It wasn't jealousy causing my mind to react this way—even though she *had* been all Rosie talked about three years ago before the radio silence. It was more the uncertainty of it all.

Would Rosie disappear again if Viv stayed in town for a long-term gig?

I knew she'd helped get Rosie into the troupe, but damn, I wouldn't have expected Rosie to lean on that situationship over what we'd had.

Yet still, I gave her the benefit of the doubt. It was what I did, after all. She needed somewhere to stay, and as raw as the wound was, I missed her.

"I'll clear out the den in the back of my apartment, and you can use the futon in there. There isn't a door, but it's pretty secluded. I lived on that thing for most of my third trimester when I couldn't get comfortable anywhere else."

Rosie's eyelids lowered. "If your water broke on that futon, I'm staying with Jude."

"You are absolutely not!" he shouted, the hammer pounding a nail into one of the few walls not made of brick.

I peered down at Mae to make sure she wasn't startled. Drumming her back with the heel of my hand, I wished I'd grabbed a muslin cloth from my backpack so I wouldn't have to throw another spit-up covered sweatshirt into the wash when I got home.

"If you can handle me taking over your den, I can handle your tiny human screaming every hour," Rosie said, leaning around the counter so she could see Mae's tiny, tan face peeking above my shoulder. "She *is* cute, Nel. You did good."

"She has Landon's complexion and his big eyes, for sure." I felt her little chest lift slightly against my shoulder as the tiniest burp escaped her lips. It was the cutest damn sound I'd ever heard. "I was just the incubator."

"She has your dimples," Jude said in passing. It was hard hiding those dimples while he washed his hands in the sink behind us. They practically poked holes straight through my olive skin the second my lips twitched into any kind of shape.

I shifted Mae around and sat her slouchy little body on my lap to find Rosie still watching Mae's every move. This was the longest I'd seen Rosie acknowledge my daughter since her grand return to Merlin Heights. I swear I even saw her lips twist into a faint smile as she leaned closer.

And then, Mae released a vomit volcano of formula right onto Rosie's jacket.

Chapter 4

Rosie

After half an hour standing beneath scalding water, scrubbing dried formula from my hair while Jude dragged in duffel bags from my car, it hit me: Nel and I were roommates again. This time, though, we weren't college students staying out too late and barely making it to morning classes.

We were now broke, jobless adults in need of direction.

Maybe my fallout from The Bare Assentials was a sign. Maybe the burning pain in my arches was supposed to happen for a reason—a reason I still couldn't get a grasp on. Thinking this way made me queasy because that troupe kept my heart—and sanity—from falling apart. It was where I felt unapologetically myself, constantly surrounded by people who embraced every flawed edge of me. When those scarlet lights hit my skin and the audience howled, I felt as radiant as the main character of a steamy romance novel during their first big sex scene. Every fear and flaw dissipated, and all that was left onstage was pure, raw confidence.

That raw energy was now drained. Zesty Zi drowned in every shot of Patron I'd consumed over the last two days, leaving a shell of a person in her wake. I wasn't even sure who Rosie Little was without the tit tassels, headpieces, and fishnets.

I didn't want to believe this was the push I needed to move onto something bigger, better...but maybe it was. Maybe I was supposed to get inebriated so that Andy at Thirsty Theodore's called my brother the other night. In truth, I was grateful the bartender called him instead of the cops. Jude knew better than to put me in a hotel or force me to stay at our cousin's place in Greyport against my will—he'd experienced angry, drunk Rosie a few too many times before trekking across the country. The place above Java Jude's he rented with Sebastian and Riley was small. Riley had set up camp on the living room futon, which left me with the floor...because I had a feeling Sebastian would try to woo me into his bed with his mandolin before giving the bed up for me.

Nel was Jude's only option.

He also knew I couldn't get mad at Nel. My body and brain wouldn't allow it. I'd tried being pissed at her in college—for petty reasons as an experiment, of sorts. It only led to me growing soft in her presence. There was something about our connection, our friendship, that synced my emotions with hers to create a state of rare stability.

I'd felt that same syncing of emotions last night when I woke up in this apartment.

Now, here I was, walking into a kitchen with a specific drying rack for bottles and breast pump tubes while a six-month-old lay whining in a bouncer stationed in the middle of the floor. When Mae looked at me, she smiled.

Even to Mae, I was a complete joke.

That or she saw me as a walking burp cloth.

Nel stopped moving for the first time since I walked in the kitchen, pausing by the sink with one hand inside of a pot overflowing with suds. "She likes you."

"It must be some fucked up form of hazing babies do," I said, realizing my words and meeting Nel's unfazed expression. "Am I allowed to say shit like that?'

Fuck, this was going to be hard.

"She found her feet for the first time last month, Rowe. You can say whatever the hell you want for the next few months." Nel faced the sink, scrubbing the inside of the metal pot before setting it into a separate drying rack. I was absolutely going to mess the drying rack situation up. "Was the shower okay? Jude left fifteen minutes ago after dragging in that garbage bag of sequined headpieces. You can try fitting all your stuff in the entryway closet."

Had they looked in my blue duffel bag where I stored all the heels I'd broken off my burlesque shoes?

I was sure that wouldn't look suspicious at all.

I needed to find a way to make money so I could buy appropriate clothes, or I'd be diving into Nel's closet of oversized sweatshirts, maternity jeans, pumping bras, and mesh hospital briefs.

Oh, and the seven pairs of overalls she swore by.

All in different colors and denim washes, of course.

"The closet will be fine. Everything is fine," I said, giving Mae a once-over before walking toward the stool on the other side of the kitchen island. "Once I find a job, everything will be fucking fine."

Nel huffed a laugh from the sink before turning off the faucet and drying her hands. "Isn't *that* the statement of the year?"

"I honestly don't even know where to begin looking, Nel! I'm back at square one. No, I'm below square one," I whined, peering across the kitchen. "Is there still coffee in that thing?"

Nel looked at the pathetically empty coffee machine by the windowsill. "Nope."

"Can there be?" I begged, flopping my body over the counter so my hands dramatically dangled off the opposite edge. "Maybe caffeine will stir up some ideas on how the hell we can survive these next six months before we sell our bodies."

Nel laughed, scooping some coffee into the machine. After a few seconds, the room filled with a familiar, nutty aroma. Subtle hazelnut made its way into the kitchen air, and the scent smacked me with nostalgia. It was the same roast—the same scent—that originally brought us together at Merlin Community.

It immediately brought me back to the book club.

"Remember how pissed you were that first night at SultReads?" A snort burst out as I replayed the scene. We always promised to leave it in the past but never did. Clearing my throat, I slid my body off the counter and back onto the stool in the smoothest way I could. It was definitely the opposite of smooth. "You should have been as pissed at me last night as you were that first night we met. I deserved that after ghosting you over these years."

Ghosting.

Had I really said it aloud?

It was a truth I avoided because it was a punch to the gut. I'd been in such a dissociative state three years ago that Viv's attention and my joining The Bare Assentials won over everything—and everyone—else.

Including Nel.

"You're saying, the other night, I should have spilled hot coffee all over you after bulldozing down the door you were standing directly in front of?" Nel's articulation was pristine every time we brought this conversation up. She shook her head, the oversized mass of chestnut hair barely staying in the bun as she looked down at Mae. "You weren't conscious enough the other night to fully experience the embarrassment, coffee withdrawal, and third-degree burn pain I endured that night at SultReads."

"They were *first*-degree burns, Nel. I will forever correct—and infuriate—you with this fact."

Expression drained from her face.

I knew her blood was boiling.

Nel rolled her light eyes, turning around to watch the coffee finish dripping into the carafe. One of her elbows met the countertop, and her chin fell onto her hand, her ass slowly rocking back and forth as the sweatshirt wrapped around her hips swayed with her movement. As her free hand appeared behind her and her middle finger flew up, she shouted, "They felt like third-degree burns, so I will forever say they were!"

"Nel."

She raised her middle finger higher into the air, her back still to me. "How you feel matters more than the truth."

I hopped off the stool and rounded the island corner before wrapping my arms around Nel's waist, forcing her into a stubborn embrace. Though she was taller than I was by a few inches, my determination gave me an advantage with these famous bear hugs she hated. She tried yanking my hands away from her midsection, and with how her fingers fumbled against mine, I could tell she didn't want me so close to her belly. She'd hinted at this post-partum insecurity earlier, before redirecting the conversation, the memory making me loosen my grip a tiny bit.

"If I hadn't run so fast into that book club," I said, rocking her side to side playfully in my arms, her fingers still clawing at the tops of my hands. "We never would have fallen so deeply in love and lived happily ever after together as roommates for the next two years."

"Ew. Don't touch me. My third-degree burns are still healing," Nel said, wiggling out of my grip and rising onto tiptoes to grab two clay, polka-dot mugs from the shelf. Without looking me in the eye, she shoved the red polka-dotted mug into my chest. With her back facing me as she poured herself some brew, she said, "I miss that."

"You miss what?" I asked, pouring myself some coffee once she stepped aside. "My aggressive hugs?'

"No. I absolutely do *not* miss you hugging me without my consent."

"Lies."

"Shut up. Well, it's only a partial lie," she said. "I miss SultReads. I miss the book club. I haven't finished a romance book in, like, months."

My eyes shot open at her confession. If it weren't for the grossly explicit romance novels we'd read at SultReads, we wouldn't have become the unstoppable force we were at Merlin Community College. Well, I guess we *really* did have the tragic coffee spill dilemma to thank. That sent us to the infirmary before book club even started, cold compresses against her chest, shoulder, and arms. That night, we discovered that, even though I was an extroverted loud-mouth, and she was an introverted klutz, we both had one thing in common: smut was life.

Even though we both despised the word *smut*, we were both equally obsessed with reading it.

After our night in the infirmary, we met every other Wednesday night at SultReads to talk about the book we'd all read, the tropes we drooled over, and the hidden messages forcing our brains awake at night. Once fall turned into early winter, we'd run into each other more often outside of the book club—sometimes the hallways or cafeteria, sometimes a house party or a bar we'd both snuck into. We'd find ourselves in the kitchen of some random guy's apartment, drinking stale IPAs out of red cups while talking about the unrealistic proposal scene in some book's epilogue.

Lunch became a regular meet-up for us, which turned into going to almost every college party together and, ultimately, becoming roommates for the next two years in the college's suite-style apartments.

We were damn proud of the three-year route we took at a two-year college.

"You didn't read Nessa Brady's recent release?" I asked, jaw dropped. "I heard she just moved to Rockberry!"

Nel rolled her lips together. "I wanted to. Just never got to it."

"What about the new Beckie Rosa romantasy?" My heart sped up just thinking about that novel as I dramatically fanned my face. "There's one scene that completely blew my mind...and it takes a *lot* to blow my mind."

Nel shook her head, her coffee mug meeting her lips.

"You *must* have read the—"

"I haven't read in almost a year, Rowe! Okay?" Nel shouted mid-sip, her chin now covered in hot, russet liquid. She wiped the coffee from her chin, drying her hand on the shirt wrapped around her waist before returning to bounce Mae with her foot.

I blinked, absorbing what Nel had said. She had been the super reader of the group—not because of her reading speed, but because of how well she understood the themes and tropes and language once finishing that last page. She probably knew the stories she read better than the author did. Knowing she hadn't read at *least* fifty books over the last year almost brought me to tears.

Almost.

Was motherhood the reason behind this? It made sense she'd want to nap whenever Mae finally did, instead of turning on an audiobook or flipping open a new paperback.

But it was the look in her solemn eyes—that mix of deep, tired gray-green—telling me it was more than motherhood pushing her passion aside.

Somehow, she'd lost the fire in her eyes she'd once had.

"I'm sorry, Nel," I cautiously said. "Want to read something together again? Since I'm here?"

Nel looked up over her glasses. "Actually, yeah. That might help."

I slid my coffee mug to the other side of the island and jogged back over, placing myself directly in front of her. "Okay, good. Great! I actually have a few new releases in my car from some local authors I'd hoped to get to during the tour."

Now I had all the time in the world for those books.

It was a blessing and a curse.

"It may distract us from hyper-focusing on the job search," Nel said as Mae softly whined from the bouncer at our feet—a bouncer she definitely had outgrown already. Nel unbuckled her and placed her over her shoulder, drool dripping over her precious, plump lips. "I wish we could just get paid to read books like all the influencers do. We just post a picture or a video, and BAM—sponsors and followers and whoever bow at our feet."

My stomach dropped.

My brow furrowed.

My eyes shot open wide.

A hypothetical lightbulb appeared above my head. Thoughts and ideas bounced around in a way I hadn't experienced in a while.

Our combined obsession with romance novels.

Nel's superhuman reading skills.

My burlesque background.

The thoughts rushing through my brain slowed to become one solid idea just as Nel noticed my smile growing.

"What's with your face?" Nel asked, leaning back. "I know that face. It's a terrifying face I've seen way too many times."

My palms slapped together, and I placed my chin on my fingertips. "One, my face is not terrifying. You love it. And two, I have an idea."

"I can tell," she said, shifting from foot to foot to keep Mae from fussing.

"I do," I said, rubbing my palms together in a wicked, satisfying, way. "I know how we can make money."

Chapter 5

Nel

Once Mae finished her bottle, spit up all over my flannel, shit through her diaper, and eventually went down for a nap, I finally took a long, soothing sip of coffee. I'd taken a liking to coffee that sat stagnant between hot and cold. I could always microwave it, but that depended on whether I had the energy to walk to the microwave and wait.

So, lukewarm coffee it usually was.

Rosie was sprawled across my living room floor, scribbling quickly in a notebook with her laptop open in front of her. The second she heard my socked feet whisper through the kitchen, she beckoned me over, patting the floor beside her.

When I sat down, all I saw were tits.

"What the fuck, Rosie?" My head snapped away, and I knew my neck would reap the consequences later. "You really thought it was a good time for porn?"

"Why are you whispering? Mae can't hear us," Rosie said. "And it's *always* a good time for porn."

I leaned forward, my open hand darting toward the screen. "But...it's before noon!"

Rosie smiled, setting her pen on the notebook, which was already covered in bullet points and arrows and notes in the margins. She'd filled up the whole page with gibberish I couldn't figure out in the time it took me to get Mae down for her nap. "It's not porn. It's YourEyesOnly."

I lowered my eyelids, my head falling to the side. "Isn't that the same thing?"

"Don't tell me you're *not* a subscriber?" This made Rosie switch from lying on her belly to mimicking my crisscross position on the floor. She was now directly facing me, her nose mere inches from my own.

I hated how perfectly straight and tiny her nose was.

Bitch.

"I mean, I've scrolled through some free tiers a few times," I admitted, shrugging my shoulders. "The livestreams where those guys do handstands and take their clothes off at the same time are entertaining."

Rosie nodded slowly. "Oh, yeah. The AcroDaddies, right?"

I turned away so she couldn't read my facial expressions. "Yeah. I guess so."

They were 100% the AcroDaddies.

"Okay, so you *are* familiar with the site…and it's *not* porn! It's more of an, I don't know, artistic, sexual outlet where like-minded people can interact in a safe space."

My gaze fell back on her. "You couldn't have just come up with that."

She pointed her finger at a scribble in the notebook. "I came up with it when you were cleaning Mae's shit. It's part of my pitch."

"What pitch?" I asked, peering back at her laptop. Two annoyingly gorgeous women were on the screen, the blonde lay on a purple yoga mat while a redhead kneeled beside her holding a foam roller and talking to the screen. Their thin, gemstone-lined sports bras left nothing to the imagination—circular, perky breasts spilling over and out the sides—and their vaginas were eating the spandex shorts they wore. As the redhead modeled how to appropriately use the foam roller to release muscle tension, she'd occasionally squint to read the comments rolling in at the side of the screen.

To my surprise, the comments were actually related to the foam rolling technique she was walking the viewers through and not whether they were going to take their tops off.

Well, to be fair, some dirty comments were *definitely* sprinkled in.

"My pitch on how we can make money!" Rosie shouted, forcing my focus back on her.

"You want us to wear sheer spandex and do yoga?"

Rosie laughed, exiting the livestream and returning to the YourEyesOnly homepage where a grid of mini livestreams appeared. Just from where I sat, I could see at least four sets of tits and three very erect penises.

I hadn't gotten this much action since my one-night stand with Mae's father…and I was just *looking* at a damn screen.

"They're *actually* physical therapists, but no. We're not doing that." When she faced me, the glint in her eyes was wicked. "We're going to read."

I pressed my lips together, cocking my head to the side. "We're going to read?"

"Yup. We're going to start our own book club," Rosie said, flipping her toned legs around so she was back on her stomach again, her body hovering above her notebook. "On YourEyesOnly."

"How would we get paid to sit around and talk about books?" I asked.

To be honest, I was intrigued. I didn't know how us starting a book club would pay our bills *and* pay for Mae's formula and diapers every month. But the idea of reading again with Rosie ignited a flicker of excitement I couldn't ignore.

As Rosie jotted a few more ideas onto a page, aggressively underlining occasional words, I said, "I'll listen."

I swear her eyes looked almost cartoonish staring back at me. "Really? Okay!" She pointed her pen at the top of her notebook page before slowly turning to look at me through thin eyes. "But you need to have an *open* mind. Can you do that?"

"My mind is open."

Rosie set the pen down and placed her chin on the top of her hands, grinning. "We're going to start a book club on YourEyesOnly where, every week, we read a chapter of some steamy romance novel on a livestream. We post on our community page beforehand and let people know what book we're reading so they can read with us if they want. You can borrow some of my garter belts and corsets to wear until you feel comfortable wearing—"

"Whoa, *what*?" I exclaimed, hoping Mae hadn't woken up. I took a deep breath and yanked my glasses off, rubbing my eyes with the scratchy, scabbed palm of my hand. My skin could stop being dry and cracked any day now. "We're wearing *what*?'

"Nel, it's YourEyesOnly. You have to be a little spicy to get followers, or we won't make any money."

"I am *not* wearing anything *spicy* on camera! I mean, come on." My hands rapidly moved across my body, skimming my chest and neck and belly and thighs. "I am nowhere near ready for a one-piece bathing suit, let alone some of your burlesque costumes. And what if someone recognizes us—recognizes *me*? Hallie is all over social platforms—TwoBloomsHal ranks high on Panormama and LaundryList and—"

"Your sister may be a social media queen, but those are the worst names for platforms ever," Rosie added with a painful eye roll.

I lowered my gaze. "And she has so many connections. She's good at what she does and she knows it. I'm sure she would find out I'm on something like this and officially disown me as her sister. I want...*need* her to be proud of me. I know you don't care if people see you, but I do."

Rosie's face dropped. "First of all, your sister is *not* perfect. If Hallie finds out we're on YourEyesOnly, she'll be jealous her mom-fluencing platforms aren't as successful as she makes them out to be. Second, you can wear a mask or something...make a new persona for yourself. There are some cute masks at Velvet in Greyport, and I have a few wigs you can try on. Nobody would know, and you could cover your tits with the book you're reading if that makes you feel better."

"I don't know if that makes me feel better. I'd feel better if we were just starting a normal, donation-based book club," I said, placing the glasses back on my nose. Inhale, exhale. I needed to breathe. "Isn't it, I don't know, *illegal* to read books without the author's permission? And make money from it?"

Rosie cleverly smiled and clicked one of the tabs at the top of her screen until her email popped up. "I already contacted five local, indie authors—Tessa Brady being one of them. I explained the idea and mentioned how it could help with their marketing and improve their sales...since followers would have to purchase books. So far, all five of them are on board. I have about four others on my list to still contact."

I needed to give Rosie credit. She really was checking off all the boxes.

"Okay...I like the idea of helping indie authors get more eyes on their books," I said hesitantly. "But how will you make money from this?"

Rosie clicked back to the YourEyesOnly tab, bringing us to a dashboard. "This is a *we* situation. I'm not doing this without you. The subscription rules are all right here. There are different subscription tiers for people to join. Hell, if people subscribe to the highest paying tier, I could read a sex scene out loud while masturbating and make majorly big bucks!"

"Rowe! Gross!"

Rosie rolled onto her back and slapped a hand to her chest, laughter echoing through the room. "Okay, okay. I wouldn't go that far...maybe. But I'd be fine doing some of the crazier shit and still splitting whatever comes in with you. We can iron out all those details once you agree that you're in."

"I am absolutely *not* in."

Even though part of me was still curious.

"I have a gut feeling this...this could be something big. You could just read in a sexy little outfit and talk to people in the chat. It would pretty much just be a virtual book club with something pretty for people to look at. You could hold down the fort in the lower tiers."

"Rowe. I'm *not* something pretty to look at."

My blood froze.

Air lodged in my throat.

Grant's face popped into my vision.

His voice sounded in my ears.

"You're not naturally pretty like those other girls. It just makes sense to stay with me."

"Why even do your make-up if it won't make a difference?"

"Just keep your shirt on. I don't want to look at all that when I'm fucking you anyway.

His smug expression.

His dark hair.

His words laced in venom.

I'd tried so hard to erase his damage over the years, but I couldn't wipe away the verbal cuts like the ones my first boyfriend—my first *love*—sliced me with.

It was as if I'd shot Rosie straight through the heart with a poisonous arrow. The edges of her eyes angled downward as she got up onto her knees, crawling toward me. Her knees settled onto the throw rug in front of us, and she cupped my face. "You've *always* been more than just something pretty to look at. You're more than that insane head of hair you force into that bun. You're more than that olive skin that makes you look like a fucking Greek goddess. You're more than those cute little dimples I have to hold myself back from poking constantly."

"But I—" Before I could finish, one of Rosie's hands slid from my cheek to my lips, her index finger stopping my words.

"The Nel I know used to rock the same pair of overalls almost every day to class and then transform into a Queen of the Night when we went out. No matter what you wore or how you looked, it was your spirit that drew people in. *That's* the beauty that matters. I may seem superficial most of the time, but I know it's the other shit that makes a difference. That's what you'd bring to the table with something like this—your spunk and, yes, something cute to look at. Because, Nel, you're fucking cute, and to be honest, it's kind of annoying how adorable you are. I hope the whole world is jealous of me because of how perfect my best friend is."

Best friend.

Would she stick around long enough to wear that title like one of her embellished headpieces?

I sucked in a hard breath, doing everything I could to avoid the dam from shattering. "I don't know, Rosie. It's been months since my personality came out to play, and this cuteness you speak of is nonexistent these days. I just...I don't know."

"What's stopping you from at least trying?" she asked, releasing her hands and leaning against the coffee table.

The only thing stopping me were my own insecurities. I knew that for a fact. It had taken years of therapy to get myself into the confident armor I'd worn at Merlin Community. I'd gone from dressing in whatever the hell I wanted to in my twenties, to hiding my stretch marks and extra belly skin beneath oversized sweatshirts tied at the waist. Ten years ago, I would have jumped on this idea as quickly as Rosie used to jump on all the singles at MCC.

I knew I needed to dive back into reading stories that lit my soul on fire. I needed income to start rolling in on a *very* regular basis. I needed to step outside my comfort zone, because I used to thrive outside of it.

I wanted to feel that fire again.

I just needed to light the match.

Rosie sat beside me, so still and focused. Taking a deep breath, a smile pinched my lips. "I'll do this on one condition."

Rosie's eyes practically jumped off her face. "Anything! What?"

"I wear overalls when we're streaming until I feel more comfortable."

As if already prepared, she curled her lips into a grin. "You can wear your damn overalls, but only with one of my bralettes underneath. Lace ones. The overall straps will hide almost everything anyway."

Silence hugged us for a few heavy seconds as I tried picturing the path we were about to walk down. This metaphorical path was still covered in rocks and sticks with a few poisonous berries. There were mud puddles strewn across the trail, and I wasn't wearing rainboots.

But the fact I could envision this path leading somewhere surprised me.

I needed to follow my heart and get out of my head.

My tired, swollen eyes met Rosie's wild ones. "I'll do it."

Chapter 6

ROSIE

My body, my mind, my emotions—everything was whirring wildly below my skin. I hadn't felt this revved up about something since I'd started with The Bare Assentials. Maybe it was the idea of getting back onstage, in a virtual sense, or creating something rooted in all my passions.

This high tasted better than the perfect shot of tequila.

Nel and I decided on a start date and the first book we'd read all before Mae's cries flooded the apartment. Once Mae was in her sixth fresh diaper of the day—all before 3:00 PM—we discussed who would read what chapters aloud and brainstormed a few wrap-up questions to ask viewers once finishing the book.

We also would call ourselves The Naked Book Club.

It just made sense.

Nel would never be fully naked on camera. That was something she was adamant about, and I respected her decision. But *I* was absolutely fine sprinkling a little sex work and burlesque into the naughty scenes I'd read to hundreds—maybe thousands—of strangers.

Being naked was my forte.

And I was damn good at it.

A week after officially deciding to do the damn thing, we found ourselves at Java Jude's with our laptops open, coffee heating our palms, and Mae squirming within the wrap bound to Nel's chest. Mae had yet to drop her binky on the floor—we'd remembered her clip this time around—so we focused for a solid hour before Sebastian began snooping.

I twisted my head to face him as he hovered about our table, my eyes thin. "Didn't Jude tell you to go add those things to the website...or something?"

Sebastian collapsed onto the bench beside Nel, lounging back and bringing both of his hands behind his head. "Done."

"You already did all the things?"

He raised a light, blond eyebrow. "Oh...I did *all* the things."

"Didn't he want you to add things to social media about the soft opening?"

"I did those things too," Sebastian said.

"Stop saying *things*…and also, ew." Nel's voice caught us off guard as our eyes locked onto her slumped frame. Her thin, pink lips were curled upward, her cheeks flushed just the slightest bit. "I just don't like the phrase *soft opening*."

I sat back in my chair, furrowing my brow with a nod. "It *is* kind of weird when you think about it."

Nel nodded. "It could be the title of a porno, though."

"Ooooh, yes! Write that down in your notes," I said, tapping the notepad beside her laptop. "You never know when we may need to use that."

Sebastian got to his feet, his hands at his hips as he took a few steps away from the table. "Well, I would love to talk all day about *openings* with you ladies, but I don't feel like getting smacked in the face today. Off to do some more, er…things."

Sebastian began whistling and walking swiftly toward Jude, who stood on a ladder by the front windows, dangling pots of pothos and philodendron from little hooks on the wooden frame. I peered at Nel the second Sebastian was out of earshot—as if I cared if he heard me. "Dude…you should talk about soft openings every time he hovers."

Nel winced. "Can we *please* stop saying that."

I scoffed, pushing aside my laptop so I had full—and intense—eye contact with her. "You can't listen to *that*, but you're okay reading the office blow job scene everyone is talking about on a livestream?"

Apparently, my eye contact hadn't been as intense as I thought. Nel just casually shrugged, tapping her foot so Mae could feel the soothing movement as she lay snuggled against her chest. "I mean, I'm kind of excited to read that chapter. I'd rather read that than hear or say soft opening one more time."

"You're excited about the soft opening next week?" Jude asked, magically appearing beside our table with potting soil dotting his olive-green crewneck. He held what looked to be a spider plant in one hand while the other held a fresh cup of coffee that he quickly slid to Nel. "Your mug looked empty from my spot on the ladder."

"First off, we were talking about a big blow job scene Nel's going to read aloud sometime soon. And second, why didn't you get your sister a fucking refill?"

Jude slid into the spot on the bench where Sebastian had sat minutes before, Nel scooting over to give him space—even though his short legs didn't need it. Genetics. "Maybe if my sister told me about this business thing she's planning, I'd feel more inclined to bring over some of our beloved brew."

He cocked his head to the side and began batting his eyelashes, a close-lipped smile pressed to his face.

Nel giggled, the mug of coffee stopping the laughter once it hit her lips.

"You *really* want to know?" I asked, eyebrows lifted.

"I mean, I also want to know what that whole blow job scene statement was about, but I'll move on," Jude said.

Nel tried to swallow back another laugh.

Where the fuck were these giggles coming from?

She was *not* a giggler.

"Well, that scene is kind of related to what we're doing," she said. Nel's eyes met mine before dashing back to my brother's. "We're starting a Naked Book Club."

The plant in Jude's hands would have crashed onto the floor if it weren't for his catlike reflexes. With the spider plant safely in his grip, his wide, dark eyes darted between Nel's face and mine. "Pardon?"

I sat up straight, setting both my hands politely on my lap. "You're looking at the two newest stars of YourEyesOnly." I looked toward Nel, who was reaching into the diaper bag beside her, grabbing a bottle and a can of formula. "Well, we haven't started yet, so I'm not sure if you can technically say we're *stars*."

"Whoa, whoa, whoa. Wait." Jude's free hand flew into the air in front of him, his head shaking so erratically that his messy bun of dark hair started coming undone. "You're doing porn?"

Why was this always the reaction?

We all watched porn—that was a given. We all supported sex workers and respected—and admired—their line of work. So, why was this any different? Why so much shock?

"We're exploring a new division of the performing arts industry, in a way," I said, dramatically attempting to flip my dark hair over my shoulder—even though there wasn't much hair to flip. "We'll read romance books a few times a week and then chat with viewers about the story. It's pretty innocent, actually."

"But...you'll be naked?" Jude's gaze shifted from mine to Nel, his Adam's apple bobbing slowly as Nel finally looked up from the bottle she was scooping formula into. "You too?"

Nel shrugged, placing the bottle beside her laptop, shaking the dry formula around inside of it so it became a mini snow globe. "Absolutely not. This mom-bod isn't ready for *that* just yet. I'm sticking to overalls for now."

"With *just* a bra underneath!" I shouted, pointing an index finger into the air. "There has to be some sexiness if we want to gain a few followers. I'll go all out at first. Nel will warm up to it."

"Speaking of warming up..." Nel jabbed the bottle into Jude's chest, raising her chin with a clever, and somewhat confident, grin. "Can you add some lukewarm water in here? Like you did the other day?"

Jude's cheeks remained flushed as he stared at her, finally grabbing the plastic bottle with an uneasy nod. "Yeah, okay. I'll do that."

The moment Jude was behind the counter, his fingers running beneath the faucet, my head fell back with a snort of laughter. "Nel, I think you broke him."

"Because he's become my *bottle boy*?" Nel asked, pulling Mae from her muslin wrap. "It's funny...because he used to be my *bottle boy* in college too. It was just a *much* different bottle back then."

I lifted an eyebrow, spinning a pen in my fingers as I sat back in the chair. "You guys haven't brought anything up yet? About that last MCC weekend?"

Nel's gaze immediately darted over my shoulder, where she could see Jude behind the counter, before angling her face down toward Mae. I could feel her foot tapping against the leg of the table, subtle vibrations growing under my mug. "What last MCC weekend?"

"Nel."

Nel's tapping foot grew faster as her almond-shaped eyes peered up through her square frames. "Rowe."

I stopped spinning the pen and pointed it at her. "Don't play dumb."

"I'm not playing dumb." Nel swallowed, her eyes twitching from me to Jude and back again. "I'm just playing pretend."

"So, you're pretending you never kissed and dissed my brother the night before—"

Nel shot a finger to her lips, as if that would stop *me* from talking. "Shhh. He's done filling the bottle." If her eyes kept moving between the two of us at the speed they were, vertigo would knock her out. "And Jude and I are fine. We've always been fine! We've always had an unspoken understanding...aaaaaand thanks for being my *bottle boy*, Jude!"

Nel snagged the bottle from my brother's hand, Mae wriggling in her arms before the rubber nipple slipped between her lips. Jude's eyes were wide, his cheeks still rosy from our previous conversation. Looking at Jude standing there, casually smiling down at Nel, I had to admit—she was right. I sensed zero tension. It felt natural and normal...even a little boring.

"How come that title gives me a heavy dose of deja vu?" Jude said, reaching for the spider plant he'd placed beside Nel moments before. He rocked from side to side in his navy-blue Converse sneakers, the plant transitioning from one hand to the other.

"You were quite the *bottle boy* at Merlin. You could always sense when I needed another beer," Nel said, laughing as she, too, began rocking slightly side to side to soothe Mae…who was practically eating the bottle whole.

Was I supposed to sway side to side too?

"Call it a sixth sense. With drinks—both alcohol and coffee—I just get it." Jude backed up toward the counter, Sebastian and Riley walking out from the back office, arguing with hands flying into the air. "I'll let you guys get back to planning this book club thing. That's all I'm going to think of it as. It's juuuuust a book club."

"You think that all you want, loser." I stood up after slamming my laptop closed and stretched my arms over my head, Sebastian stopping to watch as my sweater lifted just the tiniest bit above the hem of my jeans. Typical. "We're going to head back and prep our little book club area at the apartment. Bookshelves and ring light and lingerie and all."

Sebastian's face shot in my direction, his golden, greasy hair flying. "Books are cool. I'll join."

Nel giggled from behind me, burping Mae while attempting to slide her laptop into the diaper bag like the multitasking queen she was. I swore she grew three extra hands every time we left the house.

Snagging my coat off the chair and throwing my bag over my shoulder, I walked toward Sebastian and leaned onto the counter with a hand on my hip, Jude standing at the sink behind us. "I'll send Jude the link for where you can join our book club. He will text it to you."

Shaking his head, Jude turned the faucet on full force, and water angrily hit the bottom of the farmhouse sink. "Nope. I absolutely will not."

yourEyesOnly.com
LIVE
LIKE SUBSCRIBE COMMENTS
@rollOUT1999: Is it possible to foam roll too hard? My hamstring hurts.
@CallMeMagicMike:
@rollOUT1999: There's no such thing as too hard.
FOAM FREAKS

Chapter 7

Nel

I should have canceled.

I should have put on my big-girl pants and told them I wasn't in the mood for goulash, or chicken riggies, or Hallie's homemade baklava, or whatever we were cooking. I wished Nora was here to be the buffer she always was at our sister dinners, but, instead, she'd stayed home to do some wedding planning.

I also *definitely* should have given Hallie some sort of heads-up about Rosie.

And her brother.

I opened the front door. Hallie's twins, Daisy and Dahlia, immediately raced to their baby cousin without blinking an eye at me.

Then Mae spit up all over herself.

And the twins.

"Shit..." I whispered, knowing if I said it any louder, Hallie may get annoyed. "Let me clean that up. Sorry, girls."

"Oh...it's okay. We're used to it. Tucker can go over there and keep them busy while we catch up!" Hallie said, heading toward the entryway closet as she gestured her husband toward the couch. "I'm throwing the diaper bags and the girls' extra sweaters in—"

Before I could snag the bags and sweaters from Hallie, a crotchless, red lace thong slid onto the floor followed by a silver-studded harness and about twenty nipple pasties.

No.

No, no, no, no.

I stood frozen as Daisy and Dahlia frolicked to their mom's ankles, grabbing a couple butterfly-shaped pasties from the floor and lifting them into the air.

"Open this, Mama?"

Hallie plucked the pasty from Daisy's fingers, wrangling the rest with a cautious smile. "These aren't stickers, honey."

She nudged the lingerie into the closet with her foot then closed the door, her hand lingering a moment too long on the handle. Her chest lifted and fell before running her fingers through dirty-blond waves draped over her shoulder.

My shuffling feet were slow since I didn't know how to approach this—approach *her*—when it came to Rosie and Jude.

Did I apologize for Rosie's things falling out onto the floor?

Did I apologize for forgetting to tell her that Rosie was back in town?

Did I need to apologize at all?

Sorry was a word living on the tip of my tongue because Grant had embedded it there. When I was late to a party, he forced apologies because I'd ruined the night. If I showed too much skin, I apologized to everyone who'd gotten an *unfortunate glimpse,* Grant would say. When I tripped over my words, I apologized for being a complete idiot because, according to Grant, that was exactly how I sounded.

Until him, Hallie was the sister who occasionally guilted me for getting better grades than her but also helped with my make-up before homecoming and prom. She made sure everyone knew she was top dog with anything related to make-up or style, stepping in whenever I tried adding my own *flair* to a look. It took years for Hallie to even acknowledge we had a younger sister in the house because she was always so hyper-focused on helping me with...well, everything.

I mean, Hallie *was* older than I was.

Older and prettier and less awkward.

Her help was something I couldn't push away because...why would I?

Hallie's reign leveled up once she discovered Grant's antics.

She overheard him call me pathetic or stupid or something along those lines—the details were hazy now—one night when he'd come over to watch a movie. The haunting memory of her footsteps echoed in my brain, steps leading right over to the couch we sat on.

The second she saw tears staining my cheeks, fists flew.

Hallie punching Grant's smug mouth, blood painting her pristine knuckles, was a turning point in my life. He walked out with a bloody hand covering an eye and a nose forever crooked...but he never came back to our house again. If he saw me in the hallway at school, he gave me a look that could murder but continued walking.

Hallie freed me.

I was forever grateful.

"Oh, fuck!" Rosie jogged into the kitchen, stopping at the closet when something in her brain clicked into place. She crossed her arms over the very clear nipple piercings poking through her white tank top and leaned into one hip. When she casually placed the thong and harness Hallie avoided grabbing onto a hanger, she realized everyone in the room was gawking at her.

Of course, in true Rosie fashion, her hand flew above her head, and she flicked her wrist to wave, the other hand returning to her chest. "I didn't know everyone would be here so soon! Sorry about all that. The coat closet became my own personal armoire when I moved in."

"*Moved* in? This...this is new news." Hallie covered her girls' ears and shuffled them over to their dad, Tucker, who sat reading to Mae. Grabbing her wine and spinning the liquid gently against the glass, Hallie asked, "When did you get back? I thought you were...*dancing* these days?"

"I was, yeah," Rosie said, angling her body toward the closet. "I guess now we can just use this stuff for dress up when Mae is older or—"

"Hey, Rowe. Why don't you go change, and I'll help Hallie in the kitchen with things. Join us when...you're ready," I said, elbowing her gently in the waist.

Catching on, Rosie's hands flew to her chest again as she backed out of the kitchen. "Yeah, yes! Great. I'll be right back. Carry on!"

I felt Hallie's eyes burning bullet holes through my skin the second Rosie disappeared into the den.

God, why couldn't Nora have been here?

She was always such a calming presence during these things.

Damn little sister, and her social anxiety.

"Nel, hey..." Hallie leaned in closer, her untouched wine still in hand. "What the fudge was that?"

I peered over the top of my glasses, cocking my head to the side. "Did you just say *what the fudge?*"

Hallie angled herself toward all the children who huddled together on the couch as Tucker read aloud to them.

"I did. I know it sounds *funny*, but you may want to start talking that way too...just to prepare yourself. Mae will catch on before you know it." Hallie lifted her chin in the direction Rosie shuffled off to. "Probably Rosie too, don't you think? I know you've always liked her, but she really shouldn't talk like that and walk around here...like that."

"I'm sure she will adjust," I said, hesitantly hopeful. "She just moved in a few days ago. It takes time."

"You're absolutely right, change does take time. I'm sure you will help her make the changes she needs to make." Hallie's hand fell over my forearm, and I met her soft gaze. "You know I'm only saying all of this because I care, Penny."

The nickname.

It sent my stomach plummeting every time she said it.

Hallie was so conditioned to say it that my reminders were pointless.

But I didn't react to it because, she *was* right.

Hallie *did* have her shit together—beautiful family, gorgeous home, stable career. She probably could pinpoint those who didn't have their shit together better than most.

Was Rosie one of those people?

There was no doubt I was.

Grabbing my glass of wine off the counter, Hallie followed me to the couch where Tucker was still reading to Mae. The twins lost interest minutes before and had since pulled out the cardboard box I kept in the corner with crayons and construction paper. Instead of coloring, they ripped up blue paper into tiny pieces, throwing handfuls into the air and letting the pieces fall over them like a storm of confetti.

I, too, felt a storm rolling in, my eyes growing glossy and my breathing tight in my throat.

Breathe in, breathe out.

These comments were nothing new.

"She's grown up since college, Hal," I muttered, watching Hallie flop on the opposite end of the couch next to her husband who knew better than to ever speak up.

Like ever.

"I hope so…and I'm sure she has!" Hallie said, taking a swig of wine as her emerald eyes wandered to my glass sitting on the coffee table. "Is that *your* wine? Or did you get it for Rosie?"

Breathe in, breathe out.

Lifting the glass from the table, I brought it to my lips.

Hallie scooted down the couch until she was only a few feet from me. "Don't you think it's a little too early to start drinking? I think I waited until the girls were, maybe, fifteen months before I had a glass of wine."

"Mae is almost seven months old, not seven *minutes* old." My voice was flat; my tone was bold.

Weren't we supposed to be making dinner?

Was my mood change because I was hangry?

"I know you know all of this. You have to just be careful—that's all." Hallie scooted closer, taking another sip. "I just don't want Rosie to be a bad influence on you. After what Grant did to you, I don't want my baby sister going backward if I can help it."

I took another sip…this time, it was longer than the first.

Why was Rosie taking so long?

Hallie laughed, sitting back against the couch and adjusting her deep golden waves so they fell over the opposite shoulder. "I mean…you have to admit that if I hadn't nudged you away from those other guys in college—including *her* brother, you could have taken some pretty big steps backward."

My stomach fell through my feet when Hallie glanced at the back den when saying *her brother.*

I finished my glass of wine.

"Grant was bad, yes, and maybe I don't have the best track record," I said, my voice a little bit louder than it had been before. "But let's leave the past in the past."

Hallie flapped her hand in the air, the other one lifting the glass to her lips—lips recently prodded to perfection. "I know, I know. I always feel so bad bringing this stuff up. It's just important, Pen."

I tightened my grip around the wine glass, getting to my feet. "Why don't we go make dinner? Isn't that why you guys are *really* here? To eat some chicken souvlaki and not to nit-pick every choice I've ever made, right?"

Whoa.

That came out sounding a bit sassier than I would have liked.

But I wouldn't take back my words. Not when they were the truth.

"Pen, no...I'm not nit-picking," Hallie said, standing up and shaking her head. "I really hope that's not how you feel. You know I want you and Mae healthy and not growing up in an unstable environ—"

"Unstable from *what*, exactly?" My voice echoed through the living room, surprising even me with its sharp edges. Fire clawed at my throat. The heat was unbearable. "Mae is healthy and thriving. I'm sorry, Hallie, but even with your *gentle parenting* knowledge, that's bullshit."

Hallie eyed her daughters, who added pieces of orange and pink paper into the confetti mixture, before she returned to me with callous eyes. "You really can't keep talking that way, and Rosie being here won't help with that. I'm worried."

I took a deep breath, internally screaming at my tear ducts to keep the dam intact for at least five more minutes.

Mae seemed healthy and happy and not at all unstable.

But Hallie was seeing my world through a different lens...a lens I'd always trusted.

So, why was I struggling with that trust now?

Maybe it was my hormones figuring out what the hell was going on and postpartum depression creating a home within my body, but her verbal daggers were hitting deeper than usual today.

She could call me unstable, but she would *not* bring Mae into this conversation anymore.

Wounds couldn't heal when the bandage kept getting ripped off.

I stepped around Tucker and brought Mae to my chest, my feet weights dragging me across the floor. "I'm going to go pump for a little bit and then we can get dinner going. Excuse me."

I didn't need to pump, nor did I want to.

All I wanted was out.

Out, out, out.

"Oh, I thought you were still nursing?" Hallie said, following me toward the kitchen. "Pumping is great...seriously, I'm *so* glad you're pumping. It's just that the benefits of nursing are so amazing, and I feel like you guys could use them."

Done.

I was done.

With Mae hugging my shoulder, drool dripping over my sweater, my eyes trembled as I looked at Hallie and said, "You *know* nursing isn't my thing. You *know* I feel incredibly guilty about that...and if I want to have a glass of wine once in a while, I fucking can." My eyes darted to Tucker, who was picking up tiny pieces of paper scattered across the living room floor while the twins added to the mess, oblivious to the shitshow going on around them. "And I don't care if your girls hear me swear, because they'll learn more just by listening to how you speak to me."

Tears rolled down my cheeks as I twisted on my heel and marched through the kitchen. The second I got to the bedroom door, Rosie walked out of the den clad in a floral maxi dress with a cropped denim jacket hugging her shoulders.

She looked like a gay hipster getting ready for church.

The second she saw the tears, hands were on her hips. "What did that bitch say to you?"

"I'm just going to lie in here for a bit." I pushed open the door, stepping inside. "Tell them I'm pumping."

Rosie shook her head, her lips pressed together. "Hallie still hasn't learned to shut the hell up, huh? I'll kick her out. I'll seriously kick all of them out, if you want."

"No, no. Don't. That will make everything worse." It felt wrong saying it, but the words dripped out almost automatically as I whispered, "She's...she's just trying to help."

"Well, she's always had a real fucked-up way of showing it."

I took a deep breath, shutting my eyes tight. "Just grab me another glass of wine. I'll be okay."

"Are you sure?" Rosie asked, backing up toward the kitchen as I began closing the door.

"I'm sure. Thanks."

The second Rosie stepped away and I closed the door, I slid to the floor as carefully as I could with Mae pressed against my rapidly beating heart. Rosie shouting, "Hallie, get the fuck out," were the last words I heard before my heaving, jarring sobs drowned out everything else.

Chapter 8

Rosie

"**W**here the hell did you find that?" Nel asked the second she walked in the apartment, scuffing her boots across the mat, a dusting of snow at her heels. Setting down Mae, who lay fast asleep in her carrier, Nel wandered into the living room where I stood on my tiptoes, placing another book onto the shelf.

"Outside of Three-Ring."

Nel's eyebrows shot through the muddled bun on top of her head, a bun now sliding forward to become some weird, rounded unicorn horn above her glasses. "You took one of Three-Ring's bookshelves? Ummm...did you, like, *steal* it?"

"Nel. It was on the side of the road," I said, rolling my eyes. "Plus, Three-Ring keeps throwing all their old shit out now that the Booze Buffet took over the front of their building. I don't know why they aren't selling this stuff. They'd make *great* money!"

She leaned her head to the side as I grabbed a couple more books from the cardboard box to add to the top shelf. It had taken me way more time than I wanted to admit to line these up in a somewhat color-coded and cohesive fashion.

My arms and calves would be sore tomorrow.

"Are those...*my* books?" Nel stepped closer and squinted at the spines staring back at us from the oak shelves. "Where did you find these?"

"This box was in the den, actually." I nodded toward the empty cardboard box I'd kicked across the living room floor minutes before Nel arrived. "That one was in the back of the coat closet under a pile of sweatshirts."

Her lips twisted to the side. "Maybe I wanted to add these to my bedroom shelf."

"Nel...were you *really* planning to do that anytime soon?"

She shrugged, her lips twisting to the other side of her face. "Once I have the motivation."

"You can't *really* be angry at me when I organized your books according to color and trope so you'd have one less thing on your plate."

"You organized them according to *trope*?"

I smiled, throwing a wink her way. "Sure did."

Nel stepped closer. "Oh my god, you did."

"Second shelf is enemies-to-lovers. This side of the third shelf is forbidden romance, and the other side is office romance. And..." I fell to my knees so I could see the bottom shelf in all its green to blue to purple glory before peeking over my shoulder at Nel. "These down here are mostly forced proximity."

I hadn't even finished the statement before Nel was down beside me, her fingers running up and down the spines. "No way."

"Yes, ma'am. All your favorite only-one-bed scenes are down here, looking fine as fuck for you."

Nel turned toward me, her eyes watering. "Oh my gosh, Rosie...this is—"

"Whoa, whoa, whoa, Nel...those hormones of yours are in overdrive." I crossed my legs beneath my body. "I get you're still a bit shook up from the other night...but crying over forced proximity?"

Nel's fingers ran over a teal-colored spine before bringing the book to her chest. "I haven't read *Swiping for the Enemy* since our freshman year when I found out Dana Rowan lived in Holly Hill. I need to read it again."

"Now, there's the Nel I remember!" I said, throwing my arms up and getting to my feet...even though my calves were already screaming. I should have just grabbed a damn chair to stand on when placing books on that top shelf. Stupid ego. "Also, Dana

Rowan is one of the authors who gave us permission to read her stuff on the livestream. So, we're golden. Okay, here's what I did when you were at therapy...which I still don't understand the point of going to when you could just keep doing virtual sessions."

"When I have the energy to leave the house for a session, it's kind of nice to get out," Nel admitted with a shrug before softly placing the book back into its spot on the bottom shelf. "Plus, I stopped by the bank to grab paperwork about different combined business accounts we can look into. Whatever money we make can go into that pot, and we can split it from there. Oh, and I got contacts for accountants who can talk to us about taxes."

I tapped the side of my head with a smile. "I love when you use that educated noggin of yours. Better you than me when it comes to looking at anything related to numbers. We're both mediocre math students, at best, but your B+ surpassed my C- at Merlin."

"Wow. How do you remember that?" Nel asked, following me into the kitchen toward the coffee machine spitting hot brew into the carafe.

"How do you *still* remember that quadratic formula song from middle school you taught us at MCC? That song was the only reason we survived that test."

Grabbing her polka-dot mug from the rack, she shrugged. "Touche."

"As I was saying, I did a few things this morning when you were out," I said once our mugs were full and my laptop was open on the kitchen counter. Opening the laptop was equivalent to a syringe of adrenaline being pumped into my bloodstream. The buzz was unmatched. "Our profile is confirmed, and I created three tier levels for our followers with prices. Tier one is Steamy Storytime, tier two is Rowdy Readers, and tier three is Smut Me Up."

"You live for alliteration."

"I know! It's fucking great!" My empty creativity well was slowly filling back up. "So, you'll be the Steamy Storytime librarian—I thought calling ourselves *librarians* was cute—and when you want to help with Rowdy Readers, we can split tier two. Stop me when something doesn't make sense."

"Oh, believe me, you know I will," Nel laughed, taking a sip of coffee. "Honestly, all of this sounds okay to me. Well done."

I curtsied appreciatively. "Your subtle compliments are forever my favorites. That's a lie. Whenever Viv tells me my tongue skills are top-notch, *those* compliments surpass yours."

"Okay, ew." Nel shook her head, eyes slamming shut. "Have you even talked to Viv since coming back to Merlin?"

And there went my adrenaline rush.

"We texted last week. The Bare Assentials are doing a show in Greyport next month that she wants me to go to. I don't know. I'll see."

"Would she visit you here? Maybe for a night?" Nel looked down into her coffee mug, tapping her fingers slowly on the ceramic. "Would you *want* that?"

My head fell back with a dramatic laugh. "Viv? Staying on someone's couch? Never. She won't go near a three-star hotel, and the thought of a bed and breakfast disgusts her." I leaned onto my forearms, light from the window creating a halo of hues across the bookshelf in the living room. My heart warmed just seeing our new office—of sorts—come to life. "If she hadn't pushed me to audition for the troupe, I wouldn't have made bank over those years. She's the high-maintenance bitch of my dreams who will never want anything serious, but I'll never stop thinking she might."

My eyes flicked to Nel's, and she blinked, her heavy stare snapping me back to our initial discussion as she said, "Do you have any other updates about the page?"

"You don't want to hear more about Viv's non-monogamous, sexualized lifestyle?" I asked with a wink.

"I really don't." Nel didn't look me in the eye. "It doesn't really sound like she's bringing you a ton of joy...so, tell me more about our page, since *that* seems to satisfy you more than she does."

She wasn't totally correct...but also not totally wrong.

Clearing my throat, I clicked the laptop's trackpad so the YourEyesOnly page returned to the screen. "Okay, other than making a few adjustments to the tiers, our homepage is ready to go. You can look and edit whatever you want. Next step is setting up our recording studio in front of our *beautiful* bookshelf, and then we can start streaming this Friday!"

Nel's coffee mug practically slipped from her grip. "*This* Friday."

"Yup. We agreed on this Friday."

"I thought we'd said *next* Friday."

"We said that last week." I giggled into my coffee, watching her olive skin turn pale. "Next Friday is officially this Friday now...and we will *both* be on camera for the debut. Ready or not, let the book club begin."

Chapter 9

Nel

My foot hadn't stopped tapping the cement floor for ten minutes.

Jude hadn't stopped staring at my twitching Converse sneaker since I'd walked through the doors.

The laptop screen sat naked in front of me, and I didn't know what to do with it.

Hell, I didn't know what to do with myself.

Mae had cried continuously through the night, and each time I dragged my feet into the nursery, I found her binky on the other side of the room. After playing this game of fetch for longer than necessary, I made some coffee and hoped for the best by four o'clock a.m.

Rosie hadn't fallen back asleep without a scene, though. She'd yanked every fan I owned into the den and turned them up high to give her one hell of a white noise concert just as I clicked the coffee maker on.

I'd hear about this later.

The second Mae's eyes slammed shut for their nap, I'd packed up her diaper bag—stuffed with about twelve extra binkies—set her gently in the stroller, and left a note for Rosie, letting her know I was doing *prep work* at Java Jude's.

I just didn't know what exactly I was *prepping* in regard to my new line of work.

"What's wrong?" he asked.

Blinking twice, I finally brought the coffee to my lips. Lukewarm. Just what I was used to. "Nothing."

"Uh-huh."

"*Nothing.*"

He sat back, crossing his arms. "Mm-hmm."

My foot tapped faster as word-vomit climbed up my throat, my chest growing tighter. "Tonight is our first YourEyesOnly livestream, and I'm freaking the fuck out because I have to wear your sister's stupidly see-through bralette under my overalls, and my body is *not* ready to even show shoulder skin, let alone cleavage—"

"Nel."

"—and I said I'd be brave enough to read the first page of the book we're starting, and I'm definitely *not* brave enough to do any—"

"Nel!"

With my mouth agape and tears tickling the edges of my eyes, I peered up to see both of Jude's hands covering my own. He wasn't just setting his hands—large, rough hands that smelled of ground coffee—over my trembling fingers. He was wrapping my hands within his, forcing gentle pressure around them.

For a moment—possibly the first moment since Mae's initial binky breakdown the night before—I felt my lungs swell and release.

Swell and release.

Swell and release.

Exhaling, I focused on the tops of Jude's hands still covering my own, that gentle pressure continuing. I released my thumb from the cocoon of his palms and rubbed it against ink-kissed skin camouflaged by dried paint and coffee grounds.

Instead of pointing out that he should wash his hands a little better after painting—and grinding coffee—I noticed something else.

"These," I whispered, releasing my hand from his, my fingertips running over the thin, meticulous lines of wings and stippled antennae spanning each of his hands. The line work was extraordinary, his veins shifting beneath my touch. "You didn't have these in college."

"I didn't have *any* of them then." A laugh rumbled low in his chest. "I got this moth about a week after we left—during our short stint in Nevada."

"Why?" I asked, transfixed by the detailed ink.

His eyes followed my finger as I traced the antennae of the moth on his right hand. "Why what?"

Jude became clearer before me, my gaze softening after being stuck in a mental fog. "Why the moths?"

He watched as my finger made its way back toward the wide wings. "Some moths pupate underground and—"

"Pupate?" I couldn't help the giggle. "Did you just say *pupate*?"

"I sure did. I went through an intense entomology phase as a pre-teen." Watching my finger as it shifted across his skin, he continued. "Some moths *grow* underground and climb to the surface when they're fully formed—kind of like cicadas. When I got out West, I saw a moth climbing out of the ground and kind of, I don't know, felt like I was doing the same. I was escaping for a bit, and once I truly knew who I was and who I was becoming, I'd head back home. I got the right hand tattooed in Nevada and then the left when I got back here."

The tension in his fingers softened, my fingertip releasing from its trip around the ink. His hand shifted from mine to flatten some stray whiskers hovering over his lips. His beard looked a little less unruly today—tame, but not without a hint of rebellion.

I liked this newfound wildness to Jude.

"So, it seems like now you have a better idea of who you are," I whispered, melting back into the chair. "And what you want."

Who you want.

Jude's shrug was followed by a confident nod. "I do, yes. Sometimes you have to leave who and what you love behind for a little while so, when you return, you're certain what your next move is."

I swallowed, watching his Adam's apple bob.

"But...you're deflecting," Jude said, shaking his head. "Tell me how you're going to be brave tonight."

Then my stomach sank back through my toes, and I was drowning into the cement again. "Yeah...well...I don't think I'll end up with some *moth moment* like you had. I'll probably end up freezing, and everyone watching will—"

"Nel." His voice was soft. This time, there wasn't word-vomit creating an emotional swamp between us. It was just the two of us—two friends with a past, willing to push aside any awkward memories to fill the other person's cup.

It felt nice we could start back up right where we'd left off.

Well, *sort of* where we'd left off.

"Jude," I said.

"I don't know exactly what's going on during this livestream tonight, and I *definitely* will not check it out...because, well, Rosie." He leaned forward and covered his mouth, gagging into his fist. "But what I definitely *do* know is you're brave as hell. You used to help me be brave in college, so I know for a fact it's still somewhere inside of you. Maybe you've stuffed that bravery down into some dark place, and you don't feel like digging it up just yet, but it's there. I think now may be as good a time as any to grab a shovel."

My shoulders slumped as his words hit home. Jude was one of the few people I felt safe being vulnerable around, so I didn't think twice about bringing my feet up onto the chair and hugging my knees close to my body the way I wouldn't have around, say, Hallie.

I glanced down at my coffee for strength before I met his gaze. "Jude, we haven't talked in almost a decade. I'm not that brave, fearless kid you watched dance on bartops and hide in the woods from the cops with. I have a kid now, and I don't have a job, and my body is—"

"Don't you dare say it," Jude's voice echoed through the coffee shop, his volume remaining exactly as before—relaxed without strain. This time, each word held a confidence—a power—that was missing when he would follow Rosie and me from class to party to dorm like a little duckling.

Now, certainty flowed through him.

I wanted to dig my teeth into it and suck some out.

"It's just...it's just different," I said.

Instead of him questioning my confidence, his comforting, familiar grin caused a memory to flicker to the front of my mind.

You used to help me be brave in college.

That.

That was it.

He'd once been vulnerable and trusting with me. Now, it was my turn.

"Remember, in college, when you practiced talking to me like I was some girl you had a crush on?" My hands moved abruptly with every word I spoke. "Like, I'd pretend to be at a party, and you'd flirt with me? I'd tell you when you sounded stupid and when you sounded, well...sexy. That's what you meant before, right? When you said I used to help you be brave?"

Color immediately flushed Jude's cheeks, and he rolled his eyes, lowering into his seat. "I did *not* expect the conversation to go in this direction."

I closed my laptop and pushed it aside, my hands filling the space. "We used to pregame and do this for *hours* before leaving the room...and it usually worked for you!"

"*Usually* being the key part..." Jude sat slumped in the chair, all confidence drained. "And I don't think I had crushes on any of those people. I just didn't know how the fuck to talk to anyone." His dark eyes dove into mine. "But I knew how to talk to *you*."

"Yeah...yeah, you're right," I said, stomach somersaulting at the shift in tone. "We've always been comfortable around each other. You trusted me even though we'd make complete fools of ourselves—all in the name of getting you laid, of course."

Jude's eyelids lowered. "What are you getting at, Nel?"

A soft, yet high-pitched squeak sounded from the stroller by the window, and I jumped to my feet. Mae's eyes were wide open, her mouth opening and closing like a perplexed baby bird. I unhooked her and curled her against my chest as I grabbed one of my handy-dandy pre-made bottles from the diaper bag.

Placing the knuckle of my index finger between her lips—since the original binky probably disintegrated into thin air—I turned to Jude, who now stood beside the table. "What I'm getting at is...now I need *your* help."

"My metaphors and therapeutic presence aren't enough for you?"

Shaking my head, I swayed my body side to side from my spot in the chair. "I helped you feel brave, and now I need you to help me feel the same way…but this time, with this whole Naked Book Club thing. I need you to be my…like, practice buddy."

Jude's eyes widened, and his chin lowered to his chest, the tip of his beard brushing the drawstrings of his sweatshirt. "Excuse me?"

"No…no, no, no." I shook my head just as the front door shot open, and Rosie stepped through the entryway. Her bloodshot eyes locked on us as she walked directly to the counter, an arm straight in front of her pointing at the espresso machine.

"I may need more clarification on this whole *practice buddy* thing before I caffeinate my sister," Jude whispered, stepping back toward the counter where his twin still stood, pointing toward the machine. "…and fast."

"What I mean is I can *read* to you. I can practice reading to you the way I'll read on the livestream," I said softly, my eyes darting from him to Rosie and then back. "Maybe not for tonight's stream, but for my first solo one next week. I think it'll be nice having a few practice runs under my belt before each solo livestream. With you… We will just fall back into our old rhythm, you know?"

"You don't want to practice reading with…this?" He nodded to his sister, her index finger still pointed.

"I'll probably be more anxious trying to be all sexy with you because, well, you're more like the population who will watch. No offense…if that was offensive."

Jude shrugged. "None taken."

"Espresso! Now!" Rosie shouted, bending her elbow and aggressively jabbing her finger over the counter.

"Yeah, okay. Sure, Nel. I'll help you," Jude spit out. "I can do that for you."

I grabbed the bottle off the table, adrenaline still swimming through me as I shook it in the air. "Oh, Jude!"

"Huh?" he said, backing into Rosie, who stood like a zombie beside him.

"Here." I tossed the bottle over my table, and Jude stepped forward, barely catching it as it bounced off his chest and into his grasp. "You may be *my* tutor now, but you'll forever be my *bottle boy*."

Chapter 10

ROSIE

When Mae was old enough to know what her mother and I were doing, I'd blame her for making me look high during our debut livestream.

My bloodshot eyes would be upfront and obvious when we went live at eight o'clock. I, maybe, slept a solid two and a half hours the night before. I'd dressed myself in two hooded sweatshirts, a pair of leggings, a pair of sweatpants over the leggings, and fleece socks because I'd thought surrounding myself with icy white noise would solve the problem.

I was wrong.

Still, it was *on with the show*!

"It looks so good!" I said as Nel shuffled into the living room clad in black overalls and a red, lace bralette.

She cupped her breasts and pushed them up, grimacing when she caught a glimpse. "They look floppy as fuck."

"No. They look beautifully bouncy and *natural* as fuck." I adjusted the ring light at the arm of the couch so it faced the blush shag rug in front of the bookshelf. "No one wants someone with fake tits up to their chin these days. They want the real deal...and your girls look *good*."

"You can't see my nipples, though, right? You don't think they're going to pop out the side of the overalls or anything?"

I stood back up, shooting a satisfied grin toward the ring light. "Your nips are covered, Penny Playful."

"Rowe, you know I'm *not* going by that name," she said, grabbing the short, black wig from the couch. The wig was very similar to my hairstyle: black, pin-straight hair chopped right above the shoulders with bangs cut right above the eyebrows. We were going to try out a *twin librarian* vibe, and see if it took with any of the followers.

"So, you're going with *Penelope* Playful? I'm out of breath just saying it."

Nel shrugged, adjusting the wig before grabbing the black lace mask that would cover just her eyes—eyes sans glasses. "Didn't you say Exotic Ellie was an option?"

"Yes! That's the winner!" I exclaimed, throwing my hands over my mouth when I remembered Mae was in the other room with angry teeth pushing through her gums. Gross. "Exotic Ellie and Zesty Zi. All I can say is that our alliteration is spot-on."

Alliteration was fueling my creativity because I did not have enough brain space to think of a new stage name—so, Zesty Zi was going from Bare Assentials dropout to a sassy, classy Naked Book Club librarian.

The laptop sat on a chair within reaching distance for us in case comments started coming in. My eyes scanned the screen, and I said, "So far, no one is in the lounge waiting."

"Did you expect us to have hundreds of viewers for the debut?" Nel asked, carefully pulling the mask over her eyes. "The second this thing ends, I'm yanking these contacts off my eyeballs. I forgot how much I hate these things."

"Negative Nancy, you better turn your 'tude around in the next ten minutes! You have a page to read," I said, adjusting how I sat on the rug. This would be my main position for the entirety of the debut: tits out, ass out, and a flirty gaze that was out of this world. Once we started doing our solo livestreams next week, I'd probably end up all over the place. Crawling. Arching my back. Biting my lip. Shaking my ass—all while reading, of course. "But no. I didn't expect anyone to be waiting in the lounge. If anything, we may get five viewers at most tonight. More people will probably watch the recording."

With the wig on her head, the lace mask creating a sensual black web around her eyes, and the lace bralette—fitting oddly well for being two sizes too small, Nel wandered over to the bookshelf. She clung to Laura Christian's *My Dirty To-Do List* and had already opened to the first page. Crossing her legs, she set the book upside down on her lap and met my gaze. "Are we ready?"

"Are *you* ready?" I asked, realizing we had two minutes before I pushed the little red button in the corner of the screen. A magnetic pull was reaching for my finger from the corner of the laptop, greedy little claws cracking through the screen and forcing my finger closer. "Is my lipstick okay?"

"It's perfect," Nel said with a hesitant grin. Even though uncertain, I could sense a spark of, well, *something* in the depths of her light eyes. Maybe it was a quiet thrill or a hushed hope for her confidence to return.

Whatever was hiding back there, I was determined to pull it out of her.

I extended my index finger, hovering it above the touchscreen. "You feel comfortable with your talking points? And you'll check the comments and whatnot before you read?"

"Yes, and yes." Nel reached into the bralette, pulling her breasts up and together so a little more cleavage showed above the hem of her overalls. "Let's do this."

"Aaaaand we're live! Hello to any sexy little bookworms coming out to play tonight. This is our first episode—or chapter, we should call it—of The Naked Book Club!" The red light blinked at the top of the screen like a starting gun at a race, my heart pounding. I sat back on my heels, nuzzling into Nel, who waved as *My Dirty To-Do List* slid off her thigh. "I'm Zesty Zi, and you'll see me on tier two and tier three, which we're calling Rowdy Readers and Smut Me Up. You can find out more details in our profile about what each tier includes, but you don't want us to get into that tonight, I'm sure. So, I'm going to let this cute little thing introduce her sassy self instead."

After fumbling to open the book back to the first chapter, Nel squinted at the bottom of the screen, and I could almost feel her heart slam through her chest.

Three people.

Three people were watching us, and we weren't even three minutes in.

We were sitting in front of a bookcase clad in lingerie—well, *I* was clad in very see-through lingerie—in real time, for real people.

Holy shit, this was happening.

I nudged Nel again, and she leaned back against the bookshelf with a nod and also—if I caught that correctly—a wink?

Had she just *winked* at the camera?

Pride warmed my chest.

"Yes. Hi. Hellooooo all you bad little bookworms," she said, words stumbling. "I'm Exotic Ellie...but you honestly don't have to call me that—unless you want to. If you're into it, *I'm* into it. Obviously."

My grin became a little more plastic, and I shifted off my feet to mimic The Little Mermaid pose, my right hand finding the floor near my thigh. I knew she'd shake this off. She'd always been good at putting on a façade when the time was painfully right.

I also knew that wasn't the healthiest skill for her to have in her pocket.

"Tell these three...I mean, *six,* wonderful people what they should expect at Steamy Storytime each week?" The follower increase—as small as it was—seemed to shock Nel as she peered at the screen again, her fingertips running over the pages of the book.

Just as she leaned toward the laptop, eyes thin since her contacts were obviously outdated, her tits spilled over the front hem of her overalls. Before she could shift away from the screen, she was showcasing substantial lacy red cleavage and the rounded tops of her nipples.

Alright, well, I guess the bralette was a little more see-through and less supportive than I'd thought...on top of it being two sizes too small.

She could blame these teeny tits of mine later.

"Whoa, whoa! Hey now...save *that* for Steamy Storytime!" I said, yanking her by the overall straps toward me as she smushed her chest back into place. Her olive face was as white as the feta she'd force me to try whenever I went home with her for Greek Easter.

Her face—even stunned—was more preferable than that nasty shit.

"Fuck. Fuckity fuck. That was *not* part of the plan tonight," Nel said, tightening the straps of her overalls and taking, what seemed to be, a very deep breath before looking back at the screen. And then she winked. Again. "Or was it?"

Stunned, I rolled with it. "Will those tuning into Steamy Story-time have a side of cleavage with the sexy scenes you read?"

"I guess I can throw in a little cleavage here and there! Besides, I gotta add a little heat to the free tier to prepare viewers for the fire you're bringing, Zi." Nel lifted the book back to her lap—for what felt like the twenty-seventh time. "The books we'll read in Steamy Storytime will *definitely* have spice to them. We're starting with Laura Christian's *My Dirty To-Do List* next week...and did you know she grew up in the Finger Lakes, Zi?"

My hand dramatically found my chest. "I didn't know that, Elle! Fascinating.

"Indeed. But I plan to sit here looking all...uh...sexy...and read a few chapters to you guys once a week. Then, during the last session of the month, we will have an open discussion about the book, and I'll be more interactive with the comments during those streams."

"So," I said, looking directly into the camera. "*You* should pour yourself your drink of choice, get into something cozy—maybe a little *too* cozy—and prepare to be swooned with a steamy story from this steamy little librarian right here. Right *now*."

"Yeah. Yes. Exotic Ellie is...absolutely...all about that steam," Nel stammered, covering her chest as she leaned forward to squint at the follower count again. "Holy shit. There are twelve of you hanging out with us right now. That's...that's amazing! Ro—uh, Zi...there are comments too. Look."

Nel sat back and looked from me to the screen and then back to me again. I could tell she was still sitting in the space between excitement and terror and needed my intervention. Leaning forward, I began to silently read:

@RobEatsTacos88: *I want more tits. Lean forward again, Ellie babe.*

@SpicyStef_01: *Will all the books you guys read have HEAs? I'm a sucker for a good HEA!*

@RobEatsTacos88: *@SpicyStef_01 Are you REALLY here for the books and not the boobs?*

@CallMeMagicMike: *What's the difference between the tiers? Will you JUST be reading in all of them or do we get more skin the more we pay?*

@nerdalertALLIE26: *@CallMeMagicMike If you're actually here for the books, you probably should start by READING the profile. All the details are there.*

@BrewMeDaddy69: *I'm here for both the books and boobs. Will we know what chapter you're reading each livestream? I'm a slow reader.*

@CallMeMagicMike: *@BrewMeDaddy69 Hey, dude! I didn't know you were literate. I thought you were just into watching that naked yogi sing opera on her livestream.*

> **@BrewMeDaddy69**: @CallMeMagicMike *I read about one book a week…and I can like books and boobs equally, Mike.*

> **@SpicyStef_01**: @nerdalertALLIE26: *I signed up for Steamy Storytime and Rowdy Readers. Are you logging on for Steamy Storytime next week? I'm a big fan of Laura Christian.*

"Wow…" I whispered, forgetting for a moment we were sitting silently and reading comments. I sat back onto my heels, reaching for my wine glass sitting on the side table by the bookshelf. "These are some kickass questions! Stef and Allie, I'm excited you'll join us next week!"

Nel was transfixed on the screen, the reflection of comments rolling across her vision. "Yeah…wow. Yes! This is great! It'll be so nice seeing some of you again next week when I start reading *My Dirty To-Do List*."

"Well, *actually*…we're starting that book today. You're about to read them the first page. Right, Ellie?"

Nel fumbled with the book on her thighs before confidently holding it, taking a deep breath. As she opened the book, the pages flipped against her thumb and caused air to whoosh back the hair around her face. It was as if she'd relaxed into herself, releasing her tension and loosening her posture. She grazed the edge of the cover with her index finger, biting her lip as she looked up through her mask toward the camera.

Her ability to switch from Nervous Nelly to Exotic Ellie within seconds was giving me a headache…but for all the right reasons. I just hoped it wasn't making the viewers' heads spin with personality whiplash.

If anything, it proved that Nel really was going all-in with this thing.

She continued running her finger along the paperback edge until it met with the denim of her overalls. She then ran her finger up over the straps, pausing to gently brush the lace bralette beneath. Her finger wandered up her chest and up her neck until it landed snuggly between her teeth. With a sly—and somewhat seductive—grin, Nel winked at the camera and whispered, "Let's begin."

Chapter 11

Nel

M y eye twitched all night until Mae's brain-shattering screams woke me at four in the morning.

Why had I chosen to become a professional eye winker during our livestream?

Maybe it was the contacts.

In all honesty, I was oddly okay with Mae's alarm. She'd slept from the time we put her down until four o'clock. For a seven-month-old with two teeth piercing up through her gums, that was pretty damn successful.

When I shuffled into the kitchen and opened the refrigerator, a howling Mae clinging to my side, a thawed bag of breastmilk stared at me from the middle shelf. *One* bag. I stood there for a few long seconds, the cold air crawling over Mae and me. When Mae's flailing legs kicked me out of my trance, I hugged the bag in my hand and closed the fridge door.

My frozen bags of breastmilk had slowly disappeared since deciding to end my journey with the breast pump. Nursing wasn't written in the stars for me, and I'd known my patience with pumping wouldn't last long. Even after coming to terms with these things, guilt swarmed me wherever I went. There were posts the social media algorithm thought I needed to see. There were my family's passive-aggressive comments. Hell, there were very vocal strangers who thought the baby aisle was a great place to throw their opinions at me.

Almost every choice I'd made for Mae—and for myself—over the last year had been dug into, dissected, and spit on rather than respected.

And as I stared at the bag of breastmilk in my hand—my daughter's screams vibrating against my chest—my emotions crashed into me. From all I'd experienced that week with Hallie, to the unexpected adrenaline rush during our livestream, to the damn boob juice in my hands.

Every emotion was clawing its way out.

All at once.

My knees buckled after shakily pouring the milk into a bottle. Once the rubber nipple met Mae's lips, my knees gave out from carrying so much emotional weight. My back scratched against the edge of the kitchen island and against the cabinets beneath it, numb to the divot it left in my skin.

Right before my shallow cries turned into breath-holding sobs, Rosie slid into the kitchen in socks slouched at the ankles, stopping when my slumped body came into view. Holding onto the kitchen island for balance, she lifted her eyebrows and said, "Nel...what's...what's going on? I was going to go find another fan, but...what happened?"

"It's fine. I'm fine." I just shook my head, sniffling and facing the ceiling in hopes my glasses would slide back to their spot on the bridge of my nose. Instead of Jude being there to straighten them out, his sister folded down to my level and plucked them off my face. After drying the lenses on her cotton tee, she gently set them back into place.

"This does *not* look fine," Rosie whispered, crossing her legs in front of me on the cold kitchen tile. She made a circular motion with her hand around Mae and me. "Actually, this is the exact definition of *not* fine."

My eyes shifted from Rosie to the bottle Mae's little hands wrapped around. With each wave inside the bottle, more tears dripped onto my cheeks. "This...this...is the last one."

"The last of what?" Rosie looked down at Mae, an eyebrow raised. "The last...baby? Having one baby is absolutely fine. One kid is hard enou—"

"No...no, no. The milk." I took a deep breath before opening up my swollen eyes. I peered down to see only a few drops left inside the bottle, and with every sip Mae took, part of me seemed to disappear with it. The more I tried to take deeper breaths or twist my negative mindset into a more positive one, the tears just poured with more vigor.

"The...milk?"

And the fucking flood gates flew right open. "It's the last bag! I'm done."

Rosie scooted closer until her shoulder brushed mine. "I thought...I thought you did formula because you didn't like pumping and nursing and all that?"

My head shook back and forth, hair slipping in front of my eyes. "I do. I did. I hated it."

"Then...then why—"

"I don't know!" I shouted, pressing the back of my head against the cabinet door. "It's getting to me, and I don't know why. It just... It just is."

Rosie immediately wrapped a hand around my elbow as my sobs rocked against Mae, who lay in my arms with eyelids fluttering shut. She needed to get more upright. She needed to be burped. She needed to be rocked.

But I couldn't do anything but fucking cry.

I didn't even care *that* much about the stupid breastmilk.

Good riddance. I was ready to move onto this next phase of motherhood.

Well...I thought I was.

Rosie released her grip from my elbow and placed her hands between the two of us, palms up. "Give me her."

I stared down at her hands, sniffling loud enough to shake Mae from her milk coma. "Huh?"

"Give me the human." Rosie opened and closed both hands before bending her arms into a rounded, cradle position. "Go to sleep. I'll burp her and go chill in the rocking chair and hum whatever Beatles song you want me to hum to her."

I blinked, looking down into her awkwardly rounded arms before blinking again, a lingering tear falling onto Mae's chest. "What?"

Rosie reached for Mae, placing one hand at the crook of her chubby, floppy knees and the other below her neck. Rosie's tired eyes locked on mine as she did this, waiting for me to either nod in approval or yank Mae back against my chest.

I knew this was *not* Rosie's idea of a fun night...or a fun wake-up call, at this point.

Why did she even want to help me as I sat here in a puddle of tears and drool and milk?

This was beyond fixing.

I was beyond fixing.

The tension in my arms released as Mae gently fell into Rosie's embrace, her empty bottle clicking onto the tile floor and rolling toward the counter. Rosie adjusted Mae against her shoulder, and as she set her hand flat between Mae's shoulder blades, she lifted her eyebrows. "This is where my hand goes to burp her, right? This general vicinity should get her to either burp or projectile vomit or something...right?"

An unexpected rumble climbed up from my chest. Maybe it was the beginning of a laugh. "Yeah...that's about right."

"I'd help you up, but I'm kind of afraid I'll break your child," Rosie whispered, attempting to mimic the side-to-side motion I naturally did without realizing it. "Go to sleep, Nel. Please. Go sleep and wake up with a new head on your shoulders. If she doesn't fall asleep, I'll just start making some bacon and waffles or something."

Now *that* made me laugh. "Yeah...okay. I'd love to see that happen."

The corners of Rosie's lips turned upward as she softly tapped the heel of her palm against Mae's back. "Challenge accepted. Now go to fucking sleep."

"So...how'd it go?" Jude asked the second Rosie and I finally made our way through the crowd of college students. Sebastian nodded cooly in our direction, lifting a beer into the air as Riley appeared beside us with a mojito in one hand. In his other was the most beautiful basket of crispy fries I'd ever seen—smothered in melted cheddar, jalapeños, and bacon.

I was pretty sure I was drooling.

And then I pictured Mae with her drool coating my shoulder.

It only took fifteen minutes since dropping her off at Nora's for the guilt to start back up.

Excellent.

It was cramped for a typical Wicked Wings Wednesday at Thirsty Theodore's. MCC students—probably regulars—were squeezing into booths while twenty- and thirty-somethings stood near the bar, waiting for whoever was about to grace the small corner stage. But it wasn't the overzealous lacrosse team on the other side of the bar or the group throwing their heads back with lemon drop shots making me feel a little overwhelmed.

It was the nostalgia of it all.

About a decade ago, Rosie and I were one of the newly legal college students giggling at the bar, hoping to get discounted booze. We would flirt with that guy from our literature class or that girl from SultReads, confident at least one of us would end up getting laid later that night. Rosie would knock back too many shots and cheer too loudly for the performer onstage, while I'd foot the bill for way too many pretzels, loaded fries, and Buffalo wings.

A decade later, we sat at the only table available that not only was uneven and wobbly but also had a huge speaker system set directly in front of it. All of us pulled chairs to the sides and leaned around the speaker just to see part of the stage.

I officially wasn't twenty-one anymore.

And I felt it.

Rosie plucked a cheesy fry from the basket. "It went well. *Really* well, actually." She angled her shoulders toward Sebastian, flopping the fry in his direction. "But I need to know. What's your YEO username?"

"You'd love to know, wouldn't you?" Sebastian's mouth, covered by a frosted glass of beer, muffled his voice.

Rosie's face remained expressionless. "I have a weird feeling you're hiding behind some crazy-ass username, and I just want to know who I'm showing my tits to this weekend."

"Jesus Christ," Jude whispered, slumping into his chair.

Sebastian set his beer on the table, lacing his fingers together with a cocky grin. "You'll absolutely know it's me on there when you see my name pop up. Believe me."

Shaking his head, Riley's eyes hit mine. "It's MandolinManSeb."

Sebastian's arms flew, nearly knocking over the mojito Riley was stirring. "What the fuck, man? I wanted to give them *some* sense of mystery?"

Riley shrugged. "You keep on believing you're mysterious, Seb. There wouldn't be a surprise either way with a username like that."

"The fact you're logging on and watching all of this is a little fucked up, man," Jude said as a foamy stout was set in front of him, his expression twisting from pure disgust to giddy delight. Then he remembered the topic at hand, face falling stern. "That's my sister...and Nel."

"Hey!" I exclaimed, flicking a crumb in Jude's direction and hitting him square in the forehead. That aim deserved a cheese fry, which I gladly plucked from the basket.

"No...wait...I didn't mean..." Jude countered. "It's my sister, not you. Ugh...never mind." His beer quickly hit his lips.

Sebastian shrugged. "Hey...they've been supporting us with the shop. It's our turn to help them out with their little business endeavor."

"You're not wrong," Riley said, clicking his glass against Sebastian's before adjusting the indigo tortoise-shell glasses on his nose.

I swear this guy had every color and style possible when it came to his glasses. He was like a walking advertisement. The more styles he wore, the closer I was to using my first YEO payment toward some for myself—if and when we got a payment, that was.

A waitress returned to our table and brought me the most beautiful ale. I swear she moved in slow motion as she handed the beer over, the thin line of foam barely shifting above its mahogany body. From how I hugged it between my palms and gazed down at it, I probably looked on the brink of passing out—or orgasming.

I could use one of the latter.

It had been far too long since I'd escaped my apartment for a wing night at Thirsty Theodore's, and I was living for this breath of freedom.

I lifted the frosted glass to my lips and took a cold swig, enjoying the smooth bite as it slid down my throat. I felt Jude's gaze against my cheek and met his stare. "What?"

He extended his index finger in front of him and lifted his eyebrows. "Your face is directly in front of the tiny space right there where I can actually see part of the stage." He lowered his hand, and I watched as the moth wings on his hand fluttered toward his beer. "I was just wondering where Mae was...and was thinking it must feel nice having a kid-free night. You deserve time for yourself."

Laughing, I looked around the bar as the stage lights adjusted from more relaxed hues of blue and green to vibrant shades of red and orange. "Did you expect me to bring her *here*?"

"Hell no. You're smarter than that," he said, lifting one eyebrow as he pulled the forest-green hat off his head, and dark strands of hair shadowed his face. He brushed the hair away from his eyes before popping it all into a messy bun near the base of his neck.

It was strange how we both had gone from donning short, neat hairstyles in college to consistently rocking a messy bun these days.

"I'm glad you think I'm smart, Jude." I forced my focus toward the stage we could barely see.

"Don't let it get to your head, Nel."

"It's hard for it not to," I said, bringing the beer to my lips. Damn. It was insane how satisfying every sip of this was. "But Mae is hanging out with Nora and Ari tonight. Nora has been begging me for *months* to let them hang with Mae or do a sleepover with her. When you guys mentioned Thirsty Theodore's, it seemed like as good a time as any to let her get her baby fix in."

The guilt still churned in my stomach.

I felt bad leaning on my younger sister, even if she'd wanted me to escape in the first place. A quick night out was a good way to ease into future nights away, but that didn't make it any easier.

One night away meant one step forward.

Jude nodded as a light hum sounded from the speaker system a few feet from our table. "That's good. I'm glad." He lifted his stout into the air, nodding toward it. "Cheers to you. You made a kid and started a business while still focusing on *you*."

I wrapped my hand around the frosted glass, clicking it against his before we both took a refreshing sip, the speaker buzzing with more force now. "And cheers to being brave. I'm still holding you to helping me with that. You owe me."

"Do I now?" His laugh was sweet. "Well, tell me when and where you want these lessons to take place. We don't have a stuffy dorm room anymore. After Java Jude's is officially open, I'll start lesson planning."

"We could always order pizza some night next week after Mae falls asleep and just, like, chat. I want to hear about your cross-country adventures too since I haven't seen *your* face in years!" This time, *he* flicked a crumb at my forehead...where it bounced between my brows right into my beer. Perfect. "I'm still drinking this."

"It would be a waste not to," Jude said, looking around me to where his sister sat between Sebastian and Riley with her phone screen lit up. I squinted toward Rosie's screen, and when Jude hovered closer to do the same, his jaw slackened. "Is she watching porn with my friends?"

"Jude...it's *not* porn," I whispered, cocking my head to the side to get a better look. There were three men on the screen, walking their viewers through what the perfect handstand form was...all while wearing neon-blue banana hammocks. *Only* neon-blue banana hammocks. "Those are the AcroDaddies. It's *educational.*"

"Educational porn. I'm not saying I'm against it—I'm absolutely for it. Probably more than you'd expect," Jude murmured, the bar lights dimming as a red glow lit up the corner stage. Applause and whistles rattled the room as the humming from the speaker turned into a swoony saxophone solo. "I just don't like my sister being naked for the world to see. I know it's kind of her thing, and she finds it empowering or whatever, but...it's my sister."

"I get the weirdness of that," I shouted as smooth piano sounded alongside the saxophone. "I hope I get to her level—in a way. I mean, I don't want to show the world all my lady bits when I read books live, but I do want to feel empowered. I want *my* confidence back."

The crimson stage lights set fire to the side of Jude's face as he looked at me, his beard shifting into flames. "You still have that confidence in there, Nel. You're still you. We'll pull that confidence to the surface again."

"Holy fuck!" Rosie's voice broke our eye contact. Her phone was now spinning between her feet on the filthy tile floor, both of her hands flexed open in front of her. Rosie's jaw was agape, and for the first time all day—probably since stumbling back into my life—she fell silent.

"What? Huh? What happened?" Sebastian exclaimed, sitting up straight and looking around the bar quickly. We all followed Rosie's gaze to where a petite woman stepped onto the stage.

She wore bright-red heels with straps snaking up her calves that matched the red lace ensemble hugging the slight curves of her body. Her hair was dyed cotton-candy pink with sharp, chopped bangs falling just above her eyebrows. The hairstyle was almost exactly what Rosie had, just hot pink rather than Rosie's inky black.

"Why is my sister broken?" Jude whispered, leaning closer so his breath was warm against my cheek. For a second, I lingered there, taking in the heat, before snapping back. "She doesn't freeze up when someone hot enters the room. She usually does...well...the exact opposite."

I peered at Rosie again as a smooth saxophone glissando sang from the speaker. Nodding to myself, I sat back against my chair and watched the woman onstage. "She's probably shocked because this is *very* unexpected."

"Why? What is?" Jude asked, watching as Rosie's face remained frozen in place. Her lips parted slightly as the performer stroked the microphone, her body swaying seductively.

"Jude, that's her girlfriend...well, sort of."

"Since when does she have a girlfriend?" Jude was still staring at the stage, his eyes shifting from his sister's shocked face to the stunning woman humming into the microphone.

"Well, I guess they've had some kind of situationship going on since Rosie joined the Bare Assentials. It's nothing official." And then she ghosted our friendship for her. This pink-haired vixen climbed under Rosie's skin when she was at her lowest, molding her into a puppet and taking her away from me—away from all of us. Call me selfish, but I wanted to chop those damn strings. "That's Viv."

Chapter 12

Rosie

What the actual fuck was going on?

Viv stood in front of me, wearing the red, lace ensemble that always stole my breath—the one highlighting the definition of her legs, the decadent curve of her ass, and her intoxicating hourglass shape. The colorful tattoos painting her arms, her chest, and almost her entire right leg grew more radiant as the stage lights focused. Her eyes were done up so dramatically that she could probably tear anyone's soul out with a single wink.

"Rosie...that's Viv. Right?"

I clutched Nel's knee, needing to hold onto whatever was closest to me or else I would do something drastic. So, the knee it was. "Yeah...yes. Yup. That's her."

"I thought so." Nel's voice fell flat.

"Did you know about this?" I asked, turning so my nose was mere inches from Nel's face. "Did you reach out to her? I don't hate it—don't get me wrong—but I'm just a little, um...shook. I've barely talked to her since coming back to Merlin Heights."

"No. No, I didn't reach out to her," Nel said as melodic poetry fell from Viv's lips, and the audience clapped. A few *wooed* from the bar as she continued rocking her hips to the smooth rhythm. "I doubt she'd even recognize me since we only met that one time at that random show for, like, two minutes. I don't even think I follow her on anything."

"Jesus Christ. How did her voice get even *better*?" I muttered, pushing whatever Nel said into a part of my brain I'd revisit later. I watched Viv's free hand run from her neck to her tattooed chest, to her hips and thighs. She sung a low, sultry run of notes followed by the sexiest damn vibrato I'd ever heard. "I hate that she can dance and sing and look the way she does."

I absolutely did *not* hate it.

I was fucking *obsessed* with it.

And probably not in the healthiest of ways.

"Why haven't you guys kept in touch?" Nel asked as Jude walked around the table with a beer in hand, pulling a chair over next to

Riley, who gawked at the stage. By this point, I was pretty sure Sebastian was comatose.

"We've never been official, I guess." I shrugged before leaning back in my chair and finally reaching for the drink Sebastian ordered me that I'd barely acknowledged. "We just are...I don't know...*us*."

"Is that the reason you guys have those little arguments or whatever?" Nel asked hesitantly. "Does she want to be monogamous?"

I snorted into my beer before taking a long, lukewarm gulp. "She's a fucking free spirit. I am too. I mean, *obviously*...just look at me. If my heart is vibing with someone, I can't break that vibe no matter how hard I try. She, on the other hand, seems to have several hearts in her chest all with their own unique vibes...and she's okay with it."

She's okay with it.

But was I?

"So, the answer to my question is *no*." Nel nodded just as Viv's voice cut off, and the room erupted into a roar of shouts and whistles and applause. "But are you okay with that?"

Was Nel inside my fucking head?

If so, she needed to get out.

It was a mess in there.

I shrugged as casually as I could. "It doesn't really matter, does it? I mean, look at her. I've conditioned myself to be okay with it...and now I am."

"Well, that sounds *really* healthy," Jude whispered.

Sticking my tongue out at my brother the way I used to growing up, I turned back to the stage, my eyes meeting Viv's.

When her lips curled into a subtle smile, I knew exactly what she was doing.

I watched as those deadly dimples of hers returned, her hand stroking the microphone subtly before placing it back onto the stand. Before walking off stage, Viv looked over her shoulder, and I floated my gaze from her ass to her lips that silently worded: *Hey, baby.*

Then my heart fell straight between my legs.

"Why the fuck are you sleeping on a futon?" Viv asked once she'd slipped off her ruby heels and peacoat.

I couldn't stop staring at her *stupid* heels.

I wanted to snap the heels right off and add them to my collection.

Even if the owner of said heels was Viv.

After pouring us each a glass of whatever wine Nel had in the fridge—hoping Viv wouldn't taste the price of it—I led her to my little back den. She stood over my makeshift futon bed, the glass of wine between her fingers, and stared down at the lavender-colored comforter and green striped pillow.

I slowly sat down onto the futon, one hand running across the comforter as the other carried the wine to my lips. The wine had definitely been open for *at least* a few weeks. Dammit. She was going to be able to tell. "Why haven't you told me why you're here?"

Viv giggled into her wine glass, and I held my breath while she took a sip. Her throat shifted as she swallowed, and I felt both fearful and far more turned on than I should just from staring at someone's throat.

I wanted to wrap my hand gently around it.

I wanted to watch goosebumps scatter her skin.

I wanted to comb my fingers through her pink hair and pull until—

"It was a surprise, silly," she responded, lowering herself beside me and looking down to adjust the red push-up bra holding her perfect tits in place. "I wore this one for you, by the way."

"How did you know I was here...like, back in Merlin?" I asked, my eyes absolutely not looking into hers.

How could I *not* look at her chest?

"I mean, where else were you going to go? You weren't going to stay at some random hotel in Rockberry Park with us or drive across the country like your brother did—you *hate* driving. It made sense you'd head back home," Viv said, lying back on the futon and leaning on her elbows without letting a single drop of wine fall from her glass.

Home.

Was that *really* what Merlin Heights was for me?

I tossed some wine back, swishing it around in my mouth before it warmed my throat and dulled my thoughts. "I guess... But how did you know we'd all be at Theodore's tonight? And how did you get the singing gig? I thought you'd taken a break from open mic nights...not that you should. You should always take advantage of them because you're—"

"So many questions, Zizi," Viv hummed, running her finger down my jawline. A jolt of pleasure immediately dove between my thighs at her touch. "I have my ways. I also knew I was passing through Merlin after our latest show. When I saw Thirsty Theodore's social post about needing to fill tonight's guest spot, I thought, what the hell! Maybe some magic will happen. And look...it did."

I still didn't believe her, but I was too engrossed by the touch of her skin against my cheek, my neck, my shoulder to question her any further. She ran her fingers down the length of my arm and then back up, cupping my chin while placing her wine on the small table beside the futon. Her hand never left my face with every smooth movement she made—nor did I want it to.

Even as her touch turned me into a puddle, I wished she had checked in before now. I wished I had felt this two or three weeks ago, when a bottle of tequila played the part of therapist.

I wished she wanted just a little bit more.

But right now, I'd take what I could get...because it could be another month before I tasted her or touched her or made her tremble in such delicious ways again.

Both of Viv's legs wrapped around my body, her flawless figure straddling my hips. She tipped my face up so I was forced to fall into her endless, emerald eyes, and I willingly dove into them.

"Why are you *really* here, Viv?" I whispered, my voice strained. "Because I know you. You don't just do shit on a whim or just *hope* your plans will work out—you make sure they do."

Giggling, she pressed herself lower—harder—against me, and I couldn't help but roll my hips in response. My body automatically reacted to her touch, her pressure, her presence in a way no other hook-up or girlfriend ever had. Heat dampened my inner thighs as her body pressed down with a little more force. I could already feel a spark of pleasure rising from that bundle of nerves she was grinding her hips against through my jeans.

Leaning forward, her teeth nibbled my earlobe, my breathing tense as I took in her familiar scent. "I needed you."

"You...needed me?" I whimpered as her tongue created a line from the tender spot below my ear to the hand she was holding my face still with. The heat of her mouth being so close to mine was the kind of torture I just couldn't handle tonight, knowing how sadistic Viv could be.

I didn't want the torture.

I didn't want to hold back.

I wanted to demolish her body with my own.

There was only a matter of seconds left before my patience shattered.

"Tell me, Viv." I swallowed slowly, her pupils dilating as our mouths grew even closer. "*Why* do you need me? Because if there is a God—which, we know there isn't—he knows I fucking need you too."

Her tongue slowly, gently licked my bottom lip to the top before releasing her hand from my chin so it could grip the back of my neck. "You know why I need you, sweetheart."

"Say it."

Viv leaned forward and pressed her velvet lips against my neck, creating a path of kisses from my throat to my chest as she reached for both of my wrists. She wrapped her hands around them firmly, pushing them down into the comforter beside my thighs, forcing me still. When her lips found their way to the lace bra hiding beneath my slouchy tee, her teeth—fangs, more like it—pulled the fabric down to reveal a peaked nipple begging to be bit. The second her tongue hit those nerves, my back arched against her touch.

Fuck.

My willpower was ripping at the seams.

"I need you...because no one else makes me come as hard as you do," Viv whispered. A moan slipped out when her teeth pulled at my nipple, releasing one hand from my left wrist so it could firmly work its way over my thighs until she was cupping my sex over my jeans. I looked down at her, silently pleading for more. "And...I need to taste you."

I was done.

The kraken was fucking released.

Pushing against the hand restraining my right wrist, I yanked Viv up onto the futon in an adrenaline—or orgasm—fueled sweeping motion, an annoyingly sexy giggle sounding as her back hit the mattress. I spread her knees wide before my own knees found the floor at the edge of the futon. As she lay on her back, her fingers already gripping the sheets, my nails clawed the inside of her thighs, raking them down her inked skin before they returned to the edge of the crimson, lace panties she'd worn onstage that left nothing to the imagination.

She wanted to taste me, but it wasn't going to happen until I tasted her first.

"Rowe..." Viv sang, her back arching as I pulled her panties to the side in the least-hesitant way imaginable. Holy shit, had I missed this view. "I wasn't done with you yet."

"Well, that's nice," I said, leaning closer to her as two of my fingers plunged into her heat, her body writhing against my hand as the sweetest moan sounded. I brought my free hand to my mouth, looking Viv directly in the face as I licked the tops of my fingers before lowering them over her clit. "Because you're not touching me again until I hear you fucking scream."

The second I twisted the fingers inside her so they hit the sensitive spot that would take her over the edge, I began quickly—eagerly—rubbing her clit with the other.

"Holy fuck, Rowe," she squealed, bringing one of her fists to her mouth and biting down. "Don't stop. Don't fucking stop, do you hear me?"

"I haven't heard you scream in over a month. Don't you dare hold back," I growled as I lowered my face over her pussy, flicking my tongue against her as she trembled against my hands and face.

"Shit. Oh my god, shit! Don't stop." Viv's voice echoed against the wall of the den, both of her hands grabbing for the comforter while her body grinded against me. "I'm going to come so fucking hard. Oh my god...yes—"

And then we heard the apartment door open, followed by a high-pitched scream.

I didn't want to stop, my hands still moving fiercely against her as she grabbed a pillow, pressed it hard against her face, and bit it.

I wanted to stay hidden in my little back corner of the apartment for the rest of the night—week, month—but the den didn't have a door.

Nel was walking toward us.

Mae was screaming against Nel's neck.

For one of the few times in my life, I felt the tiniest bit of guilt.

Even though Nel and I used to hook up with whomever while the other one was sleeping—or we *thought* they were sleeping—this was different. Something in my gut twisted at the thought of Nel and Mae listening so clearly to Viv's moans.

I wanted those sounds—whether hushed or wild—just for me and no one else.

Even though I knew, in the shadows of my mind, her moans *weren't* just for me.

I forced that thought aside faster than Viv had grabbed the pillow to cover her face with.

"Fuck," I whispered, slowing my hands as Viv let out an unsatisfied sigh, the sound shattering my soul. Nel walked by us just as I leaned my back against the futon, Mae still screeching like a pissed-off seal.

Nel stopped in front of the hallway leading to their bedrooms, her eyes roaming from where I sat on the floor to where Viv lay on the futon, her hand rising for a slow wave. Leaning in our direction, she quietly said, "I'm sorry," before slumping her shoulders and tiptoeing into the hallway.

I peered up at Viv as she lay on her side, her head falling onto the pillow with pink hair covering her eyes. "I...was...so...close."

I let out a frustrated groan. But as Viv's lust-drunk eyes connect-ed with mine, I brought my hand to my lips and placed a few damp fingers into my mouth, releasing them with a grin. "Touch your-self. Now. When I get back, you'll need that pillow to bite because you're going to come hard enough to make up for not seeing me this last month."

One whole month.

One month without contact was fine, right?

She hadn't ghosted me the way I'd ghosted Nel...because *that* would be worrisome.

My gut twisted at the thought, but I got to my feet.

I couldn't hyperfocus on how bad a friend I was when I had *this* in front of me.

Before she could say a word, I looked directly at the two stand-ing fans and three small ones I'd used the other night. I dragged the standing fans into the hallway and placed them between Nel's bedroom and Mae's nursery, clicking them on and adjusting them to their highest—loudest—speed. I returned to the den and grabbed one small fan, knowing there wasn't another outlet in that part of the hallway for the others to plug into.

The roaring fans sounded almost as intoxicating as Viv's voice had been onstage.

When I returned to the futon, Viv lay, stroking herself like the good girl she was. I fell onto my knees and yanked her luscious legs toward me so they were back to where they had comfortably been minutes before.

I was starving.

I slid the red lace to the side, smiling up at her. "Now...where were we?"

Chapter 13

Nel

Twice in one week.

First, it was for Wicked Wings Wednesday at Thirsty Theodore's.

Now, it was for Java Jude's grand opening.

I'm sorry...*soft* opening.

Nora was a good sister. Hell, she'd made more of an effort over the last six months than both of my parents and Hallie combined.

For a people pleaser—with a touch of social anxiety—in the middle of wedding planning, her going out of her way to create this relationship with Mae was huge.

And I remained nauseated with mom-guilt.

And this time, Mae was staying the *night* at Nora's.

Mostly because Rosie had answered the question for me when Nora asked.

"One for you…aaaand two for me," Rosie said, slipping into the seat in front of me as she set two espresso martinis in front of her. Reaching for mine, I took a long, rich sip.

Holy shit.

Jude's mixology skills were way better than they'd been in college when he'd try to concoct a Sex on the Beach for us without the peach schnapps…or the cranberry juice.

It ended up being orange juice and vodka in a plastic cup.

The effort was there.

"Why *two* for you?" I asked, peering over her shoulder to watch Jude and Riley hustling behind the counter, Sebastian serenading customers by the entrance as they walked in. From the faces of those who walked by him, he was *actually* winning some of them over. "I should be the one drinking two with how guilty I feel leaving Mae again…to drink."

Rosie flapped her hand in the air between us. "Once that line chills the fuck out, I'll get you another. I got one for myself…and the second because I'm drinking for Viv too." Rosie pushed the two glasses together before popping a straw in each martini and sipping them both simultaneously.

Did people even drink espresso martinis with straws?

I didn't think that was a thing.

"Well, maybe if she hadn't left before you woke up, she could have stuck around to drink one herself."

Rosie brought the back of her hand to her lips, snorting out a laugh. "Viv? Staying in one place for more than one day? *Please.* If she'd stuck around Merlin for the last two days, she would have lost her fucking mind."

"She could have left you a note, at least," I murmured, rolling my eyes away from Rosie's gaze. I tried not to think about how I would have loved if Rosie had left me a note years ago. A text, an email, a message…something.

But she was here now.

She sat in front of me with two straws in her mouth and apparently felt strong enough about our friendship to start a business with me.

I'd cling to that when my mind began to sway.

It was something.

"Nah…" Rosie's muffled voice brought my attention back to her and the two straws poking down from her top lip—walrus style. "She doesn't leave notes. She doesn't even text back. She ghosts you, returns to get what she wants, and then turns into a ghost again."

Huh.

Interesting.

Rosie maneuvering both straws into their own drink while staying in her top lip snapped me out of my thoughts. "That's not really fair, though, is it? She can't just *expect* to get what she wants every time."

Rosie shrugged, taking a walrus-style sip. "She's her. She just gets what she wants…and I just give it to her."

"It's because you're obsessed with the *idea* of her," I spat, surprised by my tone.

The tone felt kind of nice, actually.

"I am not!" Rosie shouted, the straws falling out from her top lip: one diving into a martini while the other rolled onto the ground toward Jude's black leather boots coming into view. "I am obsessed with *her*. There's a difference."

"You saying that definitely doesn't help your situationship," I added.

"Whoa…" Jude said, rocking back on his heels as Rosie lifted a hand to reveal her middle finger. "Are you talking about that singer?"

"She sure is." Smiling at Rosie's middle finger, I brought the edge of my martini glass to my lips.

"If I wasn't so proud of how spunky you've been since I came back to Merlin, I'd be…er…more *annoyed* at you than I am," Rosie said, finally sipping the drink the way it was intended to be sipped.

Her walrus days were over.

Chuckling, Jude looked down at his sister. "You still aren't capable of being mad at Nel, are you?"

I brought the palms of my hands to just below my chin, blinking so my eyelashes danced in Rosie's direction.

"Look at that face." Rosie sat back in her chair while gesturing toward me. "It's fucking impossible."

"You're not wrong," Jude said, looking toward the counter where Riley threw him a thumbs up, the dark skin of his hand powdered in russet coffee grounds. Jude turned back to our table, his eyes meeting mine just as I stopped fluttering my eyelashes.

Eyelash fluttering and winking.

What the fuck was going on with me?

"This should quiet down soon—it's almost ten," Jude added. "Riley is already shutting things down, and Seb better stop chatting those girls up and help too. Then we can start the first lesson."

Terror had officially entered the room my mom-guilt was sitting comfortably in.

I knew we were going to meet tonight, but my stomach lurched thinking about Jude and I being alone together for the first time in a decade.

It *really* wasn't a big deal.

We were two old friends, doing what two old friends did...which was help the other be sexy.

Dammit.

"Lesson?" Rosie asked, her eyes darting between the two of us. "Like the ones you gave him in college?"

"Er...yeah. Kind of," I stammered. "I'm going to practice reading to him tonight like I will during the livestream."

Rosie placed both hands flat on the table, almost knocking over the martini glasses. "Oh, my God, I *need* to see this!"

"No," Jude and I responded in unison. Either Rosie was freaked out by our synchrony, or a wall immediately went up.

She curled her shoulders toward her ears, lifting her hands in surrender. "Fine, fine. I'll just get the live show tomorrow night."

"Great." I rolled my eyes, watching as she finished off both of her martinis before swinging her leather jacket off the back of the chair. Between her thin jacket and the solid buzz I could see in her eyes, it was a good thing we lived within walking distance to Java Jude's...and everything else in Merlin.

Would wherever I ended up next still be walking distance to town?

We *needed* to start apartment hunting.

"You're okay walking back alone, Rowe?" Jude asked, backing up toward the counter with my empty glass between his fingers. "Sebastian could walk with you."

Immediately, Sebastian's face appeared above the shoulder of the buzzed blonde in front of him. "Huh? What?"

With a shrug, Rosie walked toward the door and gestured at Sebastian. "Let's go, Seb. Walk me home."

To my surprise, he stepped away from the blond and hopped to Rosie's side. For someone who knew Rosie would *never* go for him, he sure was enthusiastic about walking her home.

Perhaps the flirty, quirky Sebastian we saw on the outside was softer, sweeter on the inside?

In the end, maybe all he *really* wanted was friendship with Rosie.

Before exiting into the early spring night with Sebastian at her hip, Rosie's lips twisted into a clever grin as she faced Jude and me. "You guys enjoy your *lessons*. I've always admired your love for continuing education."

"If a bear sees her, let him get her, Seb," Jude monotonously said.

Rosie stuck her middle finger at us before escaping onto the sidewalk.

Sebastian nodded his head, tipping forward the front of an invisible boater hat as he said, "It will be my greatest honor."

Rosie's middle finger appeared back inside the doorway—the tip of her finger barely an inch from Sebastian's nose.

About thirty minutes after Rosie left, I sat silently at the shop while Riley organized coffee beans into containers, and Jude counted the last of the cash.

It didn't take long before Riley felt a whisper of tension in the air—or maybe *I* just felt something—and he slid out the front door with a quick wave. Then, we were alone. Alone for the first time in years.

"Okay," Jude said, locking the money box and placing it beneath the counter. "Want some rosé?"

My jaw dropped. "You've been hiding rosé from me all night? What the hell, Jude?"

"I'll take that as a yes." He yanked the cork with a *pop* before pouring us each a hefty glass. "Tonight, we kept it to coffee and espresso martinis. The shop will do wine another night...but since it's here, why not drink it?"

"You had *this*...all night?" I snagged the wine before he could set it on the table, a tiny drop cascading onto the cover of Laura Christian's *My Dirty To-Do List*.

"Maybe I was saving it because I remember you used to down a bottle of this in one sitting. Back when you used to pretend to be Maggie LaFountain for me before a night out, rosé was your go-to."

I slid the glass closer to my chest, snickering at the memory. "Oh, my God, I forgot about Maggie. I pretended to be her, like, three times. You *loved* her."

Jude cringed before taking a long swig of wine. "Nope. I absolutely did not."

"Oh, come on!" I said, my hands waving in the air and almost knocking the wine glass off the table. "I remember we met up to *practice* before that Halloween party when you dressed up like a ketchup bottle—"

"A ketchup *packet*."

"—and then again before that big concert—"

"Battle of the Bands, yeah...and you got wasted during *that* lesson. I had to practically carry you back to the dorms."

"And then when...oh, yeah. Shit. I forgot about that," I said, biting my lip and looking down.

"Of course you forgot about it," Jude muttered, the upturned corner of his lips barely noticeable behind his beard. "You never remembered it to begin with."

Lifting my glass, I nodded. "That's not false."

Jude leaned over the table, eyeing the book in front of me. "Is this what you're reading to me tonight?"

"It sure is." I thumbed the book pages quickly. "I'm reading the first chapter tomorrow. Should I just, uh...do right now what I plan to do tomorrow?"

"Sure. Yeah." Jude coughed into his fist and sat back, crossing his arms against his chest. "Should I blurt out random thoughts when they come to me like viewers will do in the chat?"

"That's not a bad idea, actually."

"I'm brilliant. College had nothing on me," Jude laughed.

"Oooh! I have an idea." Standing up, I shuffled toward the counter, the mix of espresso martinis and wine finally catching up with me as I reached into a drawer I'd seen Riley fiddling with earlier that night. Doing my best not to trip over my feet or knock my hip into the corner of a table, I slid back into the seat. A stack of sticky notes and a pen now sat in front of Jude. "Write them instead."

He eyed the notes and pen before meeting my gaze. "Huh?"

"Don't *say* your comments aloud—unless they're tips on how to make me sound sexier or something. I'll be *reading* the comments that come in during the livestream, so this will be more realistic."

Jude replaced his glass of wine with the pen, twisting it between his fingers like the world's tiniest baton as he hovered above the sticky notes. "Got it. I'm ready."

"You're ready? Really?"

Jude laughed. "Yes. Just pretend it's like any other book club you've been in—like SultReads at MCC. Except, you're reading out loud...and you'll be half naked."

"Jesus Christ..." I whimpered, covering my face with my hands, the book flopping onto the table. "I'm so *not* ready! I'm not. What the fuck am I thinking, doing thi—"

Warmth flooded the backs of my hands, and I peeked between my index and middle fingers. Jude's eyes burned directly into my own, his faint grin soft. Jude's hands curled around the edges of my palms as he gently pulled them away from my face. The scent of roasted coffee beans and something earthy—maybe even a little smokey—were left in their wake.

What happened to the boy in college who would drench himself in Axe body spray?

That boy did *not* smell like a forest river filled with coffee.

"Nel…" he hummed, releasing his grip. "Do you want to get back into reading again?"

I nodded.

"And you need to make a few bucks before your aunt kicks you out?"

I nodded again, immediately feeling nauseated.

"And you want to get your confidence back to where you know—*I know*—it can be. Right?"

"Yeah…yes," I stammered, doing all I could *not* to let the fucking flood gates open in front of Jude.

Even though he'd seen me cry many, *many* times before.

He'd also seen me puke my brains out after too much tequila more times than I'd liked to admit.

He laced his fingers together—the moths on each hand facing one another in an unexpected duel—and leaned back in his chair. "Then start reading. Just sit and read to me."

My eyes widened, my heart trying to ram its way through my sternum with every second passing.

Just sit and read to me.

I flipped to the first page of Laura Christian's book, outlining the initial few words with the tip of my finger. Keeping my face angled downward, I looked above the rim of my glasses and lifted a single eyebrow playfully. "Let's start our first Steamy Storytime session off with a bang…and I mean a *bang.*"

"Here we go," Jude whispered contently, releasing his mothed hands so one could snag the pen and the other could prepare the notes. He looked like a little boy at the dinner table, awaiting the best meal of his life.

"Content warnings..." I said, keeping my gaze just above the rim of my glasses. "Are you *ready* for them?"

Jude nodded, his gaze unshifting.

"Okay, alright," I said, my fingers tracing the words on the page. "Laura Christian's books usually have some intense scenes, so let's prepare you for—"

"Bite your lip."

I quickly looked up at Jude.

Air stilled in my lungs at the sound of his hushed suggestion.

No...not a suggestion. A *demand*.

Trying to ignore my flailing heart, I dug my top teeth into the corner of my bottom lip, my eyes never leaving Jude's. Though his Adam's apple bobbed, and he blinked twice, he didn't shift from his position in the chair—one hand still wrapped around the pen and the other holding the notes.

"Good gi...good, yeah. Yup," he stammered. "Now tell me the content warnings."

I reached forward, poking the sticky notes in his hand. "Shhh...write your comments down."

I silently kicked myself for telling him to do this.

Even though I was so emotionally scarred from the verbal demands of my past, this felt different.

Him demanding I bite my lip in such a dominant tone was shockingly out of character for Jude.

So shocking I almost wanted to hear more of it—to *feel* more of it.

Instead, he nodded and uncapped the pen, finally letting a laugh escape his lungs. "Okay, *ma'am*."

"Thanks, *sir*," I said, adjusting my position before peering down at the page. "Content warnings: use of profanity, alcohol, and mild drug use...explicit sexual content including rough sex...and...use of sex toys..."

The second I looked away from the page, I watched Jude's jaw slowly drop, and without losing a second of eye contact, the pen in his hand began moving across a sticky note.

Chapter 14

ROSIE

When I didn't hear Mae wailing from her crib or babbling during tummy time on the living room floor, I kicked open Nel's bedroom door only to find her bed empty. When I saw her shoes weren't near the entryway and the stroller wasn't leaned up against the wall, I knew she hadn't come home.

Then my brother's face popped into my mind.

Had she stayed the night with Jude?

Were they able to leave the past in the past like she'd said they could?

Or had she passed out from too many espresso martinis at Java Jude's and was asleep on their thrifted sofa?

Running back into the den, I plucked my phone from the charger to find two text messages from her:

Stayed the night at Nora's with Mae.

I'll be back in the morning. Goodnight!

Tossing the phone back onto the futon, I laughed at myself for not checking my phone before panic struck. Of *course* she'd stayed with her sister. Why wouldn't she have? I'm *sure* Jude had driven her over there after their lesson, dropped her off, and he'd driven back to his stuffy apartment with Sebastian and Riley.

After typing a quick reply, letting her know I was going for a walk, I pulled on some jeans and threw on a sweatshirt before checking to make sure the spare key was still hidden in its usual spot. Locking the door behind me, I set out into the March morning, the chill biting the tip of my fingers as I stuffed my hands into my pockets.

Though my body was pulling me toward Java Jude's—apparently, I was conditioned to go that way every morning—my feet carried me beyond Java Jude's toward Claus Lake. The air nipped my nose, and I pulled my scarf up over my face like the wimp I was. You'd think someone who grew up with the never-ending winters in Merlin Heights would be used to the cold by now.

Wrong.

I still despised any season other than the short-lived summer we got here.

Claus Lake grew closer, and Merlin Community College came into view on my right. Instead of continuing beyond the college, my body hit an invisible wall. Feet anchored in place, I was drawn to instrumental music playing from somewhere on MCC's campus lawn. Silencing the music and ignoring my stubborn feet, my eyes shifted to the green, rectangular sign in front of me.

Lakeside Lane.

I blinked a few times to make sure the sign was correct—and it definitely was. I took a deep breath before gazing down the street, mid-morning fog lingering to create a ghostly aesthetic.

I saw the small, baby-blue Cape Cod three houses down on the left.

I saw a red Jeep in the driveway and, beside it, a plastic tricycle knocked over on the dewy grass.

The house grew nearer before I realized my feet were, in fact, moving without my permission. I stepped off the sidewalk and hid behind the thick beech tree in the front yard where I'd stood time and time again after school. This was where I'd stood, waiting to be picked up and driven to ballet or lyrical classes because God knew my mom could never bring me. Running my hand between the lowest branch and the knot in the wood, I felt slight indentations of my initials before finding Jude's initials a few inches from mine.

Peeking around the tree, I wondered why the hell I was hiding.

The people living inside this house—a structure I once called home—were complete strangers.

But the strangers didn't know I'd found my mother passed out on their very lawn more times than I could count. They didn't know Jude and I would lock ourselves in his bedroom, huddling as my tears stained his T-shirt, fearing for our mother's life. These strangers didn't know that police rushed through our doors more times than I could admit, confiscating pills and heroin and whatever else she was using.

Four years after I graduated from MCC, she was forced into St. Merlin Rehabilitation.

Two days later, Viv found me slouched on the curb outside Three-Ring, my breath tequila-hot and my tits almost falling out of my shirt.

One week later, I was part of the Bare Assentials.

I hadn't talked to my mom since Viv walked me into the event center that night—washing me up, feeding me water, and introducing me to the troupe. I hadn't thought about rekindling any kind of relationship with my mother since she'd been taken away. In truth, Jude and I lost her when we were pre-teens, so rebuilding what we'd had didn't sound enthralling.

I'd learned from my past and, in a way, was grateful to stay a version of my true self through it all. I never stopped going to school, even though I never really wanted to be there. I never stopped diving into fictional pages where romance conquered all. I never stopped auditioning for that year's *Nutcracker* or performing contemporary routines at local art galleries.

My past sculpted me, but it didn't break me.

Hopping off the sidewalk, I hastily walked toward the bench overlooking MCC's tiny stone beach I used to sit at when I was locked out of the house after dance. It had also become the bench I used to smoke a few joints at once my classes ended for the day at Merlin Community.

It was funny how life continued to retrace its own steps.

I collapsed onto the bench, the instrumental music louder behind me as my back faced campus—and the past I'd run away from yet again.

Why the fuck hadn't my feet just led me to Java Jude's?

Flutes and fiddles and drums grew more upbeat behind me, and I had a weird sense Sebastian would appear from behind a tree ready to serenade me.

I was definitely *not* in the mood for that.

Plus, after our walk home the other night, I knew Sebastian wouldn't do something like that. He now understood we wouldn't be anything more than friends, and he was genuinely okay with that. He respected my sexuality and wouldn't try to change it.

I mean, he could *try*, but it would never work.

It felt good knowing I had a solid friendship brewing with him after he'd dropped me off at the apartment that night—a friendship outside of the one I was rebuilding with Nel.

He couldn't promise he'd stop flirting with me, though. It was just part of his genetic makeup and I knew *exactly* how it felt to have this gene.

Turning away from the lake, a figure came into view—and not one with a mandolin. A woman gracefully moved her body around a speaker a few yards away—not a Bluetooth but an actual boombox. She flowed along with the gentle rhythm, her body swaying and stretching and turning with both grace and grit.

Her dark, velvety skin.

Her beaded, braided hair.

Her fierce, intense movements.

The woman's lean arms showcased every muscle hiding beneath her skin, and it was obvious from her turned-out hips that she had years of technical ballet training behind her. Though her technique was gracefully articulate, her movements held emotion. Every sauté and attitude turn and calypso onto the newly trimmed grass wasn't restrained. She was turning her knowledge of the craft into a story cutting through the morning haze.

It was powerful as fuck.

I hadn't felt my feet float their way toward this stranger, but apparently, they had, because she went from being yards away to being mere feet from me. For the first time in minutes, my brain shocked me back to the present, and I pressed the heels of my gladiator boots into the grass as if they had brakes on them.

As if they had sharp heels I could rip off and burn.

The woman finished her motion as wrists kissed in the air above her head, and her neck released, her head falling back. She lowered her arms and straightened her back, her impressive height becoming even more evident. Her eyes slowly opened, and my heart lurched at the flakes of green and gray speckled throughout them. They were stunning against her dark skin, and I took a step back, forcing myself to look away.

Because, I mean, who *really* had time to dive headfirst into eyes like that?

I had Viv, and when she was around, she was more than enough.

When being the key word.

"Do you want to join me?" Her voice was hoarse, but almost rhythmic.

I looked back toward the bench before bringing my hands to my chest with a scoff. "What? Me? Why? What?"

She stepped in my direction, shaking her head with a laugh. "*Yes, you.*"

"Guilty, I guess," I said, lifting my hands in defeat. "Do you ask people to dance with you often?"

"I do. Yeah," she said with a shrug, taking another step in my direction. As she stepped closer, I noticed she had two delicate silver rings hugging her left nostril and the tiniest barbell piercing her right eyebrow. It immediately reminded me of when I'd pierced my eyebrow in eleventh grade during a study hall.

It had quickly become infected.

That was the end of that.

"Huh...okay," I stammered, rocking side to side and placing my hands on my hips. I hoped I gave off more dominant vibes than anxious ones. At this point, I couldn't tell. "Do you...dance on the lawn a lot? Are you a teacher here or a performer or something?"

She laughed, and I could listen to that sound all day. It had a soothing gruffness to it I never even knew existed. "You're cute. You know that? I mean...you must." She took a few steps away and rolled her shoulders back to the slowing drumbeat, her knees bending and then straightening below her. "I danced with the Rockberry Academy for several years but recently left. I teach some workshops at Merlin Community pretty regularly and have one in a couple hours, actually. Warming up out here always feels...energizing, you know?"

"*You* danced at Rockberry Academy?" My eyes must have tripled in size from the reaction on her flawless face. "*The* Rockberry Academy of Modern Dance? That's fucking outstanding. It's near impossible to get accepted there."

"Ha! See? You *are* a dancer. I knew it." Her laugh echoed through the morning air. "Only dancers know the intensity of Rockberry."

She wasn't wrong. "I mean, I've dabbled. I'm a dance dabbler, I guess."

What the fuck was coming out of my mouth?

I'd danced all my life, and all I could spit out was that I'd *dabbled*?

"What styles do you dabble in, *Dabbler*?" she asked, shifting her weight from foot to foot with a slight bend to her knees. Her pierced eyebrow lifted playfully, lips twisting to the side of her face.

Plump, luscious lips.

I wanted to bite and—

No. Nope. I did *not* want to do anything with them.

I had Viv's lips.

Her lips were more than fine.

"I've done some modern, but nothing like the shit you're doing. Ballet. A little lyrical, here and there," I said, wondering why I was being so nonchalant about my talent. "I am...I *was* part of the Bare Assentials until recently."

Saying it out loud was a dagger to the heart.

The dancer's body—her lean, athletic body—stopped moving for the first time since laying eyes on her. "Wait...you were a Bare Assentials dancer? No, *that's* what's fucking outstanding." She walked toward me—no, strutted. "Did you feel liberated under those lights? That energy…that empowering, explosive, sexual energy. It must have been unlike anything else."

Well, fuck.

Her saying *sexual energy* would forever be engrained in my brain.

I swallowed hard. "Yeah. Yeah, it was."

For what felt like the thousandth time that morning, I felt my body moving without my will. My hands were being led toward the boombox, and when she let go, she backed up, swaying her hips and lifting her hands above her head.

"Come on, Dabbler. Dance a little." She turned on relevé before rolling onto the grass, crossing one long leg over the other until she was sitting with both knees bent and slightly apart, her arms straight over the knees. "I promise moving a little won't break you."

Fuck it.

Who was I to turn away from something like this—as strange as it was?

I was usually one to initiate a dance party, or a karaoke night, or—hell—a naked book club.

There was absolutely no way I could just throw up a peace sign and leave.

Instead of walking away, I swayed side to side, my head subtly rolling from shoulder to chest to shoulder and back before alternating the motion. The dancer rolled backward over her right shoulder, landing far too gracefully onto her knees before standing and casually shuffling toward me.

Her casual demeanor, after doing such elegant movements, boggled my mind.

And then the dancer stood mere inches from me.

"Just loosen up a little," she whispered, setting her hands on my hips and sending what felt like a lightning bolt straight to my core.

No…straight to my fucking vagina.

Instead of focusing on the heat radiating from her fingertips, I met her gaze only to find a knowing smile sketched across her face as she whispered, "Come on, Dabbler. You danced with the Bare Assentials. I know there's more you want to let out—you *need* to let out."

Her hushed, raspy voice broke me in the best of ways. I rolled my spine, circled my hips, and slipped from her grasp. My hands ran over my body from my thighs to my chest to the underside of my hair. I ran my fingers through the short, dark strands before releasing my neck and throwing my arms into the air. I was moving in ways I hadn't in months—hips rolling, legs stretching, and even a calypso happened—a move I hadn't done since the days of dancing for the Merlin Mages.

Damn, I'd be sore tomorrow.

But I didn't care. Freedom coursed through my veins in a way it hadn't since, well…college. Even on the nights I closed out a show with the Bare Assentials. Even the weekends we performed for hours upon hours at the most prestigious venues. There was something different, more personal, about *this* movement that I never realized I missed until this very moment.

The drums slowed, and the fiddles quieted, my breathing intense as my feet gave in to the softened earth below them. This woman—this beautifully fierce stranger—stood mere feet from me in a similar stance I did. Her chest lifted and lowered with the same vigor I felt, a smile sketched across her face.

My eyes pulled away from hers and scanned the surrounding ground, running a hand over my pockets. My phone sat several feet away on the grass, probably falling from my sweatshirt pocket once I began moving. Swiping my thumb across the screen, I noticed I'd missed four calls.

They were not from Nel.

They were not from Jude.

They were from Viv.

"Fuck," I said a little louder than it sounded in my head. I peered from the woman, down to my phone, and then back. "I...I have to go. This was...this was honestly fucking amazing. Thank you."

Her smile faded slightly but not enough to falter the confidence she radiated. "Don't thank me. This was all *you*, Dabbler. We all deserve to let go."

Staring at her with the phone clenched in my hand, I was still in awe of her tone, her rough-and-tumble yet graceful energy. She was raw. She was real. There was something about—

No. Nope.

I needed to shake myself back to reality.

I quickly turned and walked away from the lake and lawn back toward Main Street where I finally opened my texts:

Um...baby, hi. I called you. Give me a call back.

You're not ghosting me, now, are you?

Zizi, for real. Call me. I'm performing in Greyport next weekend at Velvet. I need to see you.

Just like that, I was back beneath Viv's claws.

And I didn't even know the name of the dancer fading into the fog behind me.

yourEyesOnly.com
LIVE
LIKE
SUBSCRIBE
COMMENTS
@RILEmeup30: My roommates won't try this thigh stand with me.
@nerdalertallie26: All I see are and
ACRODADDIES

Chapter 15

Nel

"Okay...alright. This will be fine. This will be *great*," I said, shaking out my hands as I paced back and forth near the bookshelf. I'd chosen to wear my favorite red denim overall shorts—the ones I used to live in during summer break from college with just a bikini hidden beneath. I thought maybe they'd add a little more spice to the livestream with the deep-red denim and black bra underneath.

Didn't red automatically add flavor to everything?

The overall straps were as loose as they could go, and still my tits were kissing my chin, and the stretch marks on my ass were *definitely* showing.

I could *not* revisit the flashing incident from the week before.

My mental state was not ready for that step yet.

And my physical state? Ha!

I was going to cry.

My hands flew to the red straps, attempting—and failing—to loosen them for the seventeenth time in the last five minutes. I walked over to the couch and pulled the short, black wig up over the messy, low bun at the nape of my neck before adjusting the lace mask into place. Trembling fingers wrapped around the water bottle sitting by the laptop stool, the cool liquid sitting on my tongue for one...two...three seconds before finally sliding down my throat.

Even as I tried to focus on the cool water fueling my system—in the way Dr. Delilah always mentioned—I still wanted to itch off every piece of fabric on me.

The entire getup was uncomfortable: the mask would probably leave my face rashy; the wig didn't feel secure; I was sure my nipples were already peeking out; and the red lipstick matching the overalls was probably smudged.

Jude said red lipstick was always a winning move.

Well, he hadn't *said* it. He'd written it down.

Along with: *Smile and look at the camera when you read something uncomfortably sexual,* and *Laugh after the part about the phallic-shaped eraser...it's funny,* and *Suck on your finger before turning the next page. Slowly.*

After I'd read that last one, I'd met the most intense, soul-gripping gaze I'd ever seen come from him.

Goosebumps grew.

Breathing faltered.

Pupils dilated.

As I'd brought a finger to my mouth—my lips hugging it before I slowly pulled it out—I'd asked, "Like this?" He'd nodded without shifting his dark eyes from mine, a silent approval.

Then I wished he'd said those demands out loud.

Possible comments were written down—mimicking the livestream—but advice...I needed to hear it.

"T-minus five minutes!" Rosie whisper-shouted, shuffling across the kitchen floor in oversized socks bunching at the ankles. Her cloth shorts mimicked what my overalls were doing...just her ass looked way better than mine. "Are you ready?"

Vomit crawled up my throat. "Yup. Yeah. Definitely."

"Oh, boy," Rosie said, shaking her head and cupping my shoulder. "Nel...you'll be *fine*. Mae is passed the fuck out, and you look fine as hell. Just welcome viewers to the stream in a flirty way and start reading the first chapter! Throw in a couple winks, stop to read the comments once in a while, and you'll be golden."

"More like bronze, but okay." I snagged the wine glass from the table beside the bookshelf and took a long swig. "Let's just do this and make a few bucks."

"That's *not* the mindset, Exotic Ellie. This just won't do," Rosie mumbled before clicking on the ring light. "If you don't read this chapter tonight like you want to be there, we won't bring in the big bucks! You *do* want to read this first chapter, right?"

My shoulders dropped, and a heavy sigh escaped my lips. Of course I wanted to read this chapter. I wanted to, not only because it was a good fucking chapter but because it would make Rosie proud.

Hell, maybe I'd even make myself proud.

"Ughhhh...yesss, I want to read it. This chapter is...it's *really* hot."

"Okay. That's some of the energy we need. We're getting there." Rosie lifted her wrist up to her eyes and dramatically pulled it away. She squatted down behind the laptop positioned in front of the bookshelf, looking at the screen with wide eyes. "One minute, Nel. Get all cute and cozy...because two people are already waiting."

"No way...what?! It's probably just Seb and Riley." I rushed to the laptop screen, and indeed, two people were waiting.

Holy shit, there were now three.

I sat back onto the blush shag rug—that was definitely from our original MCC suite—and made sure I was centered in front of the bookshelf. I opened the book to the content warning page and readjusted my wig, mask, and overall straps for the final time.

Rosie took a deep breath from her spot behind the laptop, reaching around so her index finger hovered above the LIVE button. "Nel...are you ready?"

I took one final swig of wine before placing the empty glass back onto the table. My shoulders rolled back, my chin lifted slightly, and from what I could tell, my cleavage was *at least* above average. This would have to do. "Refill that glass. Let's go."

"Hey...hi! Welcome to our first Steamy Storytime!" I wiggled my fingers at the screen in the most flirtatious way possible as the red LIVE light flashed on, and my stomach plummeted. It still showed three people were watching, and I squinted down at the names—realizing I really needed to get my ass back to the optometrist. These contacts were *extremely* outdated. "Oh, hey, SpicyStef! I remember seeing your name last week. Oh, and you too, BrewMeDaddy. Hi!"

The third viewer—LittleMonsterMolly—was someone I'd never heard of before, but at least, from the looks of it, Sebastian and Riley weren't creeping on us.

Or so we thought.

"Alright, so...if you're reading along, let's jump right in! I am a *huge* fan of everything Laura Christian writes, and if you've read *It Only Takes One Swipe*, you'll *love* this one. Um...write in the comments which of her books are your favorites."

From the corner of my eye, I saw Rosie throw me a thumbs-up as she went to refill my wine glass, tiptoeing across the kitchen floor as if Mae could wake up at any second.

Which she could.

> **@SpicyStef_01**: *I think I re-read* The Un-Soulmate Summer *every July...it just feels right to start every summer off that way!*

> **@LittleMonsterMolly: @SpicyStef_01**:
> *Re-reading it strictly for the scene on the dock*
> *is absolutely worth it.*

> **@SpicyStef_01: @LittleMonsterMolly:**
> *Just the thought of that scene…*

> **@OliVERYcaffeinatedxx:** *Bend over that*
> *book a little more. I wanna see what Exotic*
> *Ellie's hiding under those straps.*

And we now had four people watching the livestream.

Though I tried to ignore the final comment, I adjusted the strap of my overalls so that my cleavage showed just the teeniest bit more.

Bite your lip.

Jude's words clung to my memory, so I followed his directions instead of shaking them away.

"That dock scene is definitely…delicious." With my top teeth pressing down into my bottom lip, I grabbed the wine glass from Rosie and took a sip, my lipstick leaving a crimson halfmoon in its wake. "Let's start our first livestream off with a bang…and I mean a *bang*. Let's get right into these content warnings, shall we?"

I read through the content warnings with only a few awkward moments getting in the way. I'd noticed halfway through that ZestyZi_NakedBookClub appeared in the comments and was responding to those I couldn't respond to—or didn't want to. She'd even called out OliVERYcaffeinatedxx when he asked if the reason I wore a mask was to hide my shitty looks or my shitty personality.

Luckily, she responded with something along the lines of how his "shitty comments must be compensating for something."

That shut him up...a little bit.

Once I got through the first page of chapter one, unexpected ease consumed me. I relaxed into the energy—the wine, the candles, the beautiful bookshelf behind me—and felt the words flow almost naturally. I giggled innocently at the sexual innuendos, adjusting my overalls so my cleavage remained on full display. I tried giving intense eye contact with the viewers when the grumpy—yet *gorgeous*—male main character entered the storyline, biting my bottom lip once the chapter ended.

Suck on your finger before turning the next page.

Slowly.

His words, his dark eyes, his soft tone.

Leaning forward—a little *too* forward—I squinted at the screen:

> **@LittleMonsterMolly:** *Holy shit. The way Andre entered the studio soaking wet from the rain? Delicious.*

> **@Spicy_Stef01: @LittleMonsterMolly:** *Right?! No wonder Stacy fell out of her downward dog.*

> **@BrewMeDaddy69:** *I'm pretty sure it'll still be fifty pages until they fuck. Let's be honest...it's a typical slow burn story structure.*

> **@nerdalertALLIE26: @BrewMeDaddy69:** *Don't be such a negative Nancy, Daddy!*

> **@hereforthecomments420:** *Show me dem titties!*

> **@BrewMeDaddy69:** **@nerdalertALLIE:** *Call me Daddy again.*

Hallie used to brag about times she'd snuck into 90s AOL chatrooms as a kid.

Was this what it was like?

And why didn't I hate it?

"I don't know, guys...Andre and Stacy may just get a little rowdy before page fifty!" I leaned back onto my wrist, letting the lace strap of my bra fall down over my shoulder. I had to puff my chest out a tiny bit more to make sure nothing else fell down.

Reaching for my glass of wine, I watched a few more comment bubbles appear on the bottom of the screen. "Oh, yes...SpicyStef, our schedule moving forward will be Mondays with me for Steamy Storytime, Wednesdays with both of us at Rowdy Readers, and Fridays with Zi for Smut Me Up. Definitely check out Rowdy Readers and Smut Me Up if you want a little more smut and a little more skin."

I looked toward Rosie, making sure I wasn't fucking up the schedule we'd finally agreed on. Rosie gave me a thumbs-up with one hand, lifting her wine with the other and finishing off the glass.

"We will add it to our profile too, so make sure you click the notification box!" I winked while simultaneously doing a weird circular motion with my finger to look like I was clicking a button. I was pretty sure the wink looked like something crawled into my eye, and my hand motion looked like I was jerking someone off because Rosie started pointing at the invisible watch on her wrist. "Alrighty...okay! Thanks, guys, for hanging out tonight. Read up this week because next week we're reading chapter seventeen which is the halfway point...and it gets *filthy*."

With my last attempt at winking, I clicked off the livestream, practically slamming the laptop shut. Opening the laptop a little bit to make sure we'd fully logged off, I closed it again, turned the power off, and collapsed onto the shag rug.

Rosie rushed over to lie with me, her body falling over mine. "Dude, Nel. You seriously fucking crushed that! Sure, there were some weird moments, but when you started reading...it was like an audiobook. Twenty-four people stuck around the whole time, and I'm sure more will watch the recording. When people watch the recording beginning to end, we get rich, bitch!"

I'm pretty sure *rich bitch* was pushing it.

The mask practically melted off my face from sweat as I turned to Rosie. "*What?* How did I miss that number?"

"Because you were so focused on the chapter, silly!" Rosie slapped my ass as I twisted onto my side to sit up.

I felt like maybe I could do this damn thing.

I felt a familiar power crawling back, pushing me to try more, be more, do more.

And between the adrenaline pumping and disbelief squeezing my heart, I felt something else whisper through my body I hadn't felt in a long, long time.

I felt the tiniest bit confident.

And that tiny bit meant a whole hell of a lot.

Chapter 16

Rosie

"**T**wenty-four people watched her *live!*" I exclaimed in my brother's direction. Nel fidgeted with Mae sitting on her lap, her tiny hands reaching for the hot mug of coffee before Nel nudged it away. Watching Mae's little fingers made me realize a couple things: Mae was sitting—not slouching—on Nel's lap, and her tiny fingers weren't the raisins they'd been almost two months ago.

Where had the infant gone?

That only meant time was passing by faster than I could believe. This gave me all the more reason to make sure The Naked Book Club became successful enough for us to make a few more bucks—and fast. My solo stream was coming up, and I needed to make it big.

"Shhh, Rowe. There are people here."

I looked over my shoulder, honking out a laugh before facing Nel. "That grandma can't hear shit. She was here the last two mornings we were. I'm pretty sure she's just watching the coffee drip and zoning the rest of the world out."

It honestly didn't sound like a horrible idea.

"Stop. What if she isn't? Maybe she can hear you," Nel whispered, her eyes dashing toward the woman and back.

Jude stepped away from the table, the hot coffee carafe in his hand. "Oh, Flora? I hate admitting this, but my sister is right. She's ninety years old and hard of hearing. She's harmless."

My hands smacked flat onto the table. "Ha! Say that again!"

"Nope." Jude shook his head, pressing his lips together and looking toward Nel. "But I'm proud you kicked ass, Nel. Such a top-notch student."

Nel shrugged, her cheeks flushing beneath her frames. "Only because my instructor was so demanding. I couldn't let him down."

"And you definitely didn't. Tomorrow night...we're still on for eight after closing?"

"Yup! Yes," Nel stammered. "I'll be here."

Jude nodded, rounding the counter to set the carafe back on the hot plate. The second he began talking to the customer in line, I leaned forward. "What the hell was that?"

"What was what?" Nel asked, crinkling her brow and adjusting Mae's rubber teether.

Octopus-shaped, of course.

"You know what I mean," I whispered, glancing over my shoulder before shifting even closer to the table. Her avoidant stare meant there was more to this than she was letting on...and I needed to know. "You guys are flirting. Like...hard."

"What? Rosie, come on. We absolutely are not," Nel scoffed. "We just jumped right back in where we left off...or a version of it. It's kind of...I don't know...nice."

Nice.

I wasn't sure how to read that.

The relationship Nel had with my brother had always been a mind-fuck. In college, I could never tell if they were about to casually get chicken wings or go back to his room. I could never tell if her giggle was flirtatious or if that was just her awkward energy shining through. I could never tell if he wanted her to genuinely help him get girls or if he just wanted to spend time around her.

One thing I *could* tell was how guilty Nel felt keeping Jude in the friend-zone back then.

The guilt Nel felt for showing interest in someone her sister didn't approve of was heart-wrenching.

The guilt Nel felt following her sister's advice that night was an even harder punch to the gut—hers, mine, and Jude's.

And I'd just stood there, listening to Nel cry in confusion as my brother disappeared.

I didn't ghost Nel then.

But my brother ghosted us.

"Where you left off at MCC was you guys making out before telling him he wasn't good enough, Nel. And those weren't even *your* words to begin with." The air between us grew heavy, and for the first time since bringing Jude up, she was looking me dead in the eyes. She was molting her skin into armor.

We'd never talked about what happened between the two of them the night before graduation. I'd hinted at it a few times, yes. But I'd never really said my thoughts out loud.

I knew it had to do with Grant.

I knew it had to do with Hallie's manipulation.

And I knew, even years later, she still wasn't sure how to handle this.

"Dabbler?" The voice forced my eyes away from Nel's, and when I looked up, all I saw was silky, sienna skin and radiant eyes.

"Hey, hi," I stammered, practically hopping to my feet. "What's up?"

Why was I standing?

I did *not* need to stand to ask her that.

"I'm good, I'm good..." As her voice trailed off, her hands began moving in slow, circular motions, those lusciously plump lips pressing together. Before I could imagine how they'd feel against my own, I caught onto what she was silently hinting at.

"Oh, sorry. I'm an asshole. I'm Rosie," I said. "Somehow we missed the whole name-exchange thing the other day."

"We weren't really focused on names the other day, though. Were we?" she said softly, stepping toward me with a knowing eyebrow raised.

Peering at Nel from the corner of my eye, I glimpsed a confused—yet curious—grin growing across her face.

Why was I stumbling? I *never* stumbled with this shit. I took control. Control was my *thing*.

Well, except with Viv.

She'd had control since the start.

"Rosie," she hummed, her tongue rolling over her lips as if to taste my name on her breath. "I'm Cadence. Cade."

"That's a fitting name," I said. "With how well you flow with music. Your parents must have just known."

"My parents...yeah. The best word to describe them is *eccentric*. That's putting it kindly." She laughed, scratching the back of her neck and causing some intricate braids to fall over her arm. "Eccentric and very passionate about music. They named me Cadence Capella and my brother Riff Ramone."

"Wait...Riff Ramone? You got to be shitting me! That's probably the *coolest* name I've ever heard," I exclaimed, my free hand flying into the air between us as I finally brought the mug up for a sip with my other. "Oh, but Cadence Capella is gorgeous too. Both are badass. I'm honestly just jealous."

How she bit her bottom lip after she laughed made my thighs clench. "Don't be jealous, Dabbler. Rosie is fitting. How you moved the other day mimicked a rose in bloom. It sounds fucking cheesy, but it makes perfect sense."

The way Cade said *fucking* made my knees practically buckle.

No.

Nope. I couldn't let this woman get to me.

"Thanks. Um…"

"Let's get dinner," Cade asked—no, *stated*—as she placed a hand on my shoulder, almost causing the mug to drop in shock. "Wine Thyme on Friday. Want to meet around six?"

"Uhhh…this Friday?"

"Yeah. Why not!" She released her grip, and I tried not to miss the comforting warmth. "I'll meet you there?"

"Um…yeah. I mean, I'm kind of—"

"She'll be there," Nel's voice cut the invisible barrier separating Cade and me from the rest of the room.

For the first time in minutes, I looked around. Sebastian leaned against the entrance doorframe, his mandolin swung over his shoulder and his smug face grinning in our direction. I saw my brother and Riley talking behind the counter, Jude's eyes occasionally flashing in our direction before returning to whatever Riley was venting about. A couple sat a few tables away, leaning close together so their mugs covered their faces as they whispered to one another.

Even Flora in the corner seemed to stare at me.

Was this what paranoia felt like?

I wasn't *dating* Viv. I wasn't even talking to her regularly.

Then why did I still feel like she was standing behind me, her breath warm against my ear, just waiting for me to ignore this moment?

"I kind of work that night…but not until nine," I said, swallowing.

"I actually bar tend at Wine Thyme most afternoons when I'm not doing workshops. I get off at six, but I also understand work getting in the way."

I'd stopped listening after she'd said *I get off.*

"Six. That should be fine. Yeah," I said, nodding a bit too rapidly.

Cade smiled, walking backward toward the counter. "Great."

"Great."

The second she turned on her heel to face Jude, I melted back into my seat, my body slowly angling around toward Nel. I knew she was staring at me with chameleon eyes bulging out of her head. When I peered up at her, I was correct.

"Rowe," she said softly.

"Yes, Nel?"

"Start talking."

Even after spending most of the morning—and afternoon—repeating to Nel that Cade was just some spunky dancer I'd met by Claus Lake who I had no feelings for whatsoever, she didn't believe me.

Even after I told her Viv forever had a chokehold on my heart—words that felt a little scratchy on my tongue to say—she still gave me a disbelieving look. I gave up trying to convince her since we needed to review the script for that night's Rowdy Reader's livestream just to ask myself: Was I trying to convince *her* or myself of all this?

Nel planned to read the first chapter of Dana Rowan's *Swiping for the Enemy,* and then I would read the second chapter where a *very* intense sexting scene happened. We'd jump back in next week at the halfway point, hoping viewers kept up with our timeline and both read a chapter during that stream as well.

We had a pretty good strategy going. From the comments on our page and the subscriber growth, having a week between streams so readers could get halfway through the book was a smart way to do it. It let us read a book a month on each tier, which was pretty realistic in the grand scheme of things. We also added a forum where those who already finished the book could chat about spoilers and theories so they wouldn't flood the livestream comments with them.

We also knew we'd have to actively scan comments for assholes who wanted to spoil the fun.

Rowdy Readers went relatively smooth. Nel squinted at the comments a few too many times—she'd gone in blind, deciding against wearing contacts or glasses because of her self-diagnosed *Tired Mom Syndrome.* I'd stumbled over a few sentences during the spicy sexting scene, having to stop and re-read a few in the sultriest way I could without losing my adrenaline.

Fifty-three people tuned in for Rowdy Readers.

Sixty were subscribed to Steamy Storytime.

Forty-nine were subscribed to Smut Me Up.

According to the views, likes, and engagement on our YourEyesOnly page, The Naked Book Club had officially brought in enough money since our premiere for us to confidently say we had a side gig.

A *small* side gig, but a side gig nonetheless.

It was one step closer to Nel and me affording our own places come September.

And finding new jobs.

"Did you decide what you're going to do about Viv?" Nel asked as she took off her wig, finally sliding on her glasses.

"What do you mean?" I asked, folding up the ring light and sliding it behind the sofa.

"Are you going to watch her at Velvet? She's performing this weekend, right?"

I'd almost forgotten about that text. "Yeah. She is. I definitely...definitely want to see her."

I wasn't exactly sure if I wanted to see her or visit Velvet more.

Yes, I liked how Viv made me feel, but I had a feeling some toys at Velvet would make me feel just as good.

Toys wouldn't ignore me for months at a time.

Why did all of this make my head hurt?

"I heard Velvet is the place to check out in Greyport these days," Nel said. "Don't they have sex toys—"

"—*and* booze. It's a sex toy speakeasy. Just add some half-naked women dancing around, and it's pretty much my description of heaven." There was no *pretty much* about it. "But if I'm going, you're coming with me."

Nel huffed out a laugh before sinking into the sofa, her half-empty wineglass in hand. From the defeated look on her face, the glass was definitely *not* half-full. "I mean, I probably can't. I'd have to ask Nora to watch Mae overnight again, and I already feel bad I've taken advantage of her these last couple of weeks."

"You're not taking advantage, Nel. You're *living*." Grabbing my wineglass, I shuffled over to the sofa beside Nel and plopped into the pile of pillows. "You're a mom, but you're also human. You're an adult who deserves time to herself—time to laugh, time to curse, time to drink, and time to freaking fall in love, if that's on your radar. You deserve all that on top of being loved unconditionally by that tiny human of yours."

I watched Nel's eyes grow glossy, her lower lip trembling. "Rosie...that may be the nicest thing you've ever said to me."

"Really? Huh. I always thought I was a pretty damn nice person," I said with a casual shrug. "You should probably take off the glasses you just put back on before the hormonal dam breaks, and it becomes a monsoon."

"Shut up." Nel reached for her glasses, ripping them from her face and wiping her eyes with the back of her hand. "I don't feel like I deserve all this time away from Mae, though. I feel guilty for wanting the time away, and then I feel like I'm doing the fucking Walk of Shame back to her after."

"But what about during?"

Nel dabbed another tear away. "Huh?"

"How do you feel *during* those moments away?" I asked. "Because it's *the during* that matters. It's how you feel in the moment that stays with you, not how you felt before or how you think you'll feel after."

"Why are you so wise?"

"So, you'll come with my wise ass to Velvet this weekend?" I nudged Nel with my elbow until she rolled her eyes and winced away from my touch. "We can make a weekend of it."

"You're just going to get wasted and swoon over Viv the whole time."

She probably wasn't wrong. "Yes...but *you* can swoon over some people too, you know. The performers, the bartenders, the hot sex toy specialist trying to sell you their double-sided dildos..."

"Are they *really* called sex toy specialists?" Nel asked. "How do you become one of those? Are there classes you have to take...like, how to use this vibrator or how to assemble a sex swing?"

"And that, my friend, is why YourEyesOnly exists. It's educational *and* hot as fuck...and the perfect platform for this type of thing, actually." My feet hit the floor, and as I headed into the kitchen to place my glass in the sink, I turned toward Nel, walking backward. "So...it's a yes? You're coming?"

"Well, I'm sure *you* will be." Slumping over her knees with a laugh, Nel got to her feet, stretching her arms above her head. "I'll see if Nora can help...again."

Chapter 17

Nel

I hung up with Nora that morning, and my phone slid from my grasp, my body melting to the floor. With Mae grinning and babbling on her belly, reaching for the dropped phone, sobs rushed out of me like a tsunami. I was trembling, and I grew dizzy from the blinding tears. Fingernails dug into my knees through my cotton sweatpants, and a salty, metallic taste coated my tongue.

Apparently, I'd bitten down on it a little too hard when trying to quiet my cries.

I'd come to terms with my uncontrollable tears. But the more Mae watched me as I collapsed into these moments, the more I tried to force the feelings away. I couldn't keep breaking down in front of her when I needed desperately to lift her up.

For the rest of her life.

I always felt too much: deep sadness, empathy, heightened joy, critical self-worth. When those feelings burrowed inside of me all at once, I couldn't force them out. There was no way to ignore or defeat them. All I could do was sit with them and let those feelings win.

Someday, my surrender would mean something, and I could turn it into healing.

But right now, I felt both hollow and filled to the fucking brim.

"—because my sister has been watching Mae once in a while...and now is watching her for a *whole* weekend. I feel like a failure. I shouldn't be just handing her off whenever I need a break and—"

"Nel...it's okay," Dr. Delilah said softly, twisting in her chair while braiding her fingers together on her lap. I hadn't come into the office for a session since the blowout at my apartment during the family dinner. "Give yourself a moment."

Since the blowout when Hallie tried nudging me in a safe, smart direction the way she always did.

But something that night made me lose my shit, and really, I never lost my shit with Hallie. She'd been the one to put me back together all those years ago, so the most I could do was stay intact.

My swollen eyes pinched shut at the memory. "Sorry. I'm sorry. It's been...it's just been a *day*."

"Never apologize. It may feel better to let it all out rather than hold onto what weighs you down." Delilah cocked her head to the side, tiny crimson curls falling in front of colorful glasses. "But I do need you to know that you are not a failure whatsoever. You're growing. You're healing. You're learning. You can't be a failure when you're figuring out who you are."

"But the thing is, I *knew* who I was. I was so damn proud of the person I used to be. I was extroverted and goofy and, well...sexy. I was confident. After...after Grant, it took me the entire span of college to finally feel comfortable in my skin. My twenties were honestly great—well, minus Rosie disappearing. But I was confident and working and *living*," I said, leaning my head back against the bright wallpaper. "Since finding out I was pregnant, I lost all of that...and I hate admitting that, because it's not Mae's fault."

"You just compared yourself to the person you were almost a decade ago. Even the person you were a few years ago isn't who you were in college or who you are now. As much as you may want to be that girl again, you can't be...and honestly, that's a good thing. As for Grant, you've proven you are stronger than how he treated you. And now, you're learning that you're also strong enough to stand your ground." Delilah leaned over her knees, taking her glasses off and holding them as she met my gaze. "I know you believe Hallie knows what's good for you, but I think the night your family visited opened your eyes a little bit. You will lean toward the direction best for you—whether or not Hallie agrees with it. Try to remember that it's *your* life, not hers, to mold."

But she'd molded me back into a person I'd been proud of before.

Maybe I hadn't agreed with all her suggestions. Maybe she came off a little brash, but she'd kept me moving forward when it hurt to take a step. Wouldn't she help me take steps forward now too?

With motherhood and with…

My throat felt raw when his face popped into my vision.

I wouldn't bring Jude into this.

"We are ever-changing," Delilah continued. "It's up to us to explore and embrace those changes as they come. It just doesn't have to happen all at once."

Mae let out a tiny coo as Delilah lifted her water bottle up to her lips, narrowing her eyes at the cup by my elbow—a silent plea to hydrate. Wrapping my hand around the water cup, I did what she didn't have to say.

"But let's get back to the original discussion," Delilah said, setting her water bottle down and placing her glasses back on the bridge of her nose. "Is Hallie watching—"

"Oh, no. No," I said, water dribbling over my bottom lip. "No…it's Nora. Hallie is too busy with her own family and her social platforms. Nora is the only family member who really helps."

"Well…your aunt also gave you the apartment, right?"

Touche.

"Yes. I'm very grateful for Theía Elena. She just lives in Greece most of the time, so I rarely see her…or hear from her."

"You have good, supportive people in your life, Nel. You're not a failure for leaning on them once in a while. Like you said, you need breaks…and you deserve them too. You're wearing so many hats right now: single mom, job seeker, apartment hunter. Take those breaks."

Her mentioning the job-seeking and apartment-hunting scenarios made a tiny clock inside of my brain tick, counting down the minutes before Mae and I would be thrown out to the wolves.

I wouldn't cry.

Nope.

"I know I do," I whispered, Jude's kind, bearded face popping back to the forefront of my mind before disappearing just as quickly.

He would not be part of this conversation today. Not until I felt a little more secure about whatever the hell I felt for him. It was too much to add to the therapy fire.

"I think what sucks the most...is my inability to push Hallie's opinions aside," I admitted. "Yes, she'd freed me from Grant's claws—we all know that. But now...now I feel like I don't have to follow her like a naive duckling as often as I used to. I just mentally can't take those strides away yet. It's a force I can't stop but can slowly lessen the strength of."

"That's called growth. It may not feel like much, but you acknowledging this is big. It's healthy, Nel. This shows you're making progress."

But why didn't it feel like progress?

Why did it still feel like she was standing there in the room with us, waiting to throw her two cents in at any moment or push me away from friendships I wanted to build back up again.

With Rosie.

Jude.

Mae's carrier burned into the crease of my inner elbow as we walked out the door, Delilah saying she would contact Dr. Trang to send another month's worth of Lamictal and Wellbutrin refills to the pharmacy. I hated myself for relying on those damn pills, but I was grateful for the tiny bit of relief they gave my brain.

Because it was exhausting in there.

"Sorry...I thought maybe Rosie could watch Mae tonight, but this will just have to do," I said, flopping down onto the shag rug in front of the bookshelf. "And since when are she and Sebastian such close friends?"

"Since he realized he can't *break her gayness*." Jude laughed, collapsing onto the couch and pulling the knit hat from his head as long, dark hair fell to just above his shoulders. Compared to the Jude I once knew, this one obviously took pride in keeping his locks, well...*luscious*. He used to keep his hair in a messy, low-fade mohawk, of sorts. But now...now he'd discovered conditioner and probably used some kind of argan oil or hydrating serum to keep it looking healthy rather than greasy.

I grabbed the hair tie from my wrist and pulled my heavy, chestnut tangles up into the messy, half-ass bun I lived in.

At this rate, Jude would need to give me lessons on hair care.

"She didn't even tell *me* they were going to Thirsty Theodore's until she texted an hour ago," I said quietly, trying to hide that I felt the tiniest bit excluded. "But good for them. There will always be more drinks to be had."

"We will just have a few extra drinks when we're at Velvet."

My head snapped toward Jude. "Wait, what? You're going to Velvet this weekend too? As in, like, three days from now?"

"Yeah. We're still figuring out the shop's schedule, so we're only working Saturday morning, and then we're all heading out there for the night. We all deserve a break...a *real* one."

"Seb and Riley too?"

"Why do I sense you're not excited we're tagging along?" Jude quirked a dark eyebrow up, leaning back onto his elbows and straightening his legs up onto the sofa.

"Oh...no...I'm excited! It's going to be a great show, and I heard the...um...*venue*... I heard it's awesome." My fingers wouldn't stop fidgeting in my lap, and I reached across the rug for my water bottle, taking a long slug.

Jude brought both his hands behind his head, leaning all the way back with a smirk. "Nel, we know it's an adult store too. That's half the reason Sebastian even agreed to go."

"I'm guessing the other half wasn't for the cocktails, huh?"

Jude shook his head. "Nope. Not at all."

Nodding in a slow-motion wave of sorts, I reached for *My Dirty To-Do List* and slipped my finger where the bookmark was.

This one was going to be a doozy.

Well, not as big of a doozy as what Rosie was reading Friday, but for this tier...this was as spicy as this story would get. While Rosie dove headfirst into books marked at the highest steam level, Steamy Storytime stuck with scenes leaning toward the third steam level side of things.

But as I looked from the page laying on my lap to meet Jude's gaze, my mind flashed back to Merlin Community College, to the night Rosie mentioned the other day.

His face nuzzled into the crook of my neck.

His hands pressed firm into my lower back.

His eyes when I told him what he didn't want to hear.

What *I'd* never wanted to say to begin with.

Yet, here he was, lying in front of me with a genuine smile hidden beneath that dark beard of his and confidence radiating off him in waves. Had he forgiven my naivete from all those years ago, or had he wiped that memory from his brain completely?

"Nel..." His voice rumbled me back to the present. "Do you?"

"Huh? Do I what?"

"The sticky notes. Do you have them?"

"Oh. Yeah. Yes." I stumbled forward and tossed a stack of notes and a pen in Jude's direction—the pen bouncing off the center of his forehead. "Oof...sorry, Jude."

"I'm pretty sure this just marked up my face," Jude said, setting both the pen and notes on his chest as he remained in his laying position. "You'll just have to look at my eyes and not my super sexy forehead."

I squinted to see if the pen actually left a mark. "I don't know...it looks like there's a dick drawn on your forehead. So, I'll just stare at that while I read all about them in this chapter."

His dark eyes widened. "While you read about forehead dicks?"

"Yup. *Forehead* dicks." I laughed and tapped the open page in front of me with the tip of my finger. "This is the chapter when Andre and Stacy get to the third point on their to-do list."

"The *dirty* to-do list, correct?"

I nodded. "Precisely."

"What's the third point."

"Hmm?" I swallowed hard, and looked down at the page, adjusting my glasses.

"Nel." Jude sat up, the notes and pen rolling off his chest. "What's the third thing they have to do…that you have to read about? Does it have to do with forehead dicks?"

At least he got a laugh out of me. "I wish…kind of. They…they just have to have silent sex."

Jude's inked hands grew tighter around the pen. "Silent…sex?"

"Mm-hmm." I flipped the pages a few times only to return to the beginning of the chapter. "One point on her list is to have sex without either of them making a sound."

"Why the hell would anyone want to do that?"

My cheeks flushed. "I mean, I'm not sure. Maybe some people like…a challenge? Maybe Andre and Stacy find this kind of thing…I don't know…hot."

"Do you?"

"Do I what?"

"Stop playing the clueless card, Nel. That doesn't work on me anymore." Jude shook his head, a hand running through his hair as he yanked it up into his go-to bun, snapping a hair tie around it. "Do you like that kind of challenge—staying quiet? From your reaction, I don't think this is a kink of yours."

I felt my cheeks burn, the book rolling off my lap as I fumbled to find the correct chapter. Never had Jude been so forward about something like this. We used to joke about the hook-ups we'd had at college or kid about certain things we liked in bed, but never had he been so direct before.

"I mean…I do like a good challenge, I guess," I stammered. "It can be pretty hot…but I don't know."

Jude lay back onto his elbows, setting the notes and pen onto his chest. "I want to hear more about Andre and Stacy. Let's get started, *Ellie*."

Fuck.

Why did I like how he said that?

I was born Penelope.

Hallie made me hate the name Penny.

I'd grown used to Nel.

But Ellie?

Maybe I liked this version of myself more than I thought.

"Okay, so…here we go." Sitting up straighter, I set the book comfortably in my lap, pushing my chest out just the tiniest bit before looking directly at Jude. "Welcome back, friends, to Steamy Storytime! And boy, is it going to get *steamy* tonight."

Jude nodded from his spot sprawled on the couch, clutching the notes and pen atop his chest so they wouldn't roll away again.

"If you've been keeping up with the story, you should be about halfway through *My Dirty To-Do List*. If you've already read the damn thing, don't comment! Go hang out in the forum we set up and come back next week so we can talk about it. Comment if you did—"

Jude lifted a note into the air, and I had to crawl forward to see what it said. Snatching it from his hand, I squinted down at his chicken scratch:

Show some shoulder, professor.

"*Professor?* Am I acting too...educational? I'm supposed to give sexy librarian vibes," I asked. Jude grabbed another note, and before he could lift the pen, I shook my hands in front of me. "No, no. You can talk for this one."

Setting the notes down, he nudged himself back up onto his elbows. "You sound like Dr. Flanders from that human sociology course we were forced to take."

I swear my eyes rolled all the way to the back of my head the moment he mentioned her name. "Dr. Freaking. Flanders? *Really?* Come on...I'm *way* sexier than her."

"I mean, yes. You definitely are." Jude swallowed. "But you're speaking too robotically. Loosen up a little. Do you need one of those gummies we used to take when—"

"You're *really* going down memory lane tonight, aren't you?" I leaned back against the bookshelf, stretching my long legs in front of me. "If we had any edibles, I'd absolutely be down for one right now. Well...maybe. I have a child in the other room, so it may not be the most *adult* choice to make."

"Well...then pretend. Bring yourself back to how relaxed those things made you feel. Or just picture yourself as the complete opposite of Dr. Flanders."

"I hated her. Ugh!" I ran my thumb over the page edges before pressing the back of my head against the shelf. "It's been such an emotional day. I don't know if I can pretend to be high *and* Dr. Flanders' alter ego in one sitting."

Jude shuffled off the sofa, setting the notes and pen aside as he joined me on the shag carpet. He sat so close, his heat and scent adding more fog to my mind. Setting his hands on my thighs, his serious gaze met mine, and he whispered, "I'll listen to you all day if you need me to, Nel. Shit's been hard...I can sense that. You'll be so happy getting through this chapter, but if you need to—"

"No, you're right. This is therapeutic, in a way, but this isn't another therapy session. Hell, the one this morning was more than enough!"

His hands released from my thighs, and he leaned against the sofa, snagging the notes and pen. "Onward. Silent sex awaits."

Clearing my throat, I closed my eyes and exhaled, feeling my shoulders loosen. Bringing the book onto my lap, I flipped it to the chapter and slowly opened my eyes. "We left off last week with Stacy and Andre almost—*almost*—making out in the elevator after a night of steamy body shots. They checked *that* box off, so now let's see if they can check off the next one."

I let my slouchy sweatshirt slip off my shoulder, wiggling it in Jude's direction with a clever grin that made him grab the pen and notes. As he wrote, I looked down at the pages in front of me until an oddly familiar, high-pitched sound shook me. I peered behind Jude's shoulder toward Mae's nursery, my brow furrowing when I heard the sound again.

"Did you hear that?"

Jude's head shot up, moving quickly back and forth as if spooked. "Huh? No. What was what?"

"Did you say something?"

"I didn't say anything."

Then I heard it again.

"Didn't you hear that? That, right there. I heard it again." Setting the book down, I walked by Jude into the hallway leading toward Mae's nursery. I cautiously wrapped my fingers around the door's edge, dipping my head into her room. There, in her crib, Mae's tiny fingers curled around the crib edge to help her balance. Her eyes were alert and wide, as if she'd never slept at all.

"Mahhhhhm," she cried, her knees bending slightly to give her a little bounce. "Mahhhhm mahhhmy mahhhhm."

My breath caught in my chest.

My heart palpitated.

Again, she said it.

Again and again and again.

I wanted to throw myself into the crib with her, but all I could do was stand there as tears painted my cheeks. I would not force these tears away. These were tears I wanted to feel. These were emotions I'd always *dreamed* of feeling.

Whether Mae realized it, she'd called for me.

She'd finally said her first *real* word.

And it was all for me.

I flew into her room and wrapped her in my arms, swaying side to side and kissing her cheeks like the crazy person I was. She continued to coo my name in my ear, some drool—and probably snot—sliding down to meet the salty tears pooling around my neck.

"It's me. I'm Mama. Hi, baby," I whispered, kissing her cheeks and shifting my weight side to side. "I'm here. I'm here."

"Maaahmmmmy," she blubbered, her little hand escaping my own and angling it toward the ground by her crib. My eyes followed her chubby fingers until I saw one of her stupid pacifiers laying just slightly beneath her crib. I rubbed the binky on my sweatshirt and placed it between her lips. It clicked in my brain that she probably called more for the binky than for me.

But I didn't care.

If she wanted to call her damn binkies *Mommy*, so be it.

I'd listen to her scream that word all day and night if I had to.

Placing her back into her crib, I gently rubbed her back and hummed "All My Loving" until her breathing grew relaxed, her chest lifting and falling with ease. I tiptoed out of the room, closing her door so only a tiny sliver of night light brightened the hallway. Turning on my heels, I walked into the kitchen to find Jude bent over the island, his hands cupping a glass of water. His expression shifted from joyous to confused as I flew my body into his embrace. My tears fell onto the chest of his button-up as he hugged me, the faint scent of coffee beans lingering on the flannel.

"She said my name. For the first time," I sniffled out, doing my best not to rub a snot bubble all over him. "I never thought I'd be one of *those* moms who cared about these silly things...but apparently, I'm one of those moms."

The warmth of his hand against the side of my cheek forced me upright. With both hands cupping my face, his thumb wiping a tear from my cheek, Jude said, "You can cry when she hits milestones, and you can cry because you're exhausted and losing your shit. Both reasons are valid. Both reasons make you a great mom, Nel."

I wasn't sure if it was the tiniest pull of his hands against my face or my uneven stance in front of him, but within a blur of seconds, his lips were on mine.

His taste was so familiar. So refreshing. So needed. It was as if I'd gotten a tiny taste of some drug for the first time after being sober for so long.

It was dangerous.

I needed to quit while I was ahead.

But I already craved more.

Chapter 18

Rosie

"What the fuck is this?" I slid the note across the kitchen island the second Nel walked in. She'd struggled putting Mae down for a nap, and somehow, over the course of the day, our paths barely crossed. The apartment wasn't that big. Before I left for dinner with Cade, I needed to see her for at least five minutes so she could explain *this* to me...and convince me that this very date-like date was not an actual date.

It was just dinner with a friend.

A hot friend.

It was a non-date with a hot friend.

That was all.

Nel placed an index finger over her lips and grabbed the note from the counter. Her olive cheeks flushed as she slowly set the note back down. "Yeah...I didn't see this one last night. Where'd you find it?"

"On the couch this morning," I said, looking over Nel's shoulder to see the digital clock staring at me from above the stove. I had to leave in ten minutes.

Did I want to leave? Yes.

Was I stalling? Also, yes.

"Explain, please. I have to go on this non-date with Cade in, like, five seconds."

Nel tipped her head downward, rolling her eyes. "Rowe...you're going on a date."

"Nope."

"She asked you to dinner. It's a date."

"You're still not telling me why this note says, *Fuck me with your eyes, professor.*" I tapped the tip of my finger on top of the messy script as I leaned farther over the counter. "And please confirm this is *not,* in fact, my brother's shitty-ass writing."

"It's your brother's shitty-ass writing."

"Nel! What are you guys doing?" I exclaimed, my arms flailing into the air as she looked toward Mae's room. "I've always supported that weird, flirtatious tension between you guys, but what if you break his damn heart again?"

Nel paused, creasing her brow. "How would... What do you mean?"

She was playing the clueless, naive card again. Did I have to always be the bitch in these scenarios? Shoulders slumping with a sigh, I said, "What if Hallie says something again? What if she tells you that you can do better? That you don't *deserve* to be with someone so similar to Grant...even when she's making a shitty assumption based on looks and your track record and—"

"She was trying to help..." Nel whispered, not daring to look me in the eye. "I know it doesn't seem like it, and she should have gotten to know him more, but she's always wanted—"

"Nuh-uh. Nope. This time around, I won't let you stand up for her." My index finger flew into the air, wagging between us. "Back then...okay. You were getting out of a shitty relationship, and she was *helping* you. Now, Nel...now it's your turn to help yourself."

Nel couldn't hide the mix of hurt and reality hitting her as her features softened, and her eyes darkened. I wasn't sorry. If any-thing, I was glad I said it out loud because she *needed* to hear it. I just didn't like seeing her look like a kicked kitten.

It was her *kicked kitten* look that always got me.

I set my hand on hers. "I love you, Nel. And as much as I hate admitting it, I love my brother too." Her giggle was necessary to clear the air...and a way to redirect this dark conversation back toward the light. "I just need...*need* to know why you want to fuck my brother with your eyes."

"*He's* the one asking *me* to fuck him with my eyes!" Nel shouted, quickly covering her mouth. Releasing her hand from mine, she swung around to look at the baby monitor by the stove.

"I know, I know," I whispered, curling forward over the counter and placing my head in my hands. "You guys have always fucked with my head. Sometimes in a good way, because I always thought it was cute. Sometimes in a not-so-good way, because you fuck with each other's heads too. I just want everyone to end up okay...and everyone to think for themselves."

There was a hiccup of silence before Nel sighed and said, "I get it. Hallie still thinks every guy I get feelings for is some version of Grant, but I'm not twenty-one and impressionable anymore. I'm a thirty-year-old depressed mom, trying to figure out my shit, and I don't need anyone's opinions getting in the way. I know what's best for me, and I need to stop handing my heart over to her. She can make suggestions, but I'm the one who decides what to do with those suggestions. No one else."

My jaw dropped.

Had Nel admitted her need to take back control?

I knew it was hard for her. I knew she felt like she owed the world to her sister. Hallie had conditioned Nel into thinking she knew what was best for her over all these years, and when you're that far down, when someone throws down the rope, you take it.

Huh...why did this sound like advice I too needed to listen to?

I gradually bent my knees, lowering myself beneath the island and opening the cabinet until I found what I was looking for...without really looking. Standing back up, my jaw still slightly ajar, I set two shot glasses on the counter followed a bottle of Jose Cuervo. I popped open the top and poured.

"Uh...what? What's happening here?" Nel looked from the shots, to the bottle, and then back to me as I finished pouring the second shot, sliding it toward her. "Since when is there a bottle of tequila in the cereal cabinet?"

"Since I moved in." I lifted the glass into the air, finally shaking myself back into focus. "Cheers."

"Um..." Nel looked down at the shot. "Why?"

"Because..." I lifted the glass a little higher. "Because I'm admitting out loud that I'm going on an actual date with someone other than Viv...but *really* we're cheers'ing because you just stood up for yourself. Every other time you've attempted to confidently stand up for yourself, you sound a little like a scared, dying cat. This time, though, you sounded like a fucking lioness who knows what she wants. That's worth cheers'ing to, my friend."

Nel looked back down at the shot as she fiddled with a damp napkin. Her knuckles grew white around it, and she let go of the cloth, grabbing the shot and clicking it against mine. "You're right."

Winking, I said, "Say that again."

Nel's shot was gone within seconds.

"Zizi...is a play on Rosie, right?" Cade stirred the straw, decorated in a wrapped orange peel, around the outside of her cocktail glass.

"Yeah. It is. Yup."

She laughed, bringing the straw to her lips...lips that my eyes now couldn't look away from...as she said, "Clever. I like that."

"Zizi has been my go-to name for all things burlesque over the years," I explained, sitting back with my cocktail in hand and watching the single oversized ice cube float in the liquor. "Zesty Zi. It's always kind of worked, you know?"

"*Zesty*, huh?" Cade laughed low, still stirring her straw around her lavender thyme spritz. "Is it required to give yourself an alter ego when you perform? That must be a nice change of pace...getting to switch into a new character, of sorts. Become someone you aren't."

If she was quietly asking if I liked role-playing, the answer was yes.

Yes, I will role-play with you, Cade.

Wait...where was my brain veering?

Focus, Rosie.

Focus on your non-date.

"The funny thing is, I'm very much like Zizi. A lot of performers like the idea of living this protected life during the day and becoming this over-the-top sex icon at night. For me? I like being that on *and* off stage. I think it's just part of who I am...and I kind of live for it."

Cade's face remained angled down toward her drink, but her eyes gazed above the rim of her glass. "Embracing your sexuality and sensuality is empowering. Your confidence with that is hot as hell. Even though you were hesitant about dancing on the lawn, once you were moving, I could feel that confidence."

"I don't know if my confidence was *really* showing that day," I admitted as steaming plates were set in front of us. I practically drooled into the rigatoni pasta that was smothered in creamy, tomato sauce and hot and sweet peppers hiding beneath tender cubes of chicken. Cade convinced me to try the chicken riggies since the recipe originated near the town she'd grown up in. Nel had mentioned this dish before too, so it was about time I tested it out for myself. Though Cade opted for the chicken alternative, I dove in hard, my teeth slicing into a juicy piece of chicken as steam poured from my mouth. I flapped my hand in front of my lips, doing all I could not to look like a fire-breathing dragon about to pass out. "Hot...it's...hot."

Cade slid my glass of water closer and, after somehow swallowing the forkful—which was probably the best damn thing I'd ever tasted—I took a long gulp.

"It has a kick to it," Cade said, scooping some onto her fork and gently blowing the steam away, curls of gray floating over my plate. "Kind of like you."

And I was choking.

Well, not *really* choking...just a little stunned.

She was forward—that was for sure—but hearing her say that in her hoarse, raspy voice was the definition of orgasmic.

The heat of the bite I'd just taken was quickly replaced with another kind of heat.

"Are you okay, Dabbler?" she asked, a knowing smirk still pinned to her lips.

"Yup. I'm definitely okay." Taking a deep breath, I lifted a forkful and blew the steam away. "Riggies were a good suggestion. I probably would have just gone with my usual childish choice of spaghetti and meatballs if you hadn't mentioned this."

"That's not a bad choice, though." She took a bite, licking sauce from her upper lip. "You can never go wrong with spaghetti and meatballs, even their beef alternatives here are top-notch."

She didn't think my food choices were weird.

She liked that I dance—well, *danced*—burlesque.

She had an intoxicating confidence and spunk that I wanted to breathe in.

"Tell me about your job."

Her question caught me off guard. "The Bare Assentials?"

"You said you don't dance with them anymore, right? What do you do now?" she asked, lifting another forkful and blowing steam away.

"Well...since leaving the troupe, I started a business, of sorts, with my friend."

"You're a dancer *and* an entrepreneur?" The piercing hugging her right eyebrow caught the light as she lifted it. "You can stop it with all this badass energy...it's too much. But really, please don't. Don't stop. What kind of business?"

I just stared at her for a second as a witty smile grew across her face.

"Do you know of...YourEyesOnly?" I swallowed hard, unsure why I felt so anxious about this. Talking to Sebastian and Riley about this was one thing, but bringing it up to the feisty goddess in front of me? It felt, just...different.

It was a mix of thrill and uncertainty.

A tinge of fear pricked my senses as I waited for her reaction.

"Ummm...of course I do," she said with a suggestive grin. "I'm a big fan of the Vegan Vixens, and I recently discovered Bette Ohm."

My jaw dropped.

She was all the things *and* actively a part of the YEO community?

I also was a top-tier subscriber of Bette Ohm's channel.

And Foam Freaks. There was just something about those physical therapists that got me going.

Okay...and maybe a little DJ Dickspin. Just because his music kicked ass.

I was *not* interested in the *dickspin* part of his channel.

Gross.

I pushed down the butterflies in my belly. "My friend and I just started a channel on there—it's called The Naked Book Club. We read chapters of steamy romance books out loud and discuss them. We've only been doing this for a few weeks—well, *officially* anyway—and only have, like, a couple hundred followers, but it's honestly been a breath of fresh air."

"I love this for you, Rosie," Cade hummed, lifting her cocktail and taking a sip. My name—my *full* name—sliding off her lips made goosebumps immediately grow. "I'll have to check you out on there. It's about time I get back into some good smut."

"Want to come watch it? My livestream?" The words fell from my mouth as fast as the steam had minutes before. "That's actually what I'm doing after this...which was why we had to meet at this time. My roommate is going over to her sister's house for another one of their family dinner things that always turns into a shitshow. So, the place is ours until she comes home."

Cade's smile was wicked on a face so soft. "You're okay with me watching?"

My expression mirrored the one on her face, the heat between my thighs growing by the second. "Absolutely."

This was my first official solo livestream.

And I had a *live* audience.

Well, I guess I had a live audience both on screen and in the room with me...but this felt more intimate. This rug was a stage, and the sofa Cade sat on was the VIP front row. She'd see my fingers trace my lace bra up close and practically feel heat float off my skin once the steamy scene began.

This was real entertainment.

It was fucking invigorating.

"*She wrapped her hand around his hard length, his breath hitching as she slowly stroked him up and down,*" I read, my hands exploring my chest as I softly said each word...wishing we'd chosen more sapphic books to add to the line-up. Biting my lip, I snuck a look at Cade, who sat cross-legged on the sofa, her lips pressed tight into a curious grin. "*But she couldn't let him have all the fun. No. She, too, deserved pleasure...and she was the only person who could get herself to the point of pure ecstasy she craved. She needed to take the night into her own hands, and that meant using her free one to get herself there.*"

As my hand wandered beneath the lace lingerie to roll a peaked nipple between my fingers, the silver barbell cool against my skin,

I glanced at the comments rolling in...and boy, were they rolling. This chapter ended on somewhat of a cliffhanger, and I was testing the waters with this first Smut Me Up stream. I would not go all out just yet. We all liked a good tease.

And from the looks of the comments—and the 103 live viewers—they *definitely* were all about the tease too.

"You guys are naughty." I sat back, wagging my free index finger toward the camera. "OliVERYcaffeinatedxx...if you want me to get through this last page, you better stop asking me to show my tits. I will when I'm good and ready. And believe me, you'll know when I am."

"Damn..." Cade whispered from the sofa, smiling against the lip of her wine glass.

I did all I could to play off my giddiness as causal. I lifted the book back into the air with one hand as my other still cupped my breast. "*My hand slowly made its way to the inside of my thighs, the tips of my fingers walking toward the damp edge of my panties before pushing the fabric aside. With the next stroke of his cock, I slipped my fingers inside my wet heat, a gasp escaping my lungs the second I hit the spot no man had ever hit before in the way I could.*"

My hand went from pinching and twisting my nipple inside my lingerie to lowering the thin strap so it fell low enough to show half my bare chest. My hand caressed my arm, my belly, my thighs until I, too, found my fingers running across my shear bottoms. I was not planning to mimic what the character in the story was doing—at least not tonight, anyway. But I *could* lightly run my fingers between my thighs. I could subtly apply pressure to the tiny ball of nerves screaming to be touched. I could bite my lip until a metallic ping roared through me.

This was a night of trial and error, after all.

When my eyes landed back on Cade's, the wine glass still pressed against her plump lips, I could have orgasmed right then and there.

I needed to get through these last couple of sentences.

"The faster my hand moved around his cock, the faster I shifted my fingers inside of myself. When his hungry eyes fell to the hand moving between my own legs, release dripped over the fingers wrapped around his cock. He let out a guttural sound of relief, meaning only one thing: I was in full control...and he knew it."

Though I wanted more than anything to keep my hand between my thighs, I forced my focus back to the screen. "That's all we got for this week, smut sluts! Next Friday, we'll chat about the first half of *Whisper My Secrets*...and maybe read a scene where things get a little freaky in a church pew. Now, go wash your hands."

I clicked off the livestream and collapsed onto the rug in a heap of adrenaline and exhaustion. The last hour was fucking invigorating. There was teasing, performing, and one hell of a story.

Nothing was better.

This was the feeling I'd missed these last couple of months.

It felt so empowering—so comforting—knowing I wasn't just making others happy, but also myself. I'd loved burlesque for exactly this reason, and getting the chance to relive that energy in a new way was exhilarating. After the Bare Assentials let me go, I'd thought about stepping away from this line of work.

But why the hell would I take a step back when I could feel accepted in a space we were creating on YourEyesOnly?

There was no more holding back now.

I knew I needed to find a new place to live soon—that was a given.

But finding a new line of work? This feeling...this was it for me.

This was end game.

Inhaling deeply, I sat up to see my tits both fully out of the lace bralette. Stuffing lefty back in—taking my time because I had zero shame—I realized the edge of the laptop hadn't fully shut. I quickly slammed the cover down fully before meeting Cade's gaze as it scanned over my face, my body, with such controlled intensity. She had set the wine glass on the coffee table and was sitting cross-legged on the couch, leaning back on one hand.

"So...what did you think?" I asked, cocking my head to the side as I kneeled at the end of the couch.

Her throat bobbed softly as she swallowed, her eyes lasered into mine. "I think..." She paused, uncrossing her legs so one hung off the sofa and the other remained beneath her. "I think you should kiss me."

My heart collided against my ribs. "Excuse me?"

Cade leaned back, propping herself up on her elbows. "You heard me, Dabbler."

I wasn't sure when I crawled up onto the sofa like some rabid creature. I wasn't sure when I shifted to straddle Cade's thigh, my lace-clad body pressing against her as she leaned back against the pillow with a waiting grin.

What I was sure of, though, was that my body and brain were craving the same thing even as my heart shook cautiously.

Cade wasn't Viv.

That I knew for damn sure.

But as I lifted Cade's chin and my lips pressed fiercely against hers, I knew I felt more comfortable—more at peace—in this moment than I had with anyone in a long, long time.

Chapter 19

NEL

Hallie's house was a fucking fortress.

I had a hard time appreciating it without some form of weird jealousy—and I wasn't even sure if jealousy was the right word for it anymore. What I did know, though, was that my emotions were on edge when Mae and I knocked on Hallie's front door.

The twins and Tucker opened the massive front door, and all eyes fell onto Mae's chubby cheeks and toothy smile—well, *toothy* was probably pushing it since it was just her two bottom teeth coming out to play. The girls yanked on her arms as we walked inside, Tucker grabbing the diaper bag sliding off my shoulder.

"Mae! See my *new* room. Please, Theía Nel?" Daisy squealed, pulling the bottom of my sweater toward the ornate staircase curling up along the left side of the entryway. "Shhh...it's a secret."

"It's blue," Dahlia said monotonously from behind me, bending over the carrier to poke Mae's cheeks. Even at eight months, I was so grateful Mae hadn't lost those gorgeous plump cheeks of hers, and I hoped she never would outgrow them.

From halfway up the staircase, Daisy dramatically whined, "Daaahliaaa...it's a *secretttt*. You tolddddd!"

"We will come see your new room in a few minutes, okay?" I said, unclicking Mae from the carrier to scoop her into my arms. "I just need to go say hi to your mom and Theía Nora first. Are Yia Yia and Papou here yet?"

"Yes. Kitchen," Dahlia said matter-of-factly.

"They're making spang-kee-top-icka," Daisy shouted as she raced up the stairs, disappearing into the darkened hallway.

"It's spy-nay-coffee-toe," Dahlia corrected with a hint of confidence—or as much as a three-year-old could have.

"You're both right. It's spanakopita. Give me a few minutes, girls," I said, escaping the entryway for the kitchen, where black olives and grape leaves sat beautifully organized on a platter in the center of the granite island. Switching Mae over to my opposite hip, I plucked an olive off the plate right as another hand came into view.

"Nel, you don't actually *eat* those. We never eat the ones on the island, remember?" Hallie stated, walking to the opposite side of the island, her phone angled above the plate as she tapped the screen a few times. "You can eat the snacks on the coffee table in the living room though. There are some great choices!"

Hi, Hallie. How's your month been? Mine was great. It was filled with lots of lingerie and smutty books. Oh, and I'm actually not as far down in the postpartum depression well as I was a few months ago. I'm still in the well, but I'm climbing my way out.

Thanks for asking.

Turning on my heel, I left Hallie to take pictures of grape leaves that would go viral in a matter of minutes once added to Panormama and LaundryList.

"What else are we making?" I whispered over Nora's shoulder as she placed the spanakopita into the oven. Facing us, she opened and closed both hands quickly in Mae's direction.

"Give me the child," Nora said, her voice robotic as she blew strands of auburn and violet hair out of her face. I handed Mae over—well, more like she was snagged from my grasp—and Nora rocked side to side as she strode through the kitchen. They plopped themselves on the couch next to Ari, Nora's fiance, who sat beside Tucker and my father, beers in hand.

"Are you sure you'll be okay this weekend?" I asked, slumping down at the end of the couch. Mae wrapped her hand around Ari's index finger as she sat contently on my sister's lap. "We're leaving tomorrow around one. So, when I drop her off in the morning, I'll go over the schedule again. I know you know it, but I want to make sure you don't have any—"

"Nel." Nora set her chin on the dark, tight curls atop Mae's head, looking me dead in the eye. "She will be fine. *You* will be fine. You deserve this."

"I'm a little jealous you're going to see The Bare Assentials...and then you're going to go party with them."

My eyes widened. "Wait, what? We are? How do you know this?"

Ari giggled as Nora rolled her eyes with a grin and said, "My fiancé is officially one of Zizi's biggest fans."

"Really? Is this a recent discovery?" I asked, watching Ari wriggle her finger from my daughter's grip.

"I mean, I've seen The Bare Assentials perform a few times." Ari shrugged. "Once Nora told me about your little business endeavor, I may or may not have signed up for Smut Me Up."

With my jaw on the floor, I turned toward Nora. "And you're okay with this?"

My sister adjusted Mae so she sat comfortably on her lap, her leg bouncing. "I mean...Rosie's hot. I get it."

"Okay, but how do you know we're partying with them after their show? *I* didn't even know this," I said, circling back to the original conversation.

Ari's phone screen almost touched the frames of my glasses. There was a post on our YourEyesOnly forum with a picture of Rosie nibbling the tip of her finger while the other hand held a copy of *Whisper My Secrets* against her bare chest.

Was that half of a nipple saying hello on the edge of the book?

Yes. It was absolutely her nipple.

It also said in the caption that the Naked Book Club Librarians were celebrating with The Bare Assentials this weekend.

Oh.

Apparently, I *was* going to an after-party.

"I guess I need to check what she posts more often," I whispered. "I should also probably start posting more of my own shit too."

"Posting what? Wait…that's not Rosie, is it?" Hallie's voice sent my stomach straight into my throat as she bent her knees to get a closer look at Ari's screen. "Is she on *that* site? Nel, did you know about this? I really think something isn't quite right with that family. I'm worried."

I wasn't sure which point to address first. "What do you mean ' *something isn't quite right with that family*?"

Hallie stood up and set a hand on her hip. "You know how I feel about those twins—and *I'm* a twin mom, so my opinion kind of means something. One goes from dancing on Merlin's dance team to slutting it up with the Bare Assentials. The other had nothing going for him other than looking like some skater kid straight from an MTV set. I know that's always been your type, but still…it's not a good look." Hallie stepped closer, setting a hand on my shoulder. "I'm glad I talked some sense into you back then so you wouldn't fall for Jude's lackadaisical advances. You've always been better than—"

"Don't you fucking say another word, Hallie." I was on my feet, standing almost nose to nose with my sister, my fists balled at my sides.

Hallie stepped back, gesturing to Mae, who I was now grabbing from Ari. "That language really isn't appropriate around your daughter. It's—"

"I...I think I'm done, Hal." Heaving Mae over my shoulder, I realized everyone in the room sat with their jaws slack and eyes pinned on me. Turning to Nora, who also sat with her mouth agape, I said, "I'll swing by your place tomorrow around eleven."

"Penny, you can't leave. We haven't even eaten din—"

"Stop with that name, Hallie. You *know* I hate it, and you throwing it around out of spite is beyond petty. I've been in your home for fifteen minutes, and you already are nit-picking my friendships."

"Pen—Nel, I'm not nit-picking. I'm just—"

"*Trying to help?* Yes, you've helped me through many, *many* situations in the past that I am grateful for, but I don't tear you down whenever a thought pops into my head. I don't jump down your throat because your social media is staged or because you scare the fuck out of your husband, do I?" As I walked toward the door, I stopped to peer over my shoulder at the couch. "Sorry, Tucker. I like you. I can easily sense fear...and you're drowning in it."

Tucker looked away as wine hit his lips, and I noticed that, much like Tucker, no one else was stepping in. No one was standing up for me or acknowledging this brave outburst I was having out of absolutely nowhere. Nora's eyes spoke a thousand words as they dove into mine, but my parents remained silent. They watched without confronting Hallie's behaviors, leaving me to look like the outspoken idiot I, honestly, was *not*. Nora constantly came to my rescue during these kinds of things, which wasn't fair since intense social situations gave her more anxiety than standing up for myself gave me.

But this time, as I slid Mae back into her carrier with shaky hands, I felt a rage grow inside of me that I hadn't felt in months. I could feel my eyes swelling with tears, but my anger overpowered my urge to break down my emotional wall.

Hallie had no right to always think the choices she made for me were superior. She'd dissected and picked apart every move I made since punching Grant in his verbally abusive face. She'd taken the control I hadn't had the strength to take back and molded it into something she could manage.

She had no right putting down my friendships—friendships that maybe, at times, were rocky, but ones that were always filled with genuine support and love in the end.

And she had absolutely no right to verbally attack Jude—or even bring him up, for that matter. Because though she'd crawled into my brain when I was in college, I now realized how she only ever saw him at surface level.

Jude wasn't Grant.

Maybe some of the men I'd dated after Grant weren't the best choices, but none of them were anything close to the monster Grant was.

She took what she saw at surface level and twisted it in her favor.

"This...it...you're being a little silly," I heard Hallie whisper from the hallway leading toward the front door. "Pen, take a second and listen to yourself. This isn't who you are. You're stronger than this—*better* than this."

With one foot out the door, I looked over my shoulder at my sister. Her figure was shaded by the porch light as she stood cross-armed in the hallway.

"I will no longer be involved in these *family* meals and gatherings." I peered beyond Hallie toward the couch where my parents sat...quietly. Without a word. Now that I was a mom, I hated pushing my own mother aside, but why maintain a relationship with anyone—even family—when they'd obviously chosen sides years ago?

Taking a deep breath, I stepped into the damp night air. "I'm so glad I have Mae, Nora, Ari, Rosie...and, yes, even her *lackadaisical* brother, Jude, to call family. Because if you're not going to treat me like family, then it's my turn to do the same."

The ride to Greyport was quiet.

I lay across the backseat of Jude's beloved Nissan Pathfinder that, apparently, hadn't broken down during his cross-country trek. Though part of me wanted to dive into the conversation he and Rosie were having in the front seat—something about a good espresso martini recipe he needed—I knew if I didn't reboot my social meter, the rest of the weekend would drain me.

And I was still empty from the night before.

As we drove into the Towpath Bed & Breakfast, my head bumping against the archaic roll-down window lever, I could tell I was spiraling. Even though I was glad I'd confronted Hallie, there was an itch in the back of my mind I couldn't help but scratch a little. It was an itch reminding me of all the other things she'd protected me from in the past or guided me through.

Had I taken it too far?

Even though I was strong enough to confront her in ways I never had before, I wasn't sure her words could just leave my mind. Her pull, her manipulation...it was such a part of me.

How could I fully set that part of me free?

I wasn't one to binge-drink away my emotions—that was Rosie's not-so-healthy coping skill in college, not mine. Right now, though, I wanted to add a liquid depressant to my already depressed system—as unhealthy as that was.

Only time would tell if a few mojitos or amaretto sours would win the battle.

"Well, Viv *definitely* isn't staying here," Rosie said, closing the car door behind her. "She's probably staying at the one ritzy hotel Greyport has. We stayed there when we performed here last year...I forget what it's called."

"She didn't tell you where she was staying?" I asked, opening the trunk and reaching for my duffel bag just as Jude got to it first, tossing it over his shoulder.

"Nah. She lives for the tease...and I apparently live for it too," Rosie said hesitantly as she walked toward the main entrance.

Unlike Rosie, I was a sucker for a cozy bed and breakfast like the pristinely landscaped, adorable cabin before us. If they had bright quilts covering each bed and homemade waffles in the morning, maybe a pool of liquor wasn't needed, after all.

Waffles and quilts and log cabins were all the medicine necessary.

Gravel under tires sounded from behind us as we watched Sebastian and Riley roll into the parking lot. Sebastian stepped out of the Jeep, immediately reaching up to release his blond locks into the gentle wind. I swear slow, melodic music was playing—only for him—as he shook his head back and forth.

We all saw him much differently than he saw himself.

If anything, his confidence was impressive.

"Wow. Beautiful mountain air. It smells like I need a cigar and a glass of whiskey," Sebastian said, grabbing his mandolin case from the backseat.

"I mean...this isn't *really* mountain air. Holly Hill is about forty-five minutes away. This is more canal country, if anything," Riley corrected, grabbing his backpack before closing the door. "But a whiskey sounds good."

"And a cigar!" Rosie shouted, yanking the front door open.

Shuffling quickly to catch up, we followed her inside and gave our names to the front desk attendee. She directed us up to the second floor where our two rooms sat across the hall from one another. Each small room had a king-sized bed filling up most of the space with massive, hand-crafted oak bedframes surrounding the mattresses—mattresses clad in the cutest damn quilts I'd ever seen.

"Do you see these headboards? The details are intricate as fuck." Rosie dragged her suitcase into the room and walked to the end of the bed. She ran her fingers over the floral carvings lining the oak and said, "I wish I could use *these* headboards with Viv later."

"Since when are you a woodworking connoisseur?" Jude asked as Riley and Sebastian opened the door to their room across the hall.

"They're handmade by that James guy in town," Riley shouted from across the hall, adjusting his glasses so he could look closer at the detail. "I've seen his work before."

"What the fuck is happening?" Jude mumbled, shaking his head and walking into his room. Jude's eyes met mine, his feet slowing. "Are you okay, Nel?"

I nodded quickly, setting my duffel into the room. "Of course. Yeah. Mm-hmm."

Jude took a step toward the door to his room as I leaned against the doorframe across from it. "I mean...are *we* okay? After the other night? We don't have to talk about anything, but I just—"

"Oh...yeah. Yes. We're fine, Jude, really," I said, flashing back to how his lips felt flush against mine. The warm feeling was a nice redirection, but I knew I couldn't focus on it—no matter how much I craved it. If I'd learned anything after losing Jude in college—or pushing him away, more like—it was to set low expectations. The lower, the less I'd get hurt this time around.

I looked over my shoulder at Rosie, who remained entranced by the bedframe—a bedframe she obviously didn't expect to be any-where near tonight. "I'm okay. It just hit me that Rowe is staying with Viv tonight and won't be back. It'll probably be nice being alone for, like, the first time in a *long* time...but still."

I sounded like a pathetic lost child, but the thought of being alone—completely alone without Mae or Rosie or Nora—shook me more than expected.

"I mean...it's better than sharing a bed with these two assholes," Jude whispered, throwing a thumb over his shoulder. "We'll all get a ride-share back from town later. It'll be okay...I promise. You won't be alone, Nel."

I couldn't hide the faint smile growing across my face or the heat warming my chest. It was crazy what a few words could do to someone—a few words, a few quilts, and a cozy cabin. If I wanted to enjoy one of my first *big* weekends away since having Mae, I had to trust those around me and free myself from any anxieties holding me back.

Hallie's words from the night before collided inside my head for a few seconds, but I closed my eyes tight and forced those thoughts away. I wouldn't let them linger and rot away the last of the positivity left in there. When I opened my eyes, I saw Jude's poignant, comforting gaze and watched as his close-lipped grin grew beneath that dark beard of his.

Fuck Hallie.

Fuck the past.

I had no one to impress.

The petty judgments of others didn't run my life.

All I had now was the present, and I was so ready to move the hell on from the past.

Chapter 20

Rosie

Walking into Velvet was like walking into Disney World...but with more ball gags, and sex swings, and edible whipped cream.

If it weren't for the sign dangling over the door, we may have asked the ride-share driver if this was the right place. Though the lounge was in a ramshackle building with a fresh coat of paint on the clapboard siding, the inside was a much different aesthetic. Hot pink lights created a sensual hue upon arrival—entering through a shop filled with every sex toy, restraint system, lube flavor, and piece of lingerie imaginable. A blonde woman stood behind a circular desk sitting in the center of the room. She wore a pink, sheer lace top and matching skirt and welcomed us with a playful grin.

"Welcome to Velvet," the woman hummed as we grew closer, Sebastian gawking at every vibrator he walked by, Riley joining him to lap the shelves we passed. "Are you here to peek at some of our favorite items or watch what The Bare Assentials have planned for you in the lounge?"

"Both. Definitely both," I responded as Nel met me at the desk, Jude standing by her side. "But I can't walk away without asking what your bestseller is?"

"I mean...*everything* here is a bestseller, in my book. It just depends what your preferences are." The woman turned on her heel—a pink heel that matched her skin-tight ensemble—and gestured to a triangular stand behind her. "Our Clone-A-Willys are a *big* hit, but I feel like it's important to focus on what peaks *your* pleasure. Some of these classic Rabbits and remote-controlled vibrators are *definitely* items you need in your collection if you don't have them already."

Looking to my side, I noticed Nel's jaw was slightly ajar, her eyes pinned to one of the remote-controlled vibrators on the shelf above the woman's head. Nel looked from the vibrator to me and then quickly back to the shelf before saying, "Does that mean...someone else can control it? While it's...*in* you?"

"It sure as fuck does," I said, wrapping my arm around Nel's shoulders and pulling her in close. I could tell she was both uncomfortable and a little intrigued...and making her feel uncomfortable was one of my favorite things to do. "How about you get me a few drinks tonight, and I'll buy you one of those babies...and I'll buy one for myself too. I can't *imagine* how that thing would feel when—"

"Okay, alright. Where's the bar?" Jude asked, clearing his throat and wandering around the front desk, slowing down in front of a mannequin with black, plastic arms tied together above its head. The mannequin's wrists had leather cuffs hugging them with a flogger in one hand and a bright-red ball gag in the other. Pausing in front of the mannequin and looking it up and down, he then looked back over his shoulder at us. "I mean, buy what you want...I just don't want to hear it from my sister."

Right as Jude said this, Sebastian walked over and slammed down three Clone-a-Willys, a vibrating butt plug, four boxes of textured condoms, and three bottles of warming lube that, apparently, tasted like cherry pie.

Oh, and Riley threw a pair of furry pink handcuffs into the pile as well.

I was learning so, so much about everyone tonight just by observing.

If this wasn't my element, I didn't know what was.

Sebastian looked up at the woman behind the desk, holding an oddly shaped box into the air so it balanced on one of his hands. "This is *probably* not for me, but I'm fascinated by it. Do you think it's based on *real* dragon biology?"

Every single one of us looked at Sebastian. The woman behind the desk slowly scanned one of the condom boxes, a smile spreading across her face as she said, "Right? These *Supreme Dragon Dildos* sure make you wonder!"

"They definitely do." Sebastian stepped forward, his fingertips curling around the edge of the counter. "And the colors...it makes sense for them to all come in these wild colors since dragons come from so many backgrounds. It would help with camouflage."

The woman scanned one of the Clone-a-Willys, nodding viciously. "These glow in the dark too. I mean, they *did* fly at night a lot, so it makes sense."

I watched as she scanned the three bottles of lube, trying to not have my jaw drop too obviously, but also not caring in the least.

Riley cleared his throat, stepping toward Sebastian. "Seb...you do know that—"

"Don't," I said, slamming the back of my hand against Riley's chest. "I'll come back and pay for my shit on the way out. Let's let him live in this fantasy a little bit longer."

The cocktail lounge at Velvet was very much like walking into a prohibition era speakeasy...if, to enter the speakeasy, the only way in was from pulling down a golden dildo lever.

Red velvet booths and couches lined the walls where brass sconces shone above marble-top tables. Visitors sat spinning cocktail goblets between their fingers as droplets occasionally hopped into a candlestick flame, melted wax pooling beneath them. Opposite the bar was a crescent-shaped stage where a woman sat cross-legged on a red-and-black wingback chair, the fingers of a black, silk glove between her teeth as she removed it slowly from her arm. The audience was clapping and hooting, a trio of middle-aged men in the corner booth whistled and drunkenly nudged one another with raised eyebrows.

I walked toward the front of the stage, both entranced and annoyed by the familiar performer who turned the chair around to straddle it. My eyes fell to her feet where four-inch, silver stilettos hugged her perfect little toes in place.

I wanted to hop onstage and crack those stupid heels right off.

Then stir them in her drink.

Instead of letting my rage fly, I distracted myself by watching her toss a bejeweled bra off stage, teasingly covering herself afterward. I sat down just as she stood up from behind the chair's coverage to reveal her perfectly tasseled tits which obviously caused the entire room to explode.

"Hell yeah!" Sebastian shouted, setting down a beer and pulling a chair out from beside me, followed by Riley. "Do you know this one?"

"I *do* know this *performer*. Yes," I said, taking a long swig of Sebastian's beer without asking. It was now the norm. "Riot Regan. She's a newbie—came on board about six months ago."

"She has great legs," Riley said, his jaw hanging above his glass. "They go on for days."

And then Cade popped into my head.

Those long, ebony legs.

That smooth, satiny skin.

The taste of her tongue piercing.

"Viv," I said, shaking myself back to reality as the stage cleared, and the chair was dragged to the corner. I wasn't here to think about Cade. I was here to support the person who'd brought me back to life three years before. That was it. "Viv should be on soon."

"Isn't that her?" Jude asked, he and Nel pulling chairs out from the table behind us.

A petite, pink-haired beauty strutted onstage, taking a seat in the corner chair as a stagehand brought her a champagne flute that she delicately pinched between her fingers. The bright-yellow ensemble hugging her body had hints of red and purple and pink gems strewn throughout, matching the colorful art covering her skin. She immediately saw me sitting near the front of the stage and threw me a savage wink just as swoony music erupted from the speakers.

"Here's your girl." Sebastian nudged his elbow into my waist before releasing an ear-piercing whistle. I looked over my shoulder, back at Nel, who sat with one hand quickly clapping her thigh as the other one brought a cocktail to her lips.

I could tell from Nel's eye contact that her mind was moving. Cogs were shifting, and pieces were clinking. Nel wanted me happy, and I wanted the same for her, of course. But I also knew that she saw Viv as someone I'd chosen over her, even if Nel would never admit to thinking that. This never really bothered me because, well...that hadn't been my motive back then.

My motive had been getting back on my feet.

Strappy heels clicked against the stage floor, and even though they were Viv's, the sound still gave me an instant headache. But as Viv shimmied and winked and bit her ruby-red lips, my mind couldn't fully focus on the sway of her hips, the curve of her ass, the softness of her skin.

Just like Nel's, my mind was on the move too.

When it should have been 100% immersed in the woman on-stage, it just wasn't.

Instead of watching Viv remove her top—revealing heart-shaped tassels dangling from her tits—I scrolled through YourEyesOnly, hoping to find that DancingQueenCade_26 liked my most recent post.

Chapter 21

Nel

After Viv exited backstage and the final performer wooed the crowd, Viv yanked us to the bar where she bought us all a round of Patron shots followed by a round of Mezcal margaritas...followed by Jagerbombs. I wasn't sure why she thought this was a good idea—unless this line-up was just something the ladies of The Bare Assentials did post-show. Rosie didn't look fazed in the slightest, downing each drink like a champ as I struggled to get through the margarita.

I liked margaritas.

And a good spicy rim.

To say I was disappointed in myself was an understatement.

I used to drink these without blinking an eye during college and into my twenties.

Mae must have stolen my appreciation for spicy margaritas when I was pregnant.

"Nope," I said after dropping the shot into my glass. I brought the edge to my lips and took a single sip before spitting it back into the drink. "Absolutely not."

"How the fuck did we do these regularly at MCC?" Jude asked once he'd finished his glass. "Because these are brutal."

"Another one!" Sebastian shouted, throwing his arms up as a tiny redhead fell into his chest. "Make it two!"

"The thought of these will make me vomit...and I'm nowhere near drunk," I whispered, watching through my peripherals as Riley chatted with a curvy brunette on the other side of Rosie and Viv.

"Looks like everyone is making some new friends," Jude said, taking a long gulp of water.

"Yeah...they are." I turned on my stool to face Jude, gently poking his chest with the tip of my finger. "But you should make some too! You should be out there flirting. Put all of our lessons to good use, sir."

Both of Jude's hands flew to his chest dramatically before he leaned toward the bar with an eyebrow raised. His face was only a few inches from mine, and I froze in place as he whispered, "Maybe I already have been. Flirting, I mean."

Stealing his glass of water, I downed the rest of it. "Yeah? Was it that blonde from the toy shop? The one into dragon dicks?"

"*Sebastian* definitely wanted to get into her pants...so he may be in a predicament tonight. I do think I saw a ring on her finger," Jude said, nodding toward Sebastian, who casually leaned against the bar, one arm wrapped around the redhead's waist. "Plus, I'm not into blondes."

"Wasn't Maggie LaFountain blonde?"

Jude shrugged. "She was...but I think you guys thought I was more into her than I was."

"I helped you get in her pants!" I exclaimed, throwing my arms into the air and almost knocking over the empty water glass.

"Well, I never *really* got into her pants," Jude admitted, placing his knit beanie back atop his head. "We kissed a little, and that was that."

"Huh...interesting," I mumbled as casually as I could, turning away from Jude and peering at our little posse surrounding the bar.

Viv leaned into Rosie, whose back pressed into the bar, her pink hair flying back as she let out a giggle. Sebastian's hands roamed the redhead's body, his lips near her ear as she bit her lipstick-stained bottom lip. Riley tried getting the bartender's attention for another round of drinks for the dancers on either side of him just as the brunette grabbed his ass.

The shots. The flirting. The shouting. The laughing.

I'd had my fill of sex toy paradise. I'd cheered on enough burlesque routines. I'd downed tequila shots.

I was in sensory overload.

"I'm kind of ready to get out of this place. The show was great, the toy shop was…fascinating, but I'm kind of over it."

"Say no more." Jude was already a few steps away, running his thumb across the screen to find a ride-share.

I placed my hand on Rosie's shoulder in passing to mention I was going the fuck to bed like the grandma I was. Her eyeroll was as genuine as an eyeroll could be, but she let me go without the Rosie reaction I usually expected—no passive-aggressive begging, no whiny guilt-tripping, no throwing her body around mine in restraint.

My hesitance must have been clear because as I slowed, she mouthed, "It's okay. Go," and I nodded, skittering back to her brother. As I followed Jude back through the shop, I pulled at his shirt to stop him from running into a glittery purple strap-on standing at full mass harnessed to a mannequin.

We both stood paralyzed, staring directly at the harness and the impossibly large dildo attached to it.

"Well, running into that thing could have been disastrous," Jude said, looking down at the strap-on and then up the body of the mannequin.

"I mean…some people may like that kind of disaster," I said, gently pulling his jacket back toward the door where the dildo lever waited for us. "Did you let Riley and Seb know we were leaving?"

Oh my God, these things were *literally* everywhere.

And really, I didn't mind.

They'd gotten me through the last year.

Chuckling, Jude wrapped his fingers around my wrist and gently pulled me toward him. "Don't worry. I texted them about forty minutes ago, saying that once you wanted out, I wanted out too. I didn't want to interrupt the flow they got going on in there. They'll get their own ride-share."

"Do you really think their flirty *flow* will make it beyond the bar?"

Jude scoffed, pulling me closer as we both side-stepped the strap-on. "I'd rather not be awake to find out."

"Do you think they'll actually be back tonight?" I asked, slipping off my suede boots as Jude unlocked his door across the hall. It was almost one in the morning when we tiptoed back into the eerily silent bed and breakfast. Our steps echoed through the stairwell, and the only sound in our hallway were our keys sticking inside century-old locks.

Jude looked over his shoulder at the lone bed in his room as he slipped off his jean jacket, hanging it in the closet. "I think maybe one of them will come back tonight with someone. The other...may end up somewhere else. I have a hunch."

I enthusiastically hopped in place, clasping my hands together. The enthusiasm *had* to be from the tequila still lingering in my bloodstream. "Oooh! Let's make a bet on who will come back and who will go somewhere. I say Riley comes back."

Jude laughed, shaking his head as he slid off his Converse sneakers. "Sebastian would *definitely* bring someone back, forgetting that I'm here. I say Riley goes to someone's place tonight and Seb shows up in an hour, completely wasted."

Shifting my weight, I nodded. "That sounds likely...but I'll stick with my guess just to make it a bet."

"What does the winner get?" Jude asked, his head angled downward as he released the bun of hair hiding beneath his beanie. Though his face was barely visible, hair gently falling to just above his shoulders, his dark eyes never left mine.

That intensity.

It was piercing.

"The winner?" I asked, shifting again from foot to foot before realizing I, too, needed to take my coat off, quickly unzipping it and hanging it up.

Jude chuckled, leaning against the doorframe again. His voice was hushed—deep and smooth—as he said, "It's a bet, Nel. Someone's going to win, and someone's going to lose. What's the winner get?"

Heat rose in my cheeks, and I placed a palm to my face, giggling against it. "Uh...hmmm...I didn't think about that when I said that. I probably should have. Hmmm..."

"What if the winner decides how the next practice session goes?"

I cocked my head to the side, adjusting my glasses and scrunching my nose. "What do you mean?"

Jude stepped into the hallway, running a hand through his hair until it all shadowed the right side of his head. "What I mean is...if *you* win, you choose what you want to wear during the practice session, what flirting tactics you want to work on, and how you want to turn on viewers."

Standard.

That was usually how the practice nights went—just with some of Jude's steamy suggestions sprinkled in.

As Jude took another step into the hallway, the heat of his body grew closer to mine, and I asked, "And…if you win?"

He placed his hand above my head against the doorframe as he gently leaned in. "I get to choose what you wear, how you flirt…and not only will I choose *how* you turn on viewers, but I'll also make it so *you* are turned on too."

Huh.

Well, fuck.

His words felt like hot wax dripping over my skin, bringing me back to the Jude from a decade ago. That Jude seemed like a stranger compared to this new version standing mere inches away.

He'd been that unconfident kid, stumbling over his words, who followed Rosie and me around and kissed me *one* time with the confidence I felt radiating off him now. All those years ago, he'd had that confidence—that power—within him, and I'd felt it the second he'd pressed his lips to mine.

Even back then, I loved the taste of it.

I just naively didn't believe it was okay to want more of it.

Now, he wasn't bottling up that power like he used to. Now, he harnessed a quiet control I saw behind his dark eyes.

Jude cupped the side of my face, and I leaned into it, covering his hand with my own and saying, "Jude. I've hurt you before. I don't want—"

"Do you agree to the stakes of this bet, Nel?" he whispered. "Because I'm not nervous around you anymore. Now...the bet."

"The bet..." I said, swallowing hard, feeling his thumb brush my bobbing throat. His words dug into my heart, leaving claw marks in their wake. I still was so angry at the girl I was back then. Yet, as his grip grew firmer and he tipped my head back so his lips brushed the underside of my neck, I knew redemption was calling.

"The bet, Nel." He paused, and for the first time in over a year, I wanted to melt into the pleasure I felt. I didn't want to ignore it or feel guilty about it anymore. I wanted to *feel* it. I wanted to step outside whatever comfort zone I'd been stuck in for the last year...with him. "Do you give me permission to make *you* feel good? Because I want to reignite your flame. I've been waiting ten years to feel that fire again."

The second heat began pulsing between my legs, I whispered, "Yes."

Jude's eyebrows rose, his focus breaking a bit. "Yes?"

I nodded quickly against his grasp, but just as I was about to repeat the word again, his lips hit mine. His hands pressed into my lower back, our bodies shuffling backward into my room as the door slammed behind him. He lowered me onto the quilt-covered bed, his lips never leaving mine as he hovered above my body, straddling my hips.

"I thought...I thought we were waiting until our next lesson? To, you know...for whatever *this* is," I whimpered against his mouth. He pulled both my hands above my head, pressing my wrists into the quilt.

He straightened his arms and looked directly at me. "Do you want me to wait? I've waited ten years to touch you again. I can wait a few more—"

"No," I gasped, pressing my head into the mattress so my neck beckoned his mouth to return to it. "I don't want you to wait. *I* don't want to wait. I want you to touch me, Jude." A devilish smirk creased the corner of his mouth. He released one of his hands to drag a finger over my lips, my chin, my throat...stopping right above the edge of my top where a faint line of cleavage peeked out. "I'm not the same soft, quiet Jude you remember, Nel. It's going to be hard holding myself back with you like I used to, and I—"

"Please, Jude. Please don't hold back," I whimpered as his palm flattened over my chest. It shifted over my right breast, which he quickly grabbed with such unexpected force that my hips bucked against him.

His tongue skimmed a line from the base of my throat up to my ear where he whispered, "Say that again."

His hard length pressed against the zipper of his jeans, causing my clit to pulse from the perfect pressure he created against it. Instead of ripping my leggings off to free the bundle of nerves beneath them, I whimpered, "Please."

Jude bit gently into my earlobe before pulling down my top to reveal both of my breasts. "Good girl, Nel," he said, my peaked, pink nipples impatiently waiting.

He dug his teeth into my sensitive flesh to create a sensation I wanted to melt into. His words hummed against my tits, and my pussy clenched and released every time his hips pressed against mine. His hands wandered from my chest to the underside of my shirt, and when I felt his fingertips slide from my ribs down to my belly, I froze.

My body grew rigid beneath his touch as I remembered a few things this moment forced me to forget.

I'd only stopped pumping a month ago. What if my supply wasn't completely drained? What if this pleasure played with my hormones in a weird, fucked-up way, causing my nipples to create some kind of gross discharge?

A road map painted my belly, my leggings forcing down extra skin I hid behind a tied shirt at my waist. When his fingers found the hem of my leggings, the extra skin jiggled as he snapped the waistband a few times, creating a sound that both heightened my anxiety and made my pussy quiver.

And though I'd shaved and neatened up my lady bits for what seemed like the first time in months, what if it ended up not being what he wanted to see or touch or taste? What if he saw my body as broken and stitched back up in a way that wouldn't give him the pleasure he sought?

"Nel," Jude said softly, the fierceness in his voice disappearing for just a moment as our eyes connected again. "Where'd you go? I can stop."

I would not let my emotions shatter this moment—a moment I'd felt so unexplainably comfortable in just seconds before. Even though I was terrified beneath his touch, I wanted to feel something real. And more than anything, I wanted to feel it with the one person who'd always made me feel safe. "No. I don't want you to stop. I just... I realized a few things."

"What did you realize?"

"I just... I'm not the same girl you kissed in college. My body may be a little...I don't know...*different* than what you may expect...or want. I just don't want it to freak you out or for you to look at me and see all the—"

"—the beauty, Nel?" he cut me off, rolling onto his side. Though he wasn't straddling me like before, his fingertips still brushed my skin at the hem of my leggings. "When I look at you, I see a stunning woman with a spectacular body and mind. I thought you were perfect back then, Nel, and you having a child hasn't changed a damn thing about how I feel. If anything, watching you slowly crack and climb out of the shell you see your body as has made me want to be with you—touch you—even more. I'm seeing the *real* you again. I'm seeing your confidence return, and that shines brighter than whatever happened in your past and whatever you're insecure about now."

I swallowed hard, doing everything I could not to add unwanted tears to this moment. He brushed his fingers along the underside of the hem. His knuckles rubbed against the soft, loose skin of my belly with each movement until he opened his hand so it laid flat against me, pressing down firmly over the fabric of my panties.

He shifted closer, his free hand forcing my gaze to his. "And don't you *ever* say I may not want *this* because of how things are different now. I've wanted to touch you, taste you, breathe you in since I tore your room up, searching for those damn glasses of yours."

His palm pressed down harder, and the tip of his middle finger grazed my clit, the fingertip creating the softest, most teasing circles over the ball of nerves. The layer of underwear separating his finger from direct contact caused a humming sensation that forced a gasp from my lips.

Jude pressed harder against my side. "Now, give me permission to make you come so hard over my fingers that you shake yourself out of that pretty little head of yours. Because I'd do anything to see you lose every ounce of control you have bottled up in there."

Before I even finished nodding, he'd pulled aside my panties and pushed a tattooed finger deep inside of me, his thumb rolling over my clit with such intense rhythm. My pussy pulsed and clenched against him, my eyes rolling back into a fog of ecstasy. As he slid another finger inside of me, he twisted his wrist to an angle, causing my hips to thrust against his hand, his fingertips hitting my most sensitive spot with every motion.

"Fuck, Jude," I moaned, biting down onto the knuckles of my free hand right as he yanked it away. Pinning both my wrists together above my head with his free hand, his other continued to circle and cause delicious pressure I wanted to bathe in.

"Don't you dare silence your screams," he growled, trailing his tongue from my neck to my left nipple, which he quickly flicked. "Drench my hand, Nel, so that after I watch you fall apart, it'll only take me a few strokes of my cock before I let everything go too."

"Oh, my fucking god," I cried, my back arching and my toes curling against the quilt I'd already made a mess of below me. No one had ever talked to me this way, and with each gruff demand, every heavy breath, every firm grasp, I couldn't hold back.

Dirty talk used to send me into a traumatic spiral.

But with Jude...I couldn't get enough of it.

And that surprised the shit out of me.

"Your pussy is pulsing." His breath was hot against my ear, the heat making my toes curl into the sheets. "Do you want me to make you come, Nel?"

"Yes. Yes, make me come," I exclaimed, my voice coming out much louder than expected as he pressed my wrists down harder.

Jude hummed against my neck. "But what does a good girl say?"

"Please. Please, Jude...holy fucking—"

My body stilled, and all I felt were vibrations of heat and pleasure stirring inside of me as his fingers continued their addictive rhythm. I didn't hold back—*couldn't* hold back—the cry I released as my body twitched against Jude's hand one final time before the sound of his zipper cut through the ringing in my ears.

I opened my eyes to see him wrap a dripping hand around himself. His eyes did not look at my bare chest or at my pussy half-hidden behind panties, but directly at me. His gaze was so fixed on my dilated pupils, my flushed cheeks, my lips parted from reckless breathing, that I couldn't break eye contact to watch his hand. It moved quickly up and down his long, solid length—a size I didn't expect him to have hidden under his jeans.

To be honest, I wasn't sure *how* he hid it.

Holy shit, had Jude *always* been this big?

I'd never judge someone's height again...not that I had.

I bit my bottom lip, shifting to straddle him so my exposed breasts hung above the head of his cock, now wet with both my cum and his pre-cum. I peered over my glasses, meeting his focused gaze, and said, "I came on your hand. Now, it's your turn to come for me."

From his expression—and the quickened speed of his hand—I could tell he didn't expect these words to come from my mouth.

I hadn't expected them to either.

Maybe this comfort—this confidence—really had been inside of me all along.

Jude helped free this empowered version of myself from their chains.

His hand moved faster, his chest wildly rising and falling. Though I wanted to wrap my hand around him, I enjoyed watching him watch me as he grew harder in his grasp. The moment I heard a quiet growl hum from his lips, I knew he was close. I felt his muscles tighten and release below me as I straddled him, a massage I never wanted to end.

And then, I remembered.

I was a good student, after all.

"Oh, how silly of me to forget." I leaned forward, meeting his eyes with a sadistic smile. "Please. *Please* come on my tits, Jude."

After saying his name, beads of cum coated my chest, drops clinging to my nipples as Jude's head fell back with a moan. I looked down at Jude's pleasure covering my body and froze for a second when I noticed my stretched skin hanging over my underwear.

I thought about pulling the leggings up and over my belly before racing into the bathroom to clean myself up. I thought about telling Jude this was a one-time situation and that it wouldn't—couldn't—go beyond this point. I thought about apologizing for whatever had come over me tonight—a version of myself I barely knew.

But as I melted down into Jude's relaxed embrace, I felt more comfortable in this moment than I had in a very, very long time. I felt safe against the heat of his body as he plucked out a handful of tissues to clean me up with. I felt completely relaxed as I sunk down against his chest after he turned the table lamp off.

And I felt bad for the credulous little girl I'd been ten years before.

If she'd known better, she could have experienced this long before now.

She'd fucking missed out.

yourEyesOnly.com
LIVE
LIKE SUBSCRIBE COMMENTS
@stagemanDAV: Deepen that stretch, babe. I know you like it deep...
@darkromMOM3: Can we try Warrior III next?
BETTE OHM

Chapter 22

Rosie

Of course The Bare Assentials weren't staying in Greyport—they were *far* too classy for any mediocre bed and breakfast or hotel in Greyport. They traveled twenty minutes in the opposite direction to Rockberry Park to stay in one of their obnoxiously swanky hotels with accommodations going above even Viv's standards.

I'd always looked forward to spending the night in whatever ritzy hotel Marley, the troupe founder, put us in for the night. I loved walking into the room to find adorably shaped towels folded over our silk pillows or bottles of wine already chilling in the kitchenette. My clothes practically fell off whenever I walked through the door and saw a bathtub already hot and filled to the brink with lavender bubbles and Epsom salts and oils.

Tonight, as I followed Viv into her room at The Rockberry Luxe, all three of those luxuries smacked me in the face...along with cherry-red, cashmere bathrobes hanging on velvet hangers in the bathroom doorway.

I was almost half-naked by the time the door closed, my clothes crawling off my body the second I took in the space.

"I asked for a second set, knowing you'd *love* this shit when you saw it," Viv said, hopping over to the bathrobes and wildly clapping her hands.

Was it wrong to be annoyed at myself for not looking away from her perfect little ass? It was near impossible to ignore as it bounced and jiggled deliciously on her way to the robes. Part of me wanted to look away, while the other part of me wanted to devour it.

What the fuck was going on in my head?

These thoughts needed to stop.

This was Viv, and I needed to embrace any free second I had with her before she slipped away again.

Didn't I?

"I worked my magic and got it included in the room's cost. Thank *God* you didn't leave the troupe on a bad note, or Marley would probably have fought me on it."

I guess fucking up my body and refusing to wear heels was a *good* note to leave on.

Pulling the cropped sweater over my head, I tossed it onto the bed and wiggled out of the faux-leather pants that felt a bit tighter in the ass than the last time I wore them. I didn't mind. I kind of liked the look of my ass after months without dancing five days a week. It was natural, and grabbable as hell.

Fuck beauty standards.

It was time we all made our own.

Viv watched as I walked over to the bathroom, snaking around the bathrobes in the doorway and making my way to the jacuzzi tub. I yanked my red lace thong off, tossing it to the side with a toe before sitting on the tub's ledge, lavender-scented steam engulfing me.

After only a few seconds of falling into an aromatherapy-induced trance, I felt Viv's bare chest press against my back and her hands wrap around to cup my breasts. The tips of her manicured, hot pink nails pressed into my flesh, and I relaxed against her as she kissed the side of my neck. The heat between my legs intensified once her hand dipped beneath the water's surface to caress me, the other hand twisting my face toward hers.

"Don't you think a month is too long, Viv?" I asked softly as her lips hovered above mine, her fingers finding their way to the bud of nerves hiding just beneath the water. The circling motion of her fingers forced my body lower into the tub, steam hitting my face as Viv lowered with me, her hand barely shifting from its position.

"The time apart makes times like these even more intense, though. Right?" she asked as she plunged two fingers into my pussy, causing my breath to hitch and my back to arch. "And I know how much you *love* intense."

She wasn't wrong.

As she gave my nipple a light tug with her teeth, I realized just how right she was. I loved the intensity that came from waiting and wanting after time away. My body trembled at the thought of watching someone get right to the edge of falling apart as I watched from afar—unable to touch or taste.

The art of the tease was a blessing and a curse.

It was pleasure and also the sweetest pain.

I couldn't get enough of it.

Yet, as the rhythm of her fingers quickened inside of me and the motion of her hips rolled against my thigh, I couldn't help but crave more—*need* more. More emotion, connection, passion. Maybe these feelings were just as freeing—and intense—as the waiting and the edging. Maybe when someone other than yourself felt them too, it became a feeling I now hungered for.

I opened my eyes to see Viv's emerald ones staring at me as I trembled toward release in an almost robotic way. The motions were happening. The intensity was there. The release was so damn close. Yet, something was missing that usually coincided with my visits with Viv.

For the first time since Viv freed me from my weakened state years ago, I didn't feel my heartstrings tearing at my chest for her. I didn't feel that ping of *need* to please her or hold her as a silent thanks for bringing me back to life.

If anything, I felt a little trapped.

A little claustrophobic.

With pleasure still spinning inside my core, I fisted my hand through Viv's hot-pink, damp hair and pulled it gently until she let out a gasp. Swallowing hard, I made one last attempt at seeing Viv's intentions—intentions that had gotten blurrier and blurrier over the years—before I couldn't hold back my orgasm any longer.

In truth, I didn't *want* to hold it back any longer, but I needed to hear her out.

Was it selfish to still want to come when the person making me wasn't who I thought I once knew?

"You *will* visit me next week. Right?" I asked, my fingers tightening around the roots. "You will come see me and fuck me until your pussy is shaking because you need and miss me. Right?"

A smile crept across Viv's pale cheeks, her dimples deepening as she let out a low giggle. "Oh, but Zi...you wouldn't come this hard next week since you're about to come so hard right now. If I didn't leave you wondering and waiting, you wouldn't have *this*. You wouldn't have this *hunger*. You wouldn't have *me*." She bit her bottom lip, a maddening glow behind wild eyes. "And you know I don't like being tied down...unless someone else is doing the tying. Now come so I can watch you scream."

With that, I didn't hold back any longer.

I came. I trembled against her hand as I fisted and pulled more of her pink hair downward. A surge of pleasure raked through my body just as my brain came to terms with a newfound realization I couldn't ignore.

Viv no longer had full control over my heart, my emotions, my body.

I was no longer dependent on her for my success, or happiness, or pleasure.

Maybe she still thought she held this control, but the truth was clearer now.

And this was both terrifying and freeing at the same time.

When the ride-share driver—whose name was Chad and looked straight out of an 80's *Playgirl* magazine—dropped me off, Jude and Sebastian were outside, already throwing bags into their trunks. They barely blinked as I shut the door of Chad's sedan and walked over to their vehicles, diving into the backseat of Jude's Nissan without so much as saying good morning. I lay across the seats, grabbing one of the three fleece blankets Jude still stored in here after his cross-country treks, and prepared to nap for the hour we had ahead of us.

Then Nel came into view.

"I take it we're switching spots for the ride home?" she asked, smiling with hands on her hips. "*Long* night, huh?"

"Tired. Just tired." It wasn't a lie. After Viv made me come in the bathtub, I'd forced all emotional thoughts from my brain—the way I'd conditioned myself to do for years—and replaced them with the robotic, lustful ones I was used to. We'd tried out the vibrating strap-on harness she'd purchased from Velvet earlier that night—which was fucking outstanding—and then we'd experimented with a glow-in-the-dark bondage set I was now obsessed with.

I was exhausted—physically, mentally, and emotionally.

Nel pushed aside my feet and slid into the backseat with me, her lanky legs dangling out the open door. "Sooo...how'd it go?"

I shrugged and yanked the blanket to below my chin. "Fine. Good. We all got off, and I got a bathrobe out of it." I nodded toward the bed and breakfast behind her. "Are my bags still up there? I'll pay you in coffee to go get my shit."

"Jude already put your stuff in the trunk, and we're just waiting on Riley to get back," she stated, cocking her head to the side. "But you're deflecting. You seem...off."

"I'm *always* on. I don't know what you're talking about," I grumbled monotonously.

"Nah, she's definitely off," Jude said from behind Nel, his head popping into the doorframe. "You're usually peppier after Viv."

"I don't think *peppy* is the right word." Letting go of the blanket, I leaned back on my elbows. "Maybe witty or devious...I'd even take rude over peppy."

The two of them lowered their eyelids, staring at me with eyes clearly screaming, *WTF is going on?*

"You look like someone either rocked your world all night or someone ran over your dog," Sebastian added, a corner of his face visible above Jude's shoulder.

I was living in a fish bowl.

"I don't know! I don't know!" I exclaimed, my elbows releasing so I could hide beneath the fleece blanket again. "I hate feeling things, and I've always felt things only for Viv, and now I'm thinking those feelings were just feelings of lust, because those feelings are not feeling all the feels anymore."

Their eyes all slowly blinked at different times.

Now, I felt like the one looking into a fish bowl.

"Six."

I turned toward Jude with a furrowed brow. "Huh?"

He held up his hands so six digits were visible. "You mentioned feelings six times."

Sebastian poked his head into the car farther. "No...not if you count *felt* too. Then it would be—"

"Guys! Shush," Nel used her *mom voice*, hands flying into the air as she hugged my curled legs covered in the mustard-yellow fleece. "Rowe. If I can be completely honest—which I will be anyway—the handful of times I've seen you and Viv hang out, she's had this manipulative trance over you. I don't know why, and I don't know how, but she's had a grasp on you like I've seen no one else have. Maybe your confusion is a good thing, you know? Maybe you're finally letting go of what you thought you wanted and seeing what you really could have."

"Just like you were always there for me in college, Viv has been by my side since Mom went away." A deep sigh engulfed my body as I slumped deeper into the fleece blanket. If this was how it felt when Nel talked to her therapist, no wonder she was always exhausted. "She was with me during the audition process, then during training, and then as a partner onstage...and off stage. I love how I feel with her. I love where she led me."

"But..." Nel whispered, raising her eyebrows as my breath hitched beneath the blankets.

Sighing again, I closed my eyes and pressed my lips together. "But I realize now that she's only ever seen me as a success she stumbled upon—a success she wants to control. The feelings I thought I felt for her are so much different from the ones I'm feeling now...but that scares me because I like who I became with her."

"Can't you just, like, ghost her? Just get rid of her?" Sebastian asked as Nel elbowed him in the chest.

"It's not that easy, Seb," Nel whispered, turning to face him. "Trauma runs deep. It may look easy to escape from on the outside, but on the inside...it's part of you. Sometimes it's easier to just leave it there than to fight it...because fighting it hurts."

My gaze met Nel's as she turned back to face me, our eyes falling into a place of silent understanding.

Was trauma really what this all was for me?

Nel knew better than anyone that everyone's demons were different.

There was never one way to kill the beast within.

Especially when you'd been numb to the beast's presence to begin with.

"You started with the Bare Assentials, what, a few years ago?" Jude asked softly. "You were a different person then. You'd just watched Mom get forced into rehab—you went from crazy in college to confused as fuck. Maybe she helped you find your spark again, but that doesn't mean you walking away from her will lessen the glow. You're not twenty-something anymore. It's okay to want something different now. To *be* someone different."

Grunting, I sat up straight and pulled my blanket-covered knees to my chest. "I don't know. I still like her—love her, even. A snapshot of my twenties would include Viv and burlesque and being this confident creature. I don't like the idea of that part of me—*all of me*—changing."

"You still can be a version of the confident creature you once were…just a more mature, knowledgeable one," Nel whispered, stepping out onto the gravel drive so she wasn't hunched in the backseat anymore. "Hell…I'm over here trying to get back to being the confident sassy-pants I once was, so my giving you advice is a little hypocritical."

"You're still a confident sassy-pants." Jude's hand fell on Nel's shoulder, and their eyes quickly met just as a car sped up the driveway, pulling in right next to ours as Riley stepped out. With a lifted brow, I slid to the end of the seat to escape my backseat cave. "And don't forget that your confidently sassy ass lost a bet, Nel."

"What bet?" I asked, looking from Jude to Nel and back to Jude again.

"Riley! My man!" Sebastian jogged over to Riley, who was adjusting his glasses as Sebastian crushed into him with a hug. "It was the brunette with that ass… Cara, right? You went back with her, didn't you?!"

"*Claire*. Her name is Claire," I corrected, watching as the slightest hint of pink warmed Riley's cheeks. "And she does have a nice ass. Riley, you two hung out?"

Riley brushed Sebastian's hand away and walked to the passenger side of the Jeep. "Yeah. I went back to her room with them."

"Uh…*them?*" I asked, all of us turning toward him as he opened the door with a knowing chuckle.

"Yes, *them*. Claire and Harper," Riley said softly, sliding into the passenger seat and closing the door behind him without another hint to throw our way.

With jaws agape, we waited to hear if Riley would open the door to continue his story, but all we heard were robins chattering in the surrounding pines and the entrance of Towpath Bed and Breakfast opening as a couple wandered outside hand in hand.

"Well, fuck," Sebastian whispered. "How come he gets to have a threesome, and all I got was a drunken blow job?"

Snorting, I scooted backward until I was sitting in the backseat yet again. "Class, Seb. Riley has class. Take note."

Chapter 23

Nel

Every little detail was hitting hard today.

Mae said my name sixteen times that morning as she half-crawled, half-scooted around the kitchen floor. There was the tiniest white hint of top tooth peeking from her gums, the bottom two teeth finally living a pain-free life. The robins and cardinals and blue jays were making nests in almost every tree I walked by during our morning venture around the block. The headache I'd had since receiving a *You can't ignore me forever* text from Hallie finally vanished, being replaced with unexpected energy.

I felt both exhausted and oddly inspired.

This mix of emotions could start a fire.

"Have you spoken to her since the argument?" Delilah asked, spinning a curl around one of her fingers.

I peered down at my phone, forcing myself to ignore the text she'd sent the night we returned from Greyport. "I have not. She texted, but I didn't respond."

"How has being quiet on your end been for you?" she asked.

I looked over at Mae sitting on her blanket, pushing around rubber blocks and drooling all over her bib. "I'm actually okay with it. From belittling nicknames as a kid, to judging everyone I had feelings for after Grant, to treating me like a basket-case mother. She did all this in such passive-aggressive ways...and I never caught on. If breaking away from her reign is best for my mental health, so be it."

Delilah lifted a purple pen to her red lips, biting the end. "Why do you think this is all coming to the surface now? Why now are you speaking your mind to her?"

Why now?

What *had* changed?

"I think...I don't know..." I started, feeling Mae's little fingers dance across my toes. Her crawling and climbing skills had improved dramatically over the last week. She was becoming a wild inchworm before my eyes. "Grant made me feel like my words meant nothing. So, when Hallie scared him off, a power transfer kind of happened that I was blind to, and all I saw was her guiding me toward a safer, smarter future. I mean, her advice is usually solid...*usually*. I think I just see the unhealthy part of our relationship now. I'm just not sure how to completely step away from it."

"I'm glad you're seeing this, Nel. That clarity is a big step." Delilah leaned closer to the laptop screen, causing me to lean closer to mine. "What do you think played a part in this realization?"

Deadpan, I said, "Lamictal."

"Nel..." Delilah rolled her eyes with a laugh. "It isn't the medication that's making you see through a clearer lens. Yes, maybe it is helping, but *you're* the one moving forward with the changes—not the meds."

Mae picked at the thick chestnut braid falling over my shoulder, and I couldn't help but giggle as she yanked it toward her mouth, forcing me to shake my head away. Her little body falling against my chest reminded me that even though motherhood played with my emotions, it also made me prioritize myself, in a way. Even though this little girl would forever be my main priority, I realized if my head wasn't in a good place, it would impact her in the long run.

"I don't want Mae growing up being easily swayed by the thoughts of others," I said, adjusting Mae so she was facing the screen, her little hands reaching for Delilah. "I don't want her to fall into a dark place someday and need someone else to fully bring her out of it. She needs to know she's had it inside of her all along to make the climb herself. I think becoming a mom added some stressors, yes, but it also cleared some things up that I hadn't realized needed clarity."

"Mae is so lucky to have you, Nel." Delilah's cherry-red lips twisted into a grin. "It's okay if Hallie, or emotions from the past, bring unexpected feelings to the surface. It's good that you're acknowledging them. Is there anything else you want to chat about today before we end the session?"

A quiet kiss in an even quieter dorm room.

A tattooed hand cupping the side of my face.

Lips heating my own.

Trembling thighs and toes curling against a crumpled quilt.

"Um..." I mumbled, blinking a few times and adjusting my glasses before focusing back on the laptop. Both Mae's and Delilah's eyes were on me, forcing the flashbacks away. "Well...so...Hallie once made a decision for me in college that I probably shouldn't have listened to."

Breathe in, breathe out.

This conversation always left a scar in its wake.

Speaking it out loud would make the truth hurt that much more, but I needed to confront this.

I needed to move beyond this regret.

Reaching for the water beside the laptop, I took a long swig. "Hallie had calmly, quietly pushed me toward a choice. Since she'd *known best* so many times before, I just believed her." I brought water to my lips again, the cold liquid numb on my tongue. "This choice she made for me had to do with a friendship in college—a friendship that could have been something more. She saw this friend and immediately saw Grant and all of my other exes—their physical features, their uncertain futures, their laid-back attitudes. She told me I deserved better...so, I listened. Fast forward ten years,

I'm seeing how her thoughts should have never overpowered my own to begin with."

Delilah nodded, her finger returning to its place inside one of her crimson ringlets. "Growth is a beautiful thing to witness happen within yourself. I think, in time, you will want to—need to—explain all of this to her."

"But why am I still so terrified to stand up to her?" I exclaimed, Mae jumping slightly at my heightened tone. "By now, I should be beyond this. I shouldn't be so naive. This lingering fear should be gone."

"Nel...this is trauma." Delilah's voice was soft, certain. "Trauma looks different for everyone. Just because some people may face those who have hurt them doesn't mean everyone moves so swiftly. Some trauma sits within you longer...especially with co-dependency. It doesn't make the way you're navigating it any less valid."

Trauma runs deep.

It may look easy to escape from on the outside, but on the inside...it's part of you.

I'd said those very words to Rosie in the parking lot in Greyport—words so similar to what Delilah was telling me.

It was my turn to believe them.

"Right now, I want you to focus on how far you've come—not on the steps you think you should have already taken," Delilah said. "You will still have moments when your emotions take control, but you're discovering how to work alongside those emotions in a healthy way."

I pressed my lips together as Mae went to grab for my braid yet again. Shaking my hair from her grasp with a laugh, I said, "I need to think about what we're going to do for this little girl's first birthday. I know it's a few months away, but I probably should start planning."

"Oh, yes." Delilah sat back in her chair. "We have five more minutes left. I think brainstorming some birthday plans is a great way to spend that time."

May's rent was paid in full by The Naked Book Club.

I looked not once, not twice, but about seven times at our bank account just to make sure I saw this clearly.

Not to say our rent was an astounding amount, thanks to Theía Elena, but still, it was something to celebrate.

Even though I'd never believed in this endeavor as much as Rosie, I still had some hope it could help financially while we figured out our next steps by September.

Which was, really, only a few months away.

And Mae would turn one in August.

Time truly moved at warped speed when you became a parent.

The fact that The Naked Book Club grew from only a few subscribers to having near two hundred regulars on *each* tier—plus thousands of random views—this quickly, was insane. We even had followers adding donations in the support center—something I hadn't expected to happen when agreeing to *try out* that option. The support center on our page included a place to type book suggestions, place reviews, and add donations. I'd expected we would maybe get a few negative reviews after I told viewers they had to wait a little longer before getting any nip slips or ass cheek glimpses during Steamy Storytime.

I didn't expect us to get solid donations coming in on a weekly basis.

Thank you, donations, for paying for formula and diapers.

"Holy fuck, Nel," Rosie said after turning the laptop back to face her. "It's only been a couple months, and we're crushing it."

"It is pretty fucking cool that this month's rent is paid. I still don't believe it." I brought the near-empty coffee to my lips as Sebastian walked outside, plucking his mandolin and nodding to passersby. Now that spring in Merlin Heights was in full bloom, Java Jude's put together a quaint front patio surrounded by greenery and floral arrangements. Rosie and I spent too much time at the Merlin Market the weekend before, gathering wildflowers and outdoor plants. Since setting the space up, Sebastian had made it a stage for himself to lure visitors into the shop.

Whether his method worked was still up in the air.

"The *numbers* say we're crushing it, Nel." Rosie brought her finger up to underline something I couldn't see from across the table. "If we keep doing what we're doing, and maybe add more teaser posts in the feed, we could each have enough to put money down on a place come September."

The thought of a down payment made my heart skitter. "A down payment. Shit. Rowe, we need to start looking, like, *now*. It's May. We need to be out by September. That's honestly not—"

"Nel." Rosie's hand reached across the table, her fingers wrapping around my wrist. Her dark eyes—eyes so similar to her brother's—stared right into mine with such quiet comfort. "There's time. We have the whole summer. Think about how much money we can save in the next few months. Think about the apartments that will pop up."

"Think about the jobs we should start applying for," I whispered, looking over her shoulder as Jude stepped away from the cash register, a mason jar in each hand.

Rosie furrowed her brow, leaning to the side of her laptop so I could see not only her eyes but also the confused twist to her lips. "Do you not think The Naked Book Club could work out long-term? I was kind of thinking it could with how things are going."

"Oh my God. Rosie. The Naked Book Club is going to only keep getting better and better! I'm honestly so glad you convinced me to try this," I explained, leaning closer to the table, this time my hand twisting to hug hers. "I feel myself becoming the person I used to be. I'm getting more comfortable and more confident with myself—something I haven't felt since having Mae. You and this experience definitely are part of that."

"Nah," Rosie said, dramatically throwing her hand in my direction as Jude set two iced lattes on the table for us. "*You* are the one making this transformation."

Déjà vu?

Rosie continued, "It's not me. It's not the steamy scenes you've been reading in an impressively sexy voice. It's not even those tits in that lingerie the viewers are drooling over—"

"Whoa," Jude said, both of his hands flying into the air at his sides. "Weird conversation to walk into."

I loved how Jude played the part of *uncomfortable brother* whenever he overheard us talking like this. Now that I'd gotten a little peek into Jude's darker side, it was obvious that whenever he reacted to us, it was an act.

Because he *definitely* wasn't uncomfortable with these topics.

If anything, he lived for them.

Rosie cocked her head and looked up at her brother. "Is it, though? Over two months in and it's still weird to hear this shit?"

"Is it still weird to know my sister is streaming herself reading smut and touching herself? Seb's words, not mine...because I'd *never* say that about you. Yes. Yup, it's still weird."

Rosie subtly nodded in my direction. "What about Nel? Is it weird knowing she's reading smut and being sexy as fuck for the world to see?"

I nearly choked on the latte. Jude's eyes darted toward mine, his hand falling into the nook between my shoulder and neck before realizing I wasn't actually choking.

But his hand that close to my neck, the warmth of his skin on mine, made me wish his fingers would slowly work their way to the other side of my throat.

His breath against my ear as he demanded I do something for him.

To him.

"No. It's not as weird," Jude said softly, his hand slowly sliding away. "It's nice to see her embracing that side of herself—even if it's for other people. I know she's doing it for herself too."

"Huh..." Rosie mumbled, bringing the latte to her lips. "Huh."

Jude ignored her reaction, keeping his gaze on mine. "Our next practice session may have to be Monday."

"Monday?" I repeated, confused. "Mondays are my solo streams, though."

A sly smile unfolded across Jude's bearded face. "Exactly."

"Exactly?"

"Mm-hmm..." Jude took a small step backward, his smile never lessening. "Exactly. That just means our next session—the one promised from the bet I won—will be live."

"How...how will that work?" I asked as he took another step backward.

"It just means you'll have to *really* stay focused. Don't worry, Nel. I promise it'll be fun."

And just like that, Jude spun on his heel, eyeing me quickly before facing the older woman who just walked up to the counter.

Instead of grabbing my hand again or jumping onto the table, Rosie crouched down, squatted around the table, and showed up directly in my line of sight. "What the fuck did all of that mean?"

Blinking a few times, I finally peered down at Rosie, who still awkwardly hunched in front of me like the curious little goblin she was. "I'm not really sure. I guess... I guess I'll find out next week."

And the wait would be brutal.

Chapter 24

ROSIE

After we wrapped up Rowdy Readers, I *needed* to dig.

Nel's winks were spot-on.

Her lip bites were perfectly timed.

She'd even let her hands roam a bit when reading.

And for the first time since starting The Naked Book Club, Nel went on-screen without overalls covering her body.

Shocked was an understatement.

"Okay, Nel," I said, blowing candles on the bookshelf out. "What's going on?"

She peered over her shoulder at me with a red-lipped grin. "Whatever do you mean, Zizi?"

"Jesus Christ." I slammed my palm to my face as I stood up and playfully ripped her wig off her head. "First you dominate Monday's stream, then you and my brother talk in some secret language, and then tonight you touch yourself on camera."

"I did *not* touch myself," Nel said, jaw dropped as she removed her lace mask. "I just got handsy...it seemed to go with the scene since Mabel and Art were getting all—"

"Handsy, yes, I get it." I said, walking directly to the bottle of wine on the kitchen counter, my ass jiggling in my pleather panties. "I get that your confidence is growing—that much is obvious. But I haven't gotten a Jude update in a bit. I need it now."

"There isn't anything to update," Nel said quickly, appearing at the opposite side of the kitchen island.

"Bullshit. Say that to my face without laughing," I asked, filling my empty glass with wine.

Nel slowly looked over the square frames she'd just placed back on her nose. "Jude and I kissed."

"I knew it." I brought the wine to my lips, taking a knowing sip. "It was when we were in Greyport, wasn't it? You guys slept together."

"Rosie, no!" Nel exclaimed, flattening both hands on either side of her wine glass. "Yes, he stayed in our room—I didn't like being alone in there. But we really only kissed and stuff."

"I won't ask what *'we really only kissed and stuff'* means. If this was anyone other than my brother, I would ask. I'm excited for you, Nel, but please be careful. I don't want the past to repeat itself, and I don't want anyone I love getting hurt."

"Believe me when I say I will *not* let history repeat itself." Her voice was certain as she lifted her wine glass, peering at the baby monitor by the bottle of pinot. "Even though I wish I could change how things went back then, I'm making things right this time around. I'm glad I can remold the past a little bit."

"That's what worries me, though." I took another sip. "You're not sure what it all means. He's always had feelings for you, Nel. From day one, when he visited our dorm, I could see it in his eyes. He was hooked. Even a decade later, I *still* see it. You both deserve to be on the same wavelength—whether that means you guys are just friends, or friends who fool around, or whatever. Maybe some clarification this time around would help. Communication and all that shit."

Nel leaned onto her elbows, the wine glass spinning between her fingers as she looked up at me again with a grin pinching her cheeks. "Hey, Rowe...you should listen to your own advice. Because it's pretty fucking spectacular."

Shit.

This wasn't meant to flip back on me.

Low and behold, it had.

"Shut up," I said, taking a long swig of wine as I swiped the phone screen. "You're right, but shut your adorable little face."

Nel giggled, pushing her glasses up the bridge of her nose before leaning against the counter. "Are you texting Viv?"

I snorted out a laugh. "You really think she'd text me only a few days after hanging out? If anything, she's waiting for me to text her."

"And...are you going to?"

"Not yet, no." Huh. The bottle of wine was magically back in my hand. Weird. "I was going to see if Cade is hanging by campus tomorrow...but it's late. I don't want to—"

"Rosie," Nel said, smiling. "Your emotions are showing."

I let the phone drop from my hand, my eyes rolling as far back in my head as I could make them. "I don't have emotions."

Nel snagged the bottle from my hand so she could top off her glass. "What's the hurt in texting her, though?"

I stepped away from the island with my glass in hand. "We'll see. Maybe I will tomorrow. I'm going to bed. It's time I try out the new suction wand I got from Velvet and think about all the ways I can spend the money we'll have pouring in soon."

Nel pretended to gag into her wine. "You're *really* going to mas-turbate in a den without a door?"

Turning into the back corner I'd called home over the last few months, I flopped onto the futon without spilling a drop of wine. "Do you *really* think I haven't been using my toys since I've been here? I have needs, Nel."

"I shouldn't be surprised," she said, running a hand over the kitchen light switch, the apartment fading to black. "Our tiny dorm room never stopped you either."

May meant it was officially spring.

This meant it was almost summer.

And summer meant it was almost September, which meant we needed to be out of the apartment.

That was my logic, and I'd stick by it.

I didn't want to rush the current state of things. In fact, I was over the moon with how well The Naked Book Club was doing, and I lived for how great it felt clicking on the livestream every week.

The adrenaline.

The energy.

The freedom.

But Nel was in my head. She was thinking more about jobs—*real* jobs, she liked to call them. Though I saw The Naked Book Club as a *real* job, the fact that she didn't see it the same way made me question myself a bit. Did I need to still fill out applications? Would this really not work long-term?

I didn't want to look elsewhere for work.

But if I had to look, I guess I knew where to start.

Clad in jean shorts, a thrifted T-shirt I'd cropped myself, and gladiator boots, I made my way to Java Jude's, grabbing two iced lattes to go. I was being ballsy—I knew that for a fact. I was also prepared to be let down the second I turned the corner to see Merlin Community College's newly cut, emerald lawn staring back at me.

But I wasn't let down.

My eyes immediately connected with the woman flowing across the corner of the campus lawn, music sounding from a boom box on the wooden bench only a few feet from her. No one else was on the lawn—no students sitting on blankets studying or lacrosse players practicing. It was just Cade, the acoustic beats, and her energy I could feel from where I stood.

She must have sensed my nerves, because the second I stepped down onto the campus lawn, her bright hazel eyes flickered with fire in my direction.

"Dabbler," Cade said, strutting in my direction in black pants hung low on her waist and a fringed top that gave both music-festival and punk-band vibes. "Look at you just casually stopping by...and with coffee."

"Yeah...well, we haven't talked much in the last week. I thought I'd just—"

"You missed me." Her tone was confident as her hips swayed to the relaxed reggae rhythm, wrists twisted upward toward the sky. "Admit it."

Locking my eyes with hers, I said, "I may have missed dancing with you...just a little bit."

"*Just* dancing with me?" Cade wondered, turning on the balls of her feet before leaping into the air with double bent legs, her chest open toward the sun. When her feet hit the grass, she gently twisted onto the ground, rolling onto her belly and slowly rounding her back until she came to a kneeling position. "If you missed dancing with me, then you should probably dance."

Though hesitant, my body accepted her invitation—hips swaying, shoulders rolling back, neck relaxing. For someone who seriously trained in burlesque over the last few years, muscle memory still left me in awe.

It began with ballet.

I discovered contemporary.

Burlesque found me.

Dance was in my blood, but she was the syringe giving me the freedom to feel that passion again.

"Follow my lead," Cade insisted, taking a few confident—almost cocky—steps back before putting her weight on the heels of her feet, hollowing out her chest and rolling her shoulders forward.

For the quickest second, it looked like she was going to fall backward, and I ran to her, my feet stopping—not behind her but right at her toes. I lifted onto the ball of my foot, leaning toward her hollowed-out body as my back leg developed into an arabesque. My arms hovered around her, but our skin didn't touch.

That tiny space between our bodies was thick with tension I could practically taste.

As quickly as the movement formed, the foot of my lifted leg found the ground, and I leaped back onto it. I became the hollowed form she had been, and she mimicked my action, her long leg lifting into a full fucking needle—her pointed foot directly into the sky above us.

"See…" she whispered, our faces close as we unraveled from our forms, bodies still swaying to the music. "You *are* a dancer. No more shit-talking yourself, Dabbler. You must have done some contemporary partnering in the past."

"A little," I admitted, flexing my foot and lifting it up to do an exaggerated step forward, my body rolling until I hung forward over my exposed legs. I felt the heat of Cade's body fall over me, her chest pressing against my back as her arms wrapped around me until they were embracing my core.

Her calming, lavender scent with the slightest hint of mint.

Her soft, ebony skin heating my own.

Her breath against the side of my neck.

"I don't believe that," she whispered just before her lips caressed the skin behind my ear—no kiss, no nip, just skin on skin.

Without letting me organize my thoughts or emotions, I felt Cade lift me up against her so my back was pressed to her chest, and she was leaning back, knees bent. My body immediately recognized the preparation, and I straightened my legs so one foot hit the ground and the other fanned over, her arms leaving my waist so I could step the foot in flight back down, turning in a soutenu.

"Holy shit," I whispered. I bent forward and pressed my hands to my knees, out of breath. "It's been a hot minute since I did any partnering work other than lap dances or chair teasers."

"That counts, though." Cade's body relaxed from dancer mode into her more casual form—the form I recognized from Java Jude's and the night she watched my livestream. She walked to the bench where her speaker was sitting and lowered the volume, grabbing her water bottle and popping it open. "Movement is movement, no matter the style."

"I know, I know. I just feel like I'm supposed to still be in my burlesque era, of sorts." Closing my eyes, I angled my face toward the sky. "Though this feels so fucking freeing, I feel like burlesque should still be my focus. Joining another troupe or traveling around doing solo gigs is probably what I should be doing."

"Why can't you do both?" Cade asked, wiping her lips with the back of her hand as she pushed the water in my direction. I grabbed the bottle and took a much-needed chug. "You can kick ass at burlesque and put energy and emotion into movement like this as well. Why do you feel the need to pick just one style when you can master both?"

She had a point.

"I think I feel like I'm leaving a part of myself behind if I switch styles up too much. I've built this sexy, empowering brand, of sorts, that I love. If I walk away from what I worked hard to create, would that work have been for nothing?"

My hesitance caused the edges of my words to tremble. Hearing these thoughts out loud after trying to ignore them over the last few months was suffocating. I wasn't sure what my lungs were doing, but I knew my breath was catching and slowing and flailing all at once. I straightened my spine and cleared my throat, doing all I could to feel ten times taller than I was feeling.

Cade slid the water bottle from my grasp and set it back on the bench before taking a step closer, her face only a few inches from mine. She had zero awareness of personal space, and I finally understood how Nel felt when I attacked her with one of my chaotic hugs.

But unlike when I invaded Nel's space, I wanted Cade to invade mine.

I wanted her closer.

"You can't compare yourself to the person you were ten years ago. Hell, you can't compare yourself to the person you were three months ago. We're ever-changing, and we don't need to force our roots anywhere if we want to keep growing."

Was that it?

Were my roots clinging to earth they wanted to break free from?

Digging up a plant and its roots without a mess was hard, but it *was* possible.

This was possible.

I wrapped a hand around the back of her neck and pulled her lips to mine. Her hands found my waist, tugging me close against her as our tongues collided. My teeth pulled gently at her bottom lip, and she immediately let out a groan I would forever hear on repeat in my mind.

I released her lip, and our foreheads pressed together, pulling me in so close that I could feel her chest rise and fall against mine.

"Well, then...if I should *grow*, why don't you show me the studio you host workshops in?"

Cade peered over her shoulder at the college before turning back. "At MCC? Do you want to go look?"

"Yeah. Growth may mean getting me back into a studio again...even though I love my bookshelf studio more than anything right now." I began flattening my hands over my ass until I realized my phone was no longer in my back pocket. Shooting my gaze back toward the corner of the lawn, I saw the tiny rectangular shape hidden in the grass.

Why the hell did this lawn like eating my fucking phone?

As I jogged toward it, I said, "Maybe...maybe I'll sign up for a class."

"Or maybe you can *teach* one." Cade's voice stopped me as the tips of my boots came into contact with the phone.

Teach a class?

Could I do that?

Was that *really* what I saw myself doing once September hit?

Most of all, what would happen to The Naked Book Club?

The thought of walking away from something else I loved only added to the mess inside my head.

I brushed my thumb over the phone screen until the notifications bar popped up…and so did Viv's name.

Four times.

Taking a deep breath, my eyes still staring at the unread texts, I slid the phone back into my pocket and met Cade at the corner of the lawn. She held the boombox in one hand and her water bottle in the other, leaning into her hip.

"Yeah…maybe I could teach." I nodded toward the college. "Let's go see this studio."

Chapter 25

NEL

The table by the window at Java Jude's was now my home.

Jude surprised me by shifting the tables around so there was a bit of extra space near the window facing the shopfront. It let me put Mae down on a blanket or pop up her compact Pack 'N Play—The Kraken Cage, as Sebastian called it—without the coffee shop looking like a daycare center.

Jude mentioned updating the little bookshelf in the corner—the one with vintage books, a typewriter, and some curling pothos—so he could fill the bottom shelf with toys and organize his comic books.

The fact that he'd even thought about this made my heart skitter.

I sat in the usual spot after setting Mae into her bouncer—something she had officially outgrown but still put up with. My legs hadn't stopped bouncing beneath the table since sitting down, my eyes darting from the doorway to Mae and then back. I wasn't entirely sure why I was spiraling like I was. No matter how much I breathed through the emotions or took another long sip of water, it seemed like this anxiety was here to stay.

"I'm not sure if espresso is a smart idea...but then again, it's never really *not*," Jude said softly, setting down an iced lavender-vanilla latte—the spring flavor I kept requesting. "I added an extra shot of espresso in there, but from the look of your leg...maybe I shouldn't have."

"Thanks. Really. I appreciate it," I said, the fresh latte meeting my lips. "I'm just meeting—"

"My baby!" Nora exclaimed, the door closing behind her as she set her shoulder bag around the back of the chair at Jude's hip.

Nora rarely *exclaimed*.

Maybe my senses were just heightened.

This anxiety was really PMS'ing today.

"You better get your coffee now before she screams and we have to do this another time," I said, my eyes darting from Nora, now squatting down by Mae, to Jude, who still stood at the table.

"I can grab something for you. What would you like?" Jude asked, his voice nowhere near as awkward or tentative as mine would have been if I were him.

But then again, this was *Nora*.

Not Hallie.

Nora faced Jude, and it took her a few seconds before everything clicked into place. "Jude? Hi! Wow...I honestly didn't recognize you. You look nothing like the boy I remember seeing at MCC during visits."

"You look nothing like the little girl who came to trivia nights with us before Nel begged your parents to pick you up," Jude said in one breath, his thin eyes hitting mine.

With a dramatic sigh, I said, "I was saving her from the night of binge-drinking we usually had in store. You were only, what, fifteen when you visited?"

"Yes...but I wasn't clueless. I knew you didn't want your little sister following you around."

"No...that was my job," Jude interjected slyly.

"He's not wrong." I nudged his hip with my shoulder.

Nora's eyes narrowed at the exchange. "But it's been...a while, huh? Congratulations on this place, by the way!"

"It *has* been a while, yeah...and thanks, Nora. I'm pretty proud of it, if I say so myself." Jude walked backward, pointing both fingers toward Nora. "Vanilla cold foam cold brew? Pistachio latte? Cortado? Pick your poison."

"I'll try a pistachio latte...hot, please. Thanks," Nora said as he turned on his heel to meet Riley at the espresso machine. She slowly situated herself, grabbing a small notebook and pen from her bag before meeting my gaze.

I sat straight as a board, my leg still tapping from below the table. "So...it's not weird?"

"Life, in general, is weird." Nora flipped open the first page of her notebook. "But if you're talking about you and Jude being friends again...no. I don't see it as weird. You guys always had a strong bond, and Hallie had no right plugging her two cents into your head the way she did back then."

The tension in my shoulders released. "Really? You didn't think she was trying to help by, you know, steering me away from my *type* or whatever?"

Nora huffed out a laugh, sliding a few loose strands of auburn and violet hair behind her ear. "I was too young and afraid of the world to throw my two cents at anyone back then. I'm still mad at myself for not listening close when Grant talked to you...and that was *before* your friendship with Jude. All I know is Hallie stepped in and pointed you in a direction you could have chosen yourself."

My fingers created shapes in the frosted mason jar my latte was in. "I know. Well, I know this *now*. Believe me...if I'd opened my eyes a little bit more back then, maybe I could have—"

Nora's hands covered mine still wrapped around the mason jar, and I looked up to meet my little sister's gaze. "Maybe I was young and didn't really understand what was going on back then, but I could tell you were in a fog during those years, Nel. A dissociative state. You weren't *you* for a very long time. Don't beat yourself up for not snapping out of something that takes years—maybe decades—to fully heal from."

Nodding as Nora's hands released from my own, I whispered, "I never knew you thought these things."

Nora gestured back toward the register. "Well...*he* hasn't come up in conversation in a *very* long time. Plus, I've blocked *The Grant Years* from my memory too. Bringing that dickwad up is just a waste of breath."

I smiled. "I'm glad it's not weird for you."

"Is it for you, though?" Nora looked over her shoulder to make sure Jude wasn't walking this way. "Because you two could have...*should* have been something. So, I'm sure you're feeling all the things right now."

She really thought we *should* have been something?

That was even more of a stab to the gut.

"It was a little weird at first, yeah," I admitted, readjusting Mae, who sat in her bouncer, flipping a plastic book in her hands. "But honestly, now it's back to where we were ten years ago. Probably beyond that, actually."

"Wait...what does that—"

"Pistachio latte for Nora," Jude said, setting down the steaming mug in front of her. "Your first drink is on the house. I can do that sort of thing...because it's *my* house."

"I don't need special treatment, Jude. That's far too kind." Nora snagged her latte, the steam dancing through the air. "But I'm not one to complain. Thank you."

"What are you guys meeting about?" Jude asked, walking around Nora's chair and leaning against the window frame, a wandering plant stem reaching down for the beanie on his head. "It looks like some serious work is about to happen."

"We're planning Mae's birthday, actually," I said, finishing my iced latte and pulling the second one over. Jude really needed to stop giving me all these free drinks. Yet again, he really didn't need to. "She turns one a month before Rosie and I have to move...which reminds me to get back on that site and look for rentals. Jesus...we only have a few months left. I should pack and probably apply for tutoring jobs. Why did I wait this long to start applying? I mean, this most recent paycheck from The Naked Book Club *was* pretty nice, but I should—"

"You should focus on Mae's birthday party, Nel." I felt Jude's hand fall over my shoulder, and my body stilled, memories from our weekend at Velvet sliding through my thoughts the second his skin touched mine.

His lips caressing my neck and chest.

The confidence dripping from every word he whispered into my ear.

The warm embrace I melted into for the rest of the night.

I wasn't sure if he could tell there was a slide show flipping through my mind, but when he released his soft touch, all I wanted was for it to return.

"He's right." Nora pulled Mae from her bouncer, and within seconds, she pulled herself up to standing against the chair before her little knees buckled, and she plopped down. Nora dropped a handful of plastic figurines in front of her from her bag—some holding, what seemed to be, swords or bows in their hands. Turning away from Mae, who was now hyper-focused on these new exciting toys, Nora said, "Let's figure out the best date for this thing, and then we can get to the theme—which is my favorite part."

"Are those some miniatures you use during Dungeons and Dragons with Ari?" I asked, cocking an eyebrow up as Mae grabbed one that looked like an orc holding a club.

Jude squatted down beside her, reaching into the pile of minis before lifting one into the air. "No way. Is this the Drow from the *Underdawn* book that came out last year? I forget her name, but her character sheet looked badass. Sebastian and I have wanted to play an *Underdawn* campaign for a while now."

My eyes widened. "Since when do you play D&D, Jude?"

"Since Merlin Community College, *Nel*. If you don't recall, I was the vice president of the Gamers Club on campus." The sarcastic bite to his tone was far sexier than it should have been.

"No way. I'm in the middle of an *Underdawn*-themed campaign! I'm playing a sadistic halfling. You'll have to—" Nora stopped herself when she noticed me staring curiously with both hands atop my notebook. "Jude, we *will* get back to this conversation after. Right now, we need to plan *this* little halfling's birthday."

"I'm a big romantasy fan...so, I'd be down to get a little nerdy with figurines and play pretend with adults," I added with a shrug. Peering down at the blanket Mae sat on, I watched as Jude walked two figurines in her direction before tossing them in the air with a gasp.

Mae's laugh was the most beautiful sound I'd heard in a while.

Chapter 26

ROSIE

Karma smacked me in the face for not responding to Viv's texts when I'd been with Cade.

It came in the form of her calling me an hour before my Smut Me Up stream, and I knew I couldn't ignore her again.

I was still training my body not to immediately panic and respond to her on cue.

It was a lot harder than I expected.

Before I could question myself any more, I swiped the screen and brought the phone to my ear.

"Um...hello? Is this *really* you, Zi?"

Rolling my eyes with a hollow laugh, I slid down onto the rug in front of the bookshelf, making sure my lace-and-leather ensemble didn't catch. "Yes, it's me. I've been so damn busy lately, Viv...I'm sorry. The Naked Book Club is kicking ass, and it's become my whole personality."

It wasn't a lie.

"I get that, yeah," she said, her tone a little grittier than usual. "But...come on! I miss you. I'm heading back toward Rockberry in the next month or so for a solo gig...they're still nailing down a date. But I'd love to nail *you* down and make you scream when I'm in the area."

I should have seen that coming.

"Why don't you come out here to visit before then?" I asked, seeing if she'd take a bite at the line I was throwing. Though my emotions were confusing as fuck right now, I still felt the need to try. "We could check out Caravan for dinner. I heard it's—"

"Oh, Zi...you know I'm not a *dinner* person," Viv said quickly. "Unless *you're* the dinner, that is."

A few seconds of silence ticked by.

"Yeah. I prefer *both* of those dinner options," I said, looking at the clock above the stove. "I have to start my stream, though. Maybe we can find time to *actually* get together before you visit next? My brother just opened this kickass—"

"Oh, go do your naked livestream! I'm slightly jealous the world gets to see you in the form I constantly crave," she said, quickly cutting me off. "...but then again, it's kind of hot knowing I've touched you—tasted you—in all the places everyone watching wants to."

Well, fuck.

That added a tiny bolt of heat that I couldn't ignore.

And I let myself feel it.

The heat would help during the livestream.

And the Smut Me Up squad liked it hot.

"*She ran her hand down his broad chest, every muscle flexing beneath her touch as she arrived at the edge of his sweatpants. Swinging a leg over to straddle him, she ran a teasing finger across the gleaming, sensitive skin right above the waistband. She finally wiggled her hand beneath the gray fabric, walking her fingers down the length of him until she got to the head of his cock, already beading with pre-cum.*"

As I read the words aloud, I occasionally looked away from the page to add eye contact for the viewers to drool over. I ran my hand down over my pierced nipples beneath the sheer bra, over my belly, beneath the lace lip of my thong. This outfit had a tiny, red tulle skirt around the waistband, not long enough to do anything but look innocently adorable.

And I was absolutely using this adorable act to my advantage.

In the Lacy Schore book we were reading, Sophie focused on all the different people she could have been with—*wanted* to be with—if she hadn't taken the arranged-marriage route. She was naïve, curious, and insanely sexy in the book as she explored different relationships with all types of people after her divorce was finalized. This scene was her first one-night stand after the divorce—the first one she'd ever had in her life, actually. It was a scene that flipped a switch in Sophie's head, making her realize there was so much she missed out on in the life her parents planned for her.

To make this scene realistic, I had to play the part.

I had to *be* Sophie.

And after a couple months of subtle on-camera touching, I was ready to dive in.

"She wrapped her fingers around his thick length, impressed—and, to be honest, a little nervous—as she slid her hand up and down. Her body moved along with each stroke, her hips rolling on top of him as her legs straddled each side."

We really did need more sapphic books.

Stat.

"Marcus freed his cock from his sweatpants, the erection near smacking Sophie in the face in doing so—unless that was part of his plan. He clawed at her dark waves, curling his wrist and gently pulling at the roots until their faces were so close she could taste his breath.

"'Spit on it, pretty girl,' Marcus growled, his wrist twisting a little more as a gentle cry escaped Sophie's lips. 'Spit on it and let me see how dirty that pretty little mouth can get.'

"Goosebumps erupted over Sophie's skin as Marcus pushed her toward the head of his cock. Sophie licked down the shaft and back up before parting her lips to take him as deep as she could."

My hips circled below me, my open palm pressing down to add a teasing amount of pressure to my clit as the tip of my fingers circled my entrance.

"As he thrust into her throat, a gag sounding before she repeated the motion, Sophie couldn't ignore the fire filling her. The smile wouldn't leave her lips as she parted them wider, wrapping both of her hands around the base of him before consuming him again. She'd brought this night to life, no one else. She'd agreed to go back to his apartment, and she'd initiated all that was going on.

"She felt completely in control—while also feeling so completely out of it—and it was a feeling she never wanted to let go of."

My hand pressed harder over my sex, my middle finger inching inside of me just the tiniest bit. Biting my lip, I leaned toward the camera and said, "That will be all for today. Well...all for the reading portion, that is."

I pushed a finger deep inside of me, my hand still covering myself so nothing was visible to viewers. I'd get to that point sooner or later, maybe adding a VIP tier for those who wanted one-on-one sessions. For now, they would get a peek of what was to come.

My tits were completely out of my bra—they were getting *more* than a peek.

"Do you guys think...do you think she will stay with Marcus or find someone else to fuck? Tell me...in the comments." The speed of my fingers quickened, my palm circling over my clit with a little more force as I pressed the open book to my chest, letting my head fall back.

I couldn't let myself go over the edge just yet.

I had to interact with the viewers.

Leaning forward over my spread, bent knees, I smiled at the comments flowing in:

@SpicyStef_01: *We're only in the first half of the story…Sophie will probably manhandle a few more guys before finding someone to keep around.*

@darkromMOM3: @SpicyStef_01: *I can see her getting with a girl. She was so cooped up in her marriage and this is JUST the beginning for her. Go get some pussy, Soph!*

@vviPURR: *I hope Sophie gets herself some nice toys. Don't you agree, Zi?*

@oliVERYcaffeinatedxx: *Hell yeah. I support scissoring.*

@SpicyStef_01: @oliVERYcaffeinatedxx: *Gross. You don't know what you're talking about.*

@nerdalertALLIE26: @oliVERYcaffeinatedxx: *Did you even listen to the story this week, Oliver?*

@oliVERYcaffeinatedxx: @nerdalertALLIE26: *Do I need to when I get THIS view?*

@capella.calypso: *Sophie is opening herself up to others, and that's badass. Maybe* *she'll hook up with a few other people, but in the end, she'll stay true to herself.*

@vviPURR: @oliVERYcaffeinatedxx: *It's such a good view.*

@SpicyStef_01: @capella.calypso: *Preach!*

@RobEatsTacos88: *I'm just here for the tits.*

My fingers froze inside of me, my chest rising and falling as I stopped myself only seconds away from orgasm.

Two names I'd never seen before were in the chat.

vviPURR logged on at the start of the stream.

capella.calypso showed up about halfway through the chapter, according to the timestamp.

vviPURR was talking directly to *me* about toys.

capella.calypso was thinking about the character's emotions.

"Fuck," I said out loud, my hand sliding away from the damp lace. My brain went from being on an adrenaline high to spiraling within seconds. The frustrating thing was, I didn't know exactly why the spiral was happening.

Was I shocked Viv went out of her way to watch me? Was I impressed she was chasing *me* for once and not the other way around? Was I angry she was in the chat at the same time as Cade, adding unnecessary—and unknown—drama to the mix?

A door squeaked open from the hallway, and I met Nel's wide eyes, her phone in hand and lips shaped in a small, knowing O.

"Are you okay?" she whispered from the kitchen counter, a sleepy Mae bundled up against her chest. Nel's eyes went from mine to the phone screen in front of her and back to mine again. I wasn't sure if Nel knew Cade had officially joined the stream, but it was as obvious as my bare nipples that she knew Viv had.

Subtly nodding, I popped my breasts back into the bra before taking a deep breath and ruffling up my hair a bit. "I agree...Sophie is *definitely* exploring this new version of herself. I, uh...I also *definitely* like toys. Okay, see you next week...bye!"

I slammed the laptop shut and sat back against the bookshelf, my breathing tense.

Nel tiptoed across the kitchen, swaying her body back and forth to keep Mae from stirring. "Did you log off or just slam it shut? It's finicky."

I immediately opened the laptop to see that the red LIVE light was, in fact, still on. My finger found the OFF button faster than it had been moving inside of me seconds before, and I took a deep, relieved breath. "Jesus...thank God for your common sense. I always click the button. I'm just...distracted."

Nel sat on the couch carefully while switching Mae to the other shoulder. "Are you not okay with Viv watching your streams? Are you happy she was watching or anxious since you guys have been a little, I don't know, *weird* lately? I can't read you right now."

"I can't read me right now either," I admitted, sitting back against the bookshelf again. "I think I was just...surprised. A little shocked. She has voyeur tendencies, so I guess her logging on tracks."

"Mm-hmm…" Nel said, standing and swaying. "I almost popped into the messages to tell her and Oliver to chill out, but you always handle the weirdos just fine. *I'm* the one who usually needs your assistance in the chat."

"Thanks for keeping an eye on it all. I think it's smart we monitor it like we have been…even if you're rocking Mae to sleep as it's happening," I said, grabbing the glass of wine from the shelf above my head. "Go get some sleep. I'll make pancakes in the morning."

Nel tiptoed across the kitchen floor. "The microwavable ones?"

"Would you expect any other kind?" I said, raising an eyebrow and taking a sip of the rosé. "Goodnight, Nel. Thanks for being you."

Shooting me one last smile over her shoulder, she wandered back down the hallway and into the nursery, closing the door behind her. My phone vibrated from beside my thigh, and Viv's name appeared in the notification tab glowing on my screen.

Months ago, I would have done anything for the attention Viv was giving me. She was chasing *me*. I always chased her when she only seemed to chase me for two reasons: attention and sex.

My heart was a game to her.

My *healing* was a game to her.

I stood in the present, sandwiched between the past and a possible future. Like Sophie, I needed to embrace the odd, new emotions racing through me, pushing me toward this newfound sense of self.

Viv's name lit up the phone screen again, and as the notification tab faded, one thing became incredibly clear:

To move forward, it meant leaving Viv in the past.

I didn't know what that looked like yet, but it was a step I needed to take.

Chapter 27

Nel

I texted my mother *Happy Mother's Day* right around the time a text came in from Hallie. She'd only texted me a few times since my dramatic exit from the failed family dinner and only once had she given some form of an apology.

Today's text was simple: *Happy Mother's Day. Give Mae a hug for me. Xoxo*

As I sat at Java Jude's, one hand pushing the stroller while Mae dozed off and the other holding the phone, I wasn't sure how to respond—nor did I really want to. It wasn't in my genetic makeup to completely ghost someone—unlike Rosie, who'd done it flawlessly.

Something I was still only *slightly* bitter about.

Rather than text her back, I *liked* her message and set the phone on the table, the mimosa Jude set in front of me minutes before cooling my hand.

My chest grew tight.

My eyes grew damp.

Breathe in, breathe out.

Jude arrived at the table with two plates, snapping me back to the present. Cinnamon French toast with the cutest dallop of melting butter. Crispy bacon charred to exactly my liking. A skewer poking through two strawberries, two blackberries, and two pieces of pineapple. A hard-boiled egg sliced to look like it belonged on the cover of a magazine.

I had to physically push my jaw back into place. "Since when are you a professional chef? All I got in college from you was midnight grilled cheese and the occasional bowl of cereal."

"Be grateful you got *that* from me. I barely made anything aside from coffee and mediocre mixed drinks back then." Jude set his plate down and pulled the chair out in front of me, peeking over to look at Mae, who'd finally fallen asleep. "But I can't take accountability for this food. Riley is the one who listens to way too many culinary podcasts."

"*Riley* made this?" I cut off a piece of the French toast and took a bite as it melted on my tongue.

"Yeah, he did. Sebastian was the one who beautified the plate, though. Apparently, he has a lot of opinions on how brunch should look."

"Well, it's good. *You* did a good job carrying it out to the table, if that's what your main duty was," I said, raising an eyebrow before going back for another piece of the French toast.

"My main duty was getting you here before the Mother's Day brunch crew rolls in around ten o'clock."

"Why *before*?" I asked, plucking a strawberry from the skewer.

"So, I could celebrate Mother's Day with you."

My stomach shot straight to my chest when his electric gaze fell over me.

"I appreciate it, Jude. All of it." I peeked inside Mae's stroller before plucking a piece of bacon. "The brunch. Your support with this crazy YourEyesOnly thing. The night in Greyport."

I watched his Adam's apple bob slowly, his lips pressing together with a nod as he said, "You deserve all of it, Nel. You deserve to be pampered and appreciated. You deserved the night we had…and more of them."

"But you never deserved the way I treated you ten years ago, Jude." My voice came out hushed, my eyes fixated on the bacon between my fingers. "I see that now."

I shuddered and began wrapping my arms around myself as a mothed hand cupped my elbow. Leaning so his chest was against the edge of the table, his arm splayed out across it, he said, "We were different people then, and even though we're different people now, my feelings for you are still the same."

He wasn't hiding the truth behind his intense stares and punny banter. He was laying his heart out there with no expectations of my heart being handed over to him.

The raw reality of it all was too much.

I needed to step out of my head.

"So...you're still on for tomorrow night's stream?" I asked, redirecting as his hand fell away. "Nora said she would take Mae for the night. I told her it was going to be a long session...and I don't always trust Rosie to be around to help when Mae starts screaming."

Chuckling, Jude sat back, plucking curled bacon from his plate and taking a bite. "If you'll really let me take control of your night the way you agreed to, then yes. I'll be there at seven-thirty with wine in hand."

With wide eyes, I leaned onto my elbows, placing my head atop threaded fingers. "A bet is a bet, Jude. I'm ready to give up control."

I wasn't ready to give up control.

I wasn't sure I could read the chapter I planned for the night.

I wasn't sure the one-piece, lace bodysuit I borrowed from Rosie hugged my curves the way it was supposed to.

And I was *definitely* not ready for Jude to watch me read about a threesome while I awkwardly winked and grabbed my tits for the next hour.

When his knock sounded at the door, I practically peed myself.

Honestly, I may have.

"Hi. Hey," he said, his eyes immediately dropping to my chest before quickly darting back to my face as he stepped inside, lifting a bottle of white wine into the air. "I can't promise I won't check you out all night…because this little outfit is just…yeah."

Grabbing the wine from him, I shuffled backward so my ass was hidden from view. It was laughable how insecure I felt standing here in a lace romper. A few weeks ago, I'd completely let myself go with him in ways I didn't know I could.

"I've pretty much stuck to overalls for streams, but I changed it up tonight. I'm honestly terrified." Adjusting the dark wig itching my forehead, I nodded toward the backpack slung over his shoulder and asked, "What did you put in there? A sleeping bag?"

Smirking, Jude stepped away from the kitchen island and into the living room. Plopping down onto the sofa facing the bookshelf, he unzipped his bag. I tried to ignore the smile pinned to his cheeks as I poured us both a glass of wine.

But it was too damn cute to ignore.

"I won the bet, so I make the rules tonight…right?" he asked, reaching into his bag.

I set his glass of wine on the coffee table before I sat down on the shag rug. "Yes, I agreed to this…even though it *was* supposed to be during one of our practice sessions. But here we are."

"Here we are, indeed," he said. With his hand still in the backpack, he asked, "Do you trust me, Nel?"

I swallowed hard, looking away for half a second. "I do, yeah. I…I do trust you."

"Good." His voice was low, hushed. "Did anything stand out to you at Velvet the other weekend? Other than the performers and, well...our night together?"

It was hard to think of anything from that weekend that didn't involve us kissing and touching and licking and coming. The drive to Greyport, the performances, the shots...they were blurred around the edges.

But our time together was clear as crystal.

"Um...the girl talking about that dragon stuff with Sebastian? *That* stood out to me."

Jude's lips turned up slightly. "Close...but that's not what we're doing tonight."

My head fell back in relief. "Thank God, because I definitely am *not* into dragon dicks."

"What about this?" Jude lifted his hand from the backpack to reveal a small red box. On the cover, a U-shaped item was beside a small, oval shaped remote of sorts. When my eyes wandered to the rim of the box, I recognized the logo and branding immediately.

"Holy shit..." I whispered, bringing my hand to my lips and scooting toward him to get a closer look. The closer I scooted, the more I realized it was exactly what I thought it was. "Is this from Velvet?"

Jude nodded, placing the box onto the couch. "You looked at it a few times when we were there. I bought it on a whim...but I wasn't sure if you were into toys. I mean, I honestly wasn't sure you'd want to even hang out again after that night."

"Of course I would." The response was quick and unprocessed, but nowhere near a lie.

Jude leaned over his knees, his breath warming my face as he brought his wine to his lips without looking away. I watched his throat bob as he swallowed, his lips pressing together.

After setting the glass back down, I felt his body shift even closer to mine. His lips warmed my ear as he whispered, "But after the other weekend, I feel you might be up for trying something like this. You may not expect yourself to like it, but I have a weird feeling you just might."

My eyes darted back to the remote-controlled vibrator staring me straight in the face.

Yes, I'd seen this box at Velvet.

Yes, how it would feel crossed my mind...but *so* many other thoughts had that night too.

As Jude sat back, I realized I wanted his heat back on my skin. I wanted his lips back below my earlobe, my neck, my chest. If I felt *this* comfortable, *this* at ease, and *this* genuinely myself with this man, there wasn't a reason to stay within my comfort zone.

I'd already stepped outside of it during our weekend. Why not take a few more steps now?

Snagging the box from his grasp, I walked toward my bedroom, not caring if Jude gawked at my ass as I passed. I ripped open the box once the door closed behind me and removed the vibrator from its case, cleaning it as directed. Unbuttoning the bottom of my lace romper—grateful the designer made an easy-access opening—I slowly slid part of the vibrator inside. When the other side hugged my clit, a gasp escaped me.

The damn thing wasn't even turned on yet, but holy hell, I sure was.

Snapping the lace back into place, I cautiously walked into the living room. Jude's eyes were on me the second I walked toward the bookshelf and knelt down. I sat on my heels and pinched my knees together before opening the laptop.

The remote in hand, Jude opened a bag of batteries that were *actually* included.

Thanks, Velvet.

I sat back onto my heels a little more—a position that wasn't the comfiest but made it so viewers couldn't see the red device hugging my lady bits. The romper wasn't entirely see-through, but it was close enough to make viewers wonder.

"You sure you're ready?" Jude asked, adjusting the knit beanie on his head with one hand as the other grabbed the remote.

There was one minute until the stream went live, and over three hundred people were waiting in the comment section, chatting about the chapter I was about to read and discussing last week's session. The more seconds that went by and the more comments I read, the more I wasn't sure I could hand over control like this.

What if I couldn't hold myself back as I read the chapter?

What if I fell apart in all the wrong ways?

What if this romper made my stretch marks more prominent?

I was also terrified I'd enjoy watching Jude light up in pure ecstasy while watching me.

The thing about all those fears was that I was the only one holding myself back. My mind was buzzing on overdrive when I just needed to let myself feel. I knew it was easier said than done, but when it hit ten seconds before the recording button blinked red, my decision was made.

In truth, it had been made since slipping the vibrator inside of me.

I hovered my finger above the button, slipping off my glasses and peering blurrily at Jude, who sat gripping the remote. "I'm ready."

Chapter 28

Rosie

After Cade's hour and a half Contemporary Exploration Workshop at Merlin Community College, I realized a few things:

1. I missed this kind of movement.

2. My body was not in the same shape it was before The Bare

Assentials.

3. Cade was savage.

She'd stood at the front of the studio with that usual confident aura of hers, but there was an edge to her I'd never experienced before. A power radiated off of her. It was a power forcing you to listen, to watch, to seek more. It was the perfect mix of confidence and control, and I wanted her to drown me in it.

In a way, I felt like she already was.

I took the world's longest swig from my water bottle as exhausted dancers thanked Cade for the class and exited the studio. Being in this space brought out an energy I hadn't felt in over a decade—an energy different from the high that burlesque gave me. While burlesque brought forth a fiery, empowering vibe, contemporary brought forth a fresh set of emotions—apparently ones I'd pushed deep down until finding Cade on the college lawn. Feelings of openness and humility and uncertainty and freedom. I was touching upon a side of me I'd caged up since, what felt like, childhood.

Since my father disappeared and my mother started using.

I'd blocked out memories from my past—a coping skill I knew wasn't the healthiest.

"So..." Cade said, still out of breath from leading the same routine over and over for almost two hours straight. "How do you feel? You looked great."

"*Great*?" I snorted. "I felt like a drunk Great Dane...with way shorter legs."

"I promise you…your dancing looked nothing like a drunk Great Dane today." Cade slipped her arms into a cropped sweatshirt, her pierced belly button peeking out at the shirt's edge. "Speaking of Great Danes…do you still want to grab a drink at Thirsty Theodore's? My treat."

"You *do* know the logo for that place is a schnauzer, right?"

Cade rolled her eyes, snagging her keys from the hook by the studio exit. "Dabbler, I grew up with three rescue dogs. I *know* my breeds. Let me buy you a mojito."

Of course she rescued dogs.

She rescued dogs, danced like a fucking angel, kissed like a goddess, and wanted to buy me a drink.

Sold.

We left the college and walked a few blocks until we came to the main hub of Merlin Heights, the sky dimming as the restaurant and bar patios livened up. Thirsty Theodore's suspended sign popped into view—a dapper schnauzer, clad in a top hat, holding an overflowing brew. Wandering through a cluster of swaying college students—buzzed before eight o'clock—we found free stools at the bar, and Cade beckoned the bartender over for a round of mojitos. My hand immediately reached into my jacket pocket to set my phone onto the bar, but I forced myself to stop.

I needed to stop this habit.

My texts were not priority right now.

Cade's attention was.

"Are you ever sore after these things?" I asked, silencing my phone. "I can tell my hamstrings are going to be on fire tomorrow."

Cade slid a mojito into my palm, the brush of her fingertips sending a quick jolt through me. "I do get sore, yeah. Tonight's class wasn't as intensive as others, but when I teach high-level choreography for three or four hours straight, it's exhausting—exhausting in the best way, but tiring, nonetheless."

I lifted my mojito into the air. "Well, cheers to a kickass class, to being a kickass human, and...uhhh..."

"And to us." Cade's glass touched mine. "Cheers to us being where we need to be and *with* who we need to be with in this very moment."

My eyes didn't leave hers as she brought the edge of her glass to her lips and took a long swig. My drink still hung in the air between us, my fingers tight around the glass, as my mind spun in circles.

"What are you overthinking, right now?" Cade's voice was soft, her body closer than it was seconds before. Her plump lips glided across my cheek, and she whispered, "Whatever is going through your head, don't overthink it. Just go with it."

"I want to go back to your place." My throat tightened, swallowing heavily as Cade sat back. The grin on her face was coy, that mix of self-assuredness and surprise making my breath catch.

Her confidence did that to me every time.

I hadn't expected the word-vomit to happen so abruptly, but I had zero regrets. I didn't want to swallow them back up or shut them away. I wanted to keep them in the ether between us.

Cade took another satisfying swig before setting her glass on the bar. "Then let's go."

I couldn't keep my hands to myself.

I'd always been a bit too handsy onstage as Zesty Zi. That was just a character trait I couldn't separate myself from once the curtains were closed. When Cade told me her apartment was on the sixth floor, and the elevators were down for maintenance, I knew I wouldn't make it up those damn stairs.

I was getting wetter by the second from watching her ass bounce in front of me.

These stairs were going to become a dangerous Slip 'N Slide any second.

I would have hugged Cade's hips and dug my teeth into her delectable ass if people weren't in the hallway. A petite blonde made out with some guy beside an apartment door while another girl knelt down and finagled with the lock, dark curls falling in front of her face. As the guy cupped the blonde's face with one hand, his other hand wandered down into the curls of the girl kneeling. It looked like he was pulling at the roots of her curls…and did a gasp escape the lock picker's lips as we passed?

Where the hell did Cade live?

A brothel?

And why was I turned on by whatever the hell was going on there?

"Four more floors," Cade whispered, pushing open the heavy metal door to the stairwell with her back. I could see the tiniest glimpse of her belly button and the silver loop dangling from the top of it as I passed her to step into the stairwell.

That was all it took.

The moment the door closed, I slammed my hands against the metal behind her, my mouth consuming hers. Her breathing hitched against me as tongues collided. I couldn't stop my hands from wandering to her waist as if there was some kind of magnetic, lustful pull I couldn't—and didn't want to—stop.

She wrapped her hands around my neck.

Her tongue circled and flicked mine.

"I'm going to make you come. Right here," I whimpered, my teeth tugging at her bottom lip as I walked my hand lower, grazing the soft skin below her belly button until I found the elastic of her maxi skirt. "I will not make it up these stairs until you do."

"Demanding," Cade said softly into my mouth. "We're in a dilemma because...you see..." As quickly as this kiss started, Cade's hand flew from the back of my neck down to cup the space between my legs that was pulsing with heat and need. I pushed against her hand, pulling the elastic of her skirt down just a tiny bit to glimpse...her pussy?

Wait.

Cade was not wearing underwear?

Instead of red lace or patterned boy shorts, I saw a patch of dark hair groomed into the most adorable martini-glass shape above a glistening pussy screaming to be touched and teased and licked.

When I slowly yanked the elastic of her skirt down a little farther, she pressed her palm against me with more force, her hips jerking away from my grasp. "No...tonight is for you."

The more she pulled away, her hands sliding beneath my jean skirt, the more I wanted to rip off that fucking skirt of hers with my teeth and consume her.

"Your skirt is easier access than this jean shit," I whimpered as the tips of her fingers teased the edge of my underwear. When I tried to reach for her skirt again, she pulled back more, this time slipping a finger beneath my underwear until it found my clit.

Without hesitation, she gently pinched and rolled the sensitive skin between her fingers and said, "You'll have time to play with me all you want...and believe me, I want that. But I can tell you're usually the giver...not the taker. I want you to give up control. Let me taste you, Dabbler."

I could have come on her hand right then and there.

Instead, I took a deep breath as Cade's lips caressed the side of my neck, working their way down over my chest. Her tongue piercing clashed against the barbell hugging my nipple, sending intense sensation straight to where her hand still was, pinching and stroking.

"You're okay...doing this in the stairway?" I asked softly, her lips trailing downward until her knees were both on the cold ground.

Cade looked up at me, her free hand lifting my denim skirt up so she was at eye level with my sex. Licking her lips with eyes locked on the movement of her fingers, she said, "You're the one who wanted to make me come right here. I'm just stealing your idea. That's all."

"We weren't making it up those stairs without one of us coming," I said, threading my fingers carefully into the textured bun atop her head. "So, yes…this is okay with me. Public sex…is my forte, actually."

It was so hard to focus on what I was saying as her face moved between my thighs, a cool breath of air falling over me. Slowly, she filled me with two fingers, my back arching as Cade said, "I like to say I have pretty refined exhibitionist tendencies. But no more talking…unless you're moaning my name. I need your pretty pussy on my lips."

Before I could register what she'd said, she licked up my folds until my clit was on her tongue. The metal from her piercing shot such intense pleasure through me I feared my grip on her hair was too much, but she leaned into the pain. As her two fingers curled inside of me, finding my G-spot at the same time her tongue flicked against me, I had no other option but to completely hand myself over.

My knees grew weak.

My fingers viciously tugged at her hair.

My pussy thrust against her tongue.

"Jesus, Cade. Keep fucking doing that," I whimpered, biting my bottom lip as I watched her devour me. Cade's eyes met mine, her free hand walking around my thigh to grip my ass as the speed of her fingers quickened.

But it wasn't her nails digging into my ass or how the speed of her fingers and tongue moved in the same flawless rhythm that got to me.

It was the way her eyes quietly, tenaciously connected with mine that pushed me over the edge.

She looked at me like I was the best damn dessert she'd ever had.

She looked at me as if I was the *only* dessert she'd ever order again.

With the back of my head pressing against the brick wall, I thrust my hips forward as my release dripped over Cade's lips. I quivered against her tongue, her motions not slowing down as my body convulsed against her. Her not stopping or slowing only made the orgasm more intense as it pulled at my core, causing my knees to buckle.

I slid against the brick wall until I was a puddle on the floor with my legs straddling either side of her. After licking her fingers clean, she leaned back with a knowing grin. Her eyes wandered from my flushed face down to the denim skirt now acting as a tube top around my chest, my thighs separated and my lace underwear sloppily covering me.

"This is a good look, huh?" I laughed.

"I liked everything about how you looked before, during, and after you came all over my face." Cade licked her lips before sliding both hands up my thighs. "You should come to all of my workshops if this is the reward I get in the end."

"You must be drunk off that mojito, babe, because I think *I'm* the one who got the ultimate reward."

Then the door flew open.

The stairwell door almost smacked my shoulder as the two of us did nothing to leave our spots on the cold, cement floor. The little blonde, the dark-haired guy, and the curly-haired girl who'd been picking the apartment lock barged in, pausing for only a second when they saw the two of us straddled and sweaty on the floor.

The curly-haired woman nodded in our direction, her eyebrows lifted as she followed the other two up the stairs and said, "Nice."

The blonde peeked down at us before disappearing up the stairs and said, "If you guys need somewhere more comfortable for round two, we're down the hall. You look like fun."

With jaws dropped, Cade and I watched the three strangers vanish up the stairs before we turned back to one another, exhaustion and surprise painted across our heated cheeks.

"Your neighbors sure are friendly." I couldn't keep my eyes from falling to her lips. Those plump, delicious, talented lips. "I'd take them up on their offer…but I want you all to myself tonight. I *need* you all to myself."

Cade folded over her legs so she could cup my face with both hands, her thumb running across the underside of my chin. "You got me. I'm all yours."

Chapter 29

Nel

“**W**e're back for another week of Steamy Storytime and...it looks like most of the regulars are here!” I said, squinting toward the bottom where the viewers names were listed. “And...wow...I see a bunch of new viewers came to get in on the action tonight...and there will be some *action*. Welcome, MotherLoose365 and stanford.the.sandwich_03. Hello to Millen-nialMomMel36 and...”

Then I felt it.

A gentle ping of pleasure trembled up through me the second I tried reading another name.

It wasn't to the point of extreme distraction, but it was noticeable and...felt like fucking heaven. Jude sat on the couch, holding back a grin, his hand wrapped around the remote as the other brought wine to his lips. When he set the wine back down, his eyebrows lifted, and he cocked his head to the side. He lifted the remote a little higher as he brought his finger to the upward arrow.

A short gasp escaped my lips. The vibration was growing more intense both inside of me and out. I covered my lips and tried to focus on the screen in front of me before saying, "This may be...a shorter session tonight. But I can't wait to...read about Laney, Cal, and Juan. They...they absolutely don't hold back tonight, and since they don't...neither should we."

I couldn't help but glimpse at Jude sitting on the couch, witnessing and taking part in this torturous sensation. He was so focused on every word I was saying, so engrossed in every twitch of my body as I leaned into the pleasure.

One hand clutched the book by my thigh, and the other slid up my belly and chest, pausing at my neck. My entire body was humming, and every nerve ending felt on the brink of explosion. It was the most delectable tease.

But I didn't want to experience this alone.

If Jude was going to watch me linger on the edge all night, I wanted to watch him do the same.

"So...get comfortable. Let yourself become one of the characters. Try to feel what they're feeling." My attention migrated from Jude's wild eyes, to his hand clutching the remote, to just below where his arm balanced across his thigh. I could tell he was attempting to hide how his body felt, and from what I'd recently learned, Jude didn't hide anymore.

I didn't want him to.

Not tonight, not ever.

"And when I say *get comfortable*, I mean it. I don't want to be the...only one *really* getting into the story. I want you to listen to the story, but also...let yourself go completely. Don't hide a damn thing."

Finding the chapter we hoped to get through tonight, I could tell Jude heard—no, *listened*—to what I'd said. His arm moved aside, revealing the button and zipper of his jeans—denim that looked uncomfortably tight. With his face still angled downward, his eyes asked me a silent question, and I subtly nodded in response, my bottom lip finding its way between my top teeth yet again.

"Let's get started..." I said, forcing my attention back to the livestream. "Last week, we saw the friendship between Juan, Cal, and Laney...bloom, in a way. This week, we...we will see it get a little more intense when they take it into...the bedroom for the first time. Together."

I began reading the words on the page, soft vibration humming against my clit and making my G-spot quiver more with every sentence. For a few minutes, I didn't look up at all—not at the screen and not at Jude, who shifted on the couch. I needed to get through this damn scene without completely giving in to the sensation consuming me.

Peering away from the book to ask the viewers a question about the passage, I quickly glimpsed at Jude for the first time in about three minutes.

The second he came into view, I realized he'd understood my message loud and clear. He'd even taken it upon himself to edge *me* a little bit more.

And fuck, had he taken the assignment seriously.

He was no longer just teasing me through his control of the remote—which he clicked to a higher intensity the second I looked up. He was also teasing me by being several feet away—completely out of reach—with his hard length in his hand, stroking himself as he clicked the remote two more times.

This time when the vibration grew hungrier, I reached down and cupped the vibrator, the book dropping from my grasp. The pressure of my palm against it only heightened my arousal, and when I looked up at Jude, his smile was feral.

Savage.

Wild.

His hand moved up and down at a speed matching the vibration between my legs as I noticed the head of his cock growing damp and impatient.

Viewers were probably wondering if I was having a heart attack or if I'd peed myself. Without even scrolling through the comments, I looked into the camera and said, "We are experienc-ing...uh, technical difficulties. I...I will finish this chapter during Rowdy Readers...on Wednesday."

Once I tapped the OFF button to end the livestream—my trembling finger missing it the first couple of tries—I slammed the laptop shut and unbuttoned the bottom of my lace romper. I yanked out the vibrator with a high-pitched moan. Grabbing my glasses and shaking off the wig, I watched the dark hair fall to the ground easily—a reminder to add more bobby pins next time.

On all fours, I crawled around the closed laptop. "Are you trying to make me lose followers, sir?"

"Never," he whispered, watching as I placed my hands at the edge of the sofa.

"Oh, really? Because I'm pretty sure I just lost a few while I was completely losing my mind."

"Was it worth it?" His voice was so hushed that the words barely escaped his lips.

But I'd heard them as if he'd screamed them at the top of his fucking lungs.

Pulling myself onto the couch and straddling his knees as his hand continued to pump, I dipped down slowly and licked the head of his cock, savoring the beads of pre-cum. "What do you think?"

I didn't wait to hear his response before running my tongue from the base of his cock up to the glistening head, my ass in the air and back arched as I wrapped my lips around him. His hands released, making way for my own hands to take over his motions. I took him deeper, a soft gag sounding as I repeated the action again and again.

His fingers dove into my mess of hair and tightened at the roots, pulling me away from him. My eyes were teary behind crooked frames, my lips swollen and dripping in pre-cum and saliva and need.

For someone who'd never been very keen on giving blow jobs, I didn't want to be done with him yet. I wanted to taste him until he couldn't hold back any longer. I wanted to watch him squirm just like he'd watched me.

"I'm not done, Jude," I whispered as his grip on the roots of my hair tightened, tasting his breath as his face grew closer.

"No. You're not, but I can't wait any longer to know how it feels to be inside of you." He released my hair, and I gasped, his hand trailing down the side of my face and along my jawline. Running his thumb over my swollen lips, he whispered, "I've held back for ten years, Nel. I can't anymore."

"Don't. Don't hold back." When I tried folding back over to taste him, one hand quickly returned to my hair, as the other brushed a knuckle from my chin to the center of my throat.

Jude chuckled in a way that was both maniacal and trusting—a combination I never knew existed.

"Please, Jude..." I whimpered, his hand widening over my throat, fingers tightening. "No more holding back."

"Say it again," he growled.

Swallowing against the pressure of his hand, I whispered, "Please."

A ravenous grin pinched his cheeks, one that his beard could never mask. He pressed his lips to mine, his tongue winding into my mouth. Sparks of heat shot directly between my legs in a way no vibrator could ever mimic.

When he released his lips from mine, our foreheads pressed together, and he whispered, "Good girl. Now, get on your back. If

I don't bury my cock inside you in the next minute, I'll completely fucking lose it."

"Maybe I want you to lose it," I teased, wiggling out of his grasp and sliding off the couch.

"Floor. Now."

The faux-fur rug tickled my back as I lay down, Jude following my lead and stepping over my body in a standing straddle above me. He hadn't fully stuffed himself back into his pants, and I didn't blame him. If I had a cock that hard, stuffing it back in my pants would be the last place I'd want it. So, all I could do was lie there and stare up at his throbbing erection as he slipped off his jeans and boxer briefs, throwing them onto the chair behind us.

Yanking his beanie off and tossing it into the pile, he ran tattooed hands through his dark hair and said, "That lace thing needs to come off before I completely rip it off you...and it looks like that would take me a whole two seconds to do."

He yanked his crewneck up over his head in one motion. His messy locks barely touched his lean shoulders—shoulders covered in black-and-gray illustrations of flowers and insects and characters I didn't recognize. The ink didn't stop at his shoulders. It continued down over his chest and lessened the lower it got on his stomach, more tattoos wrapping around his ribs and scattering across his back.

I wanted to outline every one of them with the tip of my tongue.

"Do it," I whispered.

Jude lowered himself to his knees, the base of his cock pressing against my entrance barricaded by lace. "Do what, Nel?"

"Rip it off."

Jude barely hesitated, his fingers digging into the lace at my sternum and swinging his arm into the air. The sound of ripping fabric echoed through the living room as both of his hands tore the lace off my body, leaving only my thin, black bra and thong visible.

I wasn't brave enough to go commando under this stuff just yet.

But the more fabric Jude ripped, the more I felt my confidence growing. He didn't care about the stretch marks staring up at him. He didn't care that my tits drooped a little into my armpits as I lay on the floor.

All he cared about was how I felt in this moment—how *we* were feeling.

Nothing and no one else.

"You know there were buttons down there," I said as he pressed the lace shreds into a ball and tossed it onto the chair. "You could have just unbuttoned it and had your way with me, you know. I'm going to have to make a story up about how this got ripped to your sis—"

He brought a flattened hand into the air. "No. Nel. Don't bring her up right now. Nope."

I giggled, rolling my hips against him.

I really would have to figure out how to explain to Rosie that her lace romper was no more.

He buried his face into my neck, one hand yanking down my bra to pinch one of my nipples between his fingers. My back arched in response to the mix of pleasure and pain before I heard him say, "If I'd just unbuttoned the bottom, then you would have hidden behind the fabric. I want to see *all* of you, Nel. Everything. Like you said...no holding back. No more hiding."

He unclipped my bra, adding it to our growing pile of clothes, before pinning both of my wrists onto the rug. There was nowhere for my tits to hide. There was no leaning into the dim lighting of the bed and breakfast like last time. The Edison bulbs forced an unforgiving glow over my body.

As his eyes roamed my body, I could tell he wasn't seeing the flawed, postpartum body I usually saw when I looked in the mirror. His grin didn't give off the energy of someone judging.

It was the exact opposite.

"Birth control." His lips barely moved when he said the words, his eyes still roving across my skin. "You're on it. Yes?"

I nodded quickly, my tits bouncing and forcing his attention back up my body. "I asked them to shove the strongest IUD they could up there."

Jude snorted out the sweetest laugh and dropped his head, hair falling forward and grazing my bare chest. "You *really* had to say it that way, didn't you?"

"It was worth seeing you smile." I bit my lip, trying to shrug against his firm grasp. "...and break a little bit."

He looked at me with thin, hungry eyes and said, "You've been breaking me for years, Nel. Now it's my turn to watch you fall apart. In all the best ways."

Releasing his hands from my wrists, he reached down for the thin piece of fabric between my legs and pulled it down my thighs and off my ankles before I kicked it the rest of the way off. Wrapping his fingers back around my wrists, he leaned forward so his throbbing cock pressed against my clit. I wanted to move my wrists and yank him down on top of me. With every tortuous roll of his hips, I felt the pressure and sensation inside of me building up.

Freeing one of my wrists, he reached beneath my legs and gently pushed two fingers inside as my free hand shot straight into his hair, my fingers clenching as my back arched against him. He grinned, pushing in farther and twisting his wrist.

"Holy shit. Get inside me, Jude...now." I clawed deeper into his dark hair as his fingers moved quickly inside my heat, his hips rolling with every thrust of his hand. "I...I can't take it."

"Oh, Nel..." Jude whispered, removing his damp fingers, leaving me wet, empty, and on the goddamn edge. After adjusting his hips a little more against my folds, his head fell into the crook of my neck, and he said, "But you can."

Before I could think up a response or beg him to fill me, he was already sliding into my screaming pussy, holding himself deep inside as he outlined my jawbone with the tip of his tongue. The sound I made was animalistic—a moan of pleasure and freedom and ecstasy. His breath was hot against my neck as he pushed himself deeper inside of me, my free hand racing to cover my mouth as my eyes rolled back.

He thrust forward again—two, three, four more times—before he freed my other wrist and straightened both of his arms to hover a few inches above me. He created a scooping motion with his hips, hitting my G-spot in a way that made me uncontrollably jerk against him.

"Oh my...oh my fucking God. Yes. Do that again. *Please* do that again," I begged, my fingers crawling out of his hair down to his shoulder blades where my nails left trenches in the patterns of ink on his skin.

He listened, moving himself inside of me in the same way he just had, my body convulsing against him.

I'd had orgasms before...but *nothing* compared to this. Every single nerve ending was on fire. Goosebumps sprinkled every inch of my bare skin. My back arched, my chest open to Jude as he took a nipple between his teeth.

"Tell me how it feels, pretty girl." Jude's voice rumbled against my chest before licking circles around my nipple, raw pleasure filling my body. "Tell me what it's like to feel me inside of you...because this feels even better than I imagined you to feel after all these years."

"You...you imagined this? You thought about...this...even after you left?"

His hips crashed hard into mine, and a moan dripped over my lips. He cupped the bottom of my chin, forcing my gaze back to his, and whispered, "Nel, I've wanted this—wanted you—since meeting you that first month of freshman year. I wanted you every single time you helped me flirt with a girl I didn't care about. I wanted you when I didn't come back to Merlin sophomore year—*especially* then—because I knew I'd probably lost my chance with you forever. I *knew* I had."

His fingers loosened around my chin, and the back of his hand slid up my cheek, caressing my face with such softness. I leaned into his hand, closing my eyes as he pushed himself even deeper inside of me, and his mouth fell over mine.

This time, the kiss was different.

It wasn't messy and desperate and hungry.

It was filled with warmth, and longing, and maybe even a little hope.

He pushed inside of me in slow, sensual waves. My insides screamed for release, and I wanted to both savor this feeling and completely let it go. The shift of his movements and this new, unfiltered glow in his eyes showed me he, too, was on the verge.

"You...you didn't, Jude."

Hair falling over his flushed face, he asked, "Didn't what?"

I balled both my hands into his hair and brought his forehead to mine. My breath was ragged and uneven, hands trembling as I said, "Lose your chance. You didn't lose it, because this, right here, is another one. It's...another chance to make it right this time."

His speed quickened, his face falling back into its comfortable place in the crook of my neck as his back muscles tensed and strained. "Getting another chance at making you mine... Is that what you want?"

Heat and vibration pulsed inside of me, and before I completely let go, I brushed my lips across the edge of his ear and whispered, "Jude...I'm yours."

Cries of pleasure.

Nails digging skin.

Heat of release.

We both came undone beside the bookshelf, my heart crawling out of my skin as I realized this man was finally mine.

And the opinions of others couldn't sway a feeling like this.

Chapter 30

Rosie

After Mae screamed most of Tuesday night and barely let Nel finish her chapter during Rowdy Readers, sleeping in on Thursday was a given. The mix of teething gel and Tylenol seemed to work wonders on her vampire teeth because she slept like a fucking tank for almost five hours straight.

This was all wonderful.

It was dandy.

Sleeping for five hours straight was a goddamn miracle.

What wasn't wonderful and dandy was the doorbell ringing at eight-thirty in the morning.

Even though I didn't have a kind bone in my body before noon on most days, I didn't want the noise to wake the kraken—and this went for both Nel *and* Mae. I dragged myself through the kitchen in my thin, white tank top—shorts were unnecessary now that summer had arrived—and reached for the handle before peeking out the window first. Dewy morning air caused my bare nipples to become far too noticeable through the fabric as I blocked the sun turning my eyeballs to ash.

This was hell.

I needed to start apartment hunting.

And figure out this job thing...fast.

"Well, good morning to you too," the voice in front of me hummed.

A *very* familiar voice.

Pink hair and tattooed arms wrapped around me, followed by a kiss on the cheek.

"Um...Viv?" I said as she pulled my chest tighter against hers.

"Hold on...I've missed how this feels." Viv pulled me in even closer before bringing her hands to either side of my face. "This was *definitely* how I hoped you'd answer the door."

"What...what are you doing here?" I asked, stepping back into the entryway as she followed me inside. "You know I'm comatose until, like, one."

"We had a pop-up show at Three-Ring last night...I texted you about it." Viv stepped closer and laced her fingers through mine as she bit her bottom lip, looking up at me through wide, doe-like eyes. "So, when you didn't answer...decisions were made. I wasn't leaving Merlin without giving you the pleasure of seeing...touching...me before I left."

"Huh?" I snorted, adjusting to the unforgiving sunlight. "I don't even like morning sex."

Viv pouted her lips and squeezed my cheeks firmer between her hands, shaking my head back and forth. "What is this negativity, Zizi? You tease me for weeks on The Naked Book Club, and now you're too *tired* to touch me? Tsk, tsk."

"I mean...it's kind of my job to tease everyone on there." I shook my head against her hands and stepped back, running a hand through my hair and leaning against the wall near the entryway closet.

Viv stepped closer, wrapping an arm around my waist and tugging me close. "What is with you, Zi? No texts. No calls. Not even the tiniest bit of flirting after not seeing me for a month. Are you still butt-hurt about the heels debacle?"

"Are you asking if I'm butt-hurt about being cut from The Bare Assentials? No, I am not *butt-hurt* anymore," I said, my head falling back. When my eyelids shut, I pictured the duffel bag of broken heels sitting in the closet I still needed to burn. I needed to have a bonfire soon. "You're hot. I like seeing you. I like fucking you. But I always hoped *you'd* answer *my* texts and calls too. Most of the time, I get radio silence."

"Zi, it's been this way since I got you the spot in the troupe. You help me come, I help you come, and we live our sexy little lives." Viv threaded her fingers through my hair. "We *need* each other."

"I got myself a spot in the troupe." My head shot up with a furrowed brow. "*You* helped get me back on my feet. *You* helped me learn choreography for auditions, yes. But *I* kicked my ass to get in. That was me."

Viv rolled her eyes before curling her fingers through the hair at the nape of my neck. "*Okay*, Zi. That ass definitely helped you get in."

"Viv?" Nel's hushed voice cut through the air as she appeared in the kitchen with Mae—wide-eyed and awake—in her arms. Looking from me to Viv and then back, Nel said, "Uh…hi, Viv. What…what are you doing here?"

"I had a pop-up last night. When *this one* didn't answer my calls, I took it into my own hands. She had to see me before I left." Viv's hand slid from my hair down to meet her other hand still wrapped at my waist. I was too tired—and confused and annoyed—to wriggle from her grasp. "But it seems she doesn't want to actually see *all* of me right now."

I wanted to just shut myself in Nel's bedroom and go back to fucking sleep. "The sun isn't even up yet."

Viv booped the tip of my nose. "That rarely stopped you before…but I'll let you rest. I'll be back in the area sometime in early August. I hope next time, you answer the door *completely* naked."

"I may be busy."

Viv released her grip from my waist. "With what? Your book stuff?"

"We're planning Mae's birthday party," Nel interjected, setting Mae down so she could crawl into the living room. "She turns one on August 15th."

"And then we're packing up and moving out." The words shocked both Nel and myself, our eyes locking with this realization.

We'd been so distracted with The Naked Book Club—and maybe a couple other things too...or *people*—that we'd forgotten why we started it in the first place. We needed to find apartments, make ongoing, solid income, and move the fuck forward with our lives.

But it was hard clearly seeing those steps when I didn't want to make The Naked Book Club my second or third priority.

I loved it being my first.

"That all sounds like a lot of fun...lots and *lots* of fun." Viv opened the door as more unnecessary sunlight blinded my view. This was all too much to take before nine o'clock in the morning. "The bus leaves in ten minutes, so I need to go. I'll see you in August, baby. I know by then you'll be in Viper withdrawal and *need* a taste."

Then she flipped the bottom of her skirt up so I could see her ass cheeks jiggle as she walked out the front door.

Nel and I stood there for a minute, Mae chattering to herself as she pulled her little body up to stand by the couch. We stared at the closed door, our minds not only processing Viv's very awkward visit but also the reality that we needed to figure out our next steps.

And quickly.

"Well," I said, clapping my hands together and turning on my heel to face Nel. "At least she didn't flip up the front of her skirt...am I right?"

Nel crossed her arms over her chest. "If she had, would it have turned you on?"

My hands stayed clasped together at my chest mid-clap.

My lips pressed together.

I paused.

That pause answered the question without my saying a word.

"What a psychopath!" Sebastian shouted, slamming the frosted glass of his beer onto the bar. "I mean, don't get me wrong...she's hot. But still...cheers to *hot* psychopaths!"

Rolling my eyes, I slumped over in my seat, thankful Thirsty Theodore's was smart enough to have backs on their bar stools when my bones turned to slime. I felt like a blob with a beer. "Since when did all of you think Viv was a psychopath?"

"I mean...the red flags have been there since you started talking about her," Jude said, facing me as he tossed a couple tater tots from the basket into his mouth. "That first night I dragged you out of here, you whined about how she hadn't answered your texts after they'd cut you from the troupe."

"Well...she hadn't!" I exclaimed, grabbing a handful of tater tots and stuffing them into my face, melted cheese and crispy bacon becoming a thing of beauty on my tongue. "And believe it or not,

I'm *not* a nonstop texter or caller. If you don't answer me after a couple tries, I say *fuck it* and wait a while. You know this probably more than anyone, Jude. She never responded that night, so I ended up here."

"She didn't even talk to you after getting fired?" Sebastian asked, setting his elbows on the bar so he could see around Jude.

Fired.

It sounded too final, too definite.

I'd been honest about the pain I was experiencing. I'd offered an alternative to wearing heels, and they declined.

I'd stayed true to myself.

I did nothing wrong.

"She'd told me to shake it off and that I'd be fine." The text was still burned onto the backs of my eyelids. "I'd asked her to come over to my hotel room that night, and she said she was busy but would see me soon. That was it. She didn't knock when the bus left the next morning. The next time I saw her, it was here, on that stage."

"And you didn't get pissed after that and kick her out of your life?" Sebastian asked, eyebrows lifted. "I would have deleted her number...and her."

Looking down into my beer, I nodded. I could have done just that. I could have never answered one of her texts ever again. I could have left her—and the troupe—behind me without uncertainty and loneliness weighing me down.

But I'd felt that weight on my shoulders. I'd felt this magnetic pull come back time and time again, leading me into her arms. Maybe I looked weak for running back to her every time, but she'd been my comfort. She'd helped me find a career I loved. She'd handed me hope.

"Yeah..." I whispered. "I could have. I *should* have. It's just...not that easy. And I hate admitting it's not that easy, but it's the truth."

"I don't fully understand it," Sebastian admitted. "But I still think she's a psychopath."

"You *have* to stop throwing that word around." Riley took his glasses off and rubbed his eyes. "You can't joke around with that shit. It's a serious personality disorder."

"Sorry. *Hot* psychopath."

"Nope. Not any better," Jude interjected, gesturing behind the bar to Andy, the bartender, for another cream ale. "Rowe, somehow you have to find a way to just move on. Believe me...I know it's easier said than done. Hell, I moved across the country in hopes of mentally *moving on* from...you know."

I slammed back the final swig of my beer before asking, "Well, did it help? Because from where I'm sitting with all of this, I really can't tell."

"I mean, a little," Jude said, Andy sliding a frosted glass into my brother's palm. "Am I kind of back where I started? Yes. But that time away did me some good. It helped me find myself, and I needed that. When you put the past in the past and only take it out when it benefits your future, things get better."

"You found us too, dude," Sebastian exclaimed from Jude's side, practically knocking over the brew in Riley's hands. "You found yourself *and* us."

"I think we found each other, asshole," Riley said, shaking his head.

"What about Cade?" my brother asked.

My spine went from slime to straighter than a fucking board. "Cade?"

"I'm no idiot, Rosie—even though I've dealt with enough people who think I am one," Jude said. "The dancer."

"I feel like she's fucked with a lot of dancers, so you may need to clarify," Sebastian said loud enough for the couple in the booth behind him to snicker.

He wasn't wrong.

"The one who dances on the college lawn, right?" Riley added, popping his head behind Sebastian to catch my gaze. "I've seen you guys a couple times when I run by campus."

"Like...*physically* run?" Sebastian asked, dumbstruck.

Jude's eyebrows practically hit the stupid knit hat he was still wearing, even with it being summer. I guess he had a look he wasn't willing to part with.

Blinking dramatically, Jude asked, "With sneakers? *That* kind of run?"

It was my turn. "Outside? You run outside?"

"Yes, douchebags. A physical run outside with sneakers," Riley stated monotonously. "I run before Java opens once in a while. Sometimes, I slip away at lunch."

"I thought you played video games upstairs on your lunch breaks," Jude murmured.

"What the fuck, dude," Sebastian cried. "I'd run with you if you asked!"

"You'd wake up at 5:00 AM or run during your lunch break when you typically take a nap?"

Sebastian quickly finished his beer. "You have a point."

"You never answered my question, though." Jude turned away from Riley, his gaze fixed on me.

"You never specified what you were asking." Now was as good a time as ever to order another drink. "I'll have whatever cream ale he's having, thanks."

"What's going on with her?" Jude's voice held a curiously demanding edge to it. "You go out of your way to spend time with her. Nel even said you took one of her workshops."

"Okay, yes. I spend time with her, and I took one of her workshops." My beer arrived right on cue. "She's a good person with good energy. It's good. Good, good, good."

"What about Viv?" Jude asked. "Does Viv have good energy?"

Why was my brother roasting me like this?

"Ha!" Sebastian's laugh echoed across the bar. "I'm *sure* she does."

For the first time in what felt like forever, Jude and I twinned perfectly with our eye rolls.

"Viv's energy is…different. I'm an extroverted, in-charge bitch with a personality few people can handle. She's a corrupt, persuasive nymphomaniac who introduced me to this whole burlesque world. So, it's hard freeing myself from her claws when I've been under them since the start."

"Huh." Our heads all turned toward Riley, who was finishing his beer.

"Yes…" Sebastian said, pushing his elbow into Riley's ribs. "Do you have something to share with the class?"

Riley pushed his empty glass away from where our elbows could hit it. "This sounds a little like separation anxiety—which is a nice way of saying co-dependency—with Viv *and* with burlesque. I think when you see her, you see how she *saved* you. She brought you back up high after feeling so low. Since you're seeing all this now, I think you're mad at yourself for not walking away sooner, but you're also afraid to take that step. I'm not diagnosing you or anything, but that's just my two cents."

We all stared at Riley.

Jaws slowly fell to the floor.

My hand shifted in Riley's direction, my middle finger twitching in the way it usually did when I wanted to playfully avoid difficult conversations. But this time, I forced my immature reaction aside and replayed his monologue in my head.

Riley was digging his teeth into a topic unrelated to coffee roasting or secret threesomes...or, apparently, running.

Those were the most words I'd ever heard him string together, and though I didn't want to admit it, he made a very valid point. I rarely admitted to feeling emotional or weak, but that was exactly how I felt with Viv, and burlesque, and the uncertainty of what I wanted to do with my damn life. Maybe *weak* wasn't the right word to describe the emotions twisting in my gut.

Maybe fear was.

I was scared to step into this new phase of life.

I was scared to push away a toxic relationship—situationship—that held me back from being all I could be.

Some fucked-up part of me *still* wanted the two of us to work out, to be the spicy love story I read about in my books—even though that was *never* her end goal.

But one thing I did know, was that I cared about Cade. *A lot.* Probably more than I'd genuinely ever cared for, well, anyone in this way before.

"Huh…" I responded, finally shaking myself out of the fog Riley forced me into. "You're right."

"Did you just admit to being wrong?" Jude asked, dramatically leaning away from me.

"Yeah…okay, *Dr.* Riley," Sebastian said, waving down the new bartender, a curvy redhead with tits falling out of her top that I would have drooled over months ago. "Since when did you become so fluent in this psychological mind-reading stuff?"

Riley smiled down at his fingers still tapping on the bar. "Since I got my degree in clinical social work twelve years ago." He lifted his head, the sienna skin of his cheeks flushing the slightest bit as he grinned. "But that was before I met you losers during that D&D one-shot in Arizona and decided I wanted coffee to fuel my life…not the weight of other people's trauma."

"That's probably the most selfishly satisfying thing I've ever heard," I said, lifting my glass into the air. "To coffee, dragons, and dealing with everyone else's bullshit before figuring out your own."

With fresh brews cooling our palms, we lifted our glasses and listened to the chime of change as our glasses clinked.

Now I had to figure out how the hell I was going to navigate this change.

yourEyesOnly.com
LIVE
LIKE SUBSCRIBE COMMENTS
@SaltyKaren12: Come on, Chef Lee...
that apron is unnecessary.
@feedmedaddy: Was that a
dash of salt added to the
lentils?
VEGAN VIXENS

Chapter 31

NEL

More and more subscribers joined our livestreams each week. I'd thrown a survey onto our page one week to see why people subscribed: 25% were there for the comments; 25% were there for the sexual appeal; 50% were there for the books.

I did not believe it.

How were most people not just tuning in to see some ass cheeks once and a while?

People were actually there for the stories.

That was what kept me going.

Even though, more and more, I was looking forward to going solo on Steamy Storytime each week, I also knew the reality of the situation. I couldn't rely on The Naked Book Club forever. I needed to find an actual job that, once moved into a new apartment, I could rely on. I needed something that would build my professional resume.

My stomach hadn't stopped twisting since Theía Elena's call last night. She checked in on the status of my apartment search and asked if I'd need movers, since she had a good connection. Her excitement for prettying up the place, selling it, and heading off toward the Mediterranean Sea for good was palpable and added more anxiety into the mix.

With everything going on—Theía Elena's call, Jude, The Naked Book Club, the apartment and job search, and planning Mae's party—it made sense I'd end up here.

And that was on Dr. Delilah's couch.

Well...really, I was on the floor, being used as Mae's balance support while she repeatedly tried to let go, walk a step, and fall.

"All rollercoasters must take that ride down sooner or later. You just have to be prepared for the fall," Dr. Delilah said, spinning her chair using the pointed tip of her heel. "I know you know this already. If you didn't, you wouldn't have called."

Mae fell into my chest, gurgling something against my shirt as her hands wandered back to my shoulder so she could steady herself. "I'm very grateful for last-minute cancelations."

"Indeed," she said, threading her fingers together on her lap. "So, you mentioned you've applied to some places? That's a great start on top of the freelancing you've been doing."

Freelancing.

You could call it that.

"Yeah…I applied for a tutoring position at St. Merlin Academy and filled out a form to do some copywriting for a realtor. Merlin's infamous Real Estate Ringleader wants to expand his brand and is looking for some help. Marketing isn't really my forte—I've only done some content for blogs and websites—so I'm doubtful he'd choose me for this gig." I set the side of my head on Mae's little hand as it clasped my shoulder, her fingers wiggling and tickling the edge of my ear. "I just don't think *anyone* would choose me at this point. I mean, I have the English associate's degree and just finished the online program, but I don't have a long, lengthy resume to impress anyone with. There's a huge break in my employment, which is *not* attractive. Why would they choose me over—"

"Hey, Nel." A glass of water appeared in front of my face, Delilah's fingers pressing against the dewy glass. "Breathe and take a sip. Then I want you to try this again…but do it in a way *you'll* be proud of."

I took a long swig, the liquid cooling my insides. I focused on the water in the way Delilah taught me to back when prenatal depression first smacked me across the face. At twelve weeks along, I remembered crying every morning when my alarm went off, my body unwilling to get out of bed. It was our first or second session when I listened to her explain this method and laughed at her.

How the hell could taking a sip of goddamn water calm anyone down—especially someone pregnant and beyond depressed?

The cold water sifted through my organs and muscles, hydrating them and keeping them healthy and alive.

On the next sip, I shut my eyes and thought about how that sip fueled growth within me, even if I couldn't feel it—or see it—just yet.

I focused on how, even when this glass was empty, it was still strong and sturdy enough to fill back up again.

"Okay," I whispered, setting the glass onto the corner of her desk as Mae let go of my shoulder, taking a step before falling to her knees. "Okay. I don't think I have the experience...but that doesn't mean I shouldn't try."

Every word felt like a bruise.

But at least I'd said them.

"Yes," Delilah said, setting my glass by her mini fridge—alongside three other ones. "Keep going."

"Um...so, if they call back, I'll go to the interview and just see what happens. It's better I try than give up before I get the chance. So...yeah."

"That's *much* better than before."

Mae's hands pulled at my shirt again as they made their way back to my shoulder for balance. "Before my worried word-vomit went all over your office."

"Sometimes word-vomit is necessary, though. It feels good to get it out, as gross as that sounds." Delilah laughed, wrapping a finger around a red curl before bouncing it free. "Let's shift a little bit. Jude. Things seem to be in a different place than the last time you were physically in here."

My heart dropped into my stomach the second she mentioned his name. "Yeah...yeah, a little. He's...he's, um..." My breath turned into a ball of ice in my throat. "We're in a really good place."

Why the fuck couldn't I just say it?

He was *mine*.

I was *his*.

He. Was. My. Boyfriend.

"That's great to hear, Nel," Delilah said, clapping her hands together. "I'm glad that friendship is getting back to where you want it to be."

"Yeah...it is." I felt my cheeks flush with color as the ice lodged in my throat softened. "He's helped me a little with my...my freelance work. We all went on that weekend trip together earlier this year, which was a major step for us."

Delilah nodded slowly, the corner of her pink lips turning up. "How has this shift in your friendship affected everything else you have going on?"

I hadn't stepped back to look at my situation from a distance. Instead of sifting through my emotions, I found myself crying one minute and laughing the next. I found myself giddy and smiling the second Jude texted me and then anxious as I scrolled through Hallie's latest posts.

I'd have the best orgasm of my life one minute and then, ten minutes later, roll over and question whether I deserved to feel this good after making *him* feel that bad years ago.

My eyes wandered from Mae, now crawling to her diaper bag near the door, to Delilah who sat in her chair. Though her gaze was soft, it felt like a heavy blanket fell over my shoulders—the pressure soothing but also weighing me down. I wanted to feel comfortable telling her everything. I mean, I'd never held back before.

So why was I holding back telling her about Jude?

Or the Naked Book Club?

Maybe I feared her reaction.

Or maybe it was embarrassment. Was I embarrassed to admit I enjoyed The Naked Book Club? Was I embarrassed to talk about Jude because I hated what Past Me did to him?

Or was I embarrassed because part of me still couldn't get Hallie's voice—her opinion—out of my head?

If it was embarrassment I felt, I preferred fear.

I didn't remember sticking Mae into her car seat or pulling my own seatbelt on. I didn't remember using almost all the tissues in the car to dry my eyes—eyes leaking for reasons I honestly couldn't pinpoint. I didn't realize it was raining until I stepped out of the car, covering Mae's car seat with a muslin blanket I'd yanked from the depths of my diaper bag. I didn't even remember rushing into the entryway and slamming the door behind me, setting the back of my head against the door as I set Mae down.

What I did remember, however, was the noise that woke me from my trance.

"Surprise!"

Voices shouted.

Confetti flew.

A mandolin played and...was that a harmonica?

Mae screamed.

And I fell to my knees beside her, letting my hands catch the tears I couldn't stop from falling.

"Oh, shit..." Rosie said, walking over and kneeling down beside us. She began rocking Mae in her car seat with one hand as the other wrapped around my shoulders.

"Fuck," Jude whispered, "I told you she *still* probably hates birthdays, Rosie."

"Wha...what?" I lifted my head to see Jude picking confetti out of his beard and Riley placing what was, in fact, a harmonica into his pocket.

"Chill with that shit, Seb," Jude said, his arm replacing Rosie's as his sister pulled Mae from her car seat.

Sebastian stopped playing his rendition of "Happy Birthday," the silence—minus Mae's quieting cries—piecing everything in my brain back into place.

"Holy shit. I'm thirty-one."

"Welcome to the club," Jude whispered, his lips brushing away salty tears lingering on my cheeks. Nodding toward Rosie, he said, "I *did* tell her this may not be a great idea after what happened at MCC, but she pushed."

"It's out of love, goddammit!" Rosie began setting up a line of shot glasses on the kitchen counter as Mae clung to her, reaching for the balloon tied to the neck of a bottle of Patron.

Jude's lips hovered over my ear. "I said we should have just gotten you a pygmy octopus instead and called it a day."

It felt like my tears were being sucked back into the ducts they'd come from. Wiping my nose on the back of my hand, I whispered, "You remember."

Jude kicked a cluster of confetti to the side of the entryway. "You don't forget something like that, especially when your dorm room was decorated in posters of octopodi."

"Octopodes." I stood up, clicking my overall strap back into place before pulling the denim down over my thighs.

"Octo*puses.*"

I giggled because...how couldn't you? "Octopi."

"What the fuck is going on?" Sebastian asked, swinging his mandolin over his chest.

"They obviously have a sea creature kink," Riley said quietly from Rosie's side, Mae giggling as he covered his face and then uncovered it in the most adorable game of peek-a-boo I'd ever seen.

"Weird." Sebastian began strumming softly, a light yet upbeat tune slowly coming to life, in the kitchen. "But I'm not one to judge."

"You're the one who was into that dragon dong at Velvet!" Rosie shouted from the counter. "If you guys are done *octopussing* around, let's take a shot for the birthday girl...and then we can stop celebrating if she wants. We can just say the ice cream cake is for celebrating The Naked Book Club hitting 5,000 followers. But you know...it's no big deal."

My jaw hit the confetti-covered floor. "What? Wait...*seriously*?"

Nodding, Rosie pushed a shot glass in my direction. "Serious as fuck. I'm not sure how the hell we hit that number, but that's what the dashboard says...and the dashboard is God. There was this big banner across the screen congratulating us for hitting the milestone. Apparently, now we'll *really* be pushed into the algorithm and get seen by more people. I'm going to have to reach out to some more indie authors...ones who write sapphic stories."

"Rosie!" I jogged—more like shuffled—around the counter and threw my arms around her. "That's huge! That cake should be a *thank-you* cake for you making this happen!"

"Nah...this wouldn't be a thing if it weren't for you too. We need your sassy reading voice and occasional nip slips. This has been a team effort, Nel."

My gut twisted—a little because I didn't want to take the shot she was sliding my way and because of how proud she was of all we'd done these last handful of months.

Not that I wasn't.

I was damn proud that her idea had become an unexpectedly big success.

I just couldn't keep doing this thing forever if I wanted to be taken seriously.

No matter how much joy it brought me, I needed a career that didn't include getting half naked for the world to see.

Peering back up at Rosie, her smile beaming with pride, I feared the day this conversation would happen.

Chapter 32

Rosie

"**Y**ou guys *really* went with the *ONEder the Sea* theme, huh?" I asked, setting down a tote of uninflated balloons, streamers, mermaid-shaped confetti, and ceramic centerpieces in Nora's backyard that probably wouldn't last ten minutes around toddlers.

Nora stepped back up onto the ladder as Nel passed her another roll of tape and said, "Would you expect anything less?"

"We got octopus balloons!" Ari shouted as she walked into the backyard and placed a cardboard box onto the picnic table. "Well...they're not inflated yet, but they will be by tomorrow! I have the helium tank in the truck."

"Do the green streamers actually look like seaweed, though?" Nel asked, cocking her head to the side and adjusting her glasses. "Or does it just look like poorly taped green paper?"

"Hey! I'm securing the fuck out of these," Nora shouted, ripping another piece of tape off. "And it's not supposed to rain again...so, hopefully they'll all stay put through tomorrow afternoon."

I yanked two white ceramic planters out of the tote and wiggled them in the air. "What are we doing with these, and how will we keep them out of the hands and mouths of children?"

Almost right on cue, Mae appeared at my leg, pulling herself up to standing with a somewhat toothy grin.

She looked like a miniature grandma before bingo.

Nel walked over to the table, stopping a few feet from Mae and crouching down with her hands outstretched, beckoning her to take a few steps. Mae took two overly hasty steps before falling to her knees, distracting herself with a dandelion she contently plucked from the grass.

Standing back upright, Nel grabbed the planters from my hands. "There will only be a few kids here—just some neighbors of Nora's who Mae has played with a few times. Ari is friends with the owner of WonderFlower off Main and got us a deal on some arrangements."

"Get it…ONEderFlower…" I snickered, nudging Nel in the ribs.

Nel's face fell flat. "You were definitely the first one today to make that joke."

I mimicked her facial expression. "Of course I was. I'm hilarious."

"Is this, like, a sarcasm-off?" Ari asked, looking into the tote by my elbow. "Awesome. I'll bring these over to the shop tomorrow morning when we pick up the—"

"Nora, you *need* to tell those college friends to *stop* sending letters to my place. It's been five years and—" The voice stopped mid-sentence, and I swear my throat closed up. We all turned around to see Hallie standing at the entrance of the path leading to the backyard, Dahlia and Daisy running our way and collapsing on top of Mae. "Oh. Pen. Hi. I didn't know you'd be here."

I had to curl my toes down into my combat boots to stop myself from pouncing at her. My eyes darted from Nel to Hallie and then back again, the arches of my feet cramping from the pressure I was creating.

Stupid fucking feet.

Nora walked over to Hallie, snagging the envelope from her hand. "I'll let them know again. Thanks for bringing it."

"Is this why Mom and Dad couldn't do brunch at the Willow Center with us tomorrow?" Hallie asked, her voice soft and sincere. "We were going to catch that new kid-friendly show going on but lost our chance at tickets. Honestly, Mae would have probably loved the show, Pe…Nel."

Shut up, Hallie.

She's not even one. She wouldn't know what the fuck was going on.

I wanted to rip the serene, deceptive mask right off her perfectly contoured face.

It was obvious Hallie was holding herself back. She maintained a distance from our table, which was appreciated but also surprising. Though Hallie's words held an edge to them that made me want to yank them from her throat, her body language was confidently cautious.

I think I hated this version of her more because I didn't know what her next move was.

"Yes," Nel said with a grin I could tell was half-assed and half anxiety-ridden as she reached down to rub Daisy's back. "Yup. Mom and Dad will be here tomorrow. They'll be a little late, though."

Hallie took a few steps forward, her eyes darting to the streamers around the fence and the planters on the picnic table. "For Mae's birthday party? I'm guessing that's what this is."

"Nope. It's mine." I couldn't help myself, taking a step forward and crossing my arms across my chest.

Hallie giggled, shaking her head and bending her knees so she was only a few feet from her twins who snuggled their cousin, lifting her to a stand. Hallie smiled at Mae, who stood on wobbly legs with a jack-o-lantern smile. "You're turning one, huh? You're such a big girl now."

I tried stepping forward, but before I could take a single step, Nel's fingers softly cupped my shoulder. I noticed her eyebrows rising in a secret plea to get me to stand back as we listened to her sister whisper to Mae.

"Mommy, here she comes!" Dahlia shouted, clapping her hands together as Nel and I both watched Mae taking not one, not two, not even three, but five tottering steps forward. Mae's final step landed her directly into Hallie's arms where she was scooped up, Hallie spinning the two of them in a circle.

"Oh my, Mae! You did it!" Hallie slowed down, her loose waves falling over her shoulders as if they'd never shifted to begin with. "That was her first time walking, right? I could see it in her eyes."

"Jesus fucking Christ," I said, clawing my fingers beneath Hallie's hands until I pried Mae from her grasp. I handed Mae to Nel, who had yet to say a word—her eyes large behind her glasses. "Nel. Are you okay? Do you want me to kill her for you yet?"

"Rowe, stop..." she begged, eyes watery but yet to overflow. "She's...she's fine."

"She is *not* fine walking into this backyard without as much as an apology to your face," I whispered behind gritted teeth. "She isn't your puppeteer anymore, Nel. You freed yourself. Don't hand her back the strings."

Her eyes locked to mine with a darkness I didn't expect. "Viv isn't yours either, Rowe."

I took a step back. It wasn't her tone that made my chest tighten or how blunt she sounded.

It was the truth of the statement.

Because she was right.

Nel stood there with Mae in her arms, her fingers gently stroking her daughter's dark curls. Reaching for a bottle of water on the picnic table with her free hand, she twisted the cap off with the edge of her thumb. She practically chugged half of the bottle before letting the water linger in her mouth for a few seconds, her eyes closing. After a few more seconds passed, her eyes opened.

Nel took a deep breath and smiled down at Mae before saying, "Mae. You did it. You really, *really* walked!" Nel pressed a kiss to her daughter's forehead, tossing her gently into the air as the sweetest giggle floated from her lips. "You're such a brave, big girl!"

"I could use some of that bravery, kid," I said, never expecting I'd need a one-year-old to help me step the fuck up.

Hallie stood with her hands on her hips as Daisy and Dahlia did somersaults across the lawn behind her, their chestnut hair catching every loose strand of grass as they rolled. I couldn't *wait* to hear Hallie complain about it on the way out—because she *was* on the way out. Lifting my hand into the air, I flapped my fingers in Hallie's direction. "You can leave now."

"Tomorrow," Nel's voice chirped from behind me. "Eleven o'clock."

"Nel?" I whispered over my shoulder—though whisper probably wasn't the best way to describe my tone.

Nel pinched her lips together, her throat bobbing slowly as she stepped forward so our feet were aligned. "It starts at eleven...but I'm only telling you this for your girls' sake. Mae deserves to have her cousins here. That's all."

Twisting on her heel, Nel strode toward the sliding door at the back of Nora's house and yanked it open. It only took me two seconds before I was chasing her through the door to where the air conditioning hugged us like weighted blankets.

"I get the whole cousin thing for Mae...but she could drop them off and leave," I said, the edge of the kitchen counter biting into my back as I leaned against it. "She does *not* need to be here if she makes you uncomfortable."

Nel hunched forward with her hands clutching her thighs, and from the muscles rippling beneath her tank top, I could tell tears had finally fallen. "I don't want her here. Well...I *shouldn't* want her here, but it doesn't get much worse than your daughter taking her first steps into the arms of someone who blindly manipulated you for years. If I could get through that without completely losing it, I can get through this birthday party."

@darkromMOM3: @littleLIT33: *You seriously aren't Team Luca on this one? How can't you side with Mariah after all he did?*

@littleLIT33: @darkromMOM3: *Because it's karma, Mom! He can't expect to not have everything blow up in his face after their past. It's inevitable…it was going to happen.*

@littleLIT33: @darkromMOM3: *…but at the library?*

@vviPURR: *Zizi knows all about library shenanigans, doesn't she?*

@HarperCOOLins828: *I think they'll avoid the historical romance section for a while…*

@SpicyStef_01: @HarperCOOLins828: *That's what happens when renaissance role-playing goes a little too far.*

@littleLIT33: *Exactly. Karma.*

"Yes…I like libraries. I like role-playing. I also like historical romance…but I guess we won't find out if Mariah and Luca try out a different section until next week." I leaned onto my hands, the back of my head barely missing the pink-colored spines on the bookshelf. I was completely bare from the waist up with my tits out for the world to see, my nipples perkier than usual…and not because of the chapter we'd just finished.

And also *not* from Viv entering my stream for the fifth week in a row. Maybe sixth week… I'd lost track.

Cade lay belly-down on the floor only a few feet away from me, a book open between her elbows as she balanced her head in her hands. On the recent occasions she visited my livestream in-person—not hiding behind capella.calypso in the comments, we'd played a little game of *follow the leader*. I'd flirt with the viewers, my hand wandering through my hair and down over my chest, Cade doing the same. I'd read a steamy scene, and Cade would unsnap her bra, slowly removing it as her delectable breasts bounced into my vision. I would follow her lead, sliding off my lace bralette in front of the viewers with the same teasing shimmy my body was conditioned to do when removing clothes.

By the end of the stream, my body was humming. Buzzing. Wet and hot. She'd follow along in her own copy of the book but never without her eyes occasionally meeting mine and her own hand reaching down into her underwear to play along.

Well, if she wore any that day.

"All you smuts better turn me off and get to reading." I looked over the screen at Cade, who now sat up straight, topless with her knees just enough apart for me to see the layer of sheer, pink fabric covering her. Her smile was lethal, a mix of devilish heat and innocent teasing that made me want to forget the thousands of viewers waiting for me to sign off—including Viv. As Cade separated her knees a little bit more, I watched her fingers creep beneath the hem of her panties, and a soft gasp fell over her lips—plump lips I was desperate to taste.

I focused back on the screen, grabbing the top edge of the laptop, and said, "I may turn myself off here, but I'm definitely not done turning myself on for the night. Later, smuts."

I smacked the screen down and slid back onto the shag rug, practically ripping my thong off as Cade crawled over, her body rolling onto mine. Her lips began to suck and nip their way up my leg until she got to the crease where my thigh and sex collided—a spot she always took a few extra seconds to savor.

Her tongue against that sensitive skin immediately made my pussy tremble, and I placed a hand on either side of her face, lifting her gaze. "Cade. My fucking god, I'm not coming before you this time. I will *not* let you wait."

"I like the wait," Cade whispered, her eyes not leaving mine as the cold, metal ball of her tongue piercing flicked the tip of my clit, barely touching it, but enough to send an electric bolt through every nerve in my body. "Watching you get off gets me off. Every single time."

The second time her tongue teased me, I sat up and threw a leg over her so she was forced to roll onto her back, which she did willingly and without much of a fight. The laptop toppled backward off the chair so it laid half-open on the couch—luckily not broken on the floor.

But if it had fallen and shattered, I wouldn't have cared.

If Nel came home early, I would have stayed exactly where I was.

"That toy I ordered from Velvet came in," I whispered into the crook of her neck, rolling my hips down against her, the motion putting pressure exactly where we wanted it to be—*needed* it to be. "Reach under the bookshelf. I hid the box there."

Cade giggled, reaching until her hand was hidden beneath the shelf. "How'd you know I'd be in the position to grab it right now?"

"Hopeful thinking." She pulled the rectangular box out, my pussy immediately quivering against the damp, thin fabric she still wore—fabric I needed gone. "But right now, I wouldn't want you anywhere but in this position. Right here. With me."

"And with this?"

I rolled my eyes, snatching the box from her grasp. "Okay, yes. *And* this." I dug my fingers into the tape, feeling her hips circle below mine.

Fuck.

If fighting this tape was what it felt like when a condom wouldn't open, I was glad I never had to deal with that shit.

"Rosie." Cade gazed up at me, her hands walking up to my hips as she softly set them against me. "I wouldn't want to be anywhere but right here either. With you."

"I love you." The tape finally ripped the second those three words fell from my mouth. Cade's eyes widened, her hands climbing up my arms until she cupped my face in her hands.

I couldn't tell if it was her hands trembling against my cheeks or if I was shaking in her grasp.

I'd never said those words aloud.

To anyone.

Not even Viv.

I'd loved how Viv made me feel when her skin touched mine. I'd loved how intense she was onstage, how she could draw anyone in with her eyes and hips and voice. I'd loved how she hungered for me, but looking at it now, she seemed to love it more when she made *me* hunger for *her*.

Viv thirsted for the satisfaction of feeling wanted, while Cade's focus was *my* satisfaction.

I now could clearly see the difference between love and lust.

"Hey, Dabbler," Cade said, her thumb brushing my cheek as I leaned into her touch, "I love you too."

Chapter 33

Nel

It was late.

I returned to the apartment much later than I planned the night before Mae's birthday party.

Nora watched Mae while I went to the first in-person interview I'd had in over a year, and thankfully, it was casual. I met with a lead English instructor from St. Merlin Academy at Spellbound Beans where we each had a latte and discussed the tutoring program. For the school being so prestigious, I didn't expect the meeting to be so relaxed.

The position was, honestly, perfect.

Too perfect.

If offered the position, I'd meet with students after school each day to review English literature lessons and walk through homework assignments with them. It would be part-time to start but with full-time benefits—something this little family of mine would appreciate. She'd discussed the possibility of it becoming more of a full-time position where, during the school day, students would meet with me in the library classroom during their study halls. Since the current assistant librarian shared an office with the head librarian, the classroom would be mine to utilize for all English study and tutoring needs.

I wasn't sure how I'd sat there without jumping onto the table, knocking iced lattes onto the floor and screaming about how perfect this job was.

Instead, I stayed calm until I got to Nora's house where I completely collapsed into her arms with a smile that hadn't left my face since—well, until we'd gotten halfway home and Mae completely shit through her onesie.

After stopping in the Merlin Grocery parking lot to change Mae, screaming and kicking in the car's trunk, I made it back to the apartment where all the lights were still on, and the front door was unlocked. I looked to my right to see if Rosie's jean jacket was where it usually hung—and it was. Next to it was a leather shoulder bag with patches sewn across it and eclectic pins scattering the material.

I released a breath, figuring that it hadn't been some serial killer breaking into the apartment...but Cade had just forgotten to lock the door behind her.

Or turn all the lights off.

Mae's exhausted head fell onto my shoulder, and as I walked into the living room, I stopped at the foot of the couch. The shag rug was in a messy pile in front of the bookshelf, and the laptop balanced half-open on the pile of pillows at the far edge of the couch.

Well, it sure looked like some extracurricular activities happened here tonight.

I couldn't comment...I'd been there.

Getting down onto my knees, I plopped the laptop back onto the stool it usually sat on, opening it to check the battery. The screen was on our YourEyesOnly page, comments from Rosie's Smut Me Up session looking like a blur of words at the bottom of the page. Though I wanted to scroll through the comments to see who I needed to ban from our livestreams or monitor, my eyelids were growing heavier by the second.

Squinting down at the battery icon, it was blinking red with only 2% life left. I swiped my finger alongside the laptop, held down the power button, and watched as the laptop screen darkened, a white sentence forming across the screen that read *Goodnight* before finally fading to black.

"Yeah..." I yawned, getting up to my feet and shutting the laptop. "Goodnight, indeed."

Chapter 34

Rosie

"**P**oor Mae is crying again," Cade whispered, the darkness hugging our naked bodies almost as gently as Cade hugged mine. Her skin was silk against my bare flesh, goosebumps rising as her fingertips wandered down my thigh. She cupped my ass and pulled me closer, our chests pressing together.

This would have immediately been a sexual moment months ago.

Now, I appreciated the quiet intimacy of us lying naked in the darkness.

"She's been stir-crazy lately," I mumbled, running my hand across the pinched skin of Cade's lower back as her fingers lowered to graze my heat.

Though it was hard to ignore the slickness growing between my thighs, I felt more at ease in her arms than aroused.

Mae's abrupt cry caused us to jolt as we pulled each other closer.

Cade quirked her head toward the hallway. "Is that…"

I listened for a moment, the sound of familiar, deep sniffles mixing with the sound of Mae's angry wails. "Yeah, it's Nel. She has a hard time when Mae won't fall back asleep."

Cade's body relaxed against mine, her newly twisted locs sprawling over my shoulder as her head fit perfectly into the crook of my neck. It felt like that spot was made for her.

"I wish there was something we could do to help her."

"I'll help some nights…or offer help, at least," I explained. "I'll bring her water or tissues or coffee—"

"Coffee?"

I nodded. "Yeah…she's had coffee at two in the morning before. Caffeine doesn't do shit for her…it's a mind game. But it's a mind game that helps her calm down once in a while, so it's worth getting my tired ass up to do it."

Cade's soft breathing fell into rhythm with my own, our chests rising and falling as one. "You're a good fucking friend, Dabbler. You know that?"

"Ew...don't say such nice things about me," I huffed, closing my eyes and pushing the back of my head farther into the pillow.

Cade chuckled, forcing my body to quake along with hers. "But you are, Rosie. You have this tough shell, but inside, it's all warm and gooey and good."

"Kind of like stuffed jalapeños? Or a cannoli?"

Cade pinched the side of my waist, and I flinched before melting closer to her. "I guess you're now my little cannoli. No, definitely a stuffed jalapeno." Her lips brushed the side of my temple. "All that hard exterior and gooey goodness...it's what I love about you. It's what Nel loves about her best friend."

Hearing the word *love* thrown around twice in one sentence was startling.

But as my lids grew heavier and our breathing fell back in-sync, I knew she was right.

I was lucky to have Cade in my life, but I was even luckier to still have Nel.

Chapter 35

Nel

"**I** don't know what the kids are going to eat," Rosie mumbled between bites of deviled eggs and puff pastries. "But if any of them touch a grimy finger on my plate, they're dead to me."

"Rowe...they're *kids*!" I exclaimed with a laugh, shaking my head and gesturing to the opposite end of the table. "I made some kid-sized charcuterie boards this morning that we'll put out—we can call them *child*cuterie boards. There's some fruit and veggies and cheese and goldfish. It's very on-theme."

"I mean...that *also* sounds like my kind of board. Maybe I'll just hang by this table all day. You said there's wine inside, right?"

"And coffee!" Behind us, Sebastian carried two travel boxes of hot brew, Riley and Jude walking behind him with bags of to-go cups in their arms. "Rosie, go snag the keg of cold brew in Jude's trunk, will you?"

Leaning into her hip, Rosie said, "Um...excuse me. Do you expect me to obey your every fucking demand?"

"When it comes to coffee...yes." Sebastian set the two boxes onto one of the empty picnic tables, shaking out his hands and adjusting the mandolin strung across his back.

"Fair enough." Rosie shrugged and plucked another chicken wing from the plate before slipping around the table and down the side path toward Jude's car.

Jude set the cups down on the table and stepped closer, his beard groomed a little shorter than he usually kept it and his hair pulled up into a neat bun with the sides shaved short. "Do you want to keep this stuff inside with the wine or out—"

I swung my arms around his neck, my lips pressing against his before he could finish his sentence. He tasted of hazelnut and espresso, and I wanted to drown myself in it.

"Well..." he whispered once our lips shifted apart. "I thought this was a family party, ma'am."

"Oh, it *absolutely* is," I said, loosening my arms from his neck. "I just had to kiss my boyfriend because he looks way too delicious not to right now."

Jude looked subtly side to side before a smile pinched his cheeks, and he whispered, "Boyfriend sounds so good when you say it...but

I think you better tell me where you want this coffee to go before I get too riled up."

I swallowed as he stepped away, hugging the bags of cups back against his chest. "Yes. Right. This is Mae's birthday...we have to behave."

"Where do you want the coffee, Nel?" Riley asked monotonously from his spot behind Jude, his head falling back as he let out a heavy sigh. "I can't stand here much longer and watch the beginning of this messed-up porno keep going."

"Ew...don't talk like that. This is a *kid's* thing," Sebastian stated, nudging Riley as he picked up both of the coffee boxes again. "Where do you—"

"In the kitchen!" I shouted, throwing my arms up with a laugh. "Just go put them on the counter. There should be pitchers of lemonade and bottles of wine on ice in there too."

"So, there *is* wine." Rosie's voice popped back into the backyard as she strode toward the snack table. "I'll be right in, boys."

I felt Mae's little fingernails claw into my calf as she pulled herself up to standing, wrapping her arms around me as she babbled, "Up," and, "Ma," on repeat. I pulled her up onto my hip, tightening the bows on the dark, curly pig tails spiraling off the top of her head. Tying this teeny bit of hair into pigtails for the first time that morning was an accomplishment.

It was the little things that brought me joy that I had to cling to.

"She's been grabbing every tablecloth we've put on...but she's been good," Nora said, sitting down onto the bench of the picnic table we'd all been huddling by.

"Mae is so lucky to have you. *I* am so lucky to have you. Seriously," I said, nuzzling my nose against Mae's and feeling her giggle rumble against my chest.

Nora flicked her hand in my direction. "Oh, hush. I'd rather hang out with her than mingle with any of the adults coming in. Is that a harmonica?"

I nodded without even looking over my shoulder. "Yeah. They promised they'd stick to playing renditions of *The Little Mermaid* and *Moana* songs."

"I'm intrigued, to say the least." Nora's eyes shifted over my shoulder, and darkness heavied her gaze, her back straightening as if someone pulled an invisible string upward from her skull. The energy roaring through her had frozen in place. "Hallie's here."

I didn't turn around. "I know. After inviting her, I didn't think she'd miss a—"

"No, Nel. She looks kind of...mad."

"What the fudge is this, Penny?!" Hallie's voice sounded like a record scratching at top volume, shrill and callous.

"*Seriously*...what the fudge?" Rosie stated from the snack table, taking a long sip of her wine before walking toward us at a fierce speed.

I just stared at my sister, who walked directly toward me, her daughters scattering across the lawn. "Yeah, *fudge*, Rosie. You really shouldn't swear in front of children." Hallie stopped a few feet in front of me, ripping her phone from her pocket and skimming her thumb across the screen. "You *really* think showing both your body *and* your daughter for the world to see would be the best way to make yourself money? I thought you went to *college* for a reason—to get a stable career and start a family. And this is what you chose?"

Rosie slammed her hand down on the picnic table. "Don't you do that for a living...as a momfluencer or whatever the fuck they call—"

Hallie spun on her heels so she was almost nose to nose with Rosie. "I don't mean to sound harsh, *Rosie,* but I'm not here to talk to you. I *do* blame you for this, though."

Within seconds, the air surrounding the table had gone from cozy to chaotic. I knew, sooner or later, Hallie would learn about The Naked Book Club. I knew she wouldn't understand the empowerment of sitting in front of that camera when the red light flicked on.

But bringing Mae into this when she'd never been part of it to begin with?

That was *not* fair.

"Hallie...if you're going to be like this, you can—"

My sister straightened her arm so the phone she held practically hit my glasses, forcing me to step back.

After a few seconds of staring at the screen, the anger she'd felt began rolling through my veins, little by little.

Her emotions were valid.

Her anger made sense.

Because as I stared at a screenshot of myself and Mae—our faces surrounded by a frame reading The Naked Book Club LIVE—I felt a lump crawl up my throat, my vision growing hazy.

"What...how..."

"One of the other moms in my Panormama VIP group shared it on our message board. She *shared* a screenshot of *you* in a group message that includes near five hundred local moms. Pen, do you see how this makes me look bad? How it impacts *my* career?"

"Holy shit, can you not focus on yourself for one hot minute?" Rosie exclaimed, rounding the corner of the picnic table. Her determined energy was quickly stopped when Hallie's free hand flew up in front of her face.

After all the years of my following Hallie's lead, never had she stepped away from her soft, gentle persona—one I now knew was never all that gentle in the first place. This was a version of Hallie I'd never met before. A version who'd thrown off her gentle façade and replaced it with one of a lioness running up to its prey.

Her claws were out.

I wasn't sure my skin could avoid the wound.

"Okay, if you're *really* going to interject, I'll give you something to listen to," Hallie said, lowering the phone and running her thumb across the screen.

At this point, everyone but the children were watching our table. Adults had stopped nibbling snacks. Sebastian and Riley had stopped tuning their instruments. Even the background ocean sounds I'd put on the Bluetooth speaker seemed to have magically turned off.

"Does this sound familiar?" Hallie lifted the screen of her phone closer to Rosie's ear, upping the volume just enough for those of us at the table to hear the faint sounds of voices. "Oh...you may also want to watch. Do you recognize the bookshelf? It's all you really see until my sister and niece come into view hours later."

Color drained from my cheeks as Mae began to wriggle against me, her cousins running our way with arms outstretched in her direction. I set her down, Dahlia and Daisy grabbing her hands as they slowly walked with her away from the table—which I was grateful for. I did *not* want any small children over here with their very impressive listening skills.

Rosie's eyebrows lifted, her lips creating a little O shape against her flushed face. "Huh. This does sound familiar. Weird."

"Wait...Rowe. What...what happened?" I asked, still trying to piece together all the thoughts buzzing in my brain. "What did she just show you?"

"I think..." Rosie stammered as she pushed Hallie's hand away from her. "I think I forgot to fully turn off the stream last night."

No.

She wouldn't have forgotten.

We always clicked off the livestream button or turned off the laptop when we finished our sessions.

It was a practice we'd made routine since discovering how finicky the platform could be.

My mind rushed back to last night when I walked into an apartment that felt a little...I don't know...off. I'd drowsily carried Mae over to the laptop when I noticed it laying ajar on the pillow.

An *active* screen.

The comments had been right there, probably with timestamps if I'd looked close enough. If Rosie logged off, the comments wouldn't have been visible unless clicking into the recording.

"Shit." There were no other words I could say. There were no other emotions to feel besides shock. If members of Hallie's group saw my face—saw Mae's face—thousands of other people had too.

How fast could news like this travel?

Had people sent this to friends outside of this little VIP club Hallie led?

Did people *really* care that much?

It hadn't even been twelve hours since shutting down that laptop, and though news moving this quickly meant people were watching our channel—which was honestly kind of great—it also meant people knew Exotic Ellie was really me.

And I'd never wanted that.

That was my one stipulation from the start.

Especially now that I was actively in the interview circuit.

I wanted to vomit.

"Nel...are you okay?" My head snapped toward the voice, my eyes linking with Jude's as he shut the sliding door and walked down into the yard.

I swear Hallie's body twisted toward Jude in slow motion, my eyes switching from Jude's to hers as I watched her expression completely rearrange.

My heart was a bass drum in my ears.

My feet felt like cinder blocks.

I was sinking.

"No..." Hallie turned back toward me. "You're taking too many steps backward, Pen. I should have seen this coming. I should have stopped you. No wonder you're doing porn now. You're hanging around all *these* people."

"Alright, now *I'm* offended," Sebastian shouted, throwing his arms into the air and setting the mandolin on his stool.

Jude stepped in close, the sides of our hips touching as my heart continued to sink through my feet. "Come on, Hallie. It's been *years*. We're all moving on. This is your niece's birthday party."

"You're standing up to me now? If anything, I'm impressed," Hallie said, sarcasm dripping off every syllable. "But that doesn't give you permission to tell me how to treat my family. You dropped out of college, and your sister barely made it through...and then she became a sex worker. *You're* Grant's clone. You *really* think you're the people I want around my sister after all Grant did to her?

Jude turned to look at me. "Who the fuck is Grant?"

With a furrowed brow, Hallie whispered, "Penny never told you?"

"Stop calling me that!" I shouted, staring down at my feet and avoiding eye contact with everyone so I could attempt to keep my shit together. Deep breaths, Nel. Breathe in, breathe out. This doesn't have to be a big deal. It is what you make it. "Just stop."

Hallie's head snapped toward me, and when I met her gaze, I thought I saw a twinge of softness return to her eyes—the softness I once trusted, the softness I once thought was genuine.

But I was wrong.

I wanted to scream at my sister for marching into this party the way she had and scream at Rosie for her carelessness during a time I needed her to be more careful than ever. I wanted to scream that I loved Jude, and I'd probably loved him since he left Merlin Heights.

But I couldn't. My voice was lodged in my throat, only allowing the hollowest whisper to escape. My head forced every damn coping skill I'd ever learned to the back of my mind and pushed away every positive emotion I needed to replace the numbness I felt.

"Nel…" Rosie's voice woke me from my trance. "I had no idea I didn't fully turn the laptop off. Cade came over, and we…we got a little reckless. I'm sure no one who really matters saw you. I'm sorry, Nel."

No one who matters.

My mind immediately raced back to the interview I'd had earlier that week—the one I *needed* for my family. I had two more interviews with different businesses lined up over the next week, and as I stood here, I mentally canceled them.

Why try if my face on a YourEyesOnly screen would pop up when searching my *real* name?

I was now officially connected to Exotic Ellie…a persona I, honestly, had grown pretty damn proud of.

But even if it was deep in the search, it would be there. I didn't doubt the power of technology.

"I just had a *really* good interview. I could get the job. This…this could fuck that opportunity up for me."

Hallie stepped forward, her aura suffocating me. "*You're* the one who made this choice, Pe…Nel. You have to take some of the blame for this. I can't save you every—"

"Won't you shut the fuck up?" Jude's voice pummeled through the air, causing Hallie to step back with a gasp—a real one, not some dramatic one she'd pulled out of her ass.

Hallie looked from Jude to me, her head shaking as she said, "You're going to let your *boyfriend* talk to me like that? Because I'm guessing that's what's happening here…right? You've fallen into such a depressive state you're *giving in* and going back to where you both left off? Apparently, you made better choices back then."

"Nel never made that choice, Hallie. You did," Jude whispered, stuffing his fists into the pockets of his jeans.

Hallie shrugged. "*She* made the choice, in the end, to follow my advice. She needs to accept that and accept that this whole YourEyesOnly situation was also *her* choice."

"You manipulated her when she was at her lowest, Hallie," Rosie said, her voice hushed for the first time in minutes. "I was there. I listened to her question herself. I watched her fall for your schemes. I tried telling her your motives then, but she was so adamant you knew what was best for her...so, I let her push my brother away. But not this time. Hell no."

Hallie shook her head in Rosie's direction, blowing off the comment with far too much ease. Then her focus was back on me. "So, is he your boyfriend, *Nel*?"

"Who cares who dates who?" Sebastian shouted from behind Jude, his hands grabbing the side of his face where a golden five o'clock shadow had formed over the last day or so. "This is soap opera shit. Why does it matter so much?"

"Because my sister doesn't need another *Grant Richardson* in her life. I stopped that shitty situation, and I will stop every shitty situation until she finds someone who can handle all of *this*—all of *her*." To say that didn't mentally take me down a notch was an understatement. Hallie turned to me and said, "But you're a big girl now. If you're dating him, you'd tell me."

I wished some of the fire I'd felt over these last few months still lingered.

Nothing was left but ash.

A buzzing sound forced us all to look at the phone on the table by Rosie's hip as she grabbed it, swiping up. Her eyes blinked a couple quick times at the screen before lifting her gaze and saying, "Viv is at the apartment."

Silence thickened the air between us.

Rosie's face looked so solemn, so hurt. Though I hated seeing my friend—someone I once saw as my *best* friend—feel such guilt, I didn't have the energy to fight her. To fight anyone.

"Go. Just...just go."

Rosie looked toward the path alongside the house and then back to the phone in her hand. "Nel...I can't leave you here with this—"

"Please. Just...go." I finally met her gaze, my eyes deciding it was then when the dam needed to break. "You left me behind once for Viv. I expected it would happen again."

Rosie took a step forward, but I winced back as if her step was a bruise to the heart. In a way, it was. "Nel...no...I'm not leaving—"

"Go," I whispered, turning away from her and clutching the edge of the picnic table until my knuckles whitened.

Rosie's steps were slow, heavy, hesitant. After a quiet few seconds, the sound of her footsteps told me she'd skittered away down the path.

To Viv.

"Nel..." Jude's hand gently wrapped around my elbow, and though I should have collapsed into his chest so I could melt into him, I did nothing. I felt nothing. The heat of his hand against my skin slowly turned to ice the longer it stayed there. "Nel, let's go inside. We can go talk and—"

"I want you to leave." The words came without permission, but I didn't take them back. "I want everyone to leave. Everyone, please."

Mae's little body came into view near the patio stairs leading to the sliding kitchen doors. She was smiling the sweetest grin, her arms reaching up with little fingers opening and closing as she proudly and confidently stood on her own. Taking a few steps away from the table, I placed Mae onto my hip, finally feeling the first positive emotion I'd felt in the last fifteen minutes. Her excited little heart pounded against my frail one as I took a step up the stairs.

"Jesus Christ," Sebastian's words sounded from behind me just as I opened the sliding door, squinting through damp eyelashes toward the path leading to the backyard where everyone stared.

Cade held a perfectly wrapped package in her arms, her eyes scanning the lawn with the brightest—and slightly puzzled—smile.

It was then when the flood gates fully opened, and I slipped into the kitchen, closing the sliding doors behind me as my knees buckled. I hoped the counter could hold my weight as I leaned onto it, clutching Mae to my chest.

With Mae snuggled close, cheerfully whispering *Mama* and *DayDay* and *hug* over and over again, I lowered myself to the linoleum floor and pressed my face to her chest. Her little arms wrapped around my head, her face nuzzling into my hair as she continued to say my name and hug me closer.

Sobs rolled through my body, a tidal wave ripping me apart, and honestly, I was freely giving in to the undertow. I wanted to sink into the floor below me. I wanted these waves to pull me under because I already felt like I was drowning.

But it was Mae's little voice keeping me afloat.

I was barely hovering at the surface, but I was hovering, nonetheless.

Chapter 36

Rosie

When my ass hit the grubby front seat of the Jeep, I dissociated my entire drive from East Merlin suburbia to downtown Merlin Heights. I had no recollection of how I'd driven twenty minutes from Nora's back to our apartment—well, to *Nel's* apartment.

I think I'd always been more of a familiar visitor with chaotic ideas rather than a roommate to her—and definitely not the roommate she'd grown to know all those years before.

My senses had completely shut down the moment I'd walked away from the backyard, leaving only a memory of Nel's numb expression staring back at me no matter where I looked.

Yes, I was angry at myself for being careless with Cade the night before.

Yes, I was beyond furious at Hallie for storming in the way she had.

But what truly made my stomach climb up my throat was the look on Nel's face when she told me to leave.

"You left me behind once for Viv. I expected it would happen again."

There was nothing behind her haunting eyes—no energy, no care, no life.

I'd seen those eyes the night she woke me with a burned grilled cheese and a bowl of hummus all those months before. Though she'd greeted my hungover—partially still drunk—ass with quiet excitement, struggle was painted across her face. Thinking back to that night with a sober head, a few things did stick out. Her eyes were swollen behind familiar frames, her hair messy and unkempt. Her skin lacked that Greek goddess glow we'd always joked about as roommates and was replaced with dry patches she'd scratched to the point of scabs.

I'd witnessed her sparks flicker back on over the last few months, adding life to the freckles of light blue hiding beneath the gray in her gaze. I knew my brother was part of the reason for those sparks, but I'd also hoped I was as well.

Now I just saw myself as the person who'd thrown too much at her, too fast, forcing the darkness to return.

When the sound of crunching gravel brought me back to the present, I looked from my boots walking away from the Jeep up toward the apartment entrance. I mentally tried to prepare myself for whatever the hell I had coming for me: a disciplining for missing her show? A passive-aggressive chat about why I needed to go down on her? A hug she hoped turned into a smash sesh?

Viv sat on the house's front stoop. Her hair was freshly dyed, and her skirt was a little too short as she sat on the cement block Nel and I joked was the world's smallest front porch. Her eyes shot to mine at the sound of my scuffing steps, and she set her phone on the stoop.

"Zizi, baby. Hi." Viv got to her feet but not without her ass being visible on her way up. "You were at Mae's party, yes?"

"Yes." My voice was cold, the ice quite obviously shocking Viv as she stepped aside to let me up onto the stoop. "I was."

"Whoa...are you okay? What's wrong?" I expected Viv to run her hands down my arms until they met my lower back, but she instead laced her fingers together in front of her. Skin to skin had always been Viv's go-to method of soothing when, in truth, it was just her way to redirect.

"Honestly, Viv. I'm not. I'm not really okay."

"Oh, Rosie. I'm sorry you're not okay." Viv took a step forward, unlacing one of her hands so her fingers gently caressed the side of my face. It felt almost robotic, as if conditioned to touch and tease when emotions of any kind were obviously running rampant. "I'm not okay either."

I huffed against her palm, my eyes rolling enough for her to notice. "How so?"

"You don't believe me?" Viv asked, poking my nose. "That makes me sad. If you'd listened to me confess my love to someone before fucking them with some fancy double-sided dildo, I think you'd be sad too."

My heart froze.

My stomach fell.

I had to do everything in my power to slow my jaw from dropping, but it dropped, nonetheless.

All this time—during the entire backyard discussion—how this could impact *me* hadn't crossed my mind. My worry had strictly been on Nel and how this was fucking up everything *she'd* deliberately tried not to. My carelessness handed Hallie fuel to dive back down Nel's throat, leading to her belittling the relationship Nel and my brother were finally trying to make work.

Once the laptop fell back onto the sofa, the focus of the screen had been at the corner of the room where the wall met the ceiling. Though I'd been out of sight, I hadn't been out of mind, because the livestream sound was never turned off. Anyone popping into the stream heard everything going on between Cade and me.

Anyone new popping in and anyone who'd stuck around.

"'I wouldn't want to be anywhere but right here either. With you,'" Viv repeated Cade's words from the night before with such ease. *"Please. Whoever this bitch is cannot be giving you what I do."*

"Alright, stop. Fucking stop!" My tone caused her emerald eyes to widen, lips pressing together in a mix of confusion and shock. I only raised my voice around her when in the bedroom, when role-playing or when things got a little out of hand—in ways we both mutually consented to, of course.

This tone was different. It was a sound coming straight from my heart, a place Viv only glimpsed at since she'd never gotten to know it the way I wished she would.

Now, it was too fucking late.

"Zi. What's...what's wrong with you right now?" Viv's voice was hushed, her hand rushing to her chest. "This is *not* you."

"The crazy thing is, Viv, this actually *is* me. You've only ever seen me as a pawn to control and fuck. That's all I've ever been to you!" I threw my hands into the air, letting out a maniacal laugh. "I've always been more than this sexual being you've helped mold. Only recently did I step back and see the big picture...and it's a *much* bigger picture than I expected it to be. I can be this sexual being while also having *real* feelings I shouldn't feel guilty about. And you know what? I don't feel fucking guilty for having those feelings, Viv."

"Zi, what are you talking about?" Viv's hand remained over her chest, her eyes blinking wider as her perfectly sculpted brow narrowed. "If it weren't for my having an in with Marley, you *never* would have gotten into The Bare Assentials. We *never* would have felt the love we've felt for each other over these years. Aren't you grateful for—"

"I'm sorry...excuse me?" I whispered, dumbfounded and shocked. "What...the actual *fuck* are you trying to say right now? You're trying to tell me that my talent alone wouldn't have gotten me into the troupe while also telling me you *loved* me? How...how can either of those things be possible? It's pure madness, Viv, and you know that."

Viv took a step forward, her gaze angled downward as her hand shifted from her chest to pin a strand of pink hair behind her ear. "I think you know as well as I do that if it weren't for me—and your, well...*obsession* with me—you wouldn't be where you are today." Her gaze lifted, the corner of her lips quirking into a sadistic grin. "Isn't that right?"

Invisible claws morphed from her gaze, and it felt like fingers wrapping around my throat, silencing everything sitting inside of me.

She was right.

Viv knew the game she'd played over all these years and the power she held.

And she fucking loved it all—the way she'd played puppeteer for most of my burlesque career, the way she gaslit me into thinking I needed her when she didn't give a fuck about needing me.

She'd plunged her way into my mind—my heart—right when my mom was at her lowest point, because she knew I, too, couldn't get much lower.

"You know it, Zi." Viv stepped forward again, this time the toes of her wedges tapping the tip of my boots. "You know I'm right. You know if it weren't for me, you'd be some stripper at a nasty run-down club. You wouldn't be dancing in Rockberry or working at some prestigious school...hell, probably not even teaching at some little Merlin dance studio. You'd be where your mom ended up. Instead, you found me—or, really, I found you."

Viv's thin fingers wrapped their way around my waist, tugging my hips toward her. "So, now you can imagine how I felt listening to you moan as this bitch of yours touched you and teased you off-screen. I knew exactly what moves you were using on her...I *know* you, Zi. You know as well as anyone that I'm far too much of a voyeur to not find what happened a little hot. I loved imagining it was me you were making scream for a little bit. But then you said you *loved* her, and it made me realize how much I hated it not being me on the other end. It was *not* hot anymore, Zi. It was infuriating. I need her gone."

I need her gone.

Those last four words set fire to the muscles Viv had turned to ice.

It wasn't *I want you back.* It was her demanding I change my emotions, change part of who I was, to benefit her.

I clawed Viv's fingers away from my hips, disgusted for letting her get anywhere close enough to touch me. "Go the fuck home, Viv. I'm done. I. Am. Done."

Shock flooded her cheeks as I stepped off the stoop, tossing the keys into the air. "What... Where are you going?"

"I'm going back to the party to find Cade, who is probably wondering where the hell I am. I should have gone to her first...to explain." The fact that I'd run to Viv first before calling Cade made my stomach churn. "She's a human being with a real name and real good fucking heart. Cade *Capella* Garfield, to be exact...in case you needed to put two and two together from my Smut Me Up streams."

"She's been in the streams with me…" Viv said, realization smacking her in the face.

Twisting on the heel of my combat boot, I tossed the keys into the air again, impressively catching them for the second time in a row. "She sure has been. But please, *you* can leave. Because I am no longer breaking whenever you snap your fingers. I *never* break for anyone, and the fact that I've continued to shatter for you each and every time you come calling disgusts me."

"But, Zi. What will you do when you can't get back into burlesque? You'll need me to—"

"I don't fucking *need* you, Viv. I never really did. You helped me get back on my feet, but it was *my* talent and *my* spunk that made me Zesty Zi. I sculpted her. You only provided a tiny bit of the clay." I tugged the handle of the door as it shot open, and I slid into the driver's seat. "And no one ever said I can't get back into burlesque. No one said I couldn't do that again, *and* get back into contemporary, *and* do The Naked Book Club. I don't have to be one kind of person. No one ever should believe they have to be."

Sticking the keys into the ignition and rumbling the Jeep back to life, I didn't want to stare at Viv as I backed out of the driveway. I didn't want to look in the rearview mirror and watch her fade into the past. All I wanted was to drive toward someone I needed in my future.

As I rolled back into the parking lot of Nora and Ari's place, I realized the line of cars parked alongside the road from an hour or so before were no longer there. A Subaru sat quietly in the driveway of the small Cape Cod, and when I pulled up beside it, shutting the door behind me, I jogged down the pathway alongside the home.

My eyes drifted across a yard of teal and green streamers reaching through gentle gusts of wind toward poorly inflated balloons tied to the fence. Half-eaten slices of cheese and deviled eggs sat on paper plates sprinkling the picnic tables, some flipped over while others frolicked across the grass with the wind's assistance. A lone highchair sat near the appetizer table in front of the balloon arch Nora had slaved over, and as I made my way toward it, I realized how clean and pristine the highchair was.

There wasn't a sprinkle or drop of frosting to be found.

"Fuck," I whispered, hanging my head and running weak fingers through my hair before setting both my hands flat onto the table. "Fuck."

Taking a deep breath and one last look at the eerily silent backyard, I ran back to the car.

Nel needed time to process everything. I was sure her brain was spiraling in the worst of ways after being mentally hit from every angle. Plus, seeing my face right now probably wouldn't slow the spiral.

I'd fix what happened with Nel and me after. She needed a little more time.

I just hoped she didn't think I was leaving her yet again.

But right now, I needed to find Cade.

Chapter 37

Nel

"Is she gone?" I whispered when Nora walked into the spare bedroom and leaned against the doorframe, Mae's little fingers wrapped around my sister's as she proudly stood beside her.

"She just left," Nora said flatly.

I wasn't sure if I was physically nodding or if the nodding was just movement in my head. Footsteps sounded, and Mae babbled some words that sounded like a mixture of *Mama* and *DayDay* and

Ohpuss—the last one being a word I absolutely understood and knew most people would just awkwardly laugh at.

But even hearing her repeat *Ohpuss* over and over and over again didn't loosen the brick lodged in my chest. My nails pressed so tightly through the fleece of the blanket that I knew imprints would soon paint my palm. The energy running through my fingertips as I clutched the blanket was the only sliver of energy left in me.

Though lids curtained my eyes, it didn't mean my brain was at rest. If anything, it was the complete opposite of at rest.

Rosie's forgetfulness.

Hallie's discovery.

Jude's confusion.

Mae's failed party.

My identity.

Too many thoughts bobbed in my head, and I couldn't just grab onto one of them, because they all needed my attention equally.

"Nel..." The edges of my toes wiggled against Nora's thigh from beneath the blanket as she sat on the end of the bed. "I know you're upset...and you can stay here for the rest of the day if you'd like. But Ari and I...we leave tomorrow for Mykonos."

That was right.

Planning for their destination wedding would soon begin.

Her reminder struck a chord in my brain: Theía Elena was flying back with them after their visit to Greece so she could officially close the sale on the house.

On top of all the conversations I needed to have, apartment searching and packing up the little life Mae and I created here needed to be pushed up the list.

The little life I'd welcomed Rosie back into.

"Yeah. Mm-hmm." Again, I wasn't sure if I was physically nodding or not.

A hand softly fell over my shoulder. "Hallie shouldn't have stormed in like that...and her bringing up Grant wasn't appropriate. She can't keep hanging that over your head. You'll never heal if she keeps opening that wound back up."

My chest burned, and it was Mae's little hands against my back that softened the fire. Mae stood at the edge of the bed, her hands now walking up my arm and chest until they got to my face. She grabbed for my glasses—something she often did, knowing I would tell her not to—but this time, I let her take them. Placing the oversized glasses on her little button nose, I felt her body jolt when realizing how warped the world around her had become.

She fumbled the glasses in her hands before placing them back on my nose. They were crooked, but her setting them somewhat gently—and somewhat messily—back on made my thoughts shift. "Jude. Is he...is he okay? I never even talked to him before he left. I just...walked away."

Nora looked down at the hands in her lap, lacing and then unlacing her fingers. "He was...quiet. Once you went inside, Sebastian and Riley picked their things up, but he just kind of stood there. Hallie started talking to him, but he ignored her and went to go help the guys get their equipment."

"Hallie talked to him after I left?" My stomach churned. "She can't talk to him. Nothing ever goes well when—"

"Nel. Stop." Nora's palms slammed onto the mattress on either side of my legs, my muscles freezing. Squaring her chest in my direction, she said, "Hallie helped you in high school. I get that; you get that; *she* gets that. But she has no right to hang that over your head for the rest of your life. You deserve to love whoever the fuck you want to love without her manipulating you. I've told her all of this once, twice, probably near a dozen times. I don't like confrontation, but I've said it, nonetheless. Your fight at her place this spring wasn't enough to get the reality of it all through her head. She still thinks she owns you, when you're the only person who has the right to own the decisions you make."

I thought I'd completely drained myself of tears, but hearing Nora raise her voice and express these thoughts to me were emotions I couldn't stop myself from feeling—and I didn't want to.

"I'm just...it's all a mess." My voice was weak as Mae's little head nudged higher on my chest until she cozied into the crook of my neck. I wiped a tear off my cheek so it wouldn't fall into her dark curls and said, "Because I'm going to go home to an annoyed Rosie and then probably open up an angry email from St. Merlin Academy, telling me to forget about the interview."

Nora rolled her eyes. "That's dramatic. I doubt anyone at that school even knows what YourEyesOnly is."

"I don't know about that." I rubbed circles across Mae's back as her breathing grew as heavy as her lids. "We all have our vices."

Nora scooted closer, my knees bending beneath the blanket so she could bring her legs up into a crisscross position. "I think you need to ask yourself a few things. The first one is, are you mad at Rosie?"

I paused, my lips pressing together as I replayed the afternoon in my head. I dove back into the emotional pool of shock and frustration that overtook my body hours before. My vision had blurred, and my brain turned to mush, but the ways my body reacted weren't purely because of Rosie's accident.

It was because of Hallie's tone and approach.

It was because Mae's party was interrupted.

It was because Jude was standing by my side, waiting for me to stand up for him.

For *us*.

The mess of emotions running through me wasn't fully because of Rosie's carelessness. I was feeling the way I felt because I couldn't close all the tabs being forced wide open inside my head.

Hell, I'd had to open an extra window to make room for them all.

"I'm frustrated. I'm definitely a little upset…but I'm not mad at her, no." Saying that aloud felt like one of the weights had been plucked from my shoulders. "Am I annoyed she walked away from me for Viv again? Yes. Am I embarrassed for Cade? Yes. But I'm more grateful for all she's done to lift me up over the last few months than disappointed."

Nora smiled, placing her hand over my blanketed knee and said, "Okay. So, when you go home tonight, you'll know how you feel when you see her. That's that." Nora lifted her index finger and brought her middle finger up to make a number two sign in the air. "Second. Hallie. It's obvious you're mad at her, but I think you need to ask yourself how much of that anger is really worth carrying.

You've carried it for too long already. If you ask me, she does all of this out of jealousy, and it's not worth giving any more of your energy toward the pettiness."

My eyes opened wide, my brows furrowing as I replayed her words in my fuzzy brain and tried to hear them with more clarity. "Jealous? There's no reason for her—"

"She's gone after you because you've always done whatever the hell you wanted. You were the extroverted introvert who both read books on some Saturday nights and danced on bars on others. She was the perfect student, who kept up this perfect persona and took advantage of maintaining that *perfect* façade when she saw how Grant treated you."

"You *really* just sat back and analyzed everything growing up, didn't you?" I asked, an unexpected giggle hiccupping out of me.

I could tell Nora noticed a sliver of light slip back into my body. "It's taken me many years—and lots of therapy—to get to a point where I can just word-vomit like this." Nora leaned over my bent legs and reached for my hand, squeezing it tight. "I've seen you thrive, and I've seen you struggle, Nel. It was painful watching you fall back into such a dark place this last year—a place I'd watched you drown in during high school. But watching you climb out of that hole over these last several months...it's been exhilarating. I *know* you're finally in a place where you can put the past behind you and move forward without the opinions of others warping your mind the way they used to. You just have to understand that trauma takes time to heal from, but you only heal when you let yourself embrace the process."

Nora's words came from a heart more genuine than any heart I'd ever known, but the thing was...I'd tried moving forward before. I'd tried erasing Hallie's opinion from my life, only for it to just continue humming in my ear. I knew the humming wasn't *just* Hallie's verbal abuse, but also Grant's—all those experiences I could never fully ignore because they'd, in a way, become part of me.

Could I ignore a past where the opinions of others sculpted my every decision and move into a future where *I* finally took center stage? It was insane how impossible that sounded after naively hanging from puppet strings for most of my life.

But the thought of ripping those strings off for good sounded like the beautiful relief I needed.

The relief I deserved.

"Yeah, I know. I just have to...do it." Hesitance still lingered at the forefront of my mind. "I think when I confront Hallie, I'll really be doing it for me. Walking up to her and confronting her isn't what I do—I can't. I'm not sure how or when it'll happen, but it'll feel right when it does."

"And when you do it, you'll feel free." Nora pushed a strand of auburn hair out of her eyes, wrapping it around her ear so the violet edges peeked out just below her earlobe. Bringing her hand in front of her chest, her ring finger met the other two fingers to make the number three. "Okay. Third. Nel...do you love Jude?"

When she said the word *love*, my heart could have snapped a rib. Even though I was trying to convince myself that I didn't know why my heart was racing, I knew the truth.

I loved him.

I fucking loved Jude.

I'd loved him since our freshman year, and I loved him now.

The heart clawing its way through my chest proved the emotions I felt were real. It was proof I had nothing left to do but feel them—*really* feel them. Because once I stopped trying to convince myself that these feelings meant something else, I could melt into them.

I could enjoy the rush.

I could lean into the butterflies.

I could just listen to what my heart had been trying to tell me all along.

"Nora..." I did all I could to hold myself together, my chest heavy and a sob rolling up my throat. "I don't think I ever stopped loving him. I just never let myself believe it was love, because Hallie was spoon-feeding me judgmental lies."

Nora sat back. "I know."

"How? How've you known?"

"Because I've never seen you free yourself the way you have over these last few months since he's been around. It's a smile I haven't seen since...hell, *before* Grant. And your confidence? It's the confidence I saw whenever I'd visit you at Merlin Community. *You* came back over these last few months. It's been a version of yourself that has more strength than the one you had when you let Hallie tell you who not to love. You know who you love. You just need to tell him that."

Damn, she should have become a therapist rather than a chiropractor.

Wrapping my arms around Mae, who now lay on my chest with tiny snores sliding from her lips, I got to my feet for the first time in what felt like hours. The sun had set, and as I peered toward the windowsill, a golden haze fell over a backyard of lone streamers and deflating balloons.

The party hadn't been what I'd hoped it would be, but I could help put the pieces back together.

I'd confront Hallie when the time felt right.

I'd make a plan on how to approach Jude later.

But right now, I needed my best friend back.

Chapter 38

ROSIE

L *awn.*

I hated sending single-word texts to people just as much as I hated receiving them, but here I was, standing on the corner of the Merlin Community College lawn with the world's tiniest Bluetooth speaker in hand. I should have thought this through a little more before digging through the trunk of my Jeep. If I had, maybe I could have stopped to grab the boombox I'd seen in the back of the coat closet that Nel and I used in college.

But I was here—dinky Bluetooth in hand—scrolling on my phone to find the best instrumental music I had.

I didn't expect her to respond. Even though she was the kindest damn person I knew, I also knew that, when she arrived to the party, Sebastian told her I'd left to see an ex-girlfriend who was in town. I was definitely more furious at myself for leaving the party before letting Cade know the situation than at him for word-vomiting these things to her.

It was Sebastian.

It was expected.

I clicked on a folk playlist and increased the volume up to as high as it would go—which, in reality, wasn't all that loud. However, the guitar strings plucking against the velvety night sky was dreamy enough that, if she didn't show, I was content experiencing this alone.

I was content experiencing this alone.

Ever since, well, forever, I'd had somebody I could lean on—whether they were always physically there or just a quick text away. I'd had Jude since birth. I'd had Nel throughout college. I'd had Viv since stepping foot into adulthood. I'd never really felt okay walking through life alone, and it had taken thirty-one years to realize this.

If Cade didn't show, I was okay with that.

My heart would sting a bit, but I'd move forward.

I had to.

"Dabbler?"

I practically fell over as the top half of my body moved faster than the bottom. I focused on the beautiful woman standing bare-foot on the lawn, her sandals dangling from her fingers. A subtle smile didn't cling to her cheeks in the way I was used to, her head nodding along to the guitar as she looked down at her feet.

"Cade. Hi," I said, stumbling over my words as much as I'd just stumbled over my feet. "You're here."

"That I am," she said, sandals dropping from her hands as she walked closer, stopping only a few feet away from my own. "You left today."

"I did…and I'd like to explain if you'll let me."

"I'm not one to assume anything before hearing all the sides," she said with a nod, finally looking me in the eyes. "I'm listening …but I'll admit that I'm a bit, well, annoyed."

"You have every right to be annoyed with me. Hell, *I'm* annoyed with me." I shuffled my combat boots across the grass, my eyes shifting to Cade's bare toes as they curled around emerald blades. "Viv and I have history. She helped me when my mom was hospi-talized, and she was part of the reason I became so successful with The Bare Assentials. I can't even say she is my ex, because we never officially dated. We just…existed. She dragged me along and gaslit me into thinking I didn't *need* love when I could thrive off lust. So, I began believing that was true."

Cade nodded, her eyes angled back at her feet.

"But since coming back to Merlin—since being cut from The Bare Assentials—I've learned a few things. I've learned it's okay to step away from what used to define you if you feel like you're growing. I've learned I can still love one thing while moving onto something better. We aren't the people we used to be. We've taken what we learned from those people and sculpted ourselves into better versions of them. It's okay to let that shit go and move the fuck forward...but it's easier said than done."

Cade took another step forward, her toes barely touching the edges of my boots as her hand wrapped around mine. "It *is* easier said than done. It's hard separating yourself from someone who was such a positive part of your life, even if that positivity morphed into something else. I get that."

"I officially told her I'm done. I'm done with our situationship, done being her duckling, done meeting her needs when she barely recognized mine. I'm done with that, Cade. I'm moving on—I *have* moved on."

Cade's eyes met mine, those specks of gold lighting up the darkness. "Have you, though? I may come off as pretty understanding, but I've also been hurt. I've been walked over, believe it or not. It's taken me a while to let my guard down, and I want to let my guard down with you. I just can't be someone's second choice, you know?"

My free hand wrapped around the back of her neck, and I pulled her forehead against mine. "There isn't another choice, Cade. You're the *only* choice. You brought my heart to life this summer. It wasn't just lust or desire; it was life. You handed me an energy Viv never could, and that's why you're the only choice."

"Okay...alright." Cade slowly swayed against my body to the sound of the guitar flowing through the world's tiniest speaker. Tipping my chin up, she asked, "What's your next step, Dabbler?"

"Other than kissing you?" My laugh cut through the space between us. "I guess, my next step is to apply for something—maybe that part-time instructor position you mentioned. My next step is to look at apartments. I'll admit, though it's hard, my next step is also figuring out what to do with The Naked Book Club. But the best step of all is the one that makes you officially my girlfriend."

Cade's black curls fell over my cheeks, her hand still cupping my chin. "What if I were to accept this title as your girlfriend but also offer some solutions to your other steps."

I stepped back, my hands running down her arms until our fingers intertwined. "What solutions do you have in mind?"

"Move in with me."

I stopped swaying as my arms straightened in front of me, Cade's fingers still locked with mine. "Excuse me?"

"Move in with me. Move in, and then I can introduce you to the creative movement board at the college...if that's what you really want. If it isn't, I can be there for you no matter what steps you decide to take." Cade pulled me in, bringing our locked fingers to her lips and kissing my knuckles.

"But...you were just mad at me. I mean, *I* am still mad at me."

"I wouldn't say mad...annoyed is a better term," Cade said with a laugh. "I'm also sure there will be more times when we're mad or annoyed, but that's why we stay honest with each other. We don't hide shit. So, what do you say? Take your next steps with me, Dabbler."

Just as she was going to kiss the top of my hand again, I pulled her lips to mine instead. Running my thumb along the smile growing across her face, I said, "Lead the way."

Chapter 39

Nel

The apartment was dark the moment I walked in and just as dark after I'd rocked Mae to sleep. I didn't bother turning any of the lights on, especially if it looked like Rosie wasn't coming back.

And that was absolutely what it looked like.

I didn't want to be dramatic and convince myself she was gone for good—again—because sooner or later, she'd have to come back for all her things. She easily could leave behind certain knick-knacks and was always fine buying a whole new set of designer make-up if need be, but she couldn't leave the lingerie.

She'd ghost me before losing the lace.

As I finished filling my water bottle and twisted the cap closed, a whisper of light caught my attention from the window above the sink. The glowing Edison bulbs from our bookshelf reflected against the glass, the luminescence brighter than usual with every light in the apartment shut off. With my extra-large water bottle in hand, I shuffled my exhausted body across the kitchen floor until I came to the shag rug we'd used as a stage for the last handful of months. The stool was in its usual place, the laptop folded on top like I'd left it.

It was right here where everything changed over the last twenty-four hours.

It was here where my love for reading returned.

It was here where my confidence began crawling back.

It was here where I realized my heart had been in Jude's hands all along.

There was something so empowering about standing in front of this bookshelf after a day flipped upside down. The fact that I was physically standing was a testament to how far I'd mentally come. A year ago, I wouldn't have made it out of Nora's house for days after being emotionally attacked like I had been that morning. Instead of my body growing heavier—weaker—and pulling me down through the floorboards, it was the lights and the book bindings and the dim room lifting me up.

Kneeling down onto the rug, I opened up the laptop. The screen blinded me for only a second before I squinted and clicked open our YourEyesOnly page. Tens of thousands of people saw the video from the night before—more viewers than we'd ever had on a livestream recording.

I brushed my fingers over the touchpad until the cursor arrived at the little red button I'd grown more and more comfortable pressing over time.

Maybe I should have thought about this a little more.

Maybe my heart had taken the reins at this point.

I didn't know or care where it was all coming from, because once I clicked that red button and the LIVE light lit up in the corner of the screen, I began to talk.

Chapter 40

ROSIE

My phone buzzed within seconds of Cade and I plopping ourselves in the Jeep.

When the screen showed Jude's name in big, bold letters, I immediately picked it up. "Jude, are you okay?"

"I mean...are *you*?" he asked hesitantly. It was a fair response.

"I'm...yeah, I'm good. I'm driving with Cade...back to the apartment," I said, her hand sliding over my thigh with a gentle, assuring squeeze.

"Oh...okay, that's *probably* a good thing."

My foot stepped on the brake as we came to the first of three cross sections in Merlin Heights. "Why do you say it like that?"

There was a breath of silence before Jude said, "The Naked Book Club just went live."

Right on cue, my phone buzzed as a notification tab from YourEyesOnly flew across the screen. Keeping Jude on speaker phone in the car, I swiped open The Naked Book Club to see Nel. Not Nel with a wig. Not Nel with a lace mask. Nel with her messy bun of waves and lopsided glasses. Nel with eyes pink from crying. Nel clad in the denim overall shorts she wore most days during the summer.

Cade leaned toward me, clenching my thigh a little tighter, and whispered, "Nel is streaming on The Naked Book Club right now? Alone?"

"She *just* started one minute ago. There are over three hundred people already watching." I angled the screen toward Cade as the light turned green. Driving down Main Street toward the second intersection with more umph than before, I realized something. "Jude...since when do you follow The Naked Book Club? I thought you were too disgusted to follow us before."

Another few seconds of silence passed. "Well...I'm definitely not there for you. No offense. I've never gone into a stream. I just...have it."

I hit the brakes again, hitting another damn red light. "Well, I'm almost to the apartment. Where are you?"

"At Thirsty Theodore's with Seb and Riley."

The second that light turned green, my foot hit the gas. "Okay, good. Get your ass to the apartment. Don't bring the guys...that would be too much for her. Too much for anyone, right now."

"You really think she wants to see *me* right now?" His voice was so cautious, so uncertain.

Powering through the yellow light at the final intersection, I said, "Yes. I think you're who she wants to see most."

Chapter 41

Nel

"I know a lot of you saw the recording of last night's Smut Me Up session...and to be honest, I'm pretty impressed so many of you watched until the end. Well, maybe some of you fast-forwarded...I'm not sure..." My eyes darted to the bottom of the screen where comment bubbles were popping up, mostly from our regulars, but many usernames I didn't recognize. "I couldn't leave you guys hanging and...uh...had to come on here to say a few things."

512 viewers.

532 viewers.

Where the fuck were these viewers coming from…and within a two-minute span?

I swallowed down the lump in my throat and mentally brought myself back to the twin-sized therapeutic bed I'd lain on at Nora's. Nora's words popped into my head, and I used them as motivation to keep talking.

I needed to let go of the past and let my heart speak.

Releasing my hair tie, I shook out my hair until it fell over my shoulders, and I adjusted the frames I'm sure sat crooked on my nose. "Guys, this is me. This is the *real* Exotic Ellie. Maybe some of you realized who I was early on, and maybe some of you didn't care, but the thing is…*I* cared. I naively cared too much about what all of you would think or how this would impact my getting a full-time job after this. The thing is, *this* job right here brings me so much fucking joy…and feeling such genuine joy shouldn't be embarrassing."

My hands fell to my belly, fingers pressing into the gray sweatshirt tied at the hips of the overall shorts I wore. "The Naked Book Club helped me embrace this body I felt trapped inside of since my daughter was born. You helped me care less about my insecurities and more about the parts of me—physical or not—that make me who I am. And it was all because we wanted to read together…isn't that crazy? Even those who just wanted to see a nip slip…you were still part of this book club community in some way, and for that, I am grateful."

I looked down at my hands still pressed against the sweatshirt and loosened the tension in my fingers, bringing my palms together so they sat balled on my lap. "First, I need to address my sister...Hallie." Breathe in, breathe out. "If...if you're friends with her in real life or if you follow TwoBloomsHal on whatever social platform you obsess over her on, I have a few things to say."

I twisted open the cap to my water bottle and took a long gulp, holding the cool liquid in my mouth for a few seconds that seemed to take much longer than they probably did. I felt the water seep through my system, breathing energy and life into me—or, if anything, hydrating me for the next few minutes.

704 viewers.

721 viewers.

I needed this closure.

This chapter needed to end.

"Hallie. I don't know if you're watching, but I'm sure if you aren't watching right now, someone will soon tell you about it. I'm here to thank you one last time. Thank you for helping me escape a verbally and mentally abusive relationship in high school. If you hadn't done what you did, I'm not sure where I'd be today. However, what I *do* know is that you can no longer control who I love. You cannot demean people close to my heart just because they remind you of someone else or because you don't trust them not to hurt me. This is your weird way of showing you love me—I see that now—but I need you to find a different, less hurtful way to show it.

"I'm...I'm not a bad person, and I am *not* a bad mother." The corners of my eyes trembled, but I welcomed the breaking dams. I wiped my eyes with the back of my wrist before taking a deep breath. "Maybe I don't pretend to live this perfect life where everything is cookie cutter and gentle, but that doesn't mean I'm less of a mother. Not everyone needs to nurse their children for two years and give them all-organic meals. Not everyone has to look happy and flawless around their children, because when you do, sometimes it gives them a false sense of reality. I'm not doing that to myself or to Mae. I'd rather *live*."

The comment bubbles at the bottom of the screen were rolling as quickly as the viewer count was increasing, but I did everything in my power not to read them. I needed to get this done and over with.

"So, Hallie...this is it. I will no longer be your pawn. I've appreciated your help over these years—because, sometimes, you did genuinely help. However, I'm taking the reins now."

A weight lifted off my shoulders, and I released a breath. Weight still lingered, but that little release felt like sunshine breaking through storm clouds.

"And Jude..." My breath caught in my throat when his name fell from my lips, and I placed my glasses back onto the bridge of my nose, pretending it was Jude's fingers straightening them out. "Jude, I need you to know that I never meant to hurt you. I didn't mean to hurt you ten years ago, and I hope I didn't hurt you earlier when I couldn't bring myself to say what I've been meaning to say for so long. I do understand if—"

A creak echoed through the darkened apartment, the front door opening as footsteps sounded in the entryway. Three shadowed figures shuffled into the kitchen, the bulbs behind me casting a dim glow over their bodies. From their stances, their breathing, and the outlines of their bodies, I knew exactly who they were. They didn't need to come any closer for recognition to hit.

The bubbles at the bottom of the screen caught my eye again, and as my breathing fell back into the similar rhythm from seconds before, I read the most recent comment:

@ZestyZi_NakedBookClub: Keep going, Nel.

"I...I do understand if you're upset, Jude. Even after ten years, I still...*still* let someone else dictate who I should care about—who I should...who I should love. All along, I knew my feelings were real. I always knew I was safe with you. I knew you wouldn't hurt me, and I let someone else convince me differently...twice."

The Edison bulbs behind me caused a slice of light to cut through the darkness, illuminating Jude's face for a quick second. That second was long enough for me to feel the power of his intent gaze as it struck me from his spot at the end of the couch.

I focused back on the screen, pressing my lips together and inhaling deeply.

"Hallie, Jude is *not* Grant. Jude is not any of my other exes who, now I see, weren't the greatest. Jude is kind and sweet and quirky and cares so damn much about everyone. I can't imagine him saying something hurtful to me—or to anyone. Unlike Grant, Jude is driven. He's passionate. Hallie, you've always pinned him to be the same lazy, negligent guy Grant was because of petty similarities like looks and preferences or whatever...and you know what? I'm not sorry I'm attracted to people who don't wear expensive suits to work or bring in six-figure salaries. I won't change who I am to make *you* happy, Hallie. I'm going to change how I react to your opinions, because I deserve to love who I love...and, dammit, I love Jude."

A soft gasp cut through the murky air, and I wasn't entirely sure who it came from.

For all I knew, the gasp could have escaped my own lungs.

"And Rowe." When that same gasp sounded a second time, Rosie's silhouette came closer to the couch. "Rosie, I'm not mad at you. In a way, I'm glad your little accident last night happened. It helped me get here...to a place where I could open up. Please know I could never hate you. I'm annoyed...but hate? I can't."

"I fucking love your face, Nel!" Rosie shouted from the edge of the couch, Jude shushing her as they looked behind them into the hallway.

Tears grazed my cheeks. "Okay. Alright. I know this wasn't the surprise storytelling session you guys may have expected...but it was part of *my* story that had to be shared. We'll be back next week with some raunchy chapters for you, but don't expect Exotic Ellie to wear her black wig and mask anymore. You'll get all this from here on out...but maybe with some cute little outfits on."

Without reading any of the comments rolling in at the bottom of the screen, I carefully clicked the livestream off—triple-checking to make sure everything was shut down as I logged off the page before fully closing the laptop.

Just as I set the laptop back onto the stool and clicked off the ring light, Rosie's body careened into mine, her arms and legs wrapping around me like a sloth to a tree. She dramatically kissed both of my cheeks, shifting from one to the other as her limbs squished around me.

"Jesus Christ…enough!" I exclaimed, quieting myself as I pushed her off me. "Okay, okay, Rowe."

She loosened her grip and slid off, the two of us getting back to our feet as Rosie put her hands on her hips and said, "I'm just so proud of you. That was…that took *balls*. Like, *big* ones. I've never seen you lay it all out there like that before, Nel." Rosie took a step forward, the lights from the shelf outlining her body in a golden glow. "And I'm glad you don't hate me. I really… I really thought that was going to be it."

"I mean…maybe if it happens again, I'll have to unfriend you in real life," I joked, rolling my eyes. "Yes…I was frustrated. But there were about twelve other points of frustration coming at me this afternoon. I couldn't untangle them all at once."

Rosie stepped away from the bookshelf, blackness cascading her body as Cade stepped forward. Cade's fingers entwined with Rosie's as Rosie said, "I get that. That was a lot to untangle. I, um…untangled a couple things too. Viv. She's no more."

Jude's eyes grew three sizes bigger, turning toward his sister. "Wait…did you kill her?"

Cade's laugh filled the room.

"What? No!" Rosie shouted at a whisper, something I didn't know was even possible. "I talked to her. I told her about Cade. I told her about her manipulation. She's done."

Cade squeezed Rosie's hand a little bit tighter, the two of them looking at each other with an aura I'd never felt come from Rosie. This was new for her. I could sense the change.

I wondered if they could sense a change in me too.

With his hands stuffed into the pockets of his black jeans and his head angled downward, Jude stepped onto the rug. He had yet to look away from his socked feet, but the memory of that quick gaze from minutes before was enough to shock me with a needed bolt of energy.

"Jude...I hope you know that—"

Before I could finish, Jude strode forward as both of his hands flew from his pockets to cup my cheeks, pulling my face toward his. His lips lingered above mine, a whisper of air between us as he softly said, "I never stopped loving you, Nel. My heart has been yours for years, and that's the only damn place I ever want it to be."

My fingers found the belt loops of his jeans, and I pulled him closer, Jude's lips pressing hard against mine with raw intensity. We'd shared vulnerable moments together—moments I'd never thought I could share with another person.

But this one? This one felt different.

There was an eagerness to his hands as they dug through my hair and a desperate hunger as his tongue brushed mine. It was as if we were tasting one another for the first time, exploring each other with such clarity. As he gently nipped my bottom lip, his free hand wrapping around the underside of my chin and angling my gaze directly at him, I couldn't help but smile.

Because he was smiling too.

"I want my heart to be yours too, Jude." My heavy lids blinked slowly, taking a deep breath. "For real this time."

His thumbs brushed my cheeks as he asked, "For real, huh?"

"For real," I repeated. "Please?"

He chuckled, looking away for a second before turning to face me with a damn smile that would forever force my heart into overdrive. "You know I can't say no to that."

When he pulled my face to his, his lips filled me with fresh energy.

Maybe it felt a little like freedom.

Maybe it felt like we were finally where we needed to be.

But I knew for sure, this felt like love.

yourEyesOnly.com
LIVE
LIKE
SUBSCRIBE
COMMENTS
@disco_dan: How did you get to the beat drop at minute two? Show me again.
@spinmeround: I want to see some
DJ DICKSPIN

Chapter 42

Nel

One Week Later

"Nope, nope, nope!" Rosie shouted, sitting down with a flailing Mae in her arms. "He's not giving you any more stupid miniatures. He's given you *all* of them."

I scooped up a handful of tiny plastic elves and ogres and gnomes that were set on the blanket by the window. "She's repeating more now, Rowe. Chill with the 'S' word."

"Is the 'S' word *stupid* or *shi*—" Rosie covered her mouth when she saw my gaze tighten. Mae grabbed the plastic figurines, making noises as she rammed one into the other atop the table. "Sorry...okay. Well, good thing you'll be rid of me next week, because I'm not sure I can keep this dirty mouth clean much longer."

The truth sunk deep into the pit of my stomach.

When she'd told me that Cade asked her to move in, I couldn't help but smile and support her. I'd never seen Rosie in love before. I'd seen her infatuated...and obsessed...but never *in love.*

It wasn't that I'd expected we'd find a place together. We'd emailed a few places the week leading up to Mae's party, but we hadn't heard back from them. I guess it made sense she'd want to either find her own place or, in this case, move in with someone who didn't have a toddler running around. She loved Mae, but she was *not* a kid person.

"I'll miss your dirty mouth, though," I whispered, looking up at her with basset hound eyes I knew she couldn't ignore.

"Oh, come the fu—" She pressed her lips together, angling her face toward Mae, who still sat on her lap. "...come on. It's not like I'm going anywhere."

I pressed my lips together and cocked my head to the side until I saw another spark of realization flicker in Rosie's eyes, her mouth opening into an *Oh.*

Was it too soon for ghosting jokes?

"I know…you're not going anywhere. You're ready to be a full-fledged, *real* adult who does all these adult things," I said, savoring the sweet vanilla latte against my tongue. "I mean, we're in our thirties. It was time anyway."

"We've *been* doing adult things, Nel! You kept a human alive for a whole year while reading books half-naked and getting paid for it. If that's not hustling, I don't know what is."

"Hustling and keeping people alive doesn't make me feel like much of an adult, but I'll take your weird-ass compliment and go with it," I said.

"*Ash, ash, ashhhhh!*" Mae exclaimed, tossing a handful of plastic minis into the air, one falling directly into Rosie's hot cup of coffee.

Rosie lifted an eyebrow in my direction, smirking.

"Noooo…not Leander!" Sebastian reached directly into Rosie's coffee, pulling out the figurine and tossing it from hand to hand as if it were on fire.

"Excuse me…what?" Rosie asked, Mae's eyes following Sebastian's hands as they danced in the air.

"Did Jude give you this guy, Mae?" He set the tiny figurine so it stood in his palm, just out of reach. "Because I need little Leander Lyric, here, for the next campaign I'm in."

"Jesus, you play that silly stuff too?" Rosie said, shaking her head as she peered into her coffee mug. Shrugging, she lifted it to her lips.

Sebastian stepped back, bringing his hand to his chest. "That *silly stuff* includes very serious scenarios where mature adults play pretend, Rosie. I thought you, of all people, would appreciate the beauty that is Dungeons and Dragons."

Rosie just stared at him as he slowly backed away, his body still facing us with the tiny figurine balanced in his palm. He'd almost made it all the way to the counter safely, walking backward, before tripping over the legs of a customer waiting for her drink. Sebastian caught himself—and caught Leander—before bowing his head at the red-haired woman.

"That was weird," Rosie said, setting Mae on her blanket, hoping she would play with one of the ten books she'd pulled from the bottom of the bookshelf.

"Was it, though? I feel like we exp—"

"Ellie?" Stunned, I slowly turned toward the high-pitched voice. The woman Sebastian had not-so-smoothly tripped over was standing near the door, coffee in hand, and smiling in our direction. Shaking her head of red curls, she said, "Oh my god, I'm sorry. You actually go by Nel, right? Jesus, I'm sorry...that's embarrassing."

"You're fine. It's okay," I mumbled, immediately taking a long, icy sip of my latte.

The woman took a step closer to our table, both of her hands carefully wrapped around the travel cup. Leaning forward, she whispered, "I saw your stream the other night...well, *obviously*, since I recognized you. I just wanted to say how badass that was, putting yourself out there like that. It was badass and..." She turned to look over her shoulder toward the cash register before turning back to face me with a grin. "...honestly, *really* romantic."

I watched Jude laugh with a customer as he took their order, running a hand across the tablet in front of him. His eyes caught mine before I could turn back toward the stranger, and the corners of his lips quirked up.

It was impossible not to smile back.

"Thank you. That...that really means a lot," I said, leaning forward onto my elbows. "What did you say your name was?"

"Oh, I didn't. I'm Stef. I've actually been part of your streams since the start. I've read all the books with you guys!"

Rosie twisted on her chair so that she was straddling the back of it—somehow making that transition far smoother than it should have been. "Holy shit, you're Spicy!"

I looked at Rosie as a slideshow of livestream comments raced across my memory until it hit me. "SpicyStef?"

"That's me!" She took a step back, playfully flipping her crimson curls over her shoulder and leaning into one hip. "And actually, I'm kind of glad I ran into you here, Ell—Nel—because I know you'd mentioned the job thing...and how you were looking for something."

The latte curdled in my stomach. "Yeah...I'm looking. I should look a little more diligently after...the other night, but yes. I'm looking."

I hadn't heard back from St. Merlin Academy.

Whether that was because of my stint on YourEyesOnly or my lack of credentials, I wasn't sure.

"Well, maybe *I* can help." Stef sing-songed, bringing the coffee to her lips for a quick sip. "It wouldn't be a lot, but I could use a little help at my shop. It could be something up your alley."

The word *shop* could mean many things.

Java Jude's was a coffee *shop*.

The Vintage Press was a comic book *shop*.

Velvet was a speakeasy sex toy *shop*.

I wasn't good at letting people down, and I felt like this would be one of those situations. With how enthusiastic Stef seemed, I felt like we'd lose a devoted fan once I declined whatever the offer was.

"What…kind of shop do you have, Stef?" I asked quietly, Mae's little hands clawing at my bare legs before I heaved her up onto my lap.

Damn, I needed to clip her fingernails more often.

Stef took a quick sip before saying, "Oh, I should have clarified. I'm opening up Love Potion Lit. It'll be Merlin's first romance-only bookshop! I'm the *crazy* person painting the brick storefront bright purple across from the college. I know it's next door to Spellbound Beans Roasters, but I *promise* I come here *way* more." Stef leaned closer, trying to whisper so Mae was out of earshot. "The barista at Spellbound is kind of a dick."

It took me a second to piece everything she had just babbled together.

We'd met SpicyStef.

She'd recognized me in public.

Because she'd recognized me, she was offering me a job at her bookshop.

Her *romance* bookshop.

What the fuck was going on?

"Dude, Nel…she wants you to work at her *smutty* bookshop!" Rosie whispered loud enough for, well, everyone around us to hear. Rosie faced Stef, her legs still straddling the back of the chair.

"What would she be doing there? What about PTO and health insurance? She will need—"

"I still get health insurance through the Finger Lakes Marketplace, Rowe. I'm a single mom...that's not changing anytime soon, so I'll still qualify."

Flapping a hand in my direction, Rosie continued her interrogation. "Okay, but what about sick time? Mae is cutting teeth, and that shit spikes her fever up real—"

"Rosie," I said, my raised voice, catching her attention. "Let Stef talk."

Stef took a sip of her coffee, and once she swallowed the warm liquid, her eyes dramatically rolled, and she said, "Oh, my god. This dark roast is *seriously* the best. Wherever they get their beans...I *need* to rub them all over my body." Stef brought the cup to her lips again, repeating the same excessive eyeroll and smile. "Okay, sorry. The shop is part of the Finger Lakes Marketplace too...but part of their business sector. So, I'm glad you're already in their system...because I am *not* a mathematician."

Rosie and I exchanged glances as Stef took another long sip.

"What I'm looking for is bookseller help. You know, placing wholesale orders, and stocking shelves, and organizing the book clubs. I think *you* would be awesome doing book club stuff since you have experience with that already. I want to put together a bunch of different clubs because not *everyone* likes spicy romance. Some clubs for sweet romance, and romantasy, so..."—another sip—"you'd kind of be an assistant bookseller and community engagement...person. I'll figure out a title eventually."

Rosie peered back over her shoulder at me, the smile on her little pale face growing. By the time her eyebrows practically hit her hairline and her teeth showed from her maddening smile, I knew I needed to tell this girl something.

And really, I had little to think about.

"Yeah..." I said, Mae's hand crawling up into my hair and wrapping strands around her fingers. "Yes, Stef. Sure. I'd love to talk more about it."

Stef gleefully hopped in place, clapping the coffee cup against her hand. "Oh, good! That's *so* good! Oh...oh, let me give you a card. I'm a dork and already made cards before the shop even opened. Marketing...am I right?" Stef slid over to the table as she reached into her leather purse and plucked out a periwinkle business card with rounded gold edges. "My number and social media platforms and all the things are on there. Do you have time to meet and chat sometime this week?"

When I flipped the card over to look at the back, a shadow fell over the table. Jude stood above me, peering down at my hands and sliding another iced latte onto the table.

"What's this? Did you guys magically make business cards over the last few days?" he asked, looking toward his sister and then back at me before squinting closer at the card. "Oh...this is—"

"It's for Love Potion Lit. It's opening across the street from the college next month!" Stef said, hopping in place again. "Nel is going to be my new *bookseller and community outreach coordinator*...well, if she decides she wants to be. *Oooooh!* Now *that's* the winning title."

Smiling, Jude ran a finger down my jawline until he lifted my chin in his direction. "Is this true? You may have a new job?"

Stef stood, elated, at the edge of our table, her exuberant energy filling up the coffee shop. I too felt an overwhelming energy engulf me, bringing my wild emotions to life—per usual.

I'd learned that emotions were meant to be felt, and being an emotional person was not a flaw—it was a gift. I didn't experience life in black and white and gray. Life was splashes of wild, vibrant colors, and I got to experience those in their true, raw form.

So, I let the tears fall.

Because these were emotions I wanted to savor, not force away.

"Yeah," I said. "Yeah, I guess I do."

Chapter 43

ROSIE

Talking to Daniella Ortiz about the part-time instructor position at Merlin Community College hadn't been terrifying. When she'd requested I do three minutes of improvised movement to a random instrumental track, I didn't blink an eye. I even added some of my more sensual moves into it, and from the look on her face, she didn't hate the flair.

That was all fine—*fun*, even.

What terrified me most was waiting.

It had been two days since the interview—audition, more like. Two days of swiping my thumb across my phone to see if she'd emailed me. Two days of anxiously packing my duffel bags and emptying out my lingerie closet at Nel's. Two days of responding to comments on The Naked Book Club's forums that I'd already checked a handful of times.

Well, I actually *enjoyed* checking the forums. So, that wasn't really something I anxiously did just to pass the time. Anything I did for The Naked Book Club was because I genuinely wanted to do it—never a stressful necessity. This damn side gig brought me more joy than I'd expected when making our profile live months earlier.

Side gig.

For some reason, that phrase didn't sit well as I waited for Daniella to call me back.

"You need to get out of here," Nel said, practically crawling onto the kitchen countertop to reach wine glasses on the top shelf. After hugging three or four to her chest, she somehow made it down without dying to wrap the glasses in newspaper. "Just come with me to meet Stef and then you can go to the next apartment showing with me."

I collapsed over my arms laying crossed on the counter, my face hidden. "Can we wait until I get the email saying I'm not good enough to be an instructor?"

"Where the hell is this negativity coming from?" Nel asked, the sound of crunchy newspaper making my brain scream. "You used to call it *Nel*gativity for a reason."

"I'm not being negative."

"That's *exactly* what you're being," she said, placing a wrapped-up glass into a cardboard box and reaching for the next one. "Just come with me. It'll be a good distraction. That or give me your phone."

"Hell no!" I shouted, standing up straight and snagging my phone from the counter, hugging it to my chest. "I'm an addicted millennial and cannot part from—"

My chest hummed, and I looked down at the buzzing phone in my hands.

The number on the screen was one I didn't recognize, and for a second, I wondered if it was Viv now that I'd blocked her number.

When that possibility crossed my mind, I almost didn't answer the call.

But I pushed that aside when I brought the phone to my ear.

"Hello, hi," I coughed out, clearing my throat. Nel rounded the kitchen island and stood a few feet away from me, her eyes wide with a glass in one hand and newspaper in the other. "Hello, yes. I'm well. How are...oh. Okay, sure. Mm-hmm. I think so too. I really appreciate you thinking that...okay, yes. Absolutely. Thank you, Daniella. Thanks."

I slowly lowered the phone from my ear as dark strands of hair fell over my face, my fingers trembling.

I just couldn't nail down exactly *why* I was trembling.

"Okay...okay. Are you alright?" Nel asked, stepping forward. "What happened?"

Blowing away a few pieces of dark hair, I sighed heavily and said, "So..."

"Rowe..."

"They want me to teach full-time. They think that my teaching a full-time contemporary class along with an Intro to Sensual Expression class would be great for both Fine Arts *and* Human Sexuality majors who need a solid elective."

"Holy shit, Rosie!" Nel's arms collapsed around me, mimicking one of the obnoxious hugs. And probably for the first time, I knew what it felt like to be Nel during one of those hugs. I felt small and a little claustrophobic, my fingers clawing away her hands. Almost immediately, she seemed to notice my discomfort and stepped aside. "Rowe...are you okay?"

"Yeah. Obviously. Maybe," I stammered, my head falling into my hands.

"That does *not* sound confident after getting such a kickass call." Nel leaned against the counter, crossing her arms over her chest. "What's going on?"

The word *side gig* flashed across my vision again.

Why had this damn phrase haunted me over the last couple of days?

"I don't know. I mean...the offer is seriously amazing. I should take it."

Nel's nod was slow, eyebrows raised. "*Should?* Isn't this what you want to do? Dance again?"

"Yes. It is! I'm freaking ecstatic about getting back into a studio!" I shouted, throwing my arms into the air just for my fingers to interlock on the top of my head. As I adjusted my stance against the counter, my eyes snapped to the bookshelf across the room. Many of the books were already packed away, and the shelf looked so...naked.

I didn't like how the shelves were so bare and how the shag rug didn't color the floor in front of it anymore.

I didn't like that the Edison bulbs were packed away, and the stool for the laptop was gone from its spot.

None of it sat well with me.

The Naked Book Club had never been just a *side gig* to me.

That was it.

"Nel, I think I want to get back into the studio, but not...not full-time."

She stood in front of me like a bobblehead, her nods never stopping. "Okay...okay, that's okay."

"I don't want to work a full-time job—even one I'd really like—just because it's the more accepted option from the outside looking in," I said, doing all I could not to peer over at the bookshelf. "I want to work a job I love because it sets my fucking soul on fire every single time I think about it. Yes...dance does that for me. It always has, and it always will. But The Naked Book Club, Nel. That's what I want to do full-time because I love who I am and how I feel when that red light turns on. Settling has never been part of my personality, and I don't think I *need* to settle. I think I can teach occasionally at the college while maintaining this empowering community of book nerds we created."

Nel stood in front of me, her head still bobbing subtly from all the nodding she'd done over the last few minutes. As if that side of the apartment was pulling her toward it as well, she looked over her shoulder at the bookshelf for a long moment before turning back. "I get it."

"You do? You're not going to push me to be a full-time professor?"

Whoa...no.

I didn't like thinking of myself as a professor unless role-playing as one.

Nel's nodding continued, and I was worried her neck may cramp up. "I do get it. I get it because I feel the same way. I...*we* don't have to fit into one specific box. We've probably learned that more over the last few months than over the course of our lives. If I want to be Exotic Ellie a few nights a week and also help Stef at Love Potion Lit, I don't see her—or anyone—stopping me. If anything, I see her supporting it."

Blinking a few times to play off the unexpected tears as dust from packing tape getting in my eye—or something—I set a hand on Nel's shoulder and said, "I'm so fucking proud of you, woman."

"Stop that..." Nel whispered, flapping her hand in my direction as I tightened my grip on her shoulder, pulling her close. "Don't say those things to me. You know how I react to sappy compliments."

Instead of pushing me away, Nel fell into my embrace and squeezed me close. Her salty tears painted my shoulder as my own painted hers, because fuck it, I was going to feel this moment the way it was meant to be felt. This was the hug—the *Nel*—I'd missed for all those years when I'd chosen Viv and lust over Nel and friendship.

It felt good closing that chapter and watching a much stronger one unfold.

Because flipping the pages of this chapter with Nel felt so damn right.

Chapter 44

Nel

“And this is the system we're going to use to keep track of the books people request and how many are in stock. Oh! And you'll want to get the hang of this right here....” Stef's magenta nails clicked quickly on the keyboard as we stood behind the refurbished secretary desk near the front of the store.

My brain was buzzing with sensory overload.

And it wasn't just from the ASMR of her acrylics on keys.

Stef had created a vibrant atmosphere in the small space she had. Built-in shelves lined the walls where book bindings were organized by color throughout. Typewriters and silver trinkets were sprinkled thoughtfully throughout the room, an assortment of pothos and snake plants and wandering dudes being used as decorative bookends. A patterned area rug filled most of the space, vivid pinks and yellows and purples brightening up the small shop.

Though my style was a bit less, well...*flashy*, there was something about this energy that let me breathe freely—even with her throwing technical details in my face at the speed of light.

"So, when you click this little star icon, it will bring you to this list of distributers, and we can order wholesale from any of these," Stef explained. After scrolling down the list and babbling on about one of her least favorite distributers, she took a step back and put her hands in the air by her shoulders. "Whew! I'm sorry. I know I'm speaking *way* too quickly. Are you catching any of this? You won't need to know it all by heart for a while, of course. I'll be here whenever you are."

I nodded. "Yeah. I'm catching some of it. Definitely not all of it, but some."

Relief flooded her face, and she leaned back against the brick wall. "Okay, great! I'm just excited and...and you jumping in like this was such an unexpected surprise. Even at twenty hours a week...I don't think you understand how much that will help."

"It would have been silly to turn this down," I said, my grin genuine. "Adding bookshop time on top of streaming solo three times a week on *top* of keeping Mae occupied will be a full-time job...but one I can't imagine being sad about."

"I *love* that you'll be on camera more often now. I am here for it," Stef whispered, even though we were the only ones in the shop. I'd mentioned we were navigating the logistics of The Naked Book Club's new schedule, and she promised to keep it hush-hush on our forums. "And I want you to know that Mae can *absolutely* hang out here when your sister or Rosie or whoever can't watch her. I wanted to set up a little kid's section anyway—mostly for mamas who stop in because, well...*lots* of mamas are smut sluts."

"Guilty," I said, my hand flying into the air with lifted shoulders as the chime above the door sang, and Jude appeared, a cold brew in each hand. My stomach dropped the second my eyes fell over his adorably rugged face.

"What are you guilty of?" Jude asked, setting the cold brews on the desk and taking in all the antiques and light fixtures surrounding him.

"Oh, she's just guilty of being one hell of a smut slut. You know...the *norm* around here," Stef said casually, sliding around the side of the desk. "I'm going to go through the boxes that just came in. I do *not* remember what the hell I ordered last week. If you don't have any questions, you're good to go, and I'll see you next Monday!"

"I think I'm okay for now. I'm sure I'll have more than enough questions next week," I said, following Jude as we walked closer to the door. "Thank you so much again for this opportunity, Stef."

"Thank *you* for being such a star on The Naked Book Club and mentioning you needed a job. I'm seriously so grateful I get to work with you *and* read with you on YourEyesOnly. How lucky am I?"

Stef lifted her cold brew to her lips and took a long sip, satisfaction warming her cheeks. "So, *so* much better than Spellbound Beans."

"I will never get tired of hearing that," Jude said, chimes singing above our heads, heat warming our faces as I brought my hand up to block the sun.

Once my eyes adjusted, our feet walked in sync down the sidewalk, and I said, "Well, I probably only absorbed maybe half of what she explained today."

"Well, she seems pretty damn happy, nonetheless." One of Jude's hands slipped from the pocket of his jeans and wove its way into mine. "But what really matters is that *you're* just as happy as she is."

I took a long sip of the cold brew before facing him, the sun still blocking most of my view. "I'm, honestly, *really* happy, Jude. I'm not happy so many other people were walking through the apartment I checked out earlier—and *really* liked...or that Rosie is moving out this weekend...but I'm happy at least *one* item is checked off my—"

"Nel?"

My head twisted forward, my hand flying to block the sun's overly enthusiastic rays from burning my eyes.

But when both Jude's and my feet stopped simultaneously and my sight adjusted to Hallie standing in front of us, I would have welcomed the burn.

"Hey...hi." I lowered my hand, and the second it dropped, it returned right back to where it had been blocking the sun.

And blocking most of Hallie.

For the first time in what felt like decades, Hallie's stance wasn't as *confident* as it usually was. She stood evenly on both feet without the usual lean into her hip, her hands clasped together in front of her chest. Her hair looked almost identical to the tangled bun of waves I adorned but with more blonde and ginger highlights throughout.

Even the bags under her eyes mimicked ones I usually had.

To put it bluntly, she looked like shit.

"I heard you got a job." Her voice came out quiet, almost hushed. "At some bookshop over by Spellbound, right?"

"Yeah. It's...it's a romance bookshop opening in two weeks." I angled my head behind us. "I'm doing about twenty hours a week."

Hallie nodded, her eyes drifting from my face down my arm and to the hand woven with Jude's. "What...what's your plan for the other twenty?"

"I'm adding more solo livestreams to The Naked Book Club." Adrenaline raced through my words the second I said them, and there wasn't an ounce of hesitance to my tone. "That'll make up for the other twenty hours' worth of payments."

"Oh...okay." I waited for her to say more, to comment about what an embarrassing idea it was for me to stay with the platform.

But she didn't.

For a few solid seconds, her gaze lingered on Jude's hand holding mine, his thumb running over my own. The moth shifted atop his hand with the slight movement of his thumb, tiny wings trying to fly.

Clearing his throat, Jude stepped forward and said, "Well, we have to—"

"Look, I'm...I'm sorry."

My eyes opened wider than they'd ever been before. Maybe the heat had whispered its way into my ears, creating some sort of feedback that blurred reality.

But when I met my sister's emerald eyes—almond-shaped eyes exactly like mine and with tears I never imagined her to have—I knew my senses were clear as crystal.

"Okay," I said, biting the inside of my cheek as my body swayed toward Jude, his fingers tightening around my own.

Hallie's chest rose and lowered as she lifted her chin and looked directly at Jude. "This apology is for you, Jude. I owe my sister about two decades' worth of apologies at this point, but I think this one may be long overdue too." She shook her hands out at her sides as her head fell back with an uncomfortable laugh. "God, I suck at this."

"You kind of do," I whispered.

"Yes. I do." Another rise and release of her chest. "Jude, I saw you as Grant's twin when I first met you. In truth, I saw every guy Nel dated as Grant's twin for the longest time. Instead of telling her I was trying to...trying to protect her, I put her down. I'd convince her to run away because everyone would just treat her like Grant did. I took advantage of her mental state and manipulated her...for years."

My fingers grew numb within Jude's grasp, and I wondered if maybe he felt the same numbness as he just stared at my sister.

"I did this instead of telling her I was scared she'd fall into that low place again. I didn't want to see her heart break again, when, really, I was breaking her heart just as much...and I see that now." Deep breath in, deep breath out. "I judged *you* hard, though, Jude. You had the same dark hair falling over your eyes as Grant, and you wore the same dumb T-shirts and Converse sneakers. I made stupid, low assumptions. Grant—and a few of her other boyfriends—never knew what they wanted to do with their lives. When you said you weren't sure what you wanted with yours, I snapped. I wasn't going to let her hurt again...and because I'd broken her down over the years, she just listened to me without hesitation. And, my God, it's pathetic that it's taken me so long to admit that I'm a manipulative narcissist, but...but that's exactly what I am."

Her eyes shifted to mine as she watched my chin move up and down in agreement.

It *was* pathetic—a little terrifying and sad, but pathetic.

It took me breaking down in front of thousands of people on a social platform for Hallie to see the person she'd become over the years.

This time, her eyes stayed on me. "Nel, I know I need help. I know what I did was never okay, and I know this isn't something I can fix after a few therapy sessions. I mean, it took Tucker practically throwing lists of therapists in my face the other night for me to admit I needed one." Hallie lifted her hands to the sides of her face, shaking her head side to side against them. "I don't want therapy. I don't want to be thrown on meds. I don't want my girls to see me struggle. They can't see me fall apart, because then—"

I placed a hand over each of hers, steadying her face and watching a tear fall over her cheek. "Hallie. It's okay for them to see you fall apart. You can't be sculpted in marble forever. When you crack, it doesn't show weakness; it shows humanity. That's what kids need to see, because then they won't feel weak or embarrassed when they start cracking too."

Her eyes melted into mine, her head shaking beneath my palms. I'd never seen this side of her. I'd never seen her so completely out of character, and now, it was obvious how trapped she felt.

Hallie blinked her damp eyes a few times before lowering our hands. "Okay, okay. Nora told me you'd be this way...which is why I came over here in the first place. But...but this whole apology or confession or whatever wasn't the main reason I needed to see you." Hallie reached into her back pocket and pulled out her phone, swiping her finger until a picture lit up the screen. Turning the phone to face me, she said, "One of Tucker's clients is moving to Greyport to expand the firm out there, but he's looking to rent his house here. It's yours. Tucker already talked to him."

I reached for Hallie's phone, lowering it with a curled brow as I made out the quaint, Tudor-style home staring up at me with vines and ivy kissing the faded red brick. The front door was painted a shocking yellow, the frame curved to almost resemble one yanked right out of a fairy tale. The landscaping around the entrance probably could use a little work, some shrubs looking a bit forlorn, and I could already feel how rough that driveway would be on my tires with all its cracks and humps in the concrete.

This house... It wasn't *just* a house. It was a home.

I didn't know how much rent would be. I didn't know what it was like inside or if there were enough rooms. I didn't even know if this guy planned to be back in a year or two, hoping to move back in.

But this home, as gorgeous and perfect as it was...it wasn't mine. In my gut, I knew I couldn't agree to this.

"That's really sweet, Hal," I said, gently pushing the phone toward her. "It's a gorgeous house. I'm a sucker for Tudors...and vines...and cute little curved doors."

"I know...which is why you *have* to take this opportunity. He said he will match the rent at the amount Theía Elena asks you to pay, and you—"

My hand flew into the air between us, and Hallie pressed her lips together. It almost looked painful for her lips to stay together and for her words to stay put in her mouth. "Hallie, I can't. This next step...finding a new place for my family? It's for me to take on."

"I know...but this neighborhood and school district? It's exactly what Mae—"

"Hallie, no." My tone had a bite to it Hallie didn't expect, and she stepped back, pressing her lips together again. Jude's grip on my hand tightened, and I took a deep breath, my eyes meeting his before I turned toward my sister. "I appreciate your help. This idea seems genuine, and that means a lot, but I have to pass on this. Hallie, I'm going to make these decisions based on what *my* heart feels is right. Not yours, not Rosie's, not even Jude's—no offense."

"None taken," he said softly, his lips turning up into the sweetest grin.

My eyes met Hallie's, and I said, "Let me move forward on my own terms. When I need your guidance, I will ask. If I don't ask, just support me. Support me without forcing *your* thoughts and opinions down my throat. We're all different, and we won't always agree with the decisions the other person makes. But if we're happy and safe...that's what matters. Okay?"

Shuffling side to side with her eyes angled at her feet, Hallie nodded. "Yeah. Okay."

I opened my mouth to say one more thing—hoping it would close out this conversation—when Hallie's arms wrapped around my shoulders. Standing there like a sculpture made of ice, I had one hand still warm inside of Jude's and the other at my forehead, blocking the sun with my cold brew. I wasn't sure if it was from all the damn hugs happening lately or the emotions circling the three of us, but my chin found her shoulder and my arms wove around her.

"Thank you," Hallie whispered, her chest rising and falling against mine in relieved breaths. I melted into my sister's arms as her lanky frame pulled me harder against her. For the first time in, well, decades, Hallie hugged me with something that felt a little like hope. Hope mixed with something else.

Maybe it was still too fresh to say this was some sort of sisterly love—something we'd never really felt with one another.

But if this was the start of something like that, I'd take it.

Chapter 45

Rosie

"So, we're not going anywhere! Well...kind of," I said, watching the comments slide across the bottom of the screen. "We'll both have our own places and our own setups, but we will rotate bookshelves for Rowdy Readers."

"Will you have enough books to fill a bookshelf *just* for yourself?" Nel asked, cocking an eyebrow.

Aghast, I said, "Ellie! You don't believe in my ability to decorate a bookshelf?"

"I mean, I definitely didn't say th—"

"Between the books I brought with me here, plus all the ones hidden in the depths of my car...*plus* the ones I'll thrift once I'm officially moved in...I think I'll be good." I shimmied my shoulders with a proud grin. "There's also always my duffel bag of broken heels I can decorate the shelves with. Imagine the figurines and statues I could create...maybe even some bookends."

Nel raised a single brow. "You think you can make bookends from the heels you've broken off stilettos?"

Flapping my hand in her direction, I turned back to the screen. "Challenge accepted."

"Well, now that we have the bookshelf drama squared away," Nel laughed, rolling her eyes. "We will leave you all tonight with a few more updates."

"We want to tell you *all* the secrets, but sorry to break it to you, we—"

Nel's giggle interrupted my thought. "Get it...*break* it to you? Because you aggressively break the heels off shoes..."

I stared blankly at her for a few long, quiet seconds. "Are mom jokes going to be your new thing? I'm sure there's an audience for that."

She shrugged, adjusting her glasses. "Maybe, but the people are waiting. Continue, Zi."

"Right, right, okay," I said, sitting back and pushing out my chest. "Our goal is to bring you a fresh stream each night of the week! It may be a little ambitious of us, but we're going to try."

"I'm still sticking to Steamy Storytime and Rowdy Readers—"

"And I'll join Rowdy Readers and Smut Me up, like we've been doing," I explained. "The only change will be both of us doing two solo streams a week instead of our usual one each."

"*Ambitious* is an understatement," Nel laughed, shaking her head.

"Hey...you went viral once. I'm sure you streaming more will make it happen again," I said, nudging her in the waist.

"I absolutely never meant to go viral, Zi."

Raising my hand into the air, I said, "I'm here for all the viral shit. Bring it!"

"Jesus..." Nel whispered, turning back toward the screen. "Okay...what questions do *you* guys have?"

The two of us sat in silence for a few seconds, staring down at the comments rolling in.

@nerdalertALLIE26: Will you add any new tiers?

@littleLIT33: @nerdalertALLIE26: Do you plan to read one book a week since you're each streaming twice? I'm a slow reader...

@oliVERYcaffeinatedxx: As long as I get tits and ass...I'll be here.

@Hereforthecomments420: @oliVERYcaffeinatedxx: Same.

@**darkromMOM3:** You guys are gross. At least be here for the tits AND the books… like I am.

@**Spicystef_01:** I'm just happy we will still get this content coming in! That's all that matters!

@**littleLIT33:** @**Spicystef_01:** I'm here for it!!

@**CallMeMagicMike:** I'm just here for the pussy.

"Well…I'm here for *all* of you." I leaned closer to the screen and shimmied my chest toward the camera. "Even you dirty sluts. I'm talking to you, Oliver and Mike."

Nel crossed her legs beneath her, probably in the least attractive way she could, and leaned in my direction. "Should you hint at the tier you may add in the future?"

My stomach twisted with a shock of adrenaline. "Perhaps. I can share a little bit just because all these fine people tuned in today."

Nel tapped the tops of her thighs quickly to mimic a drumroll.

"So…I plan to add an even *spicier* tier in the coming months!" I threw my arms into the air with a hoot as Nel did the same. "It will be called Front Rowe Readers…and if you're a Smut Me Up fan, this will be a notch naughtier."

"And…" Nel said with two index fingers pointing away from her chest, the cheesiest grin forming as she circled her fingers to mimic tassels.

"And...sometimes I may throw in a little burlesque number or striptease." I wiggled my eyebrows at the screen as the comments came pouring in. "Because...why not?

"Exactly. Why the hell not?" Nel shrugged, her gaze shifting to the clock above the stove. "Well...it may just be that time, Zi."

"Ma'am, do you have somewhere to be?" My eyes thinned as a smile spread across my cheeks. "Or do you have *someone* to be with?"

Nel's cheeks flushed as she rolled her eyes yet again. "If you count meeting with my theía to hand her over our keys, then yes."

This made my focus switch from the screen blowing up with comment bubbles to the room beyond the laptop.

Cardboard boxes were taped up and stacked on top of one another by the door.

Duffel bags and suitcases were lined up beside the couch.

Plastic bins held books from the bookshelf—books Nel and I agreed to split between houses, even though I still planned to thrift another bookshelf's worth in the next month.

The near-empty apartment had been more than just a shelter for us over the last several months. It was a space where we'd grown together, learned together, and struggled together. We rekindled a friendship within these walls that I easily could have lost. I watched Nel fall apart and fall in love with both Jude *and* herself again.

She welcomed me back into her chaotic life when she could have pushed me aside the same way I'd done to her.

That, in itself, was the power of true friendship.

"Yeah…I guess that counts," I whispered, blinking before facing Nel. Waving my hands in front of myself in an attempt to wave away all these emotions, I said, "Okay, okay. So, The Naked Book Club will be back mid-September. We will throw an official date at you in the coming week."

Nel lifted her glasses up so they balanced on top of her head, fluttering her eyelashes in a way she would have failed at months ago. "Thank you for sticking around, all you sassy smuts. Now…get out of here."

"We got things to do," I added.

"Keys to hand over."

"Partners to please."

Nel giggled, setting her glasses back on her nose. "She isn't wrong."

"And the stream will *actually* turn off right…now." I leaned forward, winked into the camera, and confidently clicked the button that I knew, for a fact, shut off the stream. Lowering the laptop screen so it fully closed, I took a deep breath and leaned back against the bare bookshelf. Pressing my hands to my eyes, I whispered, "Damn. Why does it feel like one thousand eyelashes are scratching my eyeballs?"

Nel blew a strand of hair out of her face just for it to fall back into the same spot. "Because your body is telling you to fucking cry, Rosie."

"I'm not sad."

Nel faced me, her head now leaning against the shelf behind us too. "Even good change can be emotional."

Once a tear kissed my cheek, I squeezed my eyes shut and whispered, "If we don't talk, my tears will get sucked back up into my eye sockets."

Even though I tried keeping my eyes closed, I opened a single eye and followed Nel's gaze as she scanned the room. We weren't just looking at the emptiness of the space but absorbing the memories we'd made in it. The empty entryway closet that once stored all my pasties and thongs and feathery bralettes. The back corner—the den—where the futon now laid free of crumpled blankets and sheets. The hallway leading to Mae's quiet nursery and the bedroom that once was Nel's sullen escape. The kitchen island covered in duct-taped boxes.

Nel's final focal point were my eyes. My dark, dripping eyes staring back into hers. "Thank you for getting drunk at Thirsty Theodore's all those months ago."

A pathetic laugh escaped my throat, followed by a sniffle against the back of my hand. "Thanks for letting my drunk ass in that night when you should have slammed the door on my brother's face."

"I would never do that," Nel said. "But really...thanks for coming back. Thanks for reigniting the fire I'd quieted within me. Thanks for making me see where my heart *really* needed to be—should have been—over all these years."

"That wasn't me, Nel." I set the side of my head on her shoulder, nuzzling close. "That was all you. You just needed someone to come and shake shit up a bit. *We* needed to shake shit up a bit. If we hadn't, we wouldn't have realized the beauty of moving on."

The side of Nel's head gently fell atop mine, and I swear I could feel her smile without seeing it as she said, "It's weird how moving on can be both terrifying and beautiful at the same time."

I wrapped my arms around her into a hug she wouldn't push away. "*Healing* is both terrifying and beautiful at the same time."

"But when you're healing alongside your best friend, it makes the process a little more manageable." Nel leaned into my hug. "Maybe even a little fun."

"You're right," I whispered, my smile matching the one I knew she wore. "It absolutely does."

THE NAKED BOOK CLUB

JENNIFER ALINE writes stories that combine the steamy elements of romance with the raw realities of friendship and family-focused themes of women's fiction. She loves creating quirky characters with big personalities who are forced to challenge themselves and step outside their comfort zone...while also finding love—or something like it—along the way.

Jennifer lives in Western New York with her twin daughters and grumpy miniature schnauzer. She has an unhealthy obsession with vintage typewriters, owns way too many plants, and is a self-titled coffee snob. When she isn't writing, reading, or chasing her daughters around, she can be found singing karaoke, taking dance classes, or searching for the newest local coffee shop to obsess over.

If you loved hanging out in
Merlin Heights, you'll love
visiting Greyport!

Also Written by Jennifer Aline

The Ex Project: A Merlin Heights Book